Photo: Vaughan Pilikian

Max Schaefer was born in London in 1974. *Children of the Sun* is his first novel.

Children of the Sun

Max Schaefer

Soft Skull Press
New York

Originally published in English by Granta Publications under the title *Children of the Sun*, copyright © Max Schaefer, 2010. First published in Great Britain by Granta Books 2010.

The acknowledgements on pp. 390-91 constitute an extension of this copyright page.

Library of Congress Cataloging-in-Publication Data

Schaefer, Max, 1974-
Children of the sun / Max Schaefer.
p. cm.
ISBN-13: 978-1-59376-297-1
ISBN-10: 1-59376-297-6
1. Skinheads—Great Britain—Fiction. 2. Neo-Nazism—Great Britain—Fiction.
3. Gay men—Fiction. 4. Psychological fiction.
I. Title.
PR6119.C375C47 2010
823.'92—dc22
2010013028

Cover design by Jason Snyder
Typeset by M Rules
Printed in the United States of America

Soft Skull Press
An Imprint of COUNTERPOINT LLC
1919 Fifth Street
Berkeley, CA 94710

www.softskull.com
www.counterpointpress.com

Distributed by Publishers Group West

10 9 8 7 6 5 4 3 2 1

For China

'He reads on the brickwork: "NF FUCKS MEN." And is not displeased.'

— Iain Sinclair, *Suicide Bridge*

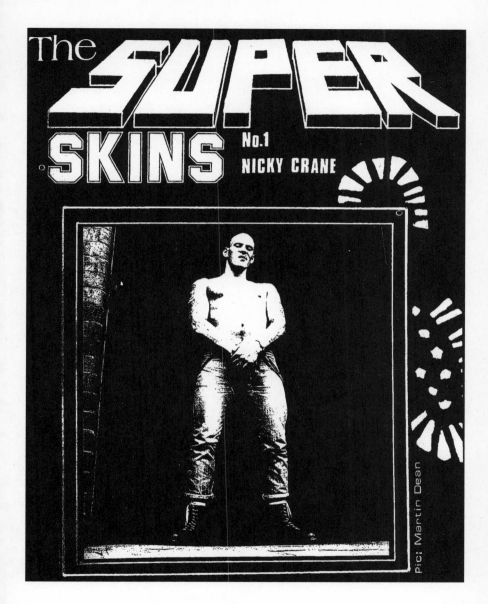

Skins International fanzine, 1983

The Woolwich Odeon

Sometimes he thinks he is already living in the future.

It is Monday, 31 August 1970. It is a bank holiday, he is fourteen, and his erection is tugging him across ground dazed by the sun. Grass barely twitches in the motionless air. The heat is amplifying: flies thud about a dog shit whose stench has overgrown it hugely, like a hothouse plant.

The tarmac path, cracked and swollen, passes a football match and a kiosk selling ice creams, which sunbathers eat contorted, to not be melted on. They watch the match or stare dumbly at a dissipating contrail. White drips gather on the ridges of their cones.

Past the bandstand, which is never used, is a depression he found years back: running ahead of his mother up a low hill he came suddenly upon it, like a place for soap, and a man and woman fucking on their sloughed clothes. Tony stared until she reared, her grin frenzied under blond hair mussed with twigs, to blow a raspberry at him. He ran from their laughter.

There is an area of unchecked growth nearby, where the ground is darkened by thick trees and bracken. It is camouflage. It is where he is heading.

This kind of horniness, like that of certain very sleepless

nights, feels like it could alter things. Last week he walked home determined to greet himself in the bathroom mirror and watch himself step through: to kiss and touch himself.

At the edge of the thicket midges vibrate in a cloud and dead leaves brush his thigh. Within it is suddenly quieter and cool. The path leads to a squat brick building and splits to symmetrical entrances. On the right is a room lit by a single ceiling lamp, its weak light marred by dust and insect carcasses. There is a chemical smell trying, like a shrill monotone, to drown out several others. Tony stops to breathe it all in. When he moves again his shoes stick slightly to the floor.

He looks in both stalls to check they are empty, then unbuttons his shorts and pushes his underpants down. He lets the pants and shorts fall to his shoes. The cool air is clammy against him.

He shuffles forward, each foot in turn describing an arc about the other to keep the shorts taut off the floor. He stands at the urinal with his feet apart and his hands by his sides. His dick bounces like a vessel planing over waves. The urine is hot as it leaves him and cool in the fine spray against his knees. He pulls his shorts up and leans against the wall, waiting.

On a window above the sink someone has drawn a penis and balls, in three loops like a cartoon cactus. Spraying from it are the words PAKI'S OUT.

A shape moves past the window and Tony quickly buttons his shorts before a man enters, stooping in the doorframe. He is very tall, middle-aged, with a monk's fringe round a head pink and sweaty from the sun. He wears spectacles, thick lenses in huge frames, above a thin and delicate mouth; the arms emerging from his short-sleeved shirt are wide and hairy. The man looks at Tony, who could wash his hands or make some other show to explain his presence, but instead leans against the sink and returns his gaze.

The man looks quickly away. He glances at the stalls, but

seems to know it would be conceding something to use one. Instead he turns to the urinal and unbuttons his fly. He lowers his head. There is a pause, and a muffled cough.

His shirt carries a vast, cruciform sweat patch on its back.

When Tony steps closer the man stiffens with the effort of feigning ignorance, his head staring fixedly down at the penis that his whole body is rigid with the desire to make urinate.

Tony stands at the urinal alongside. He aims his hard dick at the porcelain, a challenge, and whistles a couple of notes in pantomime expectation. The man stands hopelessly next to him, stoppered. His face is covered in fat pebbles of sweat, as if he has some tropical disease. It is the panic of complicity.

Deliberately, slowly, Tony turns. He affects to notice, just now, his own dick and strokes it once, curious. He glances at the man's: it is thickening nervously, in hesitant interrogation.

Tony sidesteps closer. The man lets out a tiny gasp and after a last pause takes his own penis in his left hand while his right now moves with infinite slowness across the space between them. The hand is shaking. It seems blind to any target; it is edging towards Tony's shoulder, perhaps. It stops just short of him and begins to descend, tracing his left side at an inch's remove.

When the door bangs open they spin round. A young man regards them, a teenager with heavy boots and close-cropped hair. A skinhead, realizes Tony, and as he does hears the sound of falling liquid: the shock has jump-started the man's bladder, which cast an arc of urine as he turned.

'Shit!' yells the skinhead, with an instinctive, undignified backward leap. The man reverts panicked to the urinal, his shoulders hunched. For a moment the only sound is of his gushing waste.

'Fucking disgusting,' the skin remarks, frowning at the long involuntary puddle. 'Nearly got on my boots mate.' He could be addressing himself.

5

The man is tethered in place, cradling in horror the source of an unceasing flow which a minute before he was nearly praying for, and now cannot stanch.

The skinhead repeats: 'I said that nearly got on my boots.'

The skinhead's boots are a deep dried-blood red, rising an inch or so past his ankles. His Levi's have been cut and re-sewn to stop short above them. He has thin red braces over a white short-sleeved shirt. His short hair extends in sideburns down his cheeks.

The man stuffs his penis back and scuttles to the door, steering a wide berth around the skinhead and trying not to look at him. He is still buttoning his fly, about which a wet patch blossoms.

'Yeah piss off you old fairy,' the skin calls after him. He watches the door close with a brief, punctuating laugh, then looks at Tony. 'All right?' he says.

Tony nods. The skinhead steps carefully across the slick and takes the man's place next to him at the urinal. The skin's Levi's, it turns out as he opens it, have a zip fly.

Tony watches baldly as the skinhead pisses with his hefty dick. The skin grins back at him: 'What are you staring at?'

Tony looks down: 'I like your boots.'

'Oh you do eh?'

'Yeah.'

'Yeah I bet. Want a pair do you?'

'Yeah.'

'Got six quid?'

'No.'

'Well then.'

The skin arches to face the ceiling. He shakes his dick and tucks it back without zipping his fly. Tony says: 'I like your hair.'

'Oh yeah?'

'Can I feel it?'

6

'Number-four crop that.' The skin leans forward, then seems to change his mind. 'What are you here for anyway?'

'Needed a slash.'

'Yeah? Well don't let me stop you.' The skin folds his arms expectantly. Tony faces the urinal, holding himself, willing a few drops.

'Thought you needed a piss,' says the skin.

'I did.'

'Gone away has it?'

'I suppose.'

'Got something there though haven't you?'

'What do you mean?'

'That.'

'What?'

'Come here. *That*.'

'I suppose.'

'You suppose. So what are you here for?'

'You've got one too though.'

'I have now. Whose fault is that?'

'I dunno.'

'Don't muck me about. Whose fault is that?'

.' . . Mine?'

'Well then—'

—and it is Friday, 28 March 1980 and he is twenty-three, adjusting his braces in the mirror, in the toilets of the Crown and Cushion.

'Well then,' Tony tells himself, and goes back inside the pub.

It is heaving with skins: a compact mass of boots and noise and smoke. The other punters left some time ago. He finds Steve by the bar, guarding his pint.

'Fucking buzzing in here,' Steve says, handing it over.

'Cheers,' replies Tony. 'Nicky about?'

'His do isn't it. He'll be here somewhere.'

7

Tony cranes round, looking. Right now, he thinks, it would be hard to tell. He is on his fifth pint and everyone is starting to look the same.

The bell goes for last orders. Tony calls: 'Two more here sweetheart.'

'Make it three,' says Steve. 'You met my mate Dave?'

Just arrived is a short lad, younger than both of them, with cropped strawberry hair. A few hairs emerge from the open neck of his white Fred Perry. His blue eyes shine as if with tears but he smiles uncomplicatedly, dimpling his freckled cheeks.

'Dave is it? Tony. You all right mate.'

They shake hands.

'Thought I'd missed my chance there,' says Dave. 'What do I owe you?'

'On me. You up for this are you?'

'After the day I've had.' Dave shakes his head in emphasis. 'Yeah thanks then Tony. Cheers.'

'Your health. So how do you know this' (indicating Steve) 'fucking mug?'

Dave laughs. 'He was at school with my brother.'

'I didn't know Steve went to school.' Steve waves two fingers at him. Dave is smiling and has started to say something when Steve adds:

'Well not an all-girls' one like you did.'

'You can't have two goes at a comeback,' Tony tells him.

'Come again?'

'You already gave me a V-sign. That was quite articulate for you. You can't try again when you've had time to think up something else.'

Dave laughs. Steve says: 'Cunt.'

Things are moving. People are finishing their pints and there is a sudden queue for the toilets. 'Looks like we're off,' says Tony. He crouches to check the laces on his boots, twenty-hole black Docs.

8

Steve is zipping his coat. 'Got your gear then?'

Tony looks around, thrown. 'Shit—'

'Under here, brainbox.' Vindicated, Steve hands it over: a WH Smith carrier bag. Someone near the entrance is yelling; it could be an announcement but it is hard to hear. Tony takes the bar from the bag, which he drops.

The doors are open and the exodus has started. Tony drains his glass. 'Have a good one lads,' he says. They move forward, shuffling in the crush, but as it narrows towards the exit the crowd picks up pace. Tony hefts the bar beside his thigh, feeling its weight.

They push through the doors and on to the street like a football team from the players' tunnel. Outside the night is cold. They fall into line, four abreast, spilling off the pavement into the oncoming lane, making cars swerve to avoid them. Tony looks behind him for Dave and Steve, who has thrown back his head to howl, a conscious animal sound. There are at least ten rows of skins ahead and as many following, perhaps a hundred in all. Most are teenagers, like Dave.

Some lads up front are shouting: '*Sieg heil!*' and the chant spreads down the line. Tony shoves his iron bar in the air. Others hold up knives and pickaxe handles, and those without weapons raise their arms in salute. Ahead of them Woolwich High Street curves left in a wide sweep, dipping and rising as it does, and he thinks of a rollercoaster, the deliberate accumulation of manic cranks that heave it to its brink. Few cars pass them now – they must be noticing, diverting – and one that is foolishly parked in their path, on the kerb the march straddles, has lost its windows by the time he reaches it. The *Sieg heil*s are fading out and losing rhythm, and Tony yells, 'Kill the wogs!,' bringing his crowbar down on the car's bonnet in clanging punctuation. The cry is taken up around him, and feeling good with the success of his innovation he looks back to see Steve and Dave shouting along.

9

Dave's grin seems out of place among so many purposeful scowls.

As they approach the roundabout Tony gets a clear view of the Odeon ahead, a pink 30s picture palace with its name in lights astride its tower and THE SPY WHO LOVED ME beneath its curved hoarding and there, queuing in the space below, a vast herd of blacks. It must be a gig or something, he thinks, and you have to admire Nicky's organization because there's a good hundred and fifty of the bastards. The first skins are crossing the roundabout now and Tony watches the appalled faces of the blacks as they cotton on. They're young and mostly male, like the skins, but unprepared: there is pointing, jostling, visible alarm. A few slip away and the queue loses its shape as more quickly follow, round the cinema or inside, and like chemistry as this dispersal reaches a critical point the skins break step and start running full-tilt, shouting, 'Skinheads rule' or 'Niggers go home' or just *shouting*. The ground opens up before Tony and casting a this-is-it look back at Dave and Steve he throws himself into it.

A few lads have pulled some black off a motorbike in the roundabout and are laying into him with their boots as he curls foetally to protect his head (Should have worn a helmet shouldn't you? thinks Tony) but the crowd's too big for him to get one in himself so he moves on, charging into the mêlée that spills down the steps of the Odeon.

There's fighting going on but many blacks have run, or holed up inside the building. Some lads are running up and down in front of the cinema trying to kick the doors in, and Tony joins in for a while, smashing a fanlight with his crowbar. He jumps up at it, scrambling over massing skins, and through the hole he made sees blacks in anxious conference. One girl looks him right in the eye and he starts to shout something at her but then a huge weight lands on his neck, the crowbar is yanked from his grasp and two black teenagers are on him. They bring him flat on the concrete where he can't kick easily. One boots him in the stomach and aims another at his balls. It doesn't hit full on but the pain still stalls him when he tries to lift himself. Then he spots the other raising the crowbar. He is, too slowly, changing his plan, from grabbing the leg of the one that kicked him to rolling away from the crowbar now approaching his head, when the black wielding the bar is jerked sideways as something smashes the ribcage beneath his raised arm, a voice yells, 'You all right mate?' and Tony is staring into Nicky's face, Nicky is over him in towering perspective. Sweat bounces bright light from his face and scalp and his weapon swings triumphant in his grasp. 'All right mate?' he repeats, leaning closer, and Tony wants to say something, is surely about to speak, when '*Craney!*' someone shouts and Nicky turns and the first black is coming again for Tony who scrambles to his feet and when he looks back Nicky has gone. Someone else seems to have the crowbar now and the black has lost interest so he breaks away to find another weapon. Besides, he can hear sirens and still feels dizzy from his aching bollock.

He pushes round bent almost double to the side of the cinema and follows the pavement, tracing it ape-like with his hands, as it climbs to the Mitre. The pub has closed, but he sees an empty cider bottle in the gutter and picks it up. He swings it hard at the Mitre's window, which cracks a little but doesn't break. The bottle doesn't break either, so he smashes it on the pavement instead. Then holding it tight by the neck he goes through the little gap round the side of the pub, into the church gardens. He can hear more squad cars now. He heads across the grass away from the main road, and is about to round the corner into a row of houses when someone shouts his name.

Dave is twenty feet behind, running to catch up. He's limping slightly and there is blood down his white top, a lot of it.

'Cheers,' he tells Tony, who waits to let him catch his breath but Dave shakes his head: 'Keep going, fucking load of coppers back there.' So they head fast down the street, the sirens and the noise of the fight fading with distance. Tony asks what happened to Steve, and Dave says he doesn't know. The houses are quiet, their ground-floor curtains drawn. 'You all right?' he asks Dave, 'You're fucking covered in blood,' and Dave says, 'Yeah, some cunt had a nosebleed on me.'

They zigzag through the streets, not saying much, the world trembling a little at its limits, edged with light that threatens to spill through. They are on a little hump over the railway, walking in the middle of the road, when out of nowhere they hear an engine and brightness crashes down from behind so their shadows sprout hugely before them. With a wild screech something fantastically heavy punches the back of Tony's legs and throws him forward. The tarmac zooms at his face and he intercepts it with his right arm, the cider bottle, unconsciously jettisoned, shattering somewhere close by. The impact scrapes skin from his wrist and forearm, which begin to sting as he scrambles to his feet. Dave must have been hit harder because he is lying a good few feet ahead. Tony goes to help him up, Dave muttering 'Fuck' in repeating shock and grasping Tony's arm for support with real need.

They face the car, stationary on the crest of the hump. Dave can stand by himself so Tony goes first. The driver, indistinct behind his headlights, watches them approach and raises an apologetic hand. As Tony nears the window the car tries suddenly to accelerate, then stalls. It rolls feebly forward. The driver brakes and restarts the ignition. Tony says with outrage, 'Fucking—' and leaps to open the door, behind which eyes widen beneath a turban and a hand scrabbles too slowly for the lock.

'Fuck are you doing?' demands Tony.

The man looks fifty, maybe more. 'Sorry, mate,' he offers. He cannot stop staring, trying to gauge the catastrophe.

'Christ,' says Dave, catching up. 'It's a fucking Paki.'

The man says: 'I don't want no trouble.' It's not clear if he actually talks like this or is trying to ape their language for sympathy.

'Fuck out of the car,' says Tony.

'Oh no,' the man says, 'please. I have a daughter who is waiting for me.'

Tony sighs and mutters, '*Cunt.*' He grabs the beard and pulls. The man's hands pat Tony's arm ineffectually, miming resistance but unwilling to fight. The head bends back, the body tries to follow the beard, the hands fumble for purchase on the seat. The man is angled comically towards the opening like a jack-in-the-box, tethered by Tony's grip and the seat belt. Dave says, 'Come on Tony do the cunt,' and by way of support mounts the bonnet of the car with fast-returning energy and kicks in the windshield. It hangs together in a sag: a few bits scatter over the dashboard and driver, who is grabbing at the side of his chair and the handbrake, desperate to stay inside. Tony seizes a fistful of turban with his free hand and yanks harder.

Now, whether by accident or inspiration, the driver releases the handbrake and the car rolls forward. Dave jumps off, stumbling where he lands. Tony, still holding the man's head, is pulled alongside as the car picks up speed. In rage and frustration he lets go the turban and, pulling the man's beard high until his head is half out of the gap and Tony's hand clear of it, slams the door as hard as he can with his boot. There is a muffled crack and he lets go.

They follow the car down the slope. As the road flattens the car veers left until it ploughs into another parked by the kerb. When they reach it the driver is moving slightly. Dave pulls open the door. Perhaps the padding of his turban cushioned the impact, but there is still a long deep cut down the right side of the driver's head. He is bleeding heavily behind the ear, one eye has filled with blood, and there is jawbone visible. He is mumbling something that sounds like 'No but I rather' and his hands are pawing at the steering wheel, sliding across its surface. Dave takes a wide rejuvenated kick at his head: the driver spits blood and twitches. Tony leans matter-of-factly in, pops the seatbelt and hauls him into the road. Some lingering consciousness is trying to raise the man on his elbows, so Tony steps on his chest with his left boot and presses him into the tarmac. He leans down for the turban and roughly unravels it. Silence feels inappropriate during this fiddly process, so he says, 'Hit and run will you? You fucking cunt. You fucking old Paki,' and so on. The man's turban is coming away in a wide ribbon, his long hair underneath matting with sweat and blood. He is making a low noise that occasionally sounds like it might bubble into language.

'Let's cut his hair,' suggests Dave.

'Got any scissors?'

'I'll look in the car.'

Tony waits. He kicks the man and looks about him at the silent houses.

Dave is rifling through the glove compartment. 'Prestige Cabs,' he calls.

'What?'

'Prestige Cabs. Could have fooled me with this old banger.'

'Found any scissors?'

'I'll check the boot.'

'Just a knife would do.'

'You stop that,' calls a woman in a shrill quaver from some upstairs window. 'I've called the police.'

Tony looks up. 'Yeah well,' he shouts, 'thanks for telling us you dozy cow. Come on,' he tells Dave, 'let's go.'

Dave kicks the driver twice more in the ribs and head. As

they head down the road, walking quickly but not running, he says: 'Wish we'd cut his hair off.'

'Yeah it was a nice idea.'

'I hate missing opportunities.' Dave is chatty with adrenalin. 'Prestige Cabs. Not bloody using them. Bastard nearly killed us.'

'And then he only fucking tries to drive off.'

'Jesus though he must have been pissing himself when we got up.'

'Wished he hadn't braked probably.'

'Oh my goodness gracious I have run over some skinheads.'

There are sirens approaching. Tony says, 'Get down.' They crouch behind an ice-cream van. Dave says in a loud whisper, 'It was beautiful though when you had his beard up like that. Fucking hilarious,' and Tony smiles and shakes his head at the picture. The police car passes, making the houses behind Dave pulse in electric blue. When it has gone Dave starts to move and Tony says: 'Give it a minute.'

'You think they'll come back?'

'Just give it a minute.'

They wait in silence. He hears Dave's breathing slow. Tony's bollock is aching again and the way he is crouching makes his hurt back twinge. He thinks again of the fight, the advancing black swept from his view and Nicky reaching down for him. Saved my life, he thinks, sentimentally, or maybe mutters it out loud because Dave flashes him a look. Tony frowns at the pavement, gathering himself. 'Got the time on you?' he says.

'Just gone half-twelve.'

'Where are you heading?'

'Down Plumstead.'

'They'll be out looking for a while. I'm just a couple of streets over. You can wait at mine for a bit if you want.'

They do not encounter anyone on the short walk. When

15

they enter the flat, Tony winces a bit at the smell and regrets leaving the washing-up again. Dave asks: 'Do you live by yourself?'

'Yeah. What about you?'

'Yeah with my mum.'

'Is she all right or is she a bit . . .'

'She's all right most of the time. Free food and all that.'

'Can't complain can you. Fancy a beer?'

'Cheers.'

Tony heads for the kitchen: 'Don't think I've got any cold.'

Dave calls: 'Can I read your *Patriot*? I've not seen this issue.'

'Go ahead.' Tony returns with the beers. 'Rejects all right?'

'You got the album? What's it like?'

He nods: 'It's fucking great.'

They read and listen, drink and smoke. From his bed, Tony watches Dave poring over *British Patriot*. 'I can't believe all this with Rhodesia,' says Dave.

'Nearly went out there a few months ago.'

'What to fight?'

'Good thing I didn't. Been a bit fucking late.'

'You never know. You might have turned the tide.'

They laugh. Tony says: 'Your mum be OK with that blood?'

'She'll be asleep.'

'Have a bath if you want. Might have a spare T-shirt and all.'

'Oh yeah please.'

'Go for it. There's a towel in there. Don't know about hot water.'

Dave unlaces his boots and takes them off. He slips his braces from his shoulders and pulls off his Fred Perry. Underneath, his torso is pale and thin, his chest sparse with strawberry hair. There are no wounds: the blood on the shirt really is not his.

He undoes the waist button of his jeans, looks up at Tony and grins. 'Fucking kill for a bath.' He picks up his beer, goes into the bathroom, and closes the door. Tony hears water running. After a minute Dave comes out with a towel around his waist. 'Fucking look at that,' he says, and hoists it to display the backs of his legs. He has surprisingly thick calves and thighs, which bloom red where the car hit, just above the knee.

'Jesus,' says Tony.

'Cunt,' says Dave, and closes the door again.

On the record Stinky sings:

'Where the hell is Babylon?
I've heard it's a lot of fun.
Can I get there on my bike
Or straight up the M1?'

When Dave comes out, Tony hands him a Sham 69 T-shirt. 'Sorry,' he says, 'but it's all I have clean. Which is because I never wear the fucking thing.'

Dave laughs and puts it on. 'How do I look?'

'It's a bit big to be honest. But it's better than Dracula's bib you had on.'

'I'll have Mum wash it.'

'Keep it. I'm not going to wear it.'

'No you're all right.'

Tony nods. 'You OK getting home? You can kip here if you want.'

'Won't give her the satisfaction. Cheers though. And for the bath and all that. It was good to meet you Tony. See you around yeah?'

He holds his hand out and they shake. When Tony has closed the door and changed the record, he lies back on his bed and finishes his beer.

'Racists worse than animals'

THREE LOCAL youth, members of a gang of the "ferociously racist" British Movement, who attacked a peaceful coloured family, have been found guilty at the Old Bailey of causing an affray.

Nicola Crane (21), of Plumstead High Street, was sentenced to 12 months' jail, suspended for two years, and fined £100 or one month in prison and ordered to pay £83 costs.

Bexleyheath & Welling Observer, 27 March 1980

Nazi gang leader is jailed

By GEORGE GLENTON

BRITISH Movement bully-boy Nicholas Crane was jailed for four years yesterday as a henchman gave the Nazi salute and shouted: "Sieg heil!"

Crane was found guilty at the Old Bailey of causing an affray and conspiring to lead a skinhead mob in an attack on a group of coloured youths.

The jury heard that his gang planned an ambush at Woolwich Arsenal station, South London.

Before their victims' train arrived, the thugs grew impatient and attacked two people in the street.

Then came a battle with police in which several officers were injured and eight of the mob were arrested.

Among them was Crane, a 22-year old dustman from Crayford, described as the pro-Nazi movement's North Kent organiser.

Daily Mirror, 17 June 1981

Exposed: The racist thug on the cover of this evil record

By **PAUL DONOVAN** and **PAT EVANS**

THE highly controversial record Strength Thru Oi! has been withdrawn from sale by Decca Records.

Salute

And today the Daily Mail can reveal the identity of the skinhead who appears on the cover of the record.

He is 22-year-old Nicholas Crane, a dustman from Crayford in Kent.

Last month Crane was jailed for four years at the Old Bailey for causing an affray and conspiring to lead a skinhead mob in an attack on a group of black youths. When he was sentenced a friend in court shouted 'Sieg Heil' and gave the Nazi salute.

Crane is a member of the Fascist British Movement and until his arrest was the party's North Kent organiser. He is well-known among skinheads and was once lead singer of a band called The Afflicted which sang Nazi-type songs in several Deptford pubs.

His picture on the record cover shows him in an aggressive skinhead stance — angry face, clenched fists and raised commando boots.

One of Crane's friends, 17-year-old part-time gardener Michael McKay, who also has the British Movement's sun wheel emblem tattooed on his forearm, said last night: 'Nick was in the British Movement because he didn't like niggers. But he was a good laugh and he certainly treated his mates all right'.

He produced a grubby picture which he said Crane had drawn—'he's quite an artist'—showing a bovver boy kicking a black man deep in the groin.

sounds presents for your further inebriation titillation and emancipation Oi 2

STRENGTH THRU Oi!

featuring
SPLODGE
4-SKINS
INFA-RIOT
THE STRIKE
TOY DOLLS
COCK
SPARRER
LAST RESORT
+ MANY MORE

The skinhead record . . . withdrawn from sale

Daily Mail, 10 July 1981

NAZI NICK IS A PANZI

Weird secret he kept from gay-bashers

NAZI thug Nick Crane kept an amazing secret from his gay-bashing mates — he is homosexual himself.

Nick, 34, admitted yesterday: "If they had ever found out, I'd have been beaten to a pulp."

For 10 years the bragging bullyboy kept up his pretence as a "feared and respected" member of the British Movement.

"Beating people up was part of my life then, it happened at least once a week," he said.

But he finally ditched the raving Right because he could not go on in an outfit which hated gays so much.

He explained: "I knew I had homosexual feelings, but I used to stifle them. In the end I just felt like a hypocrite carrying on in the extreme Right-wing because the movement was so anti-gay. I was a fraud."

'If my pals ever found out I'd have been beaten into a pulp'

At first, tattooed Crane's love of violence helped him make a meteoric rise through the British Movement ranks.

Within six months of joining in the late seventies he became one of leader Michael McLaughlin's elite band of minders.

Uniform

He dressed in a Nazi-style uniform and went on secret armed training weekends at country hideaways.

Crane led a war of hate against "the enemy" of blacks, Jews and left-wingers, organising violence at every opportunity.

He was involved in **BEATING UP** policemen;

PLOTTED to throw a trainload of black partygoers on to a railway track;

BATTERED Pakistanis in the East End of London; and

STAMPED repeatedly on a Left-winger's head as he lay unconscious in a pool of blood.

Crane, seen on last night's Channel 4 programme Skin Complex, went on:

Beating people up gave me pleasure. It was the power.

I used to think that people were like sheep and only took notice of power and strength.

If they didn't agree with us the only answer

EXCLUSIVE

By BRANDON MALINSKY

was to kick their heads in.

We used to drink in Brick Lane in the East End every Sunday and then go looking for targets.

One time we rampaged down the Lane turning over stalls, kicking and punching Pakistanis.

On another occasion we laid into people marching for the Jewish Remembrance Day.

We hurled insults at them and started punching and kicking as they went by.

His most vicious attack was against the Left-wing supporter he spotted on a Tube train.

He said: "Me and a few mates beat him really badly. Even though he wasn't moving we all kept jumping on his head.

Miracle

"I think he survived. It must have been a miracle."

Even now jobless bouncer Crane still looks every inch the neo-Nazi at his bedsit in Soho, Central London.

The tattoos on his arms include swastikas and slogans like: "I hate niggers."

But he insisted: "It is all in the past. I've made a dramatic change in my life."

One person who may be particularly surprised is his former close friend Ian Stewart, lead singer of the fascist band Screwdriver, for whom "Nazi Nick" handles security at concerts and who used to visit Mr Crane in jail.

Independent, 27 July 1992

Mr Nine to Five

I couldn't be sure it was Nicky who planned the attack on the Odeon, but the evidence seemed strong. It took place within days of his conviction for the bus-stop incident, and his authorship of the train ambush six months later – with its similar hallmarks – was not in doubt. Besides, Nicky was a Leader Guard in the local British Movement: and according to a skin involved in the attack, it was a Leader Guard who had organized 'the do at the Odeon.'

I found this claim in the *South East London Mercury* of 19 March 1981. 'John,' sixteen and a skinhead since he was seven, told the paper there were 200 BM members in Greenwich, Woolwich and Plumstead. He talked of unarmed combat training in Oxleas Wood and Shooters Hill, and members in the Territorial Army who knew how to use guns. They recruited at football matches and schools. They had 'something planned' for the local MP.

'I don't believe all those Jews died,' he added. 'It's just a con.'

There was more to read, but the place was closing: a librarian marshalled the stragglers, and seeing her approach I closed the paper and drew a dumb-show line under my notes. Outside, Colindale Avenue swept up from the city before me.

Even in rush hour, the traffic here was sparse and fast-moving, and the prospect of crossing held the suburban threat of real impact. I paused in the rain, wondering what to do. My plan to suggest a film to Adam had been pre-empted by his lunchtime text: *Back late if at all. If no word by lunch tomoro pls log cops into my gaydar acct! xxxA.*

I could just go home – it was an attractive option in this weather: pasta, television. But the thought of bed put me off. I could never settle when Adam was on these rendezvous: each possible position (facing the wall or the entrance; hugging a pillow or face-up; my underpants off or on; the door closed or open) seemed loaded with unintended meaning. Better to stay out for as long as possible: until he was back, or I was too tired to care. And why should his night out cancel mine?

On the tube platform, where a young couple were pressed against the wall earnestly necking, at whom I smiled to demonstrate something obscure to me and probably distasteful to them, it was announced that a suspect package had closed Euston, and there were severe delays. I sat on a bench while the station filled slowly with people and irritation. Every few minutes the news was repeated, and its announcer became more self-conscious. He began to parody, and improvise sarcastic clauses: 'As a small number of you may already be aware . . .'

In the end, after twenty-five minutes, a train did roll warily up, heavy with people scowling at us through the glass. We were packed in further at Hendon, and again at Brent Cross: I imagined Adam ringing some unfamiliar doorbell on an East London estate while in the courtyard behind him yelling kids looped in circles on their bikes. An older face, a tracksuit, grey hair on muscled arms. 'Leave your bag in the hallway.' A set of stairs. Just out of Golders Green the train heaved and braked: the mass of bodies compressed, then loosened; enervated machinery exhaled. By the time we reached it Euston had reopened, and I emerged among commuters breathing beer from their forced hiatus. I had missed the film, but it was on again at nine.

Tottenham Court Road funnelled the dregs of bad weather like a giant storm drain. The rain was now a mere dribble of grime that spattered my glasses so the headlights on the impatient herd of traffic seemed to slip and slide. I passed Spearmint Rhino, Habitat, Paperchase. A huge figure reared out of Store Street and I flinched: he asked for directions to Russell Square, but when I told him he shook his head. 'That's not right,' he said, 'that can't be right,' and strode up in the direction I'd come from. When I looked back he was asking someone else.

I killed a few minutes in Borders, where with no energy for anything new I checked on authors I had already read. They were still present, still apparently being published. I pulled a few off the shelf to see which printing they were, and flicked through vaguely remembered text. Philip's friend Mike was poorly represented by just two recent books: I put one face-out at the front of an adjacent stack.

By seven-fifteen I was on Shaftesbury Avenue, heading for the little Chinese café near the bus stop. A tall, slim boy in jeans and T-shirt stood in the window among hanging poultry, before a chopping block and simmering vat. As I entered he unhooked a piece of pork from the wall and cut off a section, which he sliced with a speed that belied his listless expression, the cleaver oscillating up and down. I ate a portion of the meat with rice at a shared table, listening to the old couple beside me. They were catching up after a long time, or had not previously met; perhaps he was visiting, because he had a strong European accent, while she, much taller than him, with crisply bunned white hair, spoke with an old-fashioned precision that was marked with the curious habit of ending assertions with a little 'nah?,' as if to make sure she was being followed. They had ordered a cliché of a meal from the menu of the restaurant downstairs: spread between them were crispy duck and pancakes, sweet-and-sour pork, and vegetables in a transparent gloop. The gaucheness of all this contrasted with their conversation, which was quite alluringly urbane. When I tuned in, the man, who I began to imagine was some poet or painter, was recounting certain ideas about womanliness, ascribed to a figure I couldn't identify. These ideas, almost shockingly essentialist to my ears, and focused on sexual arousal and the metaphysical enigma of the female orgasm, were received by his dinner partner with perfectly composed curiosity, and little nods of assent between mouthfuls of deep-fried pork. After some time the man concluded his account and said, as if it followed: 'But you are no longer in the theatre?,' to which she replied: 'Oh, I haven't been on stage in forty years.' At that point the waitress brought the bill and I was distracted, but as I stood I heard her telling him, in response to something else, 'I was in Paris once with Montgomery Clift . . .'

At the French House, where I stood at the bar with a Breton cider, the usual collection of freaks was on display. Across from me a tall, very dark-skinned black man with tiny eyes and a precise moustache, wearing a herringbone jacket and canary-yellow scarf with little dots, was lecturing a skimpily dressed blonde woman of a certain age: I imagined her in the same place, forty years earlier, a teenager in a similar, slimmer outfit, dutifully furnishing the same attention to a series of older men, journalists and the odd academic, in whose flats in Judd Street and Dolphin Square she learned how to do sex properly. This was not so bad a place to spend an hour. You could be comfortably alone, unlike in the gay bars round the corner, where solitariness, people assumed, or I always felt they did, only signalled your desire to be shot of it. Here you could look at the framed photos with real curiosity, not feigned to ward off a possible approach, or half listen to a conversation and smile at something in it without that smile being an apparent bid.

When I left the cinema the world felt delicate, like a forming scab. It had rained, and couples just emerged from pubs clutched each other teetering on the glassy streets. In Berwick Street, whose market trash had turned papier mâché in the gutter while pink lampshades glowed without irony on the floors above, I found plastic strips flapping in a porn-shop doorway, and went in.

Its walls were lined with racks of DVDs, and a display case by the counter held a selection of 'room aromas' and dildos in shrinkwrap, like popcorn and Coke by the tills at Blockbuster. Three younger boys in the corner, drunk and perhaps a bit high, glanced at me when I entered and turned back to the film they were inspecting, which they discussed with a fledgling, bitchy *esprit* that seemed to tilt on swells of adrenalin, as the mutual consequence of this still jokily hypothetical purchase made itself felt in one and then another. I watched them across the room: one was thin and very pale, with a spotty face and neck, and black hair dyed blond at its ends and a little greasy; he wore a football shirt and a gold chain, and was saying something with a grin to one of the others, a light-skinned black boy with short hair close to his scalp, who now for the second time caught my eye. I turned away, and approached the counter.

The assistant looked up from his *Empire*. He was older than me: early thirties, perhaps. I said: 'This is going to sound a bit strange . . .' and he shrugged.

'I'm writing a script, well, probably a script, about a guy called Nicky Crane. He was this very scary, violent racist skinhead back in the '80s who also starred, allegedly, in porn films. I'm trying to track them down.'

'Do you know what they were called?'

I shook my head.

'We do have some older stuff. It's popular because it's all bareback so they reissue it. But without the titles – I've never heard of the guy, so . . .' The three boys left; the strips swung back to vertical. The man said: 'If you want skinheads then Cazzo's quite good.'

I thanked him and walked to Trafalgar Square, where I found a bus heading south. It pulled away as I was climbing the stairs, and I gripped the banister, enjoying the tug as we surged into the curve. Down a deserted Whitehall and past the cathedral with its obscure familiar statues, we pressed the tapering gardens tight against the river, its water bubbling with the lights of the far bank. More people boarded under the ludicrous ski jump of Vauxhall bus station, and watching them pass me I spotted the boys from the porn shop, a few rows behind and slightly wilted now. They saw me looking but soon fell back into conversation about someone referred to as 'him,' as in 'you never should have tried that with *him*,' and '*he* wasn't going to anyway.' We were heading towards Wandsworth, which wasn't right, but there was no urgency: I could see where the bus took me for a while. When I next looked the boys seemed to be arguing: they were leaned into each other, arms tensed like mantises,' speaking with bristling muttered care.

I was seriously considering getting off, to find a way home, when someone sat next to me. It was the black boy from the group: his companions remained silently in place, ignoring his peremptory move. I looked out of the window. After a beat he said: 'Hello.'

He had a slim, serious face, high cheekbones, brown eyes with feminine lashes. He said: 'Is it all right me sitting here?'

'Um,' I said, and then politely: 'Yes, of course,' and turned away as if that was a natural end to it.

'Are you sure?' He spoke with that affected stress of some

gay men, which always makes me think of hairdressers and wonder, particularly in boys so young, how deliberately it was acquired. When I turned back I saw how beautiful he was. He repeated: 'You sure you don't mind?' and I gestured vaguely as if to indicate that it was a free country, without actually saying so, which could have been rude.

The boy asked: 'Did you find what you was looking for in that shop?'

'No.'

He giggled. 'Me neither.'

I registered an odd sensation: my realization, slightly delayed, that it was his hand on my thigh gave me a sudden and acute erection. 'Is this all right too?' he asked, and I said, 'Yeah,' and smiled back, surprising myself. He said: 'Shall we go to yours?'

'I was about to get off.'

'Was you?' The hand moved forward a little.

'I got on the wrong bus.'

'Which way are you heading, then?'

'Back to Vauxhall. I can work it out from there.'

He reached for the bell. 'I'll come with you,' he said, and before I could respond he was heading down the stairs. We stepped out by a kebab shop, where the road levelled between inclines. 'Where are we?' I asked, before the bus pulled away, revealing the station opposite: 'Clapham Junction,' he said, pointing, and as I looked in the direction of his outstretched arm he pulled it back and touched my face with his hand, and held it for a moment. Men with rugby shirts and voices swayed past us, bent on kebabs. The boy said: 'There's the bus – come on,' and ran across the road, past bereft-looking couples at a taxi rank. Once more I followed; he was right: a bus running back on the route we had taken came quickly down the hill. Upstairs his hand reappeared on my thigh and he made a noise between laughter and a squeak. A string of illuminated estate agencies below blared vertiginous prices at passing drunks. I said: 'What about your friends?'

'What's that?' He shifted closer, and I felt his breath across my ear.

I said: 'Your friends, on the bus.'

'Oh, them.' He giggled again. 'They're being arseholes anyway.'

'Weren't you on your way home?'

'No, I live north. I was going round theirs, but they can fuck off.'

'Whereabouts north?'

'Hackney. Why, you coming?'

I rolled my eyes and smiled. 'I'm going home.'

'Can I come with you?'

'No,' I said, trying to sound amused at his persistence and slightly becoming so, 'you can't.'

'Why not? Have you got a boyfriend?'

'I have, yeah. Though that isn't actually why not.'

He laughed and repeated 'actually' in a silly voice, like a child who thinks something is funny. 'What is why not then?'

'It's not something I do.'

'What isn't?'

'Meet . . . boys on buses—'

'How about in porn shops!'

'—or in porn shops – and go home with them.'

'Don't you fancy me or something?'

'No, you're very cute.' I looked at him. 'How old are you anyway?'

'Eighteen. What about you?'

'Twenty-five.'

My answer met with silence for a minute. Then he said: 'I don't do it either, you know. Meet guys like this. I just really want to have sex tonight.'

The orange glow of the Sainsbury's at Nine Elms bloomed ahead of us. I said: 'We're almost there.'

'Can't we just have a drink?' I was standing now, and he blocked my way with his legs. He said: *'Please.'*

Of course, when we stood on an island among Vauxhall's conflux of roads he looked around hopelessly. 'I'm not sure where's still open.'

'Perhaps we should both go home.'

The lights changed, and the queue of traffic from the east set off as if at a starter pistol. It came straight at us, then split into streams bent for different destinations. 'Yeah,' he said, and put his arms around my waist, pulling me against him. We kissed for a moment.

'I do turn you on, don't I?' he murmured.

I said: 'I'm not *disputing* that,' and pulled him in to me again.

'We can go to Soho,' he said. 'Just for a drink.'

On the bus he said, 'I'm Nat, anyway.' He gave 'anyway' a comic emphasis. 'What's your name?'

'I'm James.'

Now I had conceded the drink, he started chatting. He said he was studying design part-time; I wondered if I believed him. He lived alone, was somehow on housing benefit. He'd had a few boyfriends, none for long. He asked what all that was about in the porn shop, and I tried to explain my Nicky project without sounding weird. He seemed amused.

The first bar we tried was open, but charging £5 entrance. 'Can't we just come in?' Nat asked, and then: 'All right, never mind, thanks.' I was offering to pay but he pulled my elbow and said he knew where to go, a members' club. Old Compton Street was quiet, its usual crowds diminished to those desperate to stay out, or just desperate, and those who never left: in the doorway of a post-production house, a thin boy sat begging in a padded jacket. Nat stopped to speak and I realized they knew each other: the boy said, 'I've not seen you around much lately,' which made me uneasy, and a minute later I said maybe I would just go home, but Nat said, 'It's just round this corner.' He buzzed and asked if Suzie was there. He repeated himself a few times, tried to explain who he was. I heard him say, 'But Suzie said if I was ever around I should just . . .' He slumped with resignation. 'Yeah, all right then, yeah, OK.'

He turned to me: 'Can't you just come back to mine?'

'Look,' I said. 'We tried.'

'Just for a drink. We can get a cab. We don't have to do nothing.'

'I think I might go home.'

'Are you worried I'm going to rob you or something?'

'No!' I was insulted, and angry, because it was a cheap tactic to play the race card, and embarrassed, because of course he was right: I recited in my head, and imagined explaining, that it wasn't that he was black, but he *was* a bit strange, and young, and had come on to me on the *bus* (where I was beginning to wonder if he'd followed me); he had no obvious income and knew beggars we happened across in the street, and his friends had looked like junkies; besides which, any reasonable person would be concerned for their safety if they were seriously considering going home with a stranger at one in the morning when none of their friends knew where. I saw him looking at me, and considered my accent and obvious education, and where Adam might be at this moment, and how Adam come to think of it might act in a situation like this; how little I ever did that was not indemnified and caveated and warranted-for in advance; that I was probably as strong as Nat, that the minicab driver would know where he'd taken us; that this was what men had to do once and men who were not like me still regularly did; that even aware how absurd it was I nevertheless believed that I was a fundamentally good judge of character; that he was very beautiful and we had really kissed and what I was now considering could be made real also, and anyway he was black – and I said: 'Well, how far is it?'

Nat smiled and I let him kiss me again. 'Mm,' he said. Outside the minicab office he confessed: 'I don't have any money. Is it all right if you pay for the cab?' and added: 'Can we buy something to drink first?'

We found a convenience store. At the counter he asked: 'Can we have . . . what do you like? Vodka? Is Jack Daniel's OK? OK, can I . . . can we please have a bottle of JD please?'

Watching the shopkeeper, I appreciated for the first time quite how drunk Nat was. The man said: 'It's past licensed hours, mate. I can't sell you alcohol.'

'Oh,' said Nat. 'But can we . . . there's no one in here and we've been going all *over* looking. Can we, can't you just sell us just one bottle really quickly for cash or something?' He pulled what was presumably intended as a cheeky grin. I was about to apologize when the shopkeeper reached back and passed Nat a bottle, which he stuck under his sweater. He pointed to me: 'He's paying.'

The man told me: 'Seventeen fifty.' I found my wallet and handed him a twenty. 'I can't open the till for this,' he said.

I shrugged. 'Keep the change, then.' Nat took my arm, grinning.

The shopkeeper regarded us. 'Be careful, boss,' he told me quietly. This advice preoccupied me in the cab, and I stayed alert to the address Nat gave the driver and the route we took, barely reciprocating his touches on the back seat. He lived on the ground floor of a converted Victorian house. There was a living room with a bay window at the front and a kitchenette to the rear: a box of Tesco own-brand cornflakes stood on the counter. He had a sofa, to which he directed me, and a television, which he switched on. He said: 'I need a wee,' and was gone for some moments while I watched the screen. It was a cookery programme: 'And the fantastic thing,' a woman told me brightly, 'is that this is *really* easy to make.' She seemed to be frying grapes in butter.

When Nat came back he asked, 'Aren't you taking your coat off?' He found glasses and poured the whiskey: 'We should have bought mixers.' 'You don't need to keep stirring it,' said the woman, 'but you do need to make sure it doesn't burn.' Nat pushed me against the sofa. Where our hips met I felt my wallet in my pocket, and remembered the laptop in my bag. 'Is this all right?' he asked. 'Yeah,' I said, 'yeah. I just—'

'—and then just *pour* it into your sponge case.'

Nat said: 'Take this off too. Have you been with a black guy before?' A minute later he asked: 'Can I go up the road and buy some coke?'

'No.'

'I just really feel like something. Or some pills. There's a guy up the road. Have you got forty quid?'

'We don't need it.'

His bedroom had posters and raffia blinds. Every so often, at some particular movement, he would give a shuddering gasp like someone experiencing real horror, and say: 'Oh, that feels nice.' My refusal to buy the drugs seemed to have comforted him somehow; he kept looking me in the eye, his crude insistence softened into childlike affection. His body lay like calligraphy on the sheet.

At a certain point, as if he had just remembered something, he grinned and lifted his legs like a baby in a cot. He formed a spatula with his middle fingers and licked it hungrily, then applied it to the exposed part. He pulled me towards him. 'What about a condom?' I asked, and he said, 'I haven't got any.'

'I'm not doing it then.' I was secretly relieved.

He gathered himself up. 'Oh,' he said, looking around. He mumbled, apparently to himself: 'You can take it out after a bit,' and a cloud of shame passed across his face. Then it was abruptly gone and he leaned forward and grabbed me like a petitioner. 'Come on,' he said, with a determined smile, and licked himself ferociously. Even with the necessary mediation of his fingers, it made him look like a cat. 'Come on,' he said. 'Fuck me a little bit.'

'Jesus,' I said, and sat up. I told him to listen: he was a teenager with his life ahead of him; it wasn't curable, whatever he thought; people were still dying; even managed it was nasty; it would be his whole life with blood tests and side effects and Christ knows what; he was being fucking stupid.

Nat looked up at the ceiling. I thought his eyes were watering, and stroked his arm, but I might have imagined it: I was awkwardly aware of feeling righteous and grown-up. On the television in the front room the newsreader said something about video analysis, and captured aid worker's family had accepted, and there were sombre voices before a reporter's brisk recap. She said 'video' again, and 'mosque' and 'marines,' and we heard muffled urgent shouts and shots.

Nat said: 'Aww.' He smiled. 'You're sweet,' he said, and touched my face. But not long afterwards he said: 'You could fuck me though. I trust you.' I washed my penis in the bathroom sink, where a water heater was bolted. WARNING, it said: TO BE OPENED BY QUALIFIED ELECTRICIAN, and hummed when I ran the tap. I sat on the bed, pulling my socks on. Nat opened his eyes. 'Are you going?' he said. 'Don't go,' and fitted himself round me, his head on my thigh.

'I've got to,' I told him.

'Don't go,' he repeated. 'I'd feel so good in the morning.' He pronounced 'morning' like Alfred Dolittle.

When I stood he asked: 'Will you leave me your number?'

The television was showing motor racing: a camera inside one car filmed its driver's head, almost still before the juddering interior. I switched it off and screwed the lid on the Jack Daniel's. Then I sat on the sofa in my hat and scarf and waited for the minicab.

I got in shortly after five. The flat was silent, but I knew Adam was home from the envelope propped on the kitchen table. It was a letter addressed to me from the General Register Office, which apologized for the delay, and failure to locate a death certificate for Nicola Crane based on the information I had supplied. I should consider variants of the name ('the inform-ant may not have known the exact spelling or order of the deceased's forenames'), or later dates ('deaths can be registered some time after the event, if for example there was an inquest').

'A very small number of deaths are registered without a name.'

'The death could have occurred outside England and Wales.'

I deposed the cat from my place in the bed. Adam could sleep straight through the night and hardly move, but I was more restless. I'd wake several times, and need to shift, and he, apparently automatically, would adjust himself around me. Now, as he felt my touch, he woke long enough to kiss me and say, 'Hey. How are the nazis?' then rolled over, facing the wall – it was how we usually went to sleep, front-to-back, our bent knees tessellated. I wrapped my left arm round him and he clasped it to his chest with both his hands; my right, which I could neither twist behind me nor crush beneath his weight, I laid on the pillow above my head, touching Adam's crown. 'Nicky Crane,' I whispered, 'never really died.' But he was asleep again: I kissed the back of his neck. I could still taste the sweetness of his milky breath, which would be curdled by morning: he had the habit, which I found almost heart-stopping, of taking a hot chocolate to bed – after brushing his teeth with electric thoroughness. But that was his charm, I thought as I held him: with the left arm, a man to be clung to, a raft in the night's pitch, and with the right hand, a boy to stroke the head of.

The only problem with this position was my right arm. Often, as we slept, the blood would drain from it – raised as it was on pillows – and I would wake to find it dead.

A BARRAGE of milk bottles, eggs and rotten fruit was hurled at British Nazi Colin Jordan and his bride, blonde French divorcee Francoise Dior, as they arrived at his headquarters last night for a "blood-letting" pledge to celebrate their wedding.

About 150 police fought to keep back a furious, 300 - strong crowd outside the head office of Jordan's tiny National Socialist Movement, in Princedale-road, Notting Hill, London.

Some demonstrators broke the police cordon and rushed towards Jordan and his black-leather-clad bride. One man was arrested.

Jordan flung up his hand in a Nazi salute. Then, as glass smashed around him, he and the new Mrs. Jordan were hustled into the headquarters by a bodyguard of his strongarm Nazis.

The door slammed. Wreaths were hurled at it. The door reopened to let in another guest. The crowd surged forward again . . . and two more men were arrested.

Ceremony of 'blood mingling'

Swastika Flag

Inside the Nazi H Q the "blood-letting" ceremony got under way. There were about thirty guests, four of them women.

Jordan and his 31-year-old wife, who were married on Saturday at Coventry Register Office, stood below a picture of the late Adolf Hitler one-time dictator of Germany.

Over a table draped with the Nazis' swastika flag, they made a declaration that they were "pure-blooded."

Then Mrs. Jordan—wearing a gold necklace of diamond-studded swastikas — cut her wedding-ring finger with a dagger Jordan did the same.

They held hands and let their first drops of blood fall on to an open copy of Hitler's book Mein Kampf on the table.

In the background a record-player droned out Wagner's Wedding March.

Solemnly, the Nazi couple rubbed their bleeding wounds together . . and slipped a gold ring on each other's fingers.

Marching Song

Then everybody toasted them with goblets of mead, and sang the "Horst Wessel" Nazi marching song.

Absent from the ceremony was Britain's Number Two Nazi, 29-year-old John Tyndall, who was engaged to the bride earlier this year for one month.

"It doesn't mean there is a rift between John and me," Jordan explained. "He is afraid of the publicity affecting his family."

Daily Mirror, 3 October 1963

Mr Tyndall
'expelled'

Mr Colin Jordan, leader of the National Socialist Movement, issued a statement in London last night saying: "Mr John Tyndall, formerly national secretary, has been dismissed from his post and expelled from the National Socialist Movement."

Guardian, 12 May 1964

Mr Tyndall insists: 'It is Colin Jordan who is expelled'

Mr John Tyndall, who was said on Monday by Mr Colin Jordan, leader of the National Socialist Movement, to have been dismissed from the n a t i o n a l secretaryship and expelled, stated yesterday that it was Mr Jordan who had been expelled from the movement.

Mr Tyndall said:

" It is in fact Colin Jordan who has been expelled from the movement by the unanimous decision of an emergency council comprising the entire administrative staff of NSM headquarters.

" The grounds for his expulsion are woeful neglect of his duty as leader of the movement and undignified conduct in public detrimental to the good image of National Socialism. . .

" Colin Jordan knew of our intention to make this announcement and his own statement to the press is simply his way of getting in the first blow."

Guardian, 13 May 1964

The Union Tavern

'Blimey,' says the skinhead. 'Fuck.'

He leans against the wall, breathing. Tony runs the tap.

'Clever little fucker. Aren't you?'

Tony wipes his wet face on his shoulder, looks up, smiles. He turns off the water and heads for the door.

'Hang about a minute. Where'd you learn all that?'

Pausing: 'My gran taught me didn't she.'

'Yeah very funny. You got a name then?'

'Might have. What's yours?'

'Dennis. Live around here do you you cocky cunt?'

'I might do.'

'Might have, might do. What are you, fucking James Bond or something? Well if you might live around here, then it might just happen that I might see you about. Mightn't I?'

And then it is Wednesday, 9 September 1970, and Tony is late getting home from school, and there is Dennis smoking astride the low wall of a playground and scowling at the toddlers. He knows an empty house that is waiting to be demolished for flats where you can climb in the window.

And it is Saturday, 12 September. And Monday 14. And Tuesday 15.

And Dennis says: 'So do you ever just snog?'

Dennis says: 'If you're going to hang about with me we better do your hair.'

They go to Roy's, near the station.

Tony says, 'I've got no money,' and Dennis tells him, 'On me.'

'Who's your friend?' asks the girl. She wets Tony's hair and cuts it close off the back-comb.

'Bloody hell,' says Tony afterwards. 'My mum'll kill me.'

'That's what they're there for isn't it, mums? She can sew your jeans when she's finished having a go and all.'

Dennis's mum is a bit deaf and usually has the television turned up loud, so you can get away with murder or whatever.

At the market, while the man finds change for Tony's AirWairs, Dennis sings quietly in his ear:

'*Oh soldier, soldier, will you marry me,*
With your musket, fife and drum?
Oh, how can I marry such a pretty girl as you
When I have no boots to put on?
So off to the cobbler she did go
As fast as she could run.
She bought him a pair of the best that was there
And the soldier put them on.'

The salesman gives them a funny look, but warms up again when they pay extra for oxblood polish. Later Dennis teaches Tony to apply it.

'Right,' he says, when they're done. 'Now you can meet my mates.'

*

Dennis's mates are all skinheads. There are nearly twenty of them. Dennis and Tony find them at the Wilberforce estate, where they usually hang about the courtyard if the evenings are warm enough. They make a bit of noise, whistling at girls and shouting, but there's not too much bother because a lot of them live there and you don't shit in your own garden.

A few of them are Tony's age. All but a couple are younger than Dennis.

'All right?' they say to Tony. One of them murmurs to Dennis: 'Well done mate,' and Dennis looks halfway between embarrassed and chuffed.

They have a regular pub where the landlord doesn't fuss as long as the older boys do the ordering. They usually have enough money for drinks. Sometimes if they're short they'll go and roll a Paki. The bigger lads get in his face and give him a bit of aggro, and the short ones sneak into his pockets while he's distracted. Tony's too tall for that: it takes the younger boys, the eight- and nine-year-olds.

Dennis always has a bit of cash on him.

Most often they let the Paki go after a bit of a bruising, but Dennis tells him about one time when Steve, who is a bit of a psycho sometimes, not to mention a fat bastard, got carried away and lobbed a brick after the running Paki, so it landed smack on his head. He pivoted face-first into the pavement and the lads scarpered in every direction, not stopping until they were out of breath with effort and laughter. The police turned up at some of their houses later but it never came to much.

Tony says: 'How do I look?'

'You've only fucking asked ten times.'

It is Saturday, 24 October 1970. It is mid-morning, and they are standing on Victoria Embankment. The wind coming off the river flicks the sleeves of Tony's new Ben Sherman about his thin upper arms. He has goosebumps, although it's not really cold. Dennis says, 'You look good.'

Dennis is smoking. Tony puts his hands in his pockets and jumps up and down a little. He says: 'So you met him in a pub?'

'You're a fucking broken record this morning.'

'He just come up to you?'

'You can go home if you want.'

'Which pub was it?'

'*Jesus.* I can't fucking remember. Down the West End somewhere.'

'And he just come up to you and all that?'

Dennis takes a final drag on his cigarette and throws it over the wall on to the roof of a moored barge. They watch it land. He says, 'Anyway.'

'What?'

'Nothing.' He frowns at Tony, then abruptly swings his leg round to kick him up the arse. It lands round the side, ineffectually.

'What was that for?'

'So you'll shut up.'

'But I shut up already.'

'So you'll stay shut up then.'

There is a loud honk and they turn. A convertible, a Peugeot 404, has pulled up on the other side of the road. It is emerald green, newly washed, throbbing by the kerb like a fat, sated slug. A man leans out of the driver's window and calls, 'Come on then!' He has a voice like off the television.

They cross the road without looking at the traffic, daring it to hit them. Tony opens the door. In the front passenger seat is another skinhead Tony hasn't seen before: Dennis's age, with ginger hair and a long-sleeved, checked shirt rolled above the elbow. He gets out and says: 'All right Dennis?'

The driver pushes forward the vacated seat. He says: 'Christ, Dennis, he's a bit young, isn't he?'

'Yeah,' says Tony, climbing in, 'well you're a bit fucking old aren't you?'

From behind, all you can see of the man is a thick cowl of shoulder-length yellow hair, run through with frizz as if it has been scrunched up and released. A dull grey is pencilled in towards the scalp. He steers the car with his left hand and holds a cigarette in his right.

Dennis says, 'I thought you said it was OK.'

'It's cool,' says the driver. 'But I mean, you know. Fucking hell.'

Through the rear-view mirror, the other skinhead asks Dennis: 'How've you been doing, all right?'

'Yeah not bad.'

They curve through sparse traffic around Blackfriars.

'My name's Nigel,' calls the driver over his shoulder as he pulls tight round a corner. 'As Dennis isn't polite enough to introduce us.'

'Fuck off Nigel,' says Dennis.

'Tony,' says Tony.

'Ryan,' says the other skinhead. 'You all right?'

'Where are we heading anyway?' Dennis asks.

'Thought we'd start in the City. Classical architecture. Nice bit of contrast.'

Nigel pulls up by the Bank of England. He fetches his camera from the boot and arranges the three skins before the Royal Exchange. Dennis leans against a column and Ryan sits on the steps, his legs lying flat across their corners. From behind his lens Nigel says, 'Try to slouch a bit more. That's it. Tony, you're practically smiling. Look at the camera like you hate it.'

Tony yells at him: 'Fuck off. Cunt.'

'Perfect!'

Nigel's camera is strapped around his neck. He moves round them in an arc, snapping rhythmically. He photographs

45

them leaning on the railings around the tube entrance, crossing the empty street like the *Abbey Road* cover. When he has to stop and change film he asks, 'So, how would you spend an average evening?'

Ryan says: 'What do you mean?'

'How do you spend your time? When you're not, you know, down the West End. What do you do with your mates?'

They look at each other. Dennis says, 'Well we hang about don't we? Round the estate. Have a laugh and that.'

'What about facilities? Are there youth clubs you can use?'

Tony says: 'One or two.'

Dennis says: 'But they're shit really. All these rules. Like you can't drink or smoke.'

'How about bother? Do you get into fights?'

'Well I mean. You have the occasional fight don't you?'

'What about girls?'

'What do you mean?'

'Like fucking?'

He says the word with deliberate rough assertion, but it comes out sounding awkward and stupid, quarantined by the consequent silence. Dennis mutters, 'Piss off Nigel.'

They drive over to Hoxton for some different backgrounds. On the way Tony asks, 'What's this for anyway, the papers?'

Nigel tosses his cigarette. 'No, it's for a magazine. Quite a new publication, I run it with some friends of mine.'

'What sort of magazine?'

'A sort of cultural survey, really. Galleries, photographs, opinion pieces, the odd short story. Film reviews. That kind of thing.'

'Will we see it when it's done?'

'It's not easy to find in the shops. I'll pass a copy to Dennis if you want.'

By four o'clock they are finished. Nigel distributes £4 each and asks, 'Right. Who wants a drink?,' but Dennis says, 'We need to be off.'

Nigel says, 'All right then, sweetheart, take the money and run. I'll see you soon, I'm sure. Very nice to meet you, Tony.'

Ryan leans out of the passenger window. 'See you then Dennis.'

'All right sweetheart?' asks Tony.

It is a few minutes later and they are waiting for the bus.

'Oh leave it out mate I'm not in the mood.'

'What's he calling you that for?'

'He's just like that isn't he?

'He was a fucking ugly old bastard and all.'

'You didn't have to come. I thought you could do with the cash.'

'Well I could.'

'Pay for your own gear for once.'

One day Dennis tells Tony: 'We're going dancing.' They meet the rest of the mob at Mile End tube and run through the gate, yelling, 'You bloody kids!' at the ticket collector as they pass. On the train Tony swings from the straps, and a few lads sing. After Queensway someone says, 'Next stop the Congo!'

The club is in a basement flat on Talbot Road. As they approach they feel the thud of an amplified beat, and Dennis grins at Tony. 'Told you,' he says. 'If you want the good tunes you've got to follow the spades.' They cough up 3 shillings each to a black man in a mafia suit ('*Sur*charge,' he winks at them) and clamber down the stone stairs. Inside it is hot and loud, and there's a smell of strange food, overlaid with another Tony suspects is marijuana. There are no other whites in sight and he's glad they're in such a big group.

Dennis leads him through a swaying thicket of blacks – men in their twenties and thirties in suits dancing with

47

decked-out women, kids with short hair and pork-pie hats, crooking their arms as if about to break into the Lambeth Walk. At the back of the room they've dragged a table across a doorway to make a bar. A tall, limber teenager is selling beers, the beat rippling along his spine. He sees Dennis and grins.

'Going to get us raided for serving kiddies.'

'You should be bloody raided and all. His name's Tony. First time here. This big bastard's called Marcus,' he tells Tony.

'Welcome to you down there. What do you want then, two beers?'

He hands a can over the table. Reaching for it, Tony looks up at him and says, 'Ya raas.'

Marcus laughs. 'Pickney tink im nyega nuh.'

'What are you going on about?' says Dennis over the music while he pays. 'You forgotten how to speak fucking English or something?'

Marcus's response is impenetrable.

'Don't try it on with me mate, you were born in fucking Lambeth.'

'Lambeth is a fucking *dive*, man. You take me out of Africa.'

'You been at the ganja again? I haven't fucking taken you anywhere.'

'Your grandaddy take my grandaddy. Make him a slave.'

'You're having a fucking laugh mate. My grandad couldn't afford a pot to piss in, where's he going to start buying slaves from? It's Edward fucking Heath's fucking grandad you want to have words with.'

'White man all the damn same, man.'

'Yeah piss off. Come on,' he tells Tony, 'let's do some dancing.'

'Ya *raas*.'

The other lads have colonized a corner of the room near the entrance, where they're moving much like the blacks, except more fiercely, with harsh, disjointed gestures. There's a small moat of floor between the groups, but it may just be a safety margin around Steve, who is pumping his clenched fists up and down wildly as he stomps, like an accelerated King Kong.

Dennis has shown Tony how to skank in private and he starts now, following Dennis's lead. It's easy really, the casual emphatic downbeat pulling one shoulder after another into a rolling shrug, heavy boots clumping on the stone floor of the basement, hand gestures endlessly deferring each imagined interruption. He dips his head forward into the music, tilting it left and right, and rolls his eyes up, engaging the room in moody surveillance. The music's all the same really, each track the same phrase repeated again and again with some bloke rambling over it, but then that's the point: after a while you just stop thinking. Everyone's doing some version of these moves, Dennis almost lightly, betraying an easy pleasure, sneaking a quick grin at Tony as their glances briefly align, Steve still a comic raging toddler, and all the dolled-up coons like a kaleidoscope view, one endless repeated mass filling his vision and the rhythm cascading through it like dominoes, this way and that. At least you can fucking do what you like here, not like at home, none of them care anyway, just keep treading and shrugging and it all washes over you.

Another track starts now, with a piano line that's vaguely familiar, and then the voices kick in and yes, it's a song he's heard before, a hit from a few months ago, and here's the beat starting up, just more of the same. His body is picking up where it left off when he hears Dennis say, 'Oh fucking not this again,' and the chorus repeats, crisply enunciated, '*Young, gifted and black*,' which is of course the name of the song, some bollocks the blacks are actually responding to, there are more smiles now and he can see some eye-catching and a few singing along to the phrase '*open your heart to what I mean*,' Jesus

Christ they're as wet as hippies. The lads are acting up at this, jeering among themselves, and over the other end of the room he sees that Marcus cock an imaginary gun at him and winking pull the trigger, so he sticks two fingers back, and as the chorus returns Steve leads them in roaring over the top – '*Young gifted* AND WHITE!' – and some nigger bitch starts yelling back at them, so they holler it again even though it's not in time this time, and most of the blacks are shouting at them now. Dennis decides, 'I've had enough of this shit,' and he strides to the nearest speaker, a massive crate-sized thing balanced on a table, and '*There's a great truth you shou—*' yanks the cable out of the back and bolts, and now they're all fucking worked up and it's time to head up the stairs, Tony chucking his beer can in the blacks' midst as they pursue the lads into the road, hurling bottles and kicking the stragglers. The man who took their money at the door yells, 'Touch my fucking system,' as they scramble through the gate and down the street.

'Thought you were going to wake my mum.'
   'I should go in a minute.'
   It is Monday, 2 November 1970.
   'You all right?'
   'Yeah.'
   'Where are you going?'
   'Find that towel.'
   'Leave it. Come here.'
   'Bollocks it's cold.'
   'Look at that. Little animal.'
   'What?'
   'Little animal. Aren't you?'
   'No.'
   'I did that. Didn't I? Look at all this.'
   'Don't do that.'
   'You go all funny afterwards.'

50

'Get off.'

'Stay still will you?'

'I'm ticklish. Come back here.'

'All right?'

'Yeah.'

'Better?'

'Yeah.'

Outside, two cats fight. The yawn of a passing car.

'Tony boy.'

'What?'

'That Nigel geezer. You know how I know him don't you?'

'You said you met him in a pub.'

'But you know what I meant don't you?'

Tony says nothing.

'Don't you?'

'Sort of.'

'I need some extra cash sometimes. Furniture trade don't stretch to Levi's.'

'Not six pairs anyway.'

'I haven't got six pairs.'

'I've lost track.'

'You know how many pairs. I've got two pairs.'

'Yeah.'

'And I need to make sure my boy's dressed all right don't I? I can't have him dragging me down if we're going to be hanging about together.'

'Yeah.'

'So. I just don't like secrets is all.'

'I should go in a minute anyway.'

For a moment neither of them says anything.

'Here – do you want to go dancing tomorrow?'

'What,' Tony says, 'another spade club?'

'No nothing like the last place. You'll enjoy this.'

*

And it is nothing like the last place. They take the bus to Camberwell, riding at the front of the top deck, one double seat each. ('What about the others?' asks Tony as they walk to the stop, and Dennis says, 'Just us tonight.') They lean back against the sides of the bus, facing each other, boots up on the seat, and nobody says anything when it fills up, not even the conductor.

Tony looks at Dennis across the aisle. He is gazing out of the front window as the bus moves on to Tower Bridge. By seven-thirty it has long turned dark and the thin moon has been and gone; behind Dennis's profile the haze from the city lights dims somewhat above the river. As Dennis watches the road ahead, his expression blank and his mouth hanging slightly open, his boots are suddenly unconvincing. He looks vulnerable and a bit slow; you could beat him up, Tony thinks, without much trouble. His two front teeth dangle into the gap between his lips and for some reason he is swallowing repeatedly. Tony tears off part of his bus ticket and puts it in his mouth, chewing it into a ball and making it heavy with spit, then gobs it at Dennis, hitting him neatly on the cheek. Dennis gives a tiny spasm at the impact, then turns with an uncomprehending grin. 'What was that for?' he asks.

Tony says: 'Sitting with your mouth open,' and turns to look at the road. After a minute he registers a retaliatory flick, which he ignores.

The Union Tavern is on Camberwell New Road, a big building on a corner. The ground-floor windows are blacked out, but lights are visible upstairs. There is a short queue of skins waiting and you can hear the ska beat from inside.

A woman is taking money at the door, in her sixties, in a wig. She says to Tony: 'How old are you then?'

'Sixteen,' he tells her.

'Like French buggery you are. No drinking please love, eh?'

Inside it is all skins. There must be more than 200 of them.

Apart from a few hanging round the edges or buying drinks at the bar, everybody is dancing, facing the front, in strict lines. And they're all white, or nearly so: Tony looks hard and thinks he has seen a Paki, but a smack from Dennis ends his reverie. 'Come on,' he says.

And then Dennis does an astonishing thing. He takes Tony's hand in his and pulls him on to the dance floor. He does it with such ease that it's not until he's dragged him all the way into the line that Tony even notices what happened. It's his body that responds first, the whole thing suddenly bracing itself of its own accord for whatever disaster will ensue, a big panicky swill of nausea splashing up from his stomach, sudden heat on the surface of his skin. He looks up at Dennis, tries to pull away, expecting to see belated realization, the same animal horror reflected, but Dennis just grins and begins to dance, and won't let go. Tony feels his blood throb in the tight grip. He looks round anxiously but finds no reaction. People haven't seen – or rather they haven't cared. Seen, but not noticed.

The record has ended, and the rows of men are fallen nearly still, waiting for the next track. It begins with speech – *Now I want all you skinheads to get up on your feet* – and Tony recognizes it, an old one, and popular too, because the skins around are cheering and leaning slightly forward on their booted toes in anticipation, as if they will start sprinting. Buoyed on his ebbing flood of panic, Tony readies himself too, looking around him again as he does, and down the same row to his right he suddenly spots Ryan, the lad from Nigel's car, who catches his eye and nods with a little nervous smile. Along the line in front, among endless slight variations in the pattern of braces meeting the waists of jeans, he sees in one gap two hands touching, and elsewhere fingers against the small of a back, and he feels Dennis, who has never let go of his hand, give it a squeeze, and the beat begins.

*

(Ryan leaves early and gets a cab to Piccadilly – a gamble, but not a bad one. He makes the Golden Lion in plenty of time and sits at the bar with a Scotch. Tuesday is not the busiest night but there are still a few boys around, some he recognizes, more he doesn't, one that's clearly new. They don't offer you this at the Youth Employment; you find it by yourself when you're on your own one night at the pinball machines and a man in a suit comes up and subs you a few games. You learn what it was about the way you were standing that made that happen, and you do it again. Like now: already someone's next to him saying, 'Would you like another drink?'

Ryan looks up. I don't fancy you, he thinks, but then that's how this works, so he says: 'OK then, thanks.' The man is some kind of Arab. He's clean-shaven but the skin on his face carries the scars of some unspeakable ordeal, or perhaps just bad childhood acne. He has dressed to fit in, a black turtleneck under a rough tweed blazer, but his nervousness betrays him.

Ryan takes the fresh glass and says, 'Cheers.' Then he adds, as usual, 'I'm not really into wasting time.'

'No. Well. No, nor am I.'

'So what is it you're after?'

There's a silence. Ryan puts his hand over the man's, over the bar. He says, 'It's all right. You can say it.'

'Well, I was – I mean, I'm looking. For some company.'

Ryan smiles. 'Well there's a surprise.'

Ryan says: 'You want us to go somewhere private, right?'

The man nods.

'Right. And what do you want us to do?'

The man looks at him.

Ryan says: 'You want me to wank you off? You want a fuck?'

Overwhelmed, the man stares at a beermat on the bar, breaching a thin spill of drink.

'It's all right,' says Ryan. 'It just goes to the price. What's your name, anyway?'

'I'd rather not . . .'

'OK. OK. Well, you look like a Mustafa to me. Shall I call you Mustafa?'

'If you want.'

'Hello Mustafa. I'm Ryan. Pleased to meet you.'

Ryan extends his hand and the man, bewildered, shakes.

'So now. We were saying. What do you want to do?'

A tremendous sigh. 'I like . . . I suppose oral, I—'

'You want me to suck you off?'

Nothing.

'You want to suck me?'

Mustafa's eyes say yes.

'Yeah, the thing is, Mustafa mate, that's not really my cup of tea.'

This is what you do: you suggest their key desire is just a bit beyond the pale. But not that far beyond. And then you jack up the price.

'I mean, normally I wouldn't. But it's quiet in here tonight, and you've got a nice smile haven't you? When you let it out anyway – there you go! Look. What if we said a bit over the odds? Say eight quid?'

'That's a little more than . . .' No matter how desperate, they invariably haggle. 'Maybe four?' says Mustafa. Of course they settle on six.

'Where shall we go then? You got a hotel?'

'I can't.' Meaning, Yes, but my wife's there, waiting.

'Don't worry, I know a place. You'll have to pay for the room though, all right?' When the price is agreed you should get moving in case they bottle out.

In the taxi Ryan says, 'Your English is good.'

'I studied at Oxford.'

'Fuck me. Well that explains it doesn't it?'

The taxi driver mutters something that Ryan hears well enough. He says, 'Mate. If you want your fucking fare you'll keep quiet, all right? Or you can just let us out here, thank you.'

The driver finishes the journey in silence. As they get out Ryan whispers, 'Don't tip him nothing.'

The hotel is small, a converted town house near Victoria, with a plastic illuminated sign. Ryan goes up the stairs first and holds the door open for Mustafa, who is visibly readying himself for the front desk. Ryan tells him, 'It's all right.'

He says to the woman, 'We need a room. Me and my uncle,' and to Mustafa: 'It's cash up front.'

They walk up the narrow staircase in silence. When Ryan opens the door, the twin beds, little cupboard and now-familiar wallpaper wash over him like a waiting flood and he is suddenly exhausted. He tells Mustafa: 'Go on, I'll just clean up a little bit.'

In the bathroom he digs the bag of pep pills from his pocket and swallows one. It won't work fast enough, but still. He splashes cold water on his face, then undoes his Sta-Prest and washes his prick under the running tap. For this he has to stand on his toes. There's no towel again, so he dries himself on his shirt.

Ryan strokes himself. There's a trick to getting hard in this situation. You can't ignore how old and ugly the bloke is so you have to use it. You need to see yourself, here, what you're doing, what you're about to do, for money, with this man.

In the bedroom, Mustafa is affecting an interest in the now-invisible view on to the dingy internal courtyard. Ryan lies back on one of the twin beds and says, gently, 'What are you looking at?'

Mustafa looks up. He says, 'It's quite nice, the way the light . . .' and tails off, gesturing.

It's not that you want to hurry them but they tend to need encouragement. Ryan says, 'Oh yeah? The way the light?' He reopens the fly he just fastened, unveils his prepared erection. 'Come here then,' he says. 'Hey. Mustafa go. Mustafa cock. Eh?'

The room is paid for the night, and when this is finished and the man has returned to his posh hotel in Paddington, Ryan will sleep here, in clean sheets on the unused bed. He will stand under the hot shower and wash with the soap they provide, and then he will sleep. They've given up asking back home. He tells them: 'When I'm out, I'm out.' He will wake early, and he will be alone, and it will be to the sound of traffic, smart cars ferrying men to important jobs, not his father's industrious farts in the bathroom. He will have another shower, under water that will still be hot and stay that way until he turns it off. Because there are no towels he will pull the sheet from the mattress and leave it tangled on the soaking floor. Then he will walk down the stairs, leave the key on the desk, and out, slap into the middle of the fucking city, the fucking middle of it. Taking his time amid lawyers and businessmen, he will stroll down to St James's Park, crisp grass in the watery light. There's a small café on the other side where he will buy tea and a bacon roll, perhaps two. He will cross into the square and sit on a bench and have his breakfast before the Houses of Parliament.)

Right off

TROUBLES ON the Right— the National Front is being accused of going soft on the race issue. The attack comes from what we always used to call Colin Jordan's British Movement, but it now appears that Jordan's influence has waned, and the new BM boss is the national secretary, Michael McLaughlin.

The tone of the BM's propaganda is somewhat strident—the front page of its British Patriot journal says : "If you want your children to grow up in a white Britain free of commies, traitors, and coloureds, join, support, and vote for British Movement."

McLaughlin, resigned from the NF three years ago, because it "failed to recognise the spiritual leadership of Adolf Hitler." The British Movement is now inundating areas of National Front support with a leaflet which suggests that the NF is a Zionist movement.

It reproduces the front page of the Jewish Telegraph of February 15 of this year, bearing the headline: "National Front Says Protect Israel." The British Movement add "The Front is kosher." The BM policy is to repatriate all British Jews "since they are of alien race."

Guardian, 10 August 1974

Knickers fine for Jordan

COLIN JORDAN, former leader of the extreme right-wing British Movement, was found guilty yesterday of stealing three pairs of frilly red knickers.

Jordan, 51, of Tudor Avenue, Coventry, took the knickers and a box of chocolates from a supermarket in Leamington, Warwickshire.

Yesterday, he told Leamington magistrates that the knickers—which had white lace fronts—were a "surprise present" for his 89 - year - old widowed mother. Jordan said he had put them into his pocket inside the store because he was "embarrassed."

He then paid for his groceries but claimed he forgot about the knickers, and the chocolates which were in a shopping bag.

He was fined £30 with £29·42 costs.

Mirror, 17 May 1975

It is with regret that British
News notes that Colin Jordan
is retiring from politics and he
has resigned as National Chairman of the British Movement,
a kindred organisation. Although
we have disagreements in the
past, Colin Jordan was one of
the few men who had the cou-
rage to keep the flag flying in
the most difficult days of the
late fifties and early sixties
when racial-nationalism was at
its lowest ebb -let us hope
that he will soon return to the
fight.

British News 6, 1975

Voice of Britain

A crowd had gathered by the knee-high fence that separated the path from the bank of the lake. 'What's going on?' asked Sarah, so we headed down the slope to see.

It turned out to be a pelican trying to swallow: its caricaturally expressive neck swayed and stretched over its squat body, which padded gingerly beneath with small balancing movements like a unicyclist's wheel. Every few seconds the bird would face skywards and open and close its long, pale beak, and its gullet, massively distended, would ripple and shake.

'It's eating a fucking pigeon,' Sarah said.

She was right; the pelican's movements were not merely its own. Its struggling victim violently embossed the skin of its throat: you could see the arc of a wing, then a beak straining to puncture. The pelican seemed not so much panicked as frustrated. It gulped adamantly away, and now and again compressed its bulging neck, pulling its head tight against its body, as if it could force the pigeon down with its chin.

I said, 'I didn't know they did that.'

Sarah grimaced. 'I don't think they do. Let's go.'

We rounded the lake, past the flowerbeds and menacing fairytale cottage, and crossed into Parliament Square, where police in bright yellow jackets, friendlier than the riot gear I had expected, chatted by concrete barriers.

'Christ, it's cold,' Sarah said. She wore a heavy knitted coat in white and red, which in this weather matched her cheeks, and a woollen hat with earflaps. Over breakfast in Valerie, the waitress had heard us discussing the march, and handed us a couple of Danish pastries as we left. 'On the house,' she had said. 'I'd go myself if I could afford the time off.'

On the Embankment we both stopped in the same involuntary moment.

'Fuck *me*.'

Sarah asked: 'What time is it?'

'Eleven-fifteen.'

'It doesn't kick off till half-twelve.'

The view through the far distance was thick with people. A huge crowd massed backwards from the starting point under Hungerford Bridge. *Jesus!* I texted Philip: *Like this at your end too?* We followed the waiting line, past coaches parked nose to tail, as it curved away from the river, and took our place at the end, just clear of a glut of smug Lib Dems holding yellow party placards. Someone was distributing NO WAR signs on behalf of the *Mirror*: we declined and took instead a couple of the most common, DON'T ATTACK IRAQ and NOT IN MY NAME. All of a sudden Sarah shoved hers at me, muttering, 'Hold this,' and shot up the side of the queue. I saw her approach a bearded, studenty guy: a bit crusty for me, but very much her type. She said something, leaned in for his reply, threw her head back laughing. I thought, again, how obvious people were. Now he was digging out his fags and groping for a lighter. She came back with a grin and a new placard: STOP THIS BLOODY WAR.

'I've got yours here,' I said.

She made a charade of furtiveness, sliding her eyes crazily and talking from the corner of her mouth so her cigarette wiggled: 'Ditch it.'

I looked at its replacement. '*Socialist Worker?*'

'Come on, he's gorgeous. I could do with a bit of radical.'

'Slag,' I pronounced.

'You're one to talk. Let me see your palm.'

'What for?'

'Depends.' She frowned and held my hand at face level, turning it in the light. 'Hairs mean too much wanking. Rash means you've got the syph.'

'Fuck off.' I pulled away, but she gripped tighter: 'Rash *and* hairs! Score.'

This was still new for both of us. Growing up, we were close enough, but without the conspiratorial bond some siblings claim. Things had changed when her Cambridge reserve gave way to a quite different graduate studenthood. In her Edinburgh room, where tampon boxes lay in shameless chaos with her books, she had casually handed me a spliff, a gesture whose novelty we both let go unspoken. This coincided with my own self-reinvention after college, so when, on her subsequent trip to London, we got, for the first time, properly drunk together, I found myself encouraged by her endless yucky digressions on the human body – she was becoming a parasitologist, not a doctor, but it opened the same door – to confess, all of a sudden, my recent, virgin, treatment for the clap. Sexuality had been long acknowledged between us, but sex itself barely discussed, and Sarah was so delighted by my proffered gonorrhoea that insinuating a perpetual, scandalous susceptibility in me to venereal disease became her running joke. Even now she was forever diagnosing me with God-knows-what, based on the most spurious symptoms. I could not scratch myself without her crying, 'Crabs!,' and suspected her of wasting hours online in the pursuit of ever more recherché conditions to accuse me of. She had even begun to make them up – unless there really is a hepatitis F.

My text to Philip had not gone out: the network was

overloaded. I was still trying to send it when Sarah nudged me: 'Looks like we're starting.' It was not yet twelve but whistles and drums were building; the crowd ahead unpacked in stages. As I hoisted my sign my mobile buzzed. It was Philip on Gower Street saying *We're off!* – so both ends were starting early.

We saw more marchers heading along the South Bank: Sarah bounced her placard up and down at them, and somebody seemed to answer. She grinned and took my hand. Her excitement was catching; looking around, I realized it was not just the scale of the event that was affecting, but how staggeringly inclusive it was: the protest might have been cast by an ad agency, pushing soft drinks or mortgages. There were the predictable socialists and Muslim groups – who had after all arranged the thing – but church groups too, and country folk in Barbours, and everywhere the very young and very old. I pointed to an ancient couple behind us, he in veteran's uniform and medals stiffly holding a NO WAR sign (its *Mirror* logo torn off), she very properly dressed in ankle-length skirt, cardigan and padded jacket, with a purple placard that read FREEDOM FOR PALESTINE. Ahead, Sarah's beardy friend and his associates had started a chant – *'Who let the dogs out? Bush! Blair! Sharon!'* – in which some of us joined while others stayed resolutely mute, uncertain of its desirability or just self-conscious. Before we broke up I had visited Justin at MIT, where his professor had inveigled us into demonstrating against the resumption of capital punishment. We had tramped in tiny circles outside the state legislature, led by her in a rhyming chorus – *'No death penalty here in Mass.! / Keep your bill, we* won't *let it pass!'* – which sounded hopeless in our English accents. Later, collecting signatures for a petition, my only success was with older, white Cambridge liberals: I was taken aback at the lack of interest from younger blacks, whom I had neither the guts nor the statistics to lecture on the racial inequities of judicial killing in their country.

We joined in the chant of 'Blair out' by the Commons, and resumed it outside Downing Street, where Sarah's knot of socialists had managed to delay. Emerging from Haymarket, I looked for the huge window over the Criterion that marked the boardroom of the management consultancy where I'd had my token interview after college. 'How much,' they had asked, 'should someone pay for all the tea in China?' What might I now have, if I'd got the job? A mortgage; a boyfriend; subtle opinions about PFI. In Piccadilly Circus the northern tributary joined us with cheers and whistles. We fought though to the space by the doughnut shop where Philip, as promised, waited with two friends. I recognized Mike from his jacket photograph. I had read his last-but-one novel on Philip's recommendation and thought I hadn't quite understood it, but was rather awed by its manifest darkness. The other guy I hadn't seen before. He was my age, and a skinhead – not by mere dint of his haircut, but in full attire, combat jacket and trousers tucked into knee-high lace-up boots. The combined effect of these was undermined by his shy smile when Philip introduced us: 'Adam, James.' I shook hands with him, and then Mike, but decided not to mention I had read his book.

As we rejoined the march I tried to tell Philip about the pelican, but he was too worked up over his own experience: heading up Tottenham Court Road, which was closed to traffic, he had nearly been hit when a silver saloon shot from a side street. 'Fucking driver didn't even notice me. The whole country's on the streets against an illegal war, and he can't be arsed to follow a diversion. Solipsistic cunt.' We swapped descriptions of people on our marches, and the signs we'd seen. Bombing for Peace Is Like Fucking for Virginity. How Did Our Oil Get under Their Soil? Cream Your Khakis, Not Iraqis.

'Did I tell you about the lesbian contingent?' I asked. 'With the sign saying The Only Bush I Trust Is My Own?'

Philip laughed. 'We had Cunt Coven: If You Want to Spill Blood Borrow Ours. Who actually told me war was menstrual envy. And that the banner was written in their *flow*.'

A teenager in white tunic and tagiyah came up the flank of the procession. He handed out stickers that turned out to show the Israeli flag, with a swastika in place of the Star of David. I dropped mine quietly, but Philip called the boy back. 'Listen,' he said, 'I'm not wearing this. I'm against the occupation and I support the Intifada, but I don't think it helps to use Nazi imagery against Israel. It alienates a lot of people, including sympathetic Jews.'

He held out the sticker. The boy looked at him for a moment. He said: 'Yeah, OK then, bruv, thanks,' took it and headed back down the line. I told Philip: 'I wish I could do that.'

'Talk to people? Well, try it sometime.'

'Perhaps. So anyway, there was this pelican . . .'

Philip was unimpressed, but Mike seemed taken with the story. 'Imagine that, Phil,' he grinned, 'a pelican eating a pigeon. A fucking *pigeon*. Eh?'

Adam told me, 'I don't understand how it got in there in the first place.' He had an oddly deliberate way of walking, as if aware of something you were about to discover: he watched his feet as he trod, rocked forward a little on the step. Whether this secret knowledge provoked anxiety or pleasure was unclear. When I looked up his face was candidly quizzical, as if he really expected an explanation of the process by which the pigeon had got in. His eyes looked like they were watering: a recurrent illusion it would take me a while to get used to. Later he told me he worked for a brand consultancy, and I couldn't think of anything to ask about that. He said, 'What do you do?'

At the time I was working as a freelance television researcher, one of a number of jobs I'd taken since college in the hope they might lead to something creative, which so far none had. I told him: 'I'm developing a TV series,' which was not untrue, but soon confessed that I was hatefully bored, and spent my days fast-forwarding through old programmes, seeking clips from which to assemble new ones on the cheap; that while the ostensible subject was a history of food on television, the real criteria for inclusion were bloopers and wobbly sets, and the holy grail an early appearance by some subsequent celebrity. At the next desk, a bunch of kids worked on a quiz show; every now and again one would call out: 'Which of these famous daughters has *not* had a boob job?' The people they named were the same ones I was meant to find waving egg-whisks on *Why Don't You?*, but had rarely heard of – so while the quiz show would be commissioned, and the kids move on to better jobs, Channel 5 would surely pass on *Here's One I Made Earlier*. If they did it might be hard to keep my job; I found it difficult to care.

I shared a hesitant, oblique conversation with Mike, my anxious memory of whose book made anything I contemplated saying look misjudged. As we neared the Piccadilly underpass, which seemed, in the light of sunset, to throb like the mouth of the whale, he abruptly turned and said, 'Fucking hell, eh? All *this*,' and I nodded and mumbled something like 'Jesus, yes.' At the park entrance a flashing display made the extraordinary claim of two million demonstrators, and Philip passed me a flyer:

'FUCK YOUR WAR':
London artists show their disgust at the implied consensus of the inevitability of war. We determine our individual and collective responsibilities in this process.
    This exhibition, a fringe event of the 15 February anti-war march, continues for the following week as a lingering protest that won't stay mute.

We wish to make clear the ongoing and determined application of our voices in the struggle against war.
What are you doing?

'That's all right then,' he said.

The sun was below the horizon now and the speeches were winding down. We sat on the grass, among crowds dispersing even as others still arrived, and drank the beers we had picked up en route. Sarah and Philip sustained most of the conversation while the rest of us listened, Mike staring out at the darkness bleeding towards us, and me stealing glances at Adam. The rest of us, I thought, looking at him, were here a little awkwardly, like tourists in our own city, but Adam was just sitting on the grass, and when he put his hands flat at his sides and leaned back on them facing the sky, it was the sky he saw and not himself doing it. His boots were a long straight descent from his bent knees to his feet, a dark ice scarp alive with sudden glintings.

After two beers he stood: 'I need a slash.'

'Me too,' I said, and got up after him.

It was hard to see, this far from the illuminated paths, but he pointed, 'Over here,' and headed further into the dim field. Placards, abandoned by tens of thousands of departed protestors, lay scattered on the ground, and were layered in places into a vast collage over which we walked: interspersed with grass and mud, they made our footsteps sound unpredictably. In this low visibility there was a faint gloam to the white that formed the background of some signs and the text of others, and you could make out slogans in angled fragments. ENOUGH, it said in thick marker on one hand-made sign, and something about Quakers on another, and over and over again, against the murky image of a soldier, the huge capitals distributed in thousands by the *Mirror*: NO WAR, NO WAR, NO WAR. At the clearing's edge began the black scaffolding of trees, between which Adam walked confidently until we were invisible and alone. He stopped and unzipped his fly, and I saw his released flesh in his hands, pale in the dark like a strange fish. 'Caught you looking,' he said quietly, and peed against the bark. I fumbled to follow before I was too hard to manage. When we were done we stood in place for a moment, and then there was the crunch of thin roots as we moved closer, and his sudden warmth where we touched and briefly kissed.

'Philip's coming to mine for dinner after,' I told him as we walked back. 'You should join us.' I wondered if I should ask Mike too, but when we got back he was about to leave. It was almost six-thirty, and I realized I needed Parmesan, so we walked with him to Knightsbridge tube and made a surreal end to the day of protest in the food hall of Harvey Nichols. (We were not unique in this.) In my flat we watched coverage of the protests while I cooked. Another two million in Madrid; three, perhaps four million in Rome; still more in Damascus and Osaka, Christchurch and Bloemfontein, Kingston, São Paolo, Alta, Malta. 'You have a disturbing amount of Crowley here,' announced Adam, who was inspecting my books.

'Ah, you found my black shelf.'

'James,' Philip said, 'is in many ways still a teenager. It's part of his charm.'

'Cooper. Sade. You're an interesting boy.'

'He's only whoring himself in TV, you see. One day he'll be an *artist*.'

Adam came to the counter and, without asking, helped me scrape sausage meat from its skin. 'Is that true?' he said.

I flushed slightly. 'Obviously what I really want to do is write screenplays. You know, like every fucking other person.'

'So why not just do one?'

'Mainly because I've got nothing to write about.'

I burned the sauce somewhat, but by then we were too drunk to care. Adam sat across from me, stroking my calf with the toe of his boot. In a lull, as we ate, he asked: 'When are you going to take that off?'

'Take what off?'

As some corrective to the protesters, a reporter conjured al-Qaeda. We saw familiar footage of its leader on trembling video. Sarah said, pensively, 'I quite fancy Osama.'

Philip nearly squeaked. 'No! Me too!'

'Take what off?' I repeated.

'What's left of your hair.'

Instinctively I felt it, and had the odd sense of being soothed by my own hand. Bin Laden, with his rifle, mumbled at us before some neutral backdrop.

'It's the beard,' said Philip. 'It's very manly.'

Sarah said: 'I like his eyes.'

'What do you mean,' I said, 'what's left of it?'

Philip: 'I think he'd be quite a good fuck.'

'Oh, I'd give it a go.'

'What, Osama-fucking?'

Sarah giggled. 'Osama-fucking.'

'Stop kidding yourself,' Adam told me. 'Shave off the lot and put it out of its misery. What do you call it, that *style* you have?'

'Um . . . I usually say can I have it short and a bit messy on top.'

He smiled and said gently: 'There is no "on top."'

'James moves slowly,' said Philip. 'Don't you, sweetheart?'

'I think it would suit you.'

'Maybe.' I stood a little unsteadily and gathered plates. 'I was going to make pudding,' I said, 'but I'm not sure I can be arsed.'

'I want pudding,' Philip announced.

Adam said: 'Do you need a hand?'

I asked him to grease the ramekins for Nigella's molten chocolate cakes.

'What are these?' said Philip. 'They look like little tents.'

'Yeah.' Sarah prodded hers with a fork. 'Tents in Tora Bora.'

'Osama tents!' exclaimed Philip, and they both collapsed. The phrase was repeated perhaps thirty times in the next ten minutes. At around midnight he said he should be off. 'You'd better go as well,' Sarah told Adam. 'It's a studio and I'm not sleeping in the bath.'

That week he sent me an email at work:

Hi James

Got your address off Philip. I just wanted to say thanks again for dinner the other night, not to mention the rest! It was a pretty great day I thought, even without the ending. Philip says thank you too, I think he's a bit embarrassed by the whole tent fiasco.

Anyway I've been doing some Googling and I thought you might like to know there have been pelicans in St James's Park since the early 1660s, when the first ones were presented to Charles II by the Russian ambassador. It's traditional for ambassadors to give pelicans for the park, but not too many at a time, because if there's more than 4 they tend to get aggressive with the other wildlife. As you noticed! Dunno know why the poor bastard was so hungry though, the pelicans are fed every day at 3 p.m. – according to Hansard, in 1995 they were getting 4lb of whiting a day at a cost of £78.50 a week between them, not to mention vitamin tablets. Which may sound expensive, but according to myth if there are ever no pelicans left in the park things really will go to shit in this country, so I suppose it's worth it.

See, I told you research was a piss-easy job! Only joking.

Let me know if you fancy a movie or a drink sometime. When are you going to succumb to the inevitable and get a zero crop?

Adam x

We went to *8 Mile* a few days later, but I didn't succumb to the inevitable for nearly a year. It was Philip who held the clippers, and it was then that he told me about Nicky.

JOHNNY MOPED/SKREWDRIVER-Roxy Club(16/4/77).
          The back of my legs still ache,
I tell ya.I don't care there weren't more
than hundred people down there,the Roxy was
a great night on Saturday.I went ignorant of
both bands'cept in name and Steve had giving
the Skrewdriver single a fair review earlier.
When Skrewdriver come on into'Anti Social'
they were obviously gonna work hard for the
handful there.It suprised me to learn that
this was their second proper gig(Man.Poly,
supporting Li'l Bob Story-two encores).Their
songs were sharp as staypress crease,the high
points being'9 to 5'(Yeah,I thought that
enal),'Jailbait'(their own),'No Pushover'and
the great'Gotta Be Young'.The band,Phil Wal-
msley-guitar,Kevin McKay-bass,John Grinton-
drums and Ian Stuart-vocals,he's a stocky
frontman whose veins stand right out on his
forehead-he puts that much into it(mind you
he sat down once on stage,for a very good
reason-"I was knackered",he said).I'd hate
anyone to try to read anything from the fact
they're from Blackpool or go looking for a
freak show of pretenders.They shift and I
felt triffic.

Danny Baker, *Sniffin' Glue* 9, April/May 1977

Skrewdriver
DINGWALLS

AS ONE FIRMLY in the iron grip of adolescence myself, I can wholeheartedly sympathise with the growing pains at present blighting Chiswick band Skrewdriver, who played Dingwalls on Friday.

To confirm all those suspicions you had that record labels will grovel in deaf adoration at the feet of anything labelled "punk rock", Skrewdriver are at present attempting to blitzkrieg the airways with their remarkably unremarkable single "You're So Dumb".

Ever wondered why reviewers spend so much time at the bar nowadays? It's because there's less than zero going down onstage, that's why. On this occasion, however, the antics of the audience — several overweight young people bopping frenetically and falling over frantically — were enough to keep us away from the alcohol.

In contrast to this admirable show of enthusiasm, Skrewdriver's singer limited his Terpsichorean attempts to a lackadaisial shuffling from one foot to another in the manner of a small child in a public place with a desperate desire to use the can. He was wearing baggy white trousers with the legend "Skrewdriver" inscribed across the groin, and I sighed in resignation to realise that I would never have the knack of such arcane subtlety.

As the ensemble buffooned their way through "Pills" ("This is a New York Dolls song. It bores us. I hope it bores you, too") and "No Fun" (rather apt, I thought), it became clear that they had neither respect nor understanding of where they were coming from and to whom they were in debt. More importantly, they seemed to have no grasp at all on the new-wave psyche itself, as shown on songs such as "No Compromise" ("This makes fun of all the punk thing").

In studying their copy of How To Make An Audience Love You By Insulting Them, Skrewdriver had obviously bypassed the first lesson: A Parasite Should Never Bite The Neck That Feeds It *Too* Hard.   Julie Burchill

New Musical Express, 11 June 1977

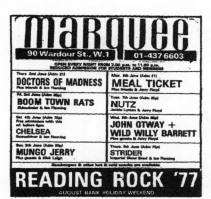

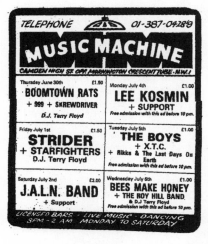

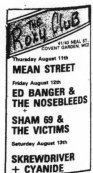

Music papers, June–October 1977

Skrewdriver back

SKREWDRIVER are back in action with a new guitarist (pictured above far right) and release a new single on Chiswick — a double A-side with '19th Nervous Breakdown' and 'Anti Social'.

Sounds, 8 October 1977: from punks to skinheads

SKREWDRIVER singer Ian Stewart went to see Fairport Convention and got 32 stitches in his back. At a FAIRPORT CONVENTION gig? Seems hardly likely. But apparently Ian was involved in a heated exchange of views with the bouncers on the way out.

Melody Maker, 14 January 1978

The Regent's Canal

It is Friday, 10 October 1975, or really Saturday 11, something like three in the morning, and Tony is nineteen, awake with his eyes closed, listening to the sounds from the bed on his right.

He hears rustling, and murmurs in two voices, magnified but distorted by the echoey room, utterly indistinct. He is on his left side and the sounds are behind him. From Jones's bed, then. Jones and who?

Feigning sleep, he rolls towards them and the noises stop. If he opens his eyes they will see and that will be the end of it. He takes long, slumberous breaths until one of them whispers again and the debate resumes with a new urgency. Tony's imagination offers speculative interpretations, hazy and metaphorical; it is still fermented by recent sleep, from which he woke to these noises with an erection, conscious of guilt and fast-obscuring dreams of heavy shapes.

It was Jones who in Tony's first week here sympathetically informed him that he had thrown himself about while sleeping, sat straight up in bed and said loudly: 'Hello? Hello?'

They are making noises like a search for something: repeating couplets of inquiry and disappointment, probing and retreat. Tony once fell asleep in front of the television and woke to an old film in a foreign language. He dozed half listening, with the sense that he understood. Now the voices sound like they are murmured too close to a microphone.

The other voice sounds younger. Harris is the one who looks fifteen, with long hair and Jagger lips. Jones and Harris?

Tony's erection persists from sleep like a token given in a dream and found on waking. It strains against the institutional sheets, impatient, heavy with meaning. Tony writhes in the sheets as if he could shake things into a different alignment, as if he and Jones and Harris could enact, beneath thick bars of extruded moonlight, the shared dream of the sleeping others.

What kind of cunt sits up in bed and shouts in his sleep? Not that anyone said anything, besides Jones. Bates sometimes snores, and will wake in a ring of boots tossed to silence him, but Tony is not Bates, and is not thrown at. The blacks especially keep their distance, but he wonders what would happen if enough of them caught him alone.

The blacks for some reason call each other by their first names, which are the names of English grandads: Arthur, Henry, George. Like when he and Dennis climbed at night into the cemetery. You take turns to find a tombstone in the dark, strike a match on it and call the name. If it's snap you pay a forfeit. There were three Freds in a row, double penalty, and Tony had to sit bollock naked on some family vault while Dennis walked away smoking with his bundled clothes. 'Don't fucking drop anything,' Tony yelled after him.

Dennis and his fucking walking away.

To be honest he feels a bit peculiar since he's been here. It's not hard on a practical level. You mainly do what the screws say, without actually looking like a cunt. You're up early but you get used to that and it's no problem going to sleep. But this sitting up and shouting is a concern. It was nearly three months ago and as far as he knows hasn't happened again but he still has nights like this, pointless fucking thoughts. And he keeps thinking of the canal.

The noise is still going on. He knows it's not what he thinks but if he opens his eyes he will be sure and he doesn't want that. And open, his eyes might betray what he thinks.

In his dream organic shadows heaved like machinery.

He's not expecting a visitor but they say he has one anyway. 'One of your skinhead thugs,' says Hodges. 'Tell him to behave himself,' and Tony's reaction must be visible because he misinterprets it: 'Don't worry, Crawford, if he wants to beat the shit out of you he'll have to wait.'

Along the corridors on the way to the room Tony tries to think of things to say. He gets as far as 'Hello.'

The grey failing light of outside leaks into the big hall like steam from a laundry, bleached in patches under hanging lamps. A grid of tables has been arranged, little islands on which the jetsam of lads' families has washed up, or maybe landed like seabirds with their urgent squawks: the cooing of maternal concern swells and falls in a relentless pulse, above the desultory croaks of fathers indistinguishable from their sons.' The rattling bulk of a tea trolley, helmed, in an emasculating apron, by one of the more docile blacks, ploughs the wide channels between.

Tony surveys from the periphery. Of course Dennis is not there. Tony knows he was never going to be but still he looks again. 'One of your skinhead thugs': that's all over mate. Don't you read the papers? It stopped years ago. They all stopped. Except a few of us.

And then he catches the deliberate, waiting smirk. And it's not Dennis, or anyone else he had imagined: it's Steve. Fat Steve, psycho Steve, from the Mile End gang, Steve the brick tosser, who Tony can't remember when he last saw, much less talked to. But there he is, same as ever, looking at Tony pin-eyed from behind a table that juts out from him like a plastic bib. More of a suedehead now, predictably, but that's a subtle distinction for the likes of Hodges.

When Tony reaches him Steve says, 'I was going to bake you a cake but I run out of sugar.'

'You haven't changed.'

'Perfect to begin with, wasn't I? You going to sit down or what?'

Tony does. They look at each other. Various nearby members of other inmates' families look at them also.

Steve says: 'Anyone topped themselves in your house yet?'

'Be too interesting.'

'That tie of yours has a twelve-pound break strain.'

'I'll bear it in mind.'

'Wouldn't stop some of these toddlers, would it? This isn't Borstal, it's a fucking one o'clock club.' The mother of a particularly young and particularly disturbed kid called Bowyer, who Tony can see killing and eating her in a few years, glares at Steve, and he winks at her.

He asks: 'Fancy a fag?' and produces a packet from his coat. When they have both lit up he says: 'Why not keep the packet.' Tony looks at him and he says: 'Go on. Don't worry about it.'

Tony shrugs. 'Cheers.'

Steve has an odd way of holding his cigarette between two fingers of his balled hand, like a cripple's claw. He keeps the hand before his mouth and blows smoke at Tony over the mound it makes, holding his gaze.

'What's your number then?'

Tony smiles. 'F72393. Crawford. Sir.'

'Shit that's long. It's a fucking phone number.'

'Took me a couple of months but I think I've got it now.'

'You the chap around here then?'

'I don't bother with all that.'

'Just do your bird eh? Very wise. If they let you anyhow.'

The black with the tea trolley rolls up. He pours out two cups with milk and puts them on the table, avoids catching their eye.

'Nice to see them putting the jungle bunnies to work,' Steve says. 'What did you do then,' he asks the server, 'mug a little old lady?'

The kid pushes the trolley on. 'Talkative bloke,' says Steve. The tea is fiercely hot.

Tony says, casually, 'You heard from Dennis?' and Steve pauses before answering, as if translating the question from another language in his head.

'Dennis? No, I haven't seen Dennis in a long time. I heard he joined the circus or something. He was always a bit of a performer.'

He takes a long draw on his cigarette and looks vaguely around the room.

'I always thought Dennis was one of them kind of lads that can never grow up. Didn't you? Most folks grow up in the end, but there's a few don't have it in them. You and me though, we're the growing-up kind, aren't we Tony?'

He crumples his fag-end in the ashtray.

'I come up here by car. Been living down in Charlton. It's a nice drive on the weekend: see a bit of countryside. I've got my own motor now, did you know that?'

Tony says: 'What are you doing here, Steve?'

'Well I thought you could do with some burn didn't I? Got a whole pack somewhere here.' He roots in his pockets. 'I know what it's like in here you see. Done it twice myself. Portland the second time. F61938 Whitcombe sir. That's probably why you and me lost touch, what with me being out of circulation. We had some right vicious screws over in Portland, some complete fucking cunts. Your lot look like cream puffs if you don't mind me saying so. Ah. Here we go.'

He hands Tony a quarter-ounce packet of tobacco, unopened. 'Anyway,' he says, while they are both holding it: 'I hear you done a nigger.'

More than a year earlier: Monday, 26 August 1974, around nine, the cemetery getting dark. In a while it would be very hard to find his way out. Still, he would stay put a bit longer: disgusting himself with his own sentimentality.

You could argue that lying all night with a bloke on some old bastard's tomb was a bit sick in the first place, let alone being a cunt about it three years later when it's not like you even want to see him again. Back then they had watched the pared moon drift and wondered, when it was gone, what the time must be; it had surprised them both when a lighter to Dennis's watch revealed not yet eleven. Then Dennis had squeezed him: 'Happy anniversary then, before it's over.'

'What are you talking about?'

'Been a year mate. August Bank Holiday Monday. It's ours. It's us.'

Tonight the moon was the same, ugly and fat; clouds drifted before it on wind that sighed like the abandoned dead. Tony got down off three women who had emerged from each other like Russian dolls to be tidied at last, with their husbands, into one neat pile, and walked back in the ebb of visibility: between slumped, cracked stones; over rotting leaves.

The gate showed itself in gaps bleeding light from beyond. It was locked, with a heavy chain fed several times around the join. Tony was considering the chain as foothold when a voice behind him said, 'It's better in here.'

The man, tall and with mad-scientist hair in an unbalanced mass, sat on the ground, leaning on one of a batch of head-stones near the wall. In his lap was a notebook and torch, which lit his face from below like in a horror film, making shadows of his slug moustache and big owl specs. Indistinct objects lay before him in a semicircle. Tony said, 'You locked in?'

'I'm working.'

'What do you do?'

'I cut grass.'

He giggled, and Tony saw the cigarette in his hand (Cancer stick, he thought suddenly, coffin nail), caught the scent of dope.

'You the gardener? You got a key?'

'Not for here.'

The man reached for one of the things disposed around him, like a rough black golfball. He touched it, as if to adjust its position.

'We cut goldfinches last week,' he said. 'With the mowers. We were eating ice cream when we found them. Babies that couldn't fly.'

'Yeah well,' said Tony, turning, 'say hi to the devil if you raise him. Think I'll just climb over.'

'What do you think of this?'

Tony looked back. The man had raised the book and torch to his face. He read: '"Dreams are back-tracked, names & symbols mated, cooked, released. It lies on the tongue like a grub. It climbs out of the book into a vertical energy—"'

For a moment the top of the gate was a fulcrum on which he heavily pivoted, pressing into him from sternum to crotch, and then he was over and down. He followed the road as it narrowed into Solebay Street, not once glancing back at the witching gardener behind his bars. A few houses here held out against the encroaching park, but they were marked for death, or dead already, having given up the lives inside. King George's Field spread across the gaps in patches, lichen over their graves, and he veered off the pavement into it. Away from the dark well of the cemetery, electric light seeped generally enough to see, and as he approached the canal the odd lit window on the other side was caught on its quivering surface like an insect in a web.

He followed the towpath beneath the bridge. He would not think of Dennis. Over the water a great desolate expanse had been partly cleared of rubble, which was piled up at its far edge by warehouses that rose like prison walls. It was maybe stupid to be here alone like this. The gardener had been doing more than writing in his book.

And then, as if formed by that thought, and heralded as he passed under it by the mantic rumble of Mile End Road, a figure: perhaps thirty feet ahead, rippling like an emanation from the water. It was the gardener again – impossibly, but still – the same tall frame, dark halo of hair. Realization chilled Tony, and the sense of a new reality clicking into place on a ratcheted dial.

The matter-of-factness, the alreadyness, of the shift rattled him, his shocked lack of surprise, as if the world had turned through a slight degree and he now saw through a gap whose breath he had always felt. It was confirmation merely: the darkness that pulsed thick in the veins of things now simply bled a little. Like the knowledge of what you could at every moment do, the violence and noise, the gardener called you from among the graves: he read, spoke, rose from the water. He led you along it, where empty houses had turned their backs and dark breaths rippled their abandoned gardens.

Without breaking his step, the gardener turned. It was as if Tony noticed immediately, in the first few degrees of the head's rotation, and watched it revolve in luxurious slow detail. He saw again the glasses and moustache in the torch's glow and awaited their actual revelation, nearly upon him now: whatever had pursued him in the graveyard, or maybe adhered three years ago to his naked body and waited. The surface of the canal spun up.

But when the hair was pulled aside, like a curtain with the

86

face following, he saw it wasn't the crazed mop of the gardener at all, but an afro, and a black youth, his own age or a little older, glanced at Tony, whose footsteps he had heard, and glanced back, and carried on walking.

The dial clicked back, and Tony's crazed hypotheses, terrifying in their immediate precision, collapsed into vagueness like a receding dream. The houses next to him gave way to industrial buildings: factories, simplified silhouettes. Here was the ground and here the sky. Here is the church and here the steeple. Tony walked forward automatically, gratefully. It's only a paper moon, he thought illogically, one of his mother's songs; and then: A silly tune, a walking coon, a big baboon. He gave a little ta-da shuffle of his feet at that, the way he had tap-danced for her as a boy when she played her records. The stuttered steps echoed beneath the railway bridge and the black turned again at the sound. He caught Tony's eye and held it for a moment. Tony didn't know what that meant. And then it happened again, too soon and for too long, and Tony remembered they were like dogs, in the eyes was a challenge, but to look down at his feet would be weak, so he defocused and looked towards the black's eyes but not at them. He counted to himself: One, two, three, four. Finally the black turned away; yet he seemed to walk more slowly now, and with intent.

From nowhere a rat scurried in front of Tony's feet, over the towpath's edge. There was nobody else around. The row of abutting factories on his right now merged into a sheer wall that admitted neither witness nor escape, and across the water bare trains slumbered in their sidings.

It had been stupid to come down here alone like this just because he was in a mopey fucking mood. The danger was not some ghost-story crap, it was real, street crime, and this was when and where it happened, and this was who did it: blacks, emerging from the shadows. Tony wasn't averse to a fight in the right circumstances, but this one was big, and he could have a weapon. A knife: its quiet slide into his flesh, his quiet slip into the canal. A retinue of nosing rodents as he sank. His knees went funny and then fixed themselves. The black turned again, the fourth fucking time.

Did he recognize Tony from the old mob? But that was two years ago. More. Tony realized he was walking in synchrony with the black, step step step step, and that seemed wrong, submissive or collusive or mocking, in any case some acknowledgement of connectedness and the looming encounter, so he stumbled his pace like another little tap ta-da, tried to establish his own independent rhythm, not accede to the other's account of what would come.

Ahead of him the black slowed. He came to a bench and sat, sprawled, his big body thrown over it with assurance, with studied casualness, like an expensive coat, his splayed legs, it became visible as Tony continued his inexorable approach, strong, in tight trousers. The black found a cigarette somewhere, lit it with a little flare, even the sound of the struck flint carrying to the nearing Tony, and now threw back his head, threw out along the back of the bench his free left arm, and gave such an exaggerated mime of calm, of confidence and readiness, of luxuriating in the summer night and the tranquil prospect of the wharf, that it could have had a caption underneath.

What followed, as Tony neared the bench, was a smooth slow motion formed along one axis, his body walking forwards, and about another, his head turning to meet the black's gaze, and locking with it like gears briefly engaged. In that moment Tony saw him in his eyes and saw there was no threat. This was not the kind to wound, but the herbivore sort, who saw only good, who went of a Sunday, with that weathered unyielding rock his mother, to a brimming church, and sang in charismatic harmony. And with this understanding, as he walked on, decoupling from their mutual scrutiny, in relief and gratitude and apology, Tony smiled.

He was past the next bridge when he heard the steps again. This time they were faster. Tony glanced back to see the black gaining, staring at him, leaning into his wake. He tried to walk on. The steps came quicker, louder, closer. His panic resumed full-blast, like a needle returned to its spinning disc. He would not show it, not speed up. He measured out a slow retarded pace, pallbearer at his funeral.

Had his smile looked a challenge? Perhaps the black had just remembered something. Had checked the time. Was running late.

And now the black began to sprint: an audible shift of gear, fast walk to all-out run, shoes no longer touching the ground at once but pounding it hard. Now it was too late there was no doubt. Tony felt air at his neck, soon to turn backdraught. Hunched his spine. The black's soles slapped the towpath stone.

He would not turn. He would not run. Here it came—

. . . past him. Ten feet, twenty feet, past him. And there: the black stopped. Slowed to an amble. Strolled forward, casual as before.

Tony trembled with uncertain relief, with nervous bewilderment, with simple anger. What the fuck, what the fucking shitting fuck, did that mean? Was this some kind of game?

Still walking slowly, the black turned to face him again. This time Tony stared back. Better for it to come than this. He willed it on: the teeth, the flashing knife.

The canal curved left, its shape disrupted by jutting wharves and sudden recesses. The black passed the cut that branched out to the River Lea, and Tony watched him leech into shadow under Old Ford Road. For an uncertain moment he was gone, then re-emerged on the far side in silhouette, where steps led to the road above. In the thick frame of the bridge he looked at Tony once more. He walked to the steps and was gone.

Was that it? Tony let himself pause. That bridge was the finish line, beyond which he could mount the rise into the park.

Maybe thirty paces to his goal. He counted down in his head as he walked. Ten, ten, ten, nine, nine, nine. Beneath the bridge, whose undersurface he could almost feel through the air above his head, even the canal disappeared. Four, four, four. Three, three, three.

And out.

The steps up which the black had gone stood empty. Tony walked, unsteady with relief, up the incline beside the lock, and where it came level with the park he jumped the fence and let its expanse unfurl before him, nestling the lake ahead. He stumbled gratefully on the sloping grass. There was space everywhere.

From a nearby tree, across the threshold of darkness, the black stepped in front of him.

Tony yelled, an involuntary childlike *ooah!*, and stumbled backwards.

The black said: 'It's OK.'

Tony said, 'Fuck. Shit. Fuck.'

He heaved, bent double, facing the grass.

'Man, I made you jump.'

He touched Tony's shoulder.

Tony looked up. Looked, for maybe the tenth time on their shared walk, into his eyes. The black smiled anxiously, said, 'I thought . . .' and stopped. He removed his hand. He said, 'It's all cool.'

Tony stared at him. With the understanding his eyes were pricking with tears. He pressed his arm over them to stifle the hot soak. 'Fuck off,' he said into it.

'Hey . . . hey man, don't cry.'

Tony shook off the careful, second touch. 'Fuck off,' he repeated, leaning on his knees, shouting through the shakes in his voice. 'Fuck off you black bastard. Fuck off coon.'

That weekend a Jamaican kid outside the station made a remark. Tony broke his cheekbone and three of his ribs, and, according to a doctor's written testimony read out in court, somehow managed to blind his right eye.

A month after his first visit, Steve returns with more tobacco and a middle-aged man in a suit called Arthur Niven. Niven has a professional air. Steve and he look like chalk and cheese, but seem to get on well enough.

Niven asks what Tony's plans are when he gets out. 'Will you stay with your parents? I imagine you'll feel a bit old for that, won't you?'

There's a network of retired Borstal officers who provide accommodation for lads on their release, while they find work. Tony has heard stories about these men. They are the ones who feel the loss of the place most personally.

Niven says that he and his wife know several people who would be keen to help out someone like Tony, who he calls a victim of the system who has displayed, however misdirected, considerable strength of character.

He gives Tony some leaflets. He says: 'Don't do anything silly in here.'

Jones holds Tony's chin and looks him in the eye. He says: 'They'll go after you for this, you know that? You'll get stop-all-privileges. Maybe the block.'

'Yeah well,' says Tony, 'I could do with some peace and quiet.'

They are locked into a toilet cubicle. Tony sits on the lowered seat.

He asks, 'How many times have you done this exactly?'

'Enough.'

The point of the straightened paperclip sways above his left eye. Jones has done his best to sharpen it by scraping it at an angle against the bricks in the yard. He says: 'It's got history, this paperclip. It's lasted well.' The end is shiny with ink where he dipped it in the biro's barrel.

Jones says: 'Hold still.'

The first prick is aimed badly: instead of being skewered straight against the cheekbone beneath, Tony's flesh is pushed over it into the well of his eye socket. The makeshift needle slips with it, and Tony, feeling this, shouts and jerks back his head. Jones reacts fast and aborts the attempt, so no damage is done.

'Sorry,' says Jones. 'Wrong angle. Try again.'

Tony swears quietly and sucks air through his teeth but it's not really too bad. Each little stab refocuses the pain away from its predecessors.

Up close, Jones's hands look older.

'How many tears shall I do you?' he asks.

New Musical Express, 29 June 1978

Skrewdriver screwed up

SKREWDRIVER have been hit by a bout of anti-skinhead hysteria. Of their planned 32-date tour only nine dates remain and all six of their London dates, including the Hope And Anchor and the Rochester Castle, have been cancelled.

Skrewdriver's manager claimed "No one will touch us because of our skinhead reputation".

Skrewdriver's remaining dates are Nottingham Sandpiper Club on August 22, Leeds Fford Green Hotel 24, Lincoln AJ's Club 26, Kirkcaldy Station Hotel 27, Oldham Tower Club September 2, and Aberdeen Ruffles Club 6.

Sounds, 19 August 1978

R·A·C·NEWS

ROCK AGAINST COMMUNISM!

For years White, British youths have had to put up with left-wing filth in rock music. They have had to put up with the anti-NF lies in the music papers. They have had commie organisations like *Rock Against Racism* trying to brainwash them.

But now there is an anti-commie backlash! R.A.C. is going to fight back against left-wingers and anti-British traitors in the music press. We hate the poseurs in R.A.R. who are just using music to brainwash real rock fans. Rock Against Communism consists of skins, mods, punks and teds, and not long haired lefty poseurs.

Over the next few months we are going to hold concerts, roadshows and tours. The message to the commie scum is clear. **Rock Against Communism has arrived and Rock Against Communism is here to stay.**

Bulldog 14, *circa* August 1979

Who, me?

I AM writing to inform you that the biased information which has appeared recently in your paper, and which RAR seem to be responsible for, is false. The news that Skrewdriver were reforming to do NF gigs is complete and utter bullshit. I formed the band and finally split it up over a year ago. I rarely see the other members of the group and have no intention of forming a band with any of them again.

Where RAR get their information beats me. Maybe they have a little KGB-type organisation within their ranks.

To suggest that we have come out in favour of the NF is also a lie. I've never voted NF and have no interest whatsoever in politics, and never had. I've also been told that RAR has solid links with the Anti-Nazi League, an organisation who, it seems, are backed heavily by the communist and Marxist parties, who in their way are just as much of a threat to this country as the NF or BM.

Why don't the two sides go and battle out their political wars in Hyde Park or somewhere, and let the people who just want to have a good time and hear some music do so in peace, without being pestered by people, pushing either communism or fascism?

I'm at present forming a new band which is not called Skrewdriver, and don't intend doing gigs for the RAR, NF or any other political organisations. — IAN STUART, Hawthorne Grove, Carleton, Poulton-Le-Fylde, Lancashire.

Melody Maker, 29 September 1979

Skrewdriver reject NF

Two months ago in a piece called 'Head-banging for Hitler' we mentioned the names of some groups who played or who were in some way connected with Rock Against Communism and the Young National Front. Since then we have heard from one of them, a band called Skrewdriver, who have asked us to make it quite clear that although they were approached by the YNF they turned them down and would not associate with them in any way.

Searchlight, October 1979

Tomorrow Belongs to Me

'Hold still,' Philip said.

The rim of his bath, over which I knelt, pressed a chill bar across my chest. Philip stood over me, operating the clippers. The pub below was only patronized by unexcitable locals, so noise was not a problem; but in this room, its expelled air, drawn by some quirk of architecture through the vent, gave the permanent atmosphere of stale cigarettes. When I rented Philip's spare room, in my first blush of proper independence, I got so used to the bathroom's smell it barely registered; now it recalled, once more, the mood I had first associated with it: a tired and introspective kind of cleanliness.

He rinsed my head and I examined myself in the mirror. 'Oh,' I said. 'I'm bald.'

'What did you expect? . . . And your nipples are hard.' He tweaked one.

'They're frozen.'

'So put your top on and make a cup of tea. I need a sit-down.'

It had been four years since I moved in here, soon after I came down from university. The radical nature of my agency in that period astonished me now: I had split with Justin – my first serious boyfriend, a year above me and the object of my parents' increasing warmth – and in short order unilaterally announced that I was leaving home to rent a room from Philip, a decade my senior and a stranger to them. The official explanation for our acquaintance, that we'd got to talking in a bar, must have been odd enough, let alone the truth, of which neither Mum nor Dad had the technical facility to guess the specifics, but which, with the dial-up bills I was then amassing, they must have imagined in some tabloid version: he had been chatting me up on an IRC channel called #gay-selfpics.

So I didn't always need the rented bed, yet my demand for it had been no mere misdirection: it was integral to the hazy but intensely felt notion of sex, politics and independence as inseparably related that was then driving me. My urgent need not only to have a room to which I could bring boys back at a rate optimistically conceived to exceed my parents' tolerance, but for that room to be held in a queer space (Philip's flat) where such tribute would be recognized, was part of the same new sense of my identity as something embedded in history and struggle that had made me susceptible to Philip's online seduction. It wasn't his older body that attracted me, nor the hilarious serial form in which he presented it, portioned and flattened against his office scanner, but what that body had seen and where it had been: the connection I made, touching it, to the OutRage! demos and art happenings of which his typed reminiscences so enthralled me. Philip had slept with *Jarman*, for fuck's sake (*don't worry*, was his cheekily presumptive rider, *i was careful*), and when, after our first IRL encounter at the Yard, where I drowned my timidity in alcopops, he took me back to the flat above the pub, I felt rooted in that same tradition.

Now, as then, his fridge was full of things I pass over in supermarkets: salad cream, carrot sticks, 'wafer-sliced' ham.

On the door hung one of those novelty aprons – a gift, I hoped – that substitute the torso of Michelangelo's David for the wearer's. His elegant, scalloped little clump of pubes looked stuck on, like a fake moustache. I called, 'Can I open these biscuits?'

Philip sat at his computer in running pants and a T-shirt, checking messages on three personals sites at once. He tested his tea gingerly, leaning his head towards the mug with his upper lip just above the liquid and sucking air across its surface so it rolled towards him in little waves. He winced, said, 'Give that a minute to cool down,' and frowned at my own mug, already a quarter empty.

'Asbestos mouth,' I said.

'So I see. How are things with Adam?'

'Good, thanks.'

'Are you fucking other people yet?'

.' . . We're very modern.'

'But maybe the haircut will get his attention.'

I ignored his smirk and pointed at the screen: 'You've got a message.'

'*Wanna be used by my mixed race cock?* Romantic sentiment, but I think not. You should join this one, you know. Lots of shaved heads on it.'

'I did,' I told him.

He gave me a look. 'Quiet little bugger, aren't you? What's your profile?'

'Bytvlight. One word. It's the name of a song.'

'Of course it is. Why not just call yourself ithinktoomuch-toshag?'

'I thought it was . . . poetically suggestive.'

'"Don't click here" is what it suggests, sweetheart. But that's a nice profile, besides the name. You'll have to update it now: *24yo, swimmer's build . . . zero crop*! You'll need new pics.'

'I might not keep the crop.'

'You should, it suits you.' He reached for his tea. 'Sometimes I think I've had everyone on here worth having.'

'Can I check my messages if you're done?'

I didn't have any. I scrolled through the list of men online. Their faces stared back, variously smiling and scowling. Philip said, 'That one's holding in his stomach.'

'How can you tell?'

He rolled his eyes. We'd never lost our master/apprentice dynamic around sexual literacy, my development in which had been, in part, his agenda in offering me the room. He'd expanded my arsenal: a technology pioneer from the days of Prestel, Philip was the first person I knew with broadband at home, an expensive cable connection on which I soon graduated from legacy Unix protocols to the 'dating' sites then swelling with network benefits. But I couldn't learn his most important lesson, which was never to chat too much: more often than not I'd ask too many questions of my latest interlocutor and uncover the feet of clay – some political or grammatical atrocity – that made the hook-up for which I'd been gunning quite unthinkable. My success rate thus never approached my bullish projections, or what Philip, with his frankly ropier toolset, was achieving down the corridor. 'Sweetheart,' he would tell me when I jealously remarked on his ability to overlook the vacuous *Weltanschauungen* blotting otherwise beautiful youths, 'you're hardly reading the fucking books on the mantelpiece when you're et-cetering the fire.'

Now he stood up and stretched. 'I'm off again next week, by the way.'

'Where to?'

Philip was a journalist on *Panorama*, and one of the more peculiar facets of being friends with him was the remote possibility of his violent death in some far-flung arena. He had been to Iraq twice: before the war, and during it.

'Zimbabwe.'

'Oh.' I shrugged. It was almost disappointing.

'If we can get in, that is.'

'Check out this guy,' I said. On screen a lawyer in Primrose Hill was proposing, with a confident smirk, that the reader meet him from his morning jog and lick his sweat off. '*To be clear, I will expect you to lick me clean from head to toe: balls, crack, pits* . . . Bet you his first draft started, *For the avoidance of doubt.*'

A man in his sixties wished to emphasize the importance of bonding on an emotional and intellectual level as well as a sexual one, and in addition *allowing mystic facets to manifest.*

A social worker from Peckham, two years older than me, peered anxiously into his webcam sporting a leather dog collar, double chin and gold-rimmed spectacles. He enumerated his 'likes': Röyksopp, pasta, Spurs, '*Sex in the City.*'

I asked Philip: 'What's WP?'

'Where?'

'Is it like watersports or something?'

The skin was in his late twenties, in braces, combats and knee-length, highly polished boots. Other photographs, in black and white, showed him without the clothes. He was looking to meet other skins for a drink and a laugh, and the occasional chat about art and politics. He concluded: *No WP.*

Philip told me: 'It's white power.'

'Like neo-nazis?'

'Yeah.'

'But why would he need to . . . specify?'

He peered at the screen. 'It's the laces.'

'On his boots?'

'They're white. Usually means nazi. He must just like the look of them, silly sod.'

I clicked through the photos. The skin grinned, then pouted; put his hands behind his head and in front of his crotch. The colour saturated, desaturated again.

I said, 'But it's a gay website.'

'So?' He leaned across me and switched off the monitor; spun my chair, lifted my chin to face him. 'It must be very interesting on your planet,' he said.

'Fuck off.'

'Look at you.' He rubbed his knuckles on my scalp. 'Little bootboy.'

I nudged the tip of my forefinger into his belly button.

Philip said: 'You've never even heard of Martin Webster, have you?'

'Who?'

'Jesus help me,' he sighed. 'Youth.'

He removed his glasses, then mine, and laid them both on the monitor. He pulled his T-shirt off and chucked it to the sofa, pressing my head against his stomach, with its thick, ticklish hair. He reached for my right hand and guided it to his crotch. 'How about Nicky Crane?' he said.

I had stayed with Philip for more than a year. In the end he asked me to find another place because of my strained relationship with the teenager he was then seeing, and with whom, he announced, he had fallen in love. When I dropped off my keys, around lunchtime on the Sunday before New Year, they were both embarked on a molehill of coke. The next few times I saw Philip the boy was ostentatiously not around, and I impressed myself with the sympathy I realized when, on Valentine's of all days, he disappeared for good, and took Philip's laptop with him.

'He's really sexy,' Adam said over my shoulder.

'Do you think so?'

The *Strength thru Oi!* album cover was the first picture of Nicky Crane I found online. Behind his wildly foreshortened boot, its vast sole aimed straight at the viewer, Nicky loomed shirtless: clenched fists raised, one warning finger extended, bearing a Neanderthal scowl. He was muscled, but hardly trim: his stomach oozed slightly over the tight waist of his jeans. It would be some weeks before I moved on from Google to the British Library; longer before I abandoned my latest TV job to pursue Nicky full-time.

'Christ, yes. Sexy as fuck.'

Adam's investment in the skin aesthetic hadn't dimmed. He could still, sometimes, bring me up short: pitching up five minutes late outside the cinema, I would spot him at once – his high bold head, his combats, tall laced boots, and the crowd around him merely vague, like water lapping a rock – and with a little rush of pride I would walk up and claim him. It still astonished me that someone could actually dress like that: could walk into the street, their job, with such overwhelming certitude. I was anxious with signs and symbols, and would prevaricate: might toy, say, with jackets in military styles, but never clothes mistakable for real uniform. Even Philip's shearing had used clippers, not a razor. Adam seemed unburdened by my constant, paralysing awareness of the interpretability of things. 'I can't help what people think,' he would say when I probed the issue. 'That's their problem.'

When I had shown him my new haircut, I'd been nervous but excited. I hadn't told him I was going to get it done. I worried he might laugh, as at a teenager pretending to a scant moustache – but imagined other consequences too: like my induction, at Adam's hands, into the look entire. He might take me to Camden market to buy boots, teach me to lace and polish them. I couldn't seriously picture myself in such a get-up, but the fantasy was powerful. Weighty things, to change your appearance for your lover, for your lover to request it.

And Philip's barb, that my cropped hair was a bid for Adam's attention, had not been entirely wide of the mark. It could feel vertiginous, the lightness of Adam's embrace. True, when he had first made clear he would not be expected to stop having sex with other people, I'd been happy to assent. After the febrile intensity of my college relationships, little orgies of overwrought performativity, and the fitful staccato that followed, it had felt rather thrillingly adult, like sliding into the spa pool at the gym. But while I was discreet in my own exploitation of our agreement, Adam approached it as candidly as he dressed. Brushing my teeth at his place I would spot a condom, say, knotted like a reminder in the bathroom bin; or later, as his explorations became more dogged, find thin lines on his buttocks, in fading red. Such artefacts signified no betrayal, but their concreteness winded me.

The marks I found on him looked like rebukes, too, for what we failed to do together, for which he had to go elsewhere. Early on we had gone through a phase of dirty emails in which Adam, encouraged by his further poking at my black bookshelf, had laid out in detail certain aspirations. Tilting my screen from my colleagues' sightlines, I responded with enthusiasm, and on the tube to his place for our next date felt hefty with momentum. But as we acknowledged, never verbally but in mutual disengagement from the idea over the weeks that followed, it didn't work. Later I wondered if the identification I had felt reading Adam's outlined scenarios had been with a role other than the one he had cast me in. In writing and reading there's a fluidity of perspective that real life doesn't easily afford.

Adam put his finger to my screen and traced Nicky's bare torso.

'Who is he, anyway?'

'I think,' I said, 'he might be my subject.'

THOSE NAKED NAZIS

Whilst on the subject of Nazis, I am somewhat pleased to see the National Front arseholes scratching each other's eyes out over the **Martin Webster** scandals. It seems fellow would-be tyrant **John Tyndal** is so upset about Webster's homosexual image that he's formed a breakaway NF organisation, and is openly slagging Webster in his publication **Spearhead**. It seems that he accuses the Front of being full of queers, and morally corrupt, and that Webster is giving the Front a **Bad Name!** I'd have thought it already had as bad a name as it was possible to get . . . But in the crazy upside-down world of the NF, it's okay to smash someone's head in, but it's the biggest crime of all to be gay.

Zipper 24, October 1980

PUBLIC EMBARRASSMENT

On the public level I was compelled repeatedly to choke with shame and embarrassment at the humiliation brought upon the party by his filthy language, bizarre gestures and frequently total loss of personal control. Internally, his presence became more and more intolerable — undermining discipline, reducing working relationships to a shambles and creating an atmosphere of rancour and poison throughout the nationwide network of regions, branches and departments. On at least two occasions I was forced to have him thrown out of Directorate meetings after he had reduced those occasions to screaming matches. Bit by bit, I became aware of his technique of working to undermine the Directorate's and my confidence in party officials around the country when the sole crime of those officials had been to cause him some personal upset; meanwhile I came to note the obverse side of this technique, which was to recommend to us for promotion people in the party who formed part of his own coterie of admirers, satellites and, in some cases, comrades of mutual sexual orientation.

Indeed if there was any moment at which I finally decided, beyond any revocation, that Webster must be removed from his position in the party it was the moment at which I recognised as true the mounting rumours in the party about his prediliction for young males. From that moment onwards it became a matter, not of whether he should be removed, but merely when and how.

John Tyndall, *Spearhead* 140, June 1980

A number of people in recent months have reminded me of the services that certain members of the homosexual fraternity have rendered to the National Front, and I have not denied these services.

I believe, however, that the greatest service that such individuals can render to the party now would be to retire from the front seat and into the shadows.

Whether they will be big enough to do this, I do not know. What I do know is that until either they retire, or are retired, no chance of unification exists.

John Tyndall, *Spearhead* 141, July 1980

Viking Youth 18, April–June 1980

Blackheath

IF YOUR MATES ASK, TELL THEM YOU'RE OFF FOR A DIRTY WEEKEND.
Basic survival course, survival school, Moreland, Cumbria
SAMPLE PROGRAMME: ARRIVAL Intro, issue of kit – DAY 1 Lectures in the theory of survival, demonstrations of techniques – DAY 2 Practical work: shelter-building, fire-lighting, skinning, trapping, cooking, navigation, edible plants and fungi – DAY 3 Continued exercises, debrief, issue of additional kit and instructions for final exercise – DAY 4+5 Put knowledge to real use in more remote exercise area. Farewell dinner, certificates.

'What do you think?'

'Yeah it looks interesting.'

It is Sunday, 20 April 1980. Dave folds the flyer into neat quarters and returns it to his pocket. He says: 'Members of the hardcore British Movement are believed to have gone to ground in the woods around the capital. These men are known to be highly experienced and could well be armed. As society collapses into civil war, communists and blacks now fear for their safety.'

Tony says: 'We look like a couple of fucking monkeys.'

'We look like waiters.'

'We do as well. We'll get asked for drinks all night.'

It is particularly true of Tony. He has ironed his white shirt with too much starch and it sits on him like stilted grammar. Dave's shirt is red, and he has not tucked it into his trousers. It makes him look, thinks Tony, even younger. Waiting in the hallway while Tony locks his door, he bounces on the balls of his feet and at one point mimes a dramatic kick: 'Goal!'

Tony says: 'We've got time to walk. Don't want to be early,' and they set off towards the common. The low sun makes silhouettes of the trees, flaring their edges. Dave says, 'If you're ever interrogated and they bring out a big file with your name on it, all stuffed with papers, bursting at the seams and that, you've got to remember there's probably nothing in it. That's an old trick, that one. Just shrug and say, "I don't know what you're talking about." And if they say they know what you done, they don't, or they wouldn't be asking.'

Dave has been reading a resistance manual. He tells Tony: 'You've got to keep everything clean all the time. Weapons, uniform. Shave every morning no matter what. Check your gun every night and clean the magazine. And never tell lies in battle. You can exaggerate to your girlfriend after but if you do it in battle your mates could end up killed.' He lobs an imaginary grenade in the direction of the sports ground.

Tony says: 'Have you got one?'

'What?'

'A girlfriend.'

'Yeah sort of between them right now. How about you?'

'I can't understand women.'

'What gets me is those white slags hanging round the discos chasing after niggers. Fucking disgusting.'

'Reckon there'll be a disco tonight?'

Dave laughs. 'Bit of Blondie.'

The streets grant each other a respectful distance as Charlton gives way to Blackheath. 'Nice round here isn't it?' mutters Dave.

When they pass a phone box, he asks: 'How are we doing for time?'

'It's a party. There's no deadline as such.'

'OK for a couple of calls? I've been carrying this around all week.' He produces another sheet, this one a newsletter.

Tony says: 'Go for it.'

'Hope it's working.' Dave digs in his pocket for a five-pence piece, propping the door with his foot. Tony lights a cigarette. While Dave waits for an answer he scratches 'BM' into the printed instructions with the end of a key.

Tony looks down the quiet street. 'Hello good evening,' says Dave. 'May I speak to Mr Wintour please?' A young woman with a pram emerges from a side road, waits with exaggerated care to cross. 'Yeah well you listen to me you commie bastard. You've been spreading your red filth round that school for long enough and your time's up, are you listening? We're not having scum like you brainwashing our kids no more so consider this your last fucking warning. We know where you live and . . .' Dave trails off. 'Fucking hung up on me,' he grins at Tony. 'Cunt. Oh well, he's not getting off that easily.'

He dials again. 'Now he's not picking up. These people have— You're fucking dead mate,' he tells the handset. 'You look over your fucking shoulder because we . . . shit. Well I think he got the message. Do you want a go?'

Tony scans the page. 'They've got the editor of *Searchlight* here.'

'Oh yeah go on.'

'It's 021, I'll be out of time before I start. Hang about. There's a commie Jew who's the new president of the National

Union of Students – oh, they don't give his number. Some lesbian in Leeds. Half these people are in Leeds. Community Levy for Alternative Projects. Donated fifty quid to something called Women Working with Girls. I bet you fucking do darling.'

'Just pick one. It don't matter too much.'

'OK here we are. The Friends of Blair Peach Committee. And she's in ANAL too . . . Ring ring. Go on, be in.'

A voice says, 'Jill Atkinson.'

'Oh hello,' says Tony. 'How are you doing then?'

There is a pause. 'Who's speaking, please?'

'We've got a friend in common. Thought I'd phone for a chat. It says here you're not married, is that right?'

'I'm sorry, who is this?'

'Live by yourself in fact. In Haddo House. That's over in Greenwich isn't it? Do your neighbours like having a nigger in the building?'

Dave, listening at the open door, grins at this flourish.

The woman says, 'Are you trying to frighten me?'

'I have to say you don't sound like a nigger, I'd never have guessed.'

'Because you don't scare me, do you understand—'

'Oh I think your voice is shaking just a bit there sweetheart.'

'—you pathetic little boy.'

'Hardly surprising you're not married is it,' Tony says.

She tells him, 'I've dealt with trash like you my whole life.'

'Perhaps you're just lonely. Would you like some company? I hope you're fucking lonely you black cunt.'

'Like the baby fascists at school. Thugs for parents and tiny pricks.'

'OK so I'll drop round later then. Haddo House. And our friend Blair Peach says see you soon. You fucking dried-up smelly old cunt.'

Her voice is properly shaking now. 'I doubt you've ever

even seen one, have you? A cunt? How old *are* you, little boy?'

Tony puts down the phone. 'She hung up,' he tells Dave. 'We should go.'

The face of Niven's wife assembles itself behind the stained glass like a shoal of fish darting into alignment. 'Hello, Tony,' she says, 'Long time no see,' and kisses him on the cheek. 'You're looking very smart. Who's your friend?'

'Dave, this is Mrs Niven. The lady of the house.'

'Pleased to meet you,' says Dave.

'Come on in,' she tells them. 'Have a drink.'

The party is already under way. There are perhaps thirty people in the front room, in twos and threes. Most of the men wear suits. The guests are all the Nivens' age. Tony mutters to Dave, 'The other kids in the nursery or what?'

Dave nudges him: '*Major* Hollywood at nine o'clock.'

Tony turns. Near the window a tall man in his sixties is talking to a shorter couple. He wears an SS uniform. He says something and all three laugh. The short man wipes his eyes. 'Gordon Bennett!' he says. 'Gordon Bennett!'

Niven's wife asks: 'Would you boys like red or white? Or there's beer if you prefer.'

'Beer please.'

They follow her to the kitchen. She takes a can from the fridge and pours it into two glasses. Dave says: 'You've got a lovely house.'

'Oh it's endless bloody work, this house.' She laughs. 'But it's nice of you to say so, love. Come back through, let's get you something to eat.'

The dining table is laid with platters of food. She gives them plates, and cutlery wrapped in paper napkins. 'There's ham, and potato salad and tuna salad, and salad salad obviously, and this is coronation chicken. There's a bit of curry in that one.' In

115

a mock whisper she adds: 'It's Mrs Thatcher's favourite dish, I read somewhere. When I told Mr Niven we nearly had to stop eating it!'

A woman nearby says: 'Shouldn't it be vegetarian, Janet, under the circumstances?' and laughs. Niven's wife answers: 'There are limits, Veronica!'

As Tony scoops potato salad on to his plate there is a ringing sound. Niven is by the bookshelves, tapping his glass with a fork. The partygoers stop talking and face him. Niven looks expectant for a moment before he speaks:

'Well, good evening, everyone, and thank you all for coming – especially those of you who have had to venture so far beyond your usual Chelsington hunting grounds and into the rather less salubrious wilds of Blackheath.'

A little laughter.

'I'm not intending to make a speech – no, no, really, I'm not! – but I have been asked to mention one or two things. Don't worry, I know this is a party and not a meeting, but the opportunity presented by having so many of you trapped in one room is far too tempting not to take advantage of.

'First of all, we have another of our semi-regular film evenings coming up next month. It's an excellent series and well worth supporting, as I'm sure anybody who attended our recent *Birth of a Nation* screening will attest. On Saturday the tenth of May we have the nuclear film *The War Game*, made and then promptly banned by the BBC for its unplanned proximity to truth. I understand it is not a little hard-hitting, but am on the other hand assured it will be gentler on the posterior than Mr Griffith's epic. Tickets are one pound fifty and available by post from the usual League address, but Douglas, who is standing over there by the drinks cabinet as is his wont, has brought a supply with him, and I'm afraid he is refusing to budge until he has either sold, or passed, out. So spare my whisky and spend a quid to prepare yourselves for the apocalypse.

'Also next month, James, who is hiding here *some*where, will continue his lecture series with a talk on Racial Elements in Contemporary Art, in which – according to this piece of paper – he will address the current vogue for piles of bricks and the art forms of primitive negroid tribes. It will take place, entirely unofficially of course, *inside* the Tate Gallery, where James informs me that many of the best works are hidden permanently in the vaults – so perhaps if he inflames us enough we might indulge in a liberating foray. It promises to be a fascinating afternoon and I encourage you all to join us in the foyer of the Tate Gallery on Millbank at 3 p.m. on Saturday the twenty-fourth.

'Finally, a note for anyone who does not yet subscribe to the *League Review*: do yourselves a great favour and have a word with Keith. It really is going from strength to strength, and anybody claiming I say so because of my own forthcoming series of articles is guilty of the most appalling slander.

'Well, I think that concludes the administrative items, and I'm not sure it was necessary to sigh with relief *quite* so loudly. So all that remains is to adjure you to avail yourselves of Janet's customarily hearty spread, and as much booze as you can handle while still being able to make it beyond our front door at the end of the evening, after which quite frankly you're on your own, and before you return to the vastly more interesting gossip from which I have so rudely detained you, to join me, please, in raising your glass to the man in whose honour we are gathered here this evening, and to offer him, wherever he might be, in this world or another, our birthday greetings and, always and for ever, our undying loyalty. Ladies and gentlemen: to the *Führer*.'

And everybody answers: 'The *Führer*.'

'Tony, I'm so glad you could make it.' Niven shakes his hand with his usual careful firmness. 'And this must be the young man we talked about.'

'Yeah this is Dave. Dave this is Arthur Niven.'

'Pleased to meet you,' says Dave.

Tony says, 'I thought Steve might be here.'

'Steve has many virtues but discretion is not one of them. There's no reason you should have noticed, but there are some important people here. When I turned my back Steve would be hawking a television off the back of a lorry to a member of the aristocracy. Come through to my study.'

He points out a bronze bust of Hitler on his desk ('My new indulgence, by the way') and they inspect it politely. Tony says, 'How much did that set you back then?' and Niven answers, 'Believe me, you don't want to know. It's quite genuine and rather rare. The challenge was getting it through customs.'

'Now that's very nice,' says Dave. 'Isn't it?'

'The first thing,' says Niven when they are seated, 'is that a certain member of our valued local Sikh community is highly unlikely to be making any further statements to the police.'

Dave glances rapidly at Tony, who smiles. 'That's good to hear. In the interests of multi-ethnic relations and all. How do you know?'

'A number of reasons, not least the remarkable disinclination of the colourful entrepreneur who runs Prestige Cabs to suffer any extended investigation of his company's bookkeeping, particularly in respect of the immigration status of his employees. Our rickshaw-wallah will need a job after his hospital sojourn, after all.'

'Thank fuck for that,' Tony says.

'As you say. Well, here's to keeping them on their toes. Chin chin.'

When they have drunk Niven asks: 'Dave, how long have you been in the Movement?'

'I signed up nearly a year ago.'

'And how old are you now?'

'Eighteen next month.'

'I assume you're clean? No silly buggers with drugs?'

'No nothing like that. I'll have the odd drink but I never done drugs.'

'Good. We can't afford to weaken our youth. And of course the niggers get the profits. Well, I don't know how much Tony told you about me . . .'

'He said you were a big help when he come out of Borstal. And it was you more than Steve got him into the British Movement.'

'Yes, I'm not as involved with the BM as I used to be. I devote most of my energy to the League these days. But I remain very supportive of the Movement, and I have a particular interest in fostering good working relations between the more useful members of the various organizations. Our enemies are busy multiplying, and we waste our energy on factional disputes. This latest mess with the Front, for example. Not so much washing our dirty linen in public as framing and spotlighting it. Buggery is a revolting hobby, but to publicize it is far more damaging.

'Dave, Tony's heard me on this particular soapbox before but I'm afraid I shall mount it again. The movement – I mean the nationalist movement as a whole – needs different people for different tasks. Some of us work best behind the scenes, with typewriters rather than guns.'

Dave says, '"A typewriter is more important than a pistol." It says so in this book I've been reading.'

'Exactly. We're thinkers and writers: developing strategy, producing propaganda. Looking after the big picture, if you will. Others, and I'd include both Tyndall and Webster in this, despite their exhausting and embarrassing catfight, are the public face. They'll lead marches, talk to the press, rally troops. They have their minions: regional organizers, good party men. They don't seek personal glory but without them we would have no members. And there are men like Steve, who take our message and make it felt on the street, a different form of struggle but a very important one. If we don't control the streets we can never win. That's something the *Führer* always understood.

'But street action – say, something like teaching a lesson to an Asian cab driver – is very messy and very public. Not all of our physical work is like that. Some of it, often the most important and the most dangerous, has to be kept secret. And you can't give that kind of work to someone like Steve – not because he couldn't do it, but because he wouldn't be able to resist bragging about it to all and sundry in the pub. That kind of work needs another kind of man. I presume you've heard of Column 88.'

Tony watches Dave as this sentence produces its intended effect. Niven goes on: 'There's been an awful lot of rubbish written about Column 88. It's been said to be a hundred different things, none remotely accurate. I can't say the hysteria has done it any harm. Anyway, all that really needs to be said on the subject is that men with discretion as well as bravery are very important to the movement, and certain activists are always on the look-out for them.'

Dave nods repeatedly and fast. 'What can I do?'

'Oh . . .' says Niven vaguely, before answering with calculated bathos: 'Don't do anything. Carry on just as you have before. Keep playing your part for the BM, which is valuable work. You needn't even bear in mind that attention may be being paid to how you conduct yourself, because if you're the kind of person I hope you are you'd conduct yourself properly as a matter of course, and if you're not no incentive will change that.

'Only bear in mind that at some time – it may be tomorrow, it may be in many years – you may be asked to do a certain thing, and that thing may place considerable demands on you. You may be required to keep it absolutely secret, even from your girlfriend – or wife, one day; it may put you at serious risk. So bear in mind that such a request may come, and think to yourself, if and when it does, how you might respond.'

'He's all right Arthur,' says Tony later in the kitchen, 'just a bit . . .' and shrugs.

'Is he really in with Column 88?'

'Fucked if I know mate. Probably knows someone who knows someone.'

'So you haven't been asked to, you know . . .'

'It's been all mouth and no trousers so far.' Tony digs in the back of the fridge for more beers. He hands Dave a can and cracks open one for himself. 'That fucking little bronze statue though. Jesus.'

'How much do you think he paid for it?'

'However much I bet you he was ripped off. I bet it was made six months ago in some Turkish sweatshop.'

The door opens, briefly unmuffling the noise of singing from the front room, and Niven's wife enters. 'I'm sorry,' she announces, 'but I draw the line at the Horst Wessel song.' She slurs the name slightly. She has a tumbler of whisky in one hand and a soda siphon in the other, which she holds up: 'Needs a new cartridge.'

As she rifles in a drawer, she asks: 'Are you boys having a good evening?'

'Yeah very nice,' says Dave. 'Thank you.'

'Got enough to drink?'

Tony holds up his can. 'We've raided your supply.'

'That's what it's there for, my lovely.'

She fills the siphon from the tap. When she unscrews the charger cap it falls and clinks on the floor. 'Whoops,' she says, bending over uncertainly.

'I've got it.'

'Thanks, love.' She mimes a kiss as she takes it from him,

then turns back to the task of inserting the gas cartridge. 'Bloody thing,' she says to it. There is a whooshing sound and she shakes it vigorously.

Dave nudges Tony and whispers, 'Does she spit or swallow?' This cracks him up.

Niven's wife spurts soda into her whisky and takes a sip. 'That's better.' She looks at Dave suppressing his laughter and smiles. 'Am I interrupting a private conversation?'

'Course not,' says Tony.

'Mind if I join you for a minute? I keep getting pounced on by Douglas for my typewriting skills. I've told him Mr Niven's leaflets take up quite enough of my time already.'

Tony says: 'Oh you type them do you?'

She slips into a mock whisper. 'Don't tell anyone but I do a bit of editing as well. He never can get his arguments on two sides himself.'

'Yeah well,' says Tony. 'Cheers.'

'Your good health.'

There is a silence, and they look vaguely around the room.

'I tell you what I do enjoy,' says Niven's wife: 'doing the headlines. I can look through that Letraset catalogue for hours. Found a lovely typeface the other day. Like on those old German posters. Blackletter, they call them.'

'"A reproduction machine is worth as much as a light machine gun."'

'Quite right, love. It is Dave, isn't it? Not something you hear very often, that. Because it's not women using the machine guns is it?'

'You've got a lovely kitchen,' says Dave. 'I like your fridge.'

'Thank you, sweetheart. I tell you, it's endless bloody work though. Keeping it clean. Shows up finger marks like nobody's business.'

'You keep it lovely. You've got a lovely house.'

'How old are you, love?'

'Eighteen. Well next month I will be.'

'Eighteen,' she repeats. 'Bugger me.' She drains her glass and then all of a sudden lunges at the floor. 'Out!' she yells, and adds mournfully, 'Bloody cat.' They watch the flap swing in the animal's wake. 'So,' asks Mrs Niven, fixing Tony with a look: 'what did you think of Mr Niven's tie?'

'His tie? Didn't notice to be honest. Was there something special about it?'

'Ah!' She holds her finger to her nose. 'There's always something special about Mr Niven's ties. He's very particular about the patterns. He has club ties, school ties, every kind of tie.' She is slurring her words quite badly now.

'How many has he got?' Tony asks.

'Oh, I've lost count! I know you men think we ladies have too many clothes, or waste time worrying what to wear, but I pale before Mr Niven and his ties. Honestly, I do. And I've given up trying to buy them for him.' She shakes her head as if someone is disputing it. 'I used to think they made good presents, but he's far too particular for me. When I give him one he's very polite, but you watch, it'll disappear in a drawer and you'll never see it again. I tell you, they're one of the wonders of the world. Mr Niven's ties.'

Tony says, 'So what did you think?'

'Oh they're all right aren't they?'

'Wouldn't want to do it every week. Got any fags left?'

'Here.'

'Listen about this training thing. Up in Cumbria.'

'What about it?'

'Well it depends how much it is to be honest. I mean it's five days or whatever and I can't really afford to go nowhere right now.'

'Yeah no worries Tony. It was just an idea.'

'Anyway how much do we need to learn? How to skin a

rabbit won't do us much good. Tell you what, we should start a London survival course. How to glass someone: Hold bottle by neck, smash on table, shove into face. Always execute in one smooth movement for maximum effect. Don't smash too far down neck, you might do your hand an injury.'

Dave laughs. 'Milk bottles are a good size for Molotov cocktails but they've got wide necks and it's hard to find a bung that fits.'

'That's a point,' Tony says. 'What time is it?'

'Just gone eleven. Why?'

'Fancy a bit of a detour through Greenwich?'

EXTREME right - wing racialists are preparing for terrorist violence in Britain—and claim they have made and tested weapons.

We have been shown a terrorism manual imported from the United States which has been used as a recipe for experiments with incendiary bombs and a one-shot, disposable firearm by members of a group calling itself 'Column 88'

Security chiefs are investigating allegations of links between these groups and serving soldiers and members of the Territorial Army.

The preparations take place against a background of a rising number of racial assaults, some by members of the openly Nazi British Movement. Members of the movement have told us about organised assaults on Jews and blacks.

The British Movement has grown to a total membership of more than 3,000 during the past two years, benefiting from the recent disintegration of the National Front into squabbling splinter groups.

Observer, 16 November 1980

Stand Proud

Adam had arranged for us to visit a man who lived an hour's train ride from London. 'I think he's a squaddie,' he said hopefully. In fact while the man, whose name was Sean, did claim to be in the military, he would not specify his branch or job. I thought this ostentatious.

'Only if you're up for it,' added Adam.

In theory, this was a refinement of our failed experiments in role play – the idea being that we might do better playing the same role. It was true that the earlier attempts had frustrated us both. But I suspect Adam also guessed that, for me, the attraction of doing such things together was hard to separate from how melancholy I found the idea of him doing them apart. Whether my jealousy was sexual or romantic, or not jealousy at all so much as egoism, I didn't know.

I stayed over at Adam's the night before our meet and woke early after dreams of maths exams. While he dozed, I opened my laptop and read through my prior conversation with Sean. I had dreaded this requirement of his, which he called an 'interview,' but he had, it turned out, a businesslike lack of imagination that curtailed both small talk and any obligation I might have felt to flirt, thus making our transaction unexpect-edly efficient: it had seemed easy, in this surreal and detached context, to concede to his stipulations. Now, seeing my late-night confessions and consent preserved in the flat reality of morning was almost giddying: a skittish, unexpected arousal grew in me.

In the bathroom, getting ready according to Sean's instruc-tions, I left my glasses on the toilet cistern. Going back to retrieve them later I found Adam readying himself in turn. 'You could have knocked,' he told me, but my mind was else-where. Crouched in his bath, the shower extension trickling round his feet, he had returned me to my gap-year trip through India, passing at dawn the last fields before some nearing city, where squatting figures dotted at polite intervals the low blue mist: facing as one my train, and the sun that rose behind.

At Waterloo, a pigeon flew in huge panicked zags in the high space above the concourse, ducking round the advertising banners that hung from the ceiling and rising baffled from the rear, as if one of them might hide the clear sky. We watched it as we queued for tickets (to a destination that sounded absurdly quaint), then bought two Evians and an *Independent* from Smiths. I drank little of my water on the journey: antic-ipation seemed to make it go straight through me, so that after every sip, taken at long intervals between pensive screwings of the cap, I felt the urge to stand and shuffle along the juddering carriage to the toilet, which banked each discharge with a loud mechanical suck.

'Are you OK?' Adam said, looking up from his paper. He was in full skinhead gear. Doubtless, I thought, observing him, Sean had masturbated in anticipation over photos of Adam like this; doubtless Adam had taken them with that in mind. I pictured him spread for Sean's consumption like the *Zipper* features I had seen in the library, hoping to spot Nicky: When

You Feel Like a Skinhead, Larry Harris Is Your Man. Porn magazines were classified 'special material' and arrived behind the counter in a locked box, to be read at certain designated desks under the gaze, for some reason, of the music librarians. Even *Gay Times* turned out to be classified, so I had been disturbed to find how much fascist material was, by contrast, unrestricted. I would join the general queue to collect bundles of the National Front's youth tabloid *Bulldog*, its massive headlines calling for RACE WAR NOW — invariably fetched for me by young black men, or women in hijabs. Nonsensically afraid they might think I approved of the stuff (which seemed to worry me less when the librarian was white, which in turn struck me as confusingly racist), I accepted them with ham expressions of disgust. Back at my desk I would tut and sigh loudly and often to dissociate myself from the material; no doubt my neighbours were more bothered by the constant noise.

The city abated behind the window (which way were we headed – south-east? south-west?) and houses swelled with the suburbs' sturdy confidence, accruing gardens of substance, hedges, gravel drives. Later they gave way to fields, over which two aircraft in fast low unison flew, pitched sharply up and banked impossibly. I knew there was a military base near our stop, and land for training exercises, and thought again quite suddenly of the man we were meeting, and our agreed agenda, and terms of engagement. Not long after, abandoning the *Independent* on our seat (having decided by unspoken consent that it risked seeming a loaded, anti-establishment accoutrement, which might sour things from the outset), we descended on to the miniature country platform dangling our Evian bottles a little feyly by their necks and sloshing around the water left inside.

The face pic Sean sent had been less than informative, a postage-stamp jpeg riven with the artefacts of aggressive compression. It was a jumping-off point for the imagination merely, and Adam must, like me, have cast a variety of types in the role. Now, as we walked through the ticket hall, where a single pasted sheet sufficed to list every train on the weekly schedule, we saw a black station wagon idling outside, and at its wheel a man older than either of us could have envisaged. Wordlessly we paused, and leaned against the railing of the raised deck. There was nobody else around. A few metres ahead of the station wagon a blue coupé sat empty, as, in the parking lot, did two cars and a transit van. Traffic sounded from some major route nearby. I looked again at the waiting car: its driver glanced at me, then away. He must have been sixty. 'Tell me that's not him,' I murmured. 'Don't stare,' Adam said, sipping his water, and gazing ostentatiously at the sky asked: 'Should we just leave?' I could sense the scaffolding of his own expectations was in collapse, falling through his chest and settling leaden in his stomach while Evian slopped round it in an icy pool.

'When's the next train?'

'Dunno.'

'He's watching us.'

'We could say you're ill. Came down with something on the train. Or pull an emergency at home. It's easy, I've done it before. Ring ring.' He fished his mobile from his pocket and mimed answering: showed me a blank look, then a frown of concern. 'Oh *no*,' he said to the phone. 'What *happened*?'

There was a loud honk and we turned: the blue car, occupied after all. 'Phew,' said Adam, dropping the phone to his side, and skipped down the few steps to the road. Watching him speak to the driver I panicked suddenly: the plan to abort all this had enabled me to relax, and its reversal was violent. I tried not to show it as I followed him to the car, the old man in the station wagon watching without interest. 'This is James,' Adam said when I arrived, but the driver barely looked up, saying merely, 'Get in,' as he pushed forward the passenger seat. Adam sat in front.

Before I could fasten my seatbelt we pulled abruptly out and accelerated quickly. The car was high-pitched, like a toy; it clung frenziedly to the tarmac that now climbed between tall grass. The driver said nothing, pulling us fast along the dips and curves of the country road. Thick hedgerows blitzed past; sunlight flared through trees in crackling patterned bursts. We rode the crest of the hill, then veered over it into a steep plunge, the sky spilling above us. 'Is it far?' Adam asked as the road flattened out. 'Not far,' said the driver, and the silence resumed, underscored by the tin roar of the engine.

Sean, as I now remembered to think of him, surveyed the road through wraparound shades, whose arms disappeared into blond curls above his ears. His face was freckled, thick and pink around his cheeks and chin.

At a roundabout we passed a heavy gate manned by soldiers. The road beyond it ran straight into the distance. Clearing my throat I said: 'Is that where you work?' and Adam caught my eye in the driver's mirror.

'Some of the time,' Sean answered.

He was thirty-five at most. His arms looked muscled enough, but his torso was hard to make out. Leaning slightly forward on the pretext of a passing sign, I saw an apparent stomach above his belted jeans. It could have been how his shirt was folded, or how he sat.

'It's nice around here,' murmured Adam.

Ten minutes later we stopped in a small, isolated development of neat brick homes on a cul-de-sac. Sean opened his front door in silence; inside he locked it again and put the keys on a shelf that held unopened post. Curtains were drawn across the windows of the living room, where two chairs, a sofa and a bare coffee table stood on the carpet like an unconvincing set. There were no shelves, but a wide TV occupied a dedicated stand: standby lights glowed on boxes beneath. The curtains filtered what little sun passed through to a greyish green that coloured the whole assembly.

'Do you want any water?' asked Sean.

Adam smiled and held up his bottle, and I realized I'd left mine in the car. 'Have some now,' Sean told him, 'and give it to me.'

Adam nodded. He drank, paused, drank again. He screwed back the cap and offered it to me, but I shook my head. 'Not thirsty?' said Sean.

'No, I'm fine, thanks.'

'You're fine what, boy?'

It took a moment for me to realize what was intended, and longer still to respond: if I were wrong I would sound ridiculous. I would anyway.

I said, 'I'm fine, thanks, sir.'

'That's better.' Sean took Adam's water bottle to the sofa where he sat. He told us: 'Strip and face the wall.'

'Boots and everything, sir?' said Adam.

'I'm not interested in your boots, boy.'

'Yes, sir,' Adam said. So this was it. We undressed in unison. At first I kicked off my trainers; but seeing Adam unlace his boots carefully and place them neatly to the side, I picked them up again and arranged them next to his. I was conscious of a desire not to offend, as if visiting some peripheral relative. The dim room had that atmosphere, with its carpet and timeless hush: there could have been tea and rock cakes on the way. I folded my T-shirt vaguely over the shoes. When I had removed my jeans I paused lest there was something else intended; but no comment came and Adam was slipping off his jockstrap, so I took off my underpants and looked at the wall. It was chilly, despite the warmth outside. My fingertips brushed my thigh. I could feel Adam breathing beside me, and see the texture of the wallpaper up close.

Sean said nothing. I supposed it was some psychological game. I looked at my feet, where the fringe of sunlight that got between curtain and window frame cut at a shallow angle across the floor. Adam, I noticed, was already hard, and I tried to will myself into anticipation, but the silent figure watching us felt as humdrum as the carpet's weave against my soles. Now I was standing naked in a green room and tomorrow at the same time I could be choosing a sandwich at Pret.

Eventually we heard Sean stand, and cross the room with evident deliberation (I pictured an exaggerated Clouseau creep). He stood behind Adam with regulated breaths. Again, the transparent pause; then he must have touched him because Adam jumped. Sean gave a small *hmpf* of satisfaction. At the edge of my vision a blindfold was lowered over Adam's eyes. 'Hands behind your back,' Sean told him, and I heard the clicks of a ratcheted fastening. He stepped behind me. 'You too, boy,' he said. I put back my arms, which he adjusted with hands that gave surprising, human warmth. I heard the clicks again and felt something thin and plastic tighten round my wrists.

Hands on my shoulders tried to rotate me and I helpfully turned. Sean put his finger under my chin and tilted my head to face him. There was a longer pause as he regarded me.

'Helpless now, aren't you, boy?'

Sean's eyes squinted hopefully. Despite his odd mix of threat and cheery observation, the cajolement was palpable. I knew what he was watching for. Beside me, facing the wall in his blindfold, I could feel Adam waiting too.

'Aren't you, boy?' he said.

'Yes, sir.'

'Hear you're new at this, boy,' he said.

I considered pointing out that we had already established that fact on IM, but it felt inappropriate.

'Bet you're wishing you hadn't got yourself into this situation, aren't you?'

'Don't know, sir,' I said. By now this comment was more polite than honest, but the disingenuous ambiguity worked, and there was another of Sean's pleased little exhalations.

'Heh! I'll bet you don't. Not sure what to think, eh?'

'No, sir,' I said.

Sean looked at me again. He glanced down and quickly back up, as if I might not notice. In our silence I could hear Adam breathing steadily.

'You're scared, but part of you's enjoying this, isn't it? Feels strange, does it boy? Nervous and excited at the same time?'

This was just irritating. If I had been feeling remotely nervous, such anxious collusion would have undermined it. I trotted out another 'Yes, sir.'

Sean produced a blindfold and placed it over me. The strap went over the top of my left ear, pressing it to my head, but the right ear remained free. The lack of symmetry felt like an itch. I could see light leaking in at one side, a slit of detail through his window. I closed my eyes.

After a moment there was a pattering on my chest.

'Ever taken a beating, boy?'

'Not really, sir.'

'But you will take a beating, won't you, boy?'

It was something I had consented to online. At the time there had been some glamour to the idea: I had thought of torture scenes in World War II films. Norton and Pitt in *Fight Club*.

'I don't know, sir, ' I said quietly. I could no longer hear Adam breathe.

Sean paused as he absorbed my rebuff. He changed tack.

'Didn't tell me you were a wimp, boy,' he said disdainfully.

I didn't say anything.

'Pathetic little wimp, are we? Sad little mummy's boy?'

'Don't know, sir.'
'You're a bloody cretin, aren't you, boy?'
'Yes, sir.'
'What are you?'
'A bloody cretin, sir.'
Sean flicked my uninterested penis.
'What's this?'
'Don't know, sir.'
'This is no bloody good, is it?'
'No, sir.'
He could not keep the disappointment from his voice.
'I'll bet you got some stick for that at school, didn't you, boy?' he said. 'Dreaded the showers, eh? I'll bet the chaps called you all sorts of names.'

'Silly snob,' I said, recalling this exchange to Adam on the journey home. It was a throwaway remark; my main theme, to which I energetically returned, was the pernickety attention Sean devoted to role play on the one hand, and his inability, on the other, to see how gauchely he was deconstructing it. It was obvious, I knew, how such conversation was deflecting my own shame.
'What do you mean,' said Adam, 'silly snob?'
'Oh, you know.' I watched the Eurostar overtake us. 'That awful public-school fantasy of chaps in showers.'
'You and I both went to public schools,' he said gently.
'Yes, but we don't get off on it. At least I don't. Besides, my place hardly involved *chaps*.'
The biggest irony, I went on, was that while the purported situation required my own arousal to go unmentioned, Sean could not conceal that it was his urgent focus. Worse, he complained of its absence: not only, thereby, underlining his own failure to produce it, but exposing his assumed persona as a campy, lascivious parody. My flaccidity, by contrast, was too

true to my role: a simulacrum that horrified Sean and showed up the dishonesty of his own eager performance.

'You think too much for this stuff,' Adam said.

Back at his place much earlier than planned, neither of us was sure what to do. I kept sitting on his sofa, then standing again. In the end we went to a movie, and then the pub, where we drank bitter and ate pie and chips, and I pawed intermittently at him beneath the table.

'You know something else?' I said, as I brought over our second pints. 'This has only just struck me, but it was all a bit Abu Ghraib.'

'You don't have to keep explaining.'

'I'm serious. All that stuff is fine as fantasy. To be honest, when we chatted online, I kept thinking of those photos in the *Mirror* and they were almost turn-ons. But when we got down there and drove past whatever that place was, it did drive it home. That he really is in the military, or claims to be, and where he works they probably train soldiers who really do end up in Iraq, so, you know, you wonder if with him the fantasy *is* just a fantasy. I mean if that's what he wants to do . . .

'And those plastic handcuff things we had on: you remember, when we stopped, he just cut them off? I realized after that I'm sure I've seen them on the news, I'm sure they're military issue. I think Amnesty complained about them, in fact. They're used because they're cheap and quick and you can carry loads so they're good for dealing with lots of prisoners. But they don't loosen at all, they only get tighter, so you end up restricting blood flow, causing damage, whatever. I think even when he put them on I sort of knew that's what they were.

'Besides,' I concluded vaguely, 'it was all such a cliché. The banality of the suburban semi, my God.'

'Silly snob.' Adam said it fondly, but I was feeling too sensitive and all at once got annoyed at having so contorted myself round his predilections. I stared at his skinhead outfit, which now looked like the most egregious drag, and had the odd sense of preparing a deliberate cruelty, like chopping ingredients for a stew. It felt slightly dizzying.

'That's what this is all about for you,' I said. 'Isn't it?'

'All of what?'

'Your whole . . . erotic make-up.' I pronounced this with more distaste than I'd intended, and he looked at me, surprised. I tried to stifle the hunter's pleasure I could feel tugging at a corner of my mouth. If only, I thought, I could produce such aggression in sexual form, we might never have got here in the first place.

'This whole sub-skin thing. You get your rocks off by dressing up as the *ne plus ultra* of the lumpenproletariat and pretending you're powerless. It's classic English class guilt.'

'I think it's more about masculinity,' said Adam quietly.

'Same difference,' I replied. 'Anyway.' We were silent after that. For my part I was wondering, rather late, if what I had accused Adam of did not apply more accurately to me. From the moment I had entered Sean's flash-looking, tin-engine car, through our arrival in his Barratt home with its oversize telly and no bookshelves, I'd had the mounting sense of his being, frankly, unbearably petit-bourgeois. Perhaps what had repelled me in Sean's line about showers, I now thought, was less his appeal to any mutual heritage than the aspiration I could taste in it. Though blindfolded, I had seen him then with terrible clarity: imitation cut glass on his parents' table; his mother's careful study of the *Mail*; his unremarkable provincial school, its house names chosen as if from a catalogue in imitation of the grand old establishments for which his masters could not hide their hankering; such petty ambitions, passed on to the boys, shown eventually in phenomena like Sean's cheap, whining car. If he had been a squaddie, it might have worked out.

*

The next morning Adam told me:

'What you said last night, about me. Your whole . . . class analysis. You've never asked me about the first time I had sex.

'When I was a kid we used to go and stay at my uncle's in the country. He had this huge house – massive garden, a paddock, horses, the whole thing. My cousin was older and I had a serious crush on him. I mean emotionally; I must have been about seven at the time, he was thirteen, fourteen. Maybe more. He'd definitely hit puberty. So we're playing some game, I can't remember the details, but we're running around outside the house. I think I'd nicked something of his and he was chasing me. So I went into the stables; there was a dead-end corridor round the side where they stored the equipment, saddles and so on, and I ran into it. Come to think of it I must have known it was a dead-end, so there you go. And of course he comes running in after me, and jumps me and takes back whatever it was, I think it might have been an air rifle, not loaded or anything, and we're sort of play-fighting and rolling around, and at some point he just pulled out his knob. I can still see it, my first close-up erection. And he said, "Suck it." And I did.'

Adam stopped. He lay on his back, with me on my side facing him: his leg between mine, my head on his shoulder.

'Jesus, Ads,' I said. 'That's child abuse.'

'We did it three times every visit for the next five years. Then he got a girlfriend. Anyway, I don't think that's why either.'

Later, as he pulled me into the tight cuddle with which he usually followed his orgasm, he told me his flatmate was going back to Denmark and asked if I wanted to move in with him.

R★A★C★NEWS

Strength through

Oi!

WHITE POWER rules at most rock venues around the country. And the communist outsiders who are trying to brainwash White rock fans are getting kicked out!

At a Selecter concert at Hammersmith Palais recently, more than two hundred racist fans chanted National Front slogans.

National Front supporters were also present at a concert given by the Specials and the Beat in Belfast. Some IRA supporters had gathered on the balcony and were spitting down on a Union Jack being carried by NF Loyalists. But the IRA scum soon shut up when a group of around 70 skinheads started to chant "National Front! National Front!"

OI! THE NEW WAVE OF SKINHEAD BANDS

A NEW WAVE of skinhead bands have risen to carry on the working class tradition which started with Slade in the early seventies. First there were the Upstarts and Skrewdriver and now there is a White Army of new bands.

SKREWDRIVER were in the forefront of the skinhead revival in 1978. Both they and Sham 69 led a legion of racist youth during the hot summers of a few years back. Unlike Sham though, Skrewdriver never betrayed their supporters and never sold out to big business. Their first album, All Skrewed Up, is a classic example of aggressive White rock. Lead singer Ian Stewart is hated by the music papers because he openly supports the National Front.

THE ANGELIC UPSTARTS are not noted for their support for the National Front, but they have nevertheless produced some really hard-hitting music. England, their recent single, is a classic patriotic song with great words. It has become one of the most popular records to be played at YNF discos.

Upstarts lead singer, Mensi, started off by playing at Rock Against Racism gigs. But now he appears to be more confused: "Who isn't confused with this government and the opposition" he recently wrote in a music paper, "the only ones who seem to have any time for today's youth are the SWP, NF and BM."

INFA-RIOT are one of the new wave of skinhead bands. They play fast aggressive rock and they are building up a large following of skins. The band are all teenagers and their music relates to the new generation of White British youth. One of their most popular numbers is the NF orientated Britain's Not Lost. White rock fans should look out for this band in the future or, better still, go and see them live.

Bulldog 22, circa May 1981

POULTON, Lancs.: There are now more than eighty members and active supporters of the Young National Front in Poulton-le-Fylde, Lancashire. Poulton is only a very small town near Blackpool but nearly all of the local youths

have joined the YNF! Much of the credit for the growth of the National Front in the area must go to local YNF Organiser Ian Donaldson who is pictured above with other Poulton members.

Bulldog 25, *circa* October 1981: Ian Stuart Donaldson

The Chamber of the Sun

Niven calls. He says: 'You're needed.'

At the pub it is only Tony and Dave. Niven buys drinks. He seems excited: the pints slop in his hands.

He tells them: 'We're having a visitor.' He will not say who. He says: *she*.

She is very important. She is passing through England, a rare visit. There are elements that would be very interested in this, and must not find out.

It is best if she moves around. She does Niven the honour of staying at his house for two nights. For this time she needs protection. Also, she is elderly. On Saturday Niven and his wife will be unable to attend to her. They have a prior engagement, a gathering at his in-laws.' (He intimates revulsion.) Dave and Tony will therefore spend the day with Niven's guest, at his house.

He says they must remain alert, and respectful. He calls them an honour guard. He says this is important. He says: an important mission.

His cheeks twitch with anticipation.

It is Tuesday, 12 October 1982.

*

They meet Niven on Friday morning and drive with him to Dover. He asks, 'Who's sitting in the front?' and 'How's your map-reading?' He pays officious attention to the speed limit and indicates diligently when he wants to overtake. There is some confusion finding the ferry terminal and he criticizes Dave's navigation. Niven says, 'You'll need to be a damn sight sharper than this when the war starts.' Dave says, 'Just turn left. Left!'

Dave and Tony stand by the car while Niven goes inside.

'Bet you it's his mum,' Tony says.

Eventually Niven emerges, struggling manfully with two large, old leather suitcases, and attentive to the frail figure beside him.

She walks slowly, with evident difficulty, her right leg trailing. She is dressed in white, thin cotton wrapped around her head and body. A sari.

Tony mutters, 'You're taking the fucking piss.'

Dave puts the cases in the boot and Tony opens the passenger door. As Niven guides the old woman towards it, Tony sees that the right side of her mouth hangs in a droop, as if someone snipped its muscle. She edges forward, brushing his thigh. Her eyes look lost and liquid. One is dead; the other stares confused and urgent through a film of milk. When it meets his gaze it blinks, and as Tony helps her into her seat she whispers: *'Heil Hitler.'*

The next morning she is sitting in an armchair in Niven's front room, nudged curiously by dust motes that hover in the sunlight. Tony watches her from the sofa. He cannot tell if she is asleep: every now and then she opens her eyes without shifting or saying anything. He feels like he has been here for hours: where is Dave? He checks the clock: ten-forty-five.

On the way back from Dover she seemed tired, responding only briefly to Niven's conversational gambits and making the odd disjointed observation. At one point, staring at the road ahead with her one struggling eye, she asked: 'Did you see what the Jews did in Lebanon?' and her voice, though thickened by the vagaries of her slumped right lip, was sharp, almost harsh.

Niven said, 'Disgusting,' and nodded. Tony wondered if he was bluffing.

At eleven-fifteen Dave arrives. The old woman does not react to his doorbell. Still, he and Tony are quiet as they discuss her in the kitchen.

Tony says, 'I can't even watch telly in case it wakes her up.'

'Sounds like fun.'

'Want to hide in their bedroom and get pissed?'

Dave laughs. 'We could see if she's up for it.' Then he says, 'Actually, I was going to ask:'

There is a rally today for this new British National Party and a lot of BM lads are going. Dave says: 'I don't want to take the piss but it don't look like she needs two of us. Would you mind? I'll tell you how it goes. The only thing is they're redirecting from Trafalgar Square soon.'

By a quarter to twelve he has gone and Tony is back on the sofa failing to concentrate on the Nivens' *Reader's Digest* and watching their cat make the rounds of resting feet. The sun is bright through the window and he can feel his crotch under his jeans. He rests his hand on it, wonders about finding somewhere for a wank. Also, he is getting hungry. Niven's wife told him, 'Apparently she's vegetarian! There's plenty of cheese in the fridge, and celery and things, and the end of the nut roast we had for dinner. I'd stick to cheese if I were you, the nut roast played all sorts of funny with me. Oh, and she doesn't drink tea, she drinks *coffee*.'

The cat keeps brushing against his boots. Tony is properly hard now and glances over at the old woman as he moves his thumb a bit under his fingers, feeling the tag of his zip. There was a photo of Nicky up at the Last Resort last time he was round there that he can still picture.

Quite suddenly the cat jumps into the old woman's lap. She gives a small jolt and instantly relaxes again. Her hand moves to the settling animal. Tony's moves to his thigh.

'Puss,' she says. 'Puss, puss.'

Tony says, 'It's like he knows you.'

'Oh, nearly all animals – and especially all cats – "know" me.' Her fingers probe the indents behind its ears. 'They *feel* that I love them. Intuitively, and' – she looks him – 'with absolute certainty.'

After a pause she adds, 'I fed stray cats in the war, you know. There was a famine in Bengal, and I would go down twice a day, with rice, fish and milk, to two or three courtyards where they'd gather.'

'How many did you look after?'

'About a hundred and fifty.'

'You're joking.'

She smiles. 'Not at all. Twice a day. And every evening, along the winding iron staircase that led to my terrace, there would be such a great queue of cats, kittens and all, waiting to be fed. I had thirty-five in my house alone! Everyone knew me as the cat memsahib.'

'Always been more of a dog man myself.'

'One time, in Calcutta Zoo, I put my whole arm into the cage of a Royal Bengal tiger. I wanted to stroke it. I still remember how it looked at me for a moment, as if making up its mind, and then just half closed its eyes, like so, and rubbed up close to me against the cage. And it purred,' she stagily confides to the animal on her lap, 'like an *enormous cat*.'

Tony says, 'A friend of mine when I was young, his mum had a thing for cats. She was a bit deaf and her husband wasn't around no more. She adopted strays a few times. I think she found them reassuring you know? Liked the company. Mind you she only ever had three or four. Not a hundred and fifty.'

'Where's the other young man?'

'Dave? He's not here yet.'

'On the contrary,' she replies, 'he came and went.'

Tony looks at her. 'Thought you was asleep.'

'Sleep, at my age, is no longer the same thing.'

Tony pauses. 'He's gone to a meeting. Don't tell Arthur though, he'll shit— Pardon me. He thinks you need two men to look after you.'

The old woman smiles, stroking her intuitive friend. She sings to it quietly: 'Nanda, Nanda,' it sounds like. 'Nanda, Rani.' Then she asks: 'What meeting?'

Tony sees no reason not to tell her.

'Oh yes,' she says. 'John Tyndall's new alliance. We were talking about it last night. Of course, I remember the old British National Party, the original. I was here in 1961 – in London. I was teaching in Lyons and I came at Easter, to see the same dear friend I am visiting tomorrow, when I leave here.

'I used to hate London.' The way this is said makes clear it is not hyperbole. 'I was here at the time of the so-called Nuremberg "Trials" . . .'

She pauses and Tony, to show he is paying attention, says, 'The war-crimes tribunals.' He is pleased with this knowledge.

She snorts. 'The greatest infamy in world history! The martyrdom of the Eleven, after *months* of moral and physical agony. And in the name of justice! Oh, the wild hatred of this ugly, Jew-ridden world . . . they killed them, you know, on one of their festival days. Such persecution. What was I saying?'

'You were telling me why you hated London.'

'Oh! Well, I was in London on that dismal day. Everywhere you went, the atrocity-campaign was at its height. Signs on Oxford Street: "Nazi Horrors. Entrance, one shilling and sixpence." Ha! Hypocrisy, stupidity everywhere. "Pity the starving

German children," cry the makers of the phosphorus bombs! And in England – England, which should never have gone to war with Germany.

'But in 1961, after fifteen years of the most vicious anti-Nazi propaganda, what should I read about but demonstrations – in Trafalgar Square! – by a new party loyal to Nazi ideals. A *British National* Party, turning back immigrants at railway terminals and standing up to the Jews, a party dedicated – I still remember the words – to "a racial nationalist folk state . . . embodied in the creed of National Socialism and uniquely implemented by Adolf Hitler!"

'Of course I wrote to them, and that summer we had a camp in the English countryside, with songs and ale round the fire. But when I was back in France, Arthur wrote to me that John had been betrayed. The BNP was embarrassed by the mention of Hitler, they thought Nazism a political liability.

'And now John is starting a new BNP – a new cycle begins. And there will be more people, more every time, ready to face the sickness of this world and defy it with their every gesture. And every time more, many more, young ones – like you! – without even the personal memory of Hitler's great days to sustain them. Yet still they come. And still, and still, we will come.'

She leans back her head, closes her eyes, and recites: '*When justice is crushed, when evil reigns supreme, then I come. For the protection of the good, for the destruction of the evil-doers, for the sake of firmly establishing righteousness, I am born, age after age.*'

She tells him of the cycle of ages, the Yugas, as laid down in the great epics of the Aryans, which repeats through all eternity. She traces the inexorable decline from the Krita Yuga, the Age of Truth – the Golden Age, whose memory all cultures, from the Greeks and Japanese to the Sumerians and Romans, somehow preserve – to the current, fourth, Dark Age, the Kali

Yuga, the Era of Gloom, in which human selfishness and conceit allows man to overrun the planet while its once-thick mantle of forest declines. Whole species of proud wild creatures are killed off, replaced by an obnoxious and expanding stream of dreary, vulgar, worthless two-legged mammals, and everything is done to encourage that mad increase in number and loss in quality. Everything is done to keep the sickly, the crippled, the freaks of nature, unfit to work and unfit to live, from dying. Thousands of innocent, healthy animals are tortured in search of 'new treatments,' so that deficient men, whom Nature has anyhow condemned to death, might last a few more months. The healthy are made unhealthy through joyless work, overcrowded homes, lack of privacy, unnatural food, their brains softened by advertising and propaganda. Lies are called truth and truth falsehood, and the speakers of truth, the God-like men, are defeated, their followers humbled, their memory slandered, while the masters of lies are hailed as saviours.

And she tells him of Kalki, the last One, the Destroyer, destined to clear the ground for the building of a new age of truth. It was Kalki of whom, with that unfailing cosmic intuition, the *Führer* said, 'I know that Somebody must come forth and meet our situation. I have sought, and found him nowhere; and therefore I have taken upon myself to do the preparatory work; *only the most urgent preparatory work.*' She tells him that Kalki, unlike Hitler, will act with unprecedented ruthlessness. He will spare not one enemy of the divine cause: not one outspoken opponent, nor even one of the heretical, the racially bastardized, the unhealthy, hesitating, *all-too-human*: not a single one of those who, in body or in character or in mind, bear the stamp of the fallen Ages.

'And we like to hope,' she says, 'that the memory of the One-before-the-last – of Adolf Hitler – will survive, at least in songs and symbols, in that long Age of earthly Perfection which Kalki, the last One, is to open. We like to hope that the Lords of the new Time-Cycle, men of his own blood and faith, will render him divine honours, through rites full of meaning and potency, in the cool shade of the endless regrown forests, on the beaches, or on inviolate mountain peaks, facing the rising sun.'

Tony helps her through to the kitchen for lunch. She holds his left arm like a bird grips a branch. Her near leg trails forward with him when he moves, so he has to stop and start alternately with the stronger one. He lowers her on to the hard kitchen chair, puts cheese and butter on plates, slices bread.

Across the table, she peers at him. 'And what is that by your eye?'

'This?' Tony fingers the tattoo. 'A "barrier to decent employment," they tell me.'

'It looks like one.'

'Where's yours?'

'What do you mean?'

Tony points to his forehead. 'Aren't you meant to have a dot here or something?'

She smiles. 'No.'

She puts the buttered corner of a slice of bread to her mouth and severs it. She chews impossibly slowly. Her face is a village hit by a mudslide: one side remains standing, functional.

When she has finally swallowed she asks: 'How old are you?'

'Twenty-six.'

'And how long have you been one of us?'

The question makes him pause. 'I've been politically active for about six years now. But I've always been patriotic.'

'And what have you read?'

'What do you mean?'

'You call yourself "patriotic." Either you are talking in a

needlessly roundabout way, or even after six years you have not embraced the entirety of our faith – so I wonder what you have read.'

'I don't really think of it as a faith.'

'A faith – *the* faith – is exactly what it is.' She considers him. 'And you have it, even if you will not admit it yet.'

He says: 'How do you know?'

'I learned to recognize it long ago.'

'Where did you go?'

'To Linz, where the *Führer* spent his boyhood. To Leonding, to his parents' burial place. Braunau am Inn, where he was born. To Berchtesgaden, Obersalzburg, Munich. To Landsberg am Lech. To Nuremberg.'

'This was after the war?'

'Eight years after. I had been several times, the first in 1948. My English friend, the one I am visiting tomorrow, was once a theatrical costumier. She found me work with a travelling dance troupe, the Randoopa Dancing Company, and I went with them to Stockholm. There I stayed up for two nights, and I wrote out by hand 500 leaflets—'

'Got enough energy haven't you?'

'I took the Nord-Express through Germany; and from its windows I distributed my leaflets to the people I met, hidden in packets of cigarettes and food.'

'What did they say?'

'They said, essentially: *We are the pure gold which can be tested in the furnace. Nothing can destroy us.* Heil Hitler.'

'What was Germany like then?'

'As I wrote. It was a furnace.'

Later he smokes in the Nivens' upstairs bathroom, the one they use themselves. Since the morning's initial boredom there has been no let-up in her conversation, and he takes the opportunity to linger for a second cigarette before dropping the fag-end in and watching it flounder. In the mirror he scans his eyes for whatever she has seen in them. They blink emptily back.

The radiator in the guest room has been left on high and there is an air of stale secretion. By her bed are some flowers and a glass of water; the afternoon sunlight shows up their dust. He has been sent for the smaller of her two cases, which stands unopened against the wall. It is very heavy, and he struggles to carry it to the sitting room, where she sits on the sofa, squinting patiently at the window.

'I don't know what you've got in here,' he tells her, 'but I'm surprised the ferry didn't sink.'

'A few books.'

'You must read a lot.'

'I can't read at all any more. These are copies of my own books, for the Americans. I will go there after visiting my friend, to give some lectures.'

'I'd like to go to America.'

'Do you know my friend's definition of an American? A mammal that cannot shut its mouth. Would you kindly open the case?'

The books occupy one half, beside a substantial folded coat. He picks one up: it is long and dense, printed on cheap, thin paper.

'You wrote all these?'

'Yes. But it is that coat I want. Please, be as careful as you can.'

It is an old trench coat in dirty cream, heavier and larger than it should be. He lifts it gently from below and places it on the sofa next to her. She turns and with her functional hand begins very carefully to unfold it.

'In 1953, after I left Berchtesgaden, I travelled on to Munich. The Bürgerbräukeller, where the *putsch* had once been planned, had become an American Service Club; and the shrines of the martyred Sixteen, which in the great days were guarded day and night, had been destroyed. But their foundation stones had withstood the dynamite. I touched them through the fence – as Christian pilgrims, or Muhammadans or Hindus, touch the tombs of their respective saints. And I repeated the names reverently in my mind. Alfarth. Bauriedl. Casella. Ehrlich. Faust. Hechenberger. Körner. Kuhn. Laforce. Neubauer. Pape. Pfortden. Rickmers. Scheubner-Richter. Stransky. Wolf.'

She takes from the coat a folded fabric, which she places on her lap. She regards him with her living eye, which glimmers like kindling.

'The friend who entrusted it to me told me that Heinrich Trambauer was carrying it, and he was shot and fell, and when Bauriedl was killed he fell over him, and stained it with his blood.'

She unfolds the flag with fingers that tremble with more than mere age. The red field, the white disk.

'At Nuremberg, at the great rallies, it would touch the new banners – thousands more every time – and, with its blood, give strength to them.'

The symbol, heavy and black, assured in its own inevitability.

'It is the Wheel of the Sun,' she says, 'and we are Children of the Sun. The world believes us dead. There is silence around us like around the dead. There is silence around Him, whose name we dare not speak, save as one speaks in a graveyard. The night of death has closed on us and the Moon sheds its livid rays. But we know we are awake. We know the Sun will rise. *Einst kommt der Tag der Rache.*'

Tony stares at her. 'You're joking.'

'If I am joking,' she asks, 'why are you afraid to touch it?'

He says quietly: 'How do you know I'm what you think I am?'

'I know you as others have known me. I feel it.' She smiles at him, and her voice becomes gentler. 'In Uelzen I met a *Sturmführer* just released from Landsberg. He talked of Auschwitz and Treblinka, and the convoys of Jews that he had himself accompanied to the place of fate. And he described the activity of the crematoria, and the "great bright-red flames" that would spring from the main chimney when new fuel fed the furnace below. The *Sturmführer* and I, we had not known each other even half an hour, but still he said to me, "*You* would have loved to see those beautiful great red flames!" Because people of the same sort *feel* one another, you see. And of course he was right: those flames were the sunset purple announcing the twilight of a world I have hated for years – for centuries, perhaps – just as other flames, lit from isle to isle, once announced the destruction of Troy. And so I say: you too, *you would have loved to see those beautiful great red flames*. Give me your hand.'

The surface of the flag feels of nothing at all.

'Blood touches blood,' she whispers, gripping him to it. '*Aum Shivayam! Aum Rudrayam! Heil Hitler!*'

She says this with mounting intensity and on the last invocation inhales sharply, and her left hand, holding his wrist, clutches it tighter. Tony, who has had to lower himself to give her his hand, remains awkwardly crouched before her in this enforced novitiate posture, waiting for the passion to pass. But instead of subsiding her excitement now seems to increase, and her nails dig into him as her breath speeds up. Her eye, which just now fixed him with atavistic witness, widens differently in confusion and creeping panic, and she begins to gasp with shock. Tony asks, 'Are you OK?' and she shakes her head tightly. He says, 'What's the matter?' but she seems unable to speak, struggling as she is to catch her breath, inhaling in violent stuttered chokes. Her hand drops his wrist and moves to the centre of her chest, where it begins to open and close, flexing like an insect, splaying then squeezing to a tight fist. She makes this gesture twice, then keeps it clenched, clutching tighter, so the wrinkles on her knuckles splay wide, opening long-sealed cracks. Between gasps she manages, 'Pressure – on my chest.' Tony says, 'Are you having a stroke?' and prods his thumb above her half-good eye, pulling the skin free of the socket, peering into its pearly swim as if things might clarify. He realizes he has no idea what to do. She shakes her head: 'Choking.' The grotesque skew of her slurring mouth is exacerbated by panic, as if her face is melting. He says, 'But you haven't eaten anything. It must be a stroke. You've had one already, haven't you?' Her eyes are watering now and her skin losing colour; she shakes her head again in desperate uncertainty, or perhaps fierce disagreement. She looks at him pleadingly. This is why Dave should be here. First-aid tips from school come back as daft non-sequiturs. If someone electrocutes themselves you have to make sure they don't choke on their own vomit. The kiss of life: he imagines the flabby seal of their lips, the taste of mucus and cheese, vigorous shoves against her frail constricted chest, like an antique roll-top. He should call a doctor, but now sweat is slathering her face, and he can at least find a tissue for that. He had one in a pocket: standing over her, he begins to go through them. There are keys and coins, an old bus ticket: too small, and not remotely absorbent. Her gasps are going on and on; it seems impossible that each one will not be the last, and yet they continue. He says apologetically, 'I thought I had a tissue somewhere,' and then, 'Must have chucked it away.'

He must make clear to the doctor she is having a stroke. He wonders what number to call. He looks about for the Nivens' address book, standing on the spot, mummingly turning his head so she knows he is doing something. She is, he notices, dropping laterally across the couch. When she is horizontal she will be in the same position that she would have, might soon have, as a corpse. She might stain the fabric; Mrs Niven is house-proud. He hears her retch and sees a spray of sputum, followed by the dribble from her mouth's dead corner of something cream-coloured, with lurid orange flecks. He realizes she might puke on the flag in her lap, and lifts it out of the way, placing it for now on a side table. He does not have time to fold it carefully. As he puts it down he looks at her again, still sliding and choking, and for the first time registers how disgusting the sight is, the shameless indiscretion of a failing body, its primitive leaks; and at the same time the old simplicity of it, nature reasserting its course. He leans down to her face and says, 'Can you hear me?' and when she answers, 'Yes,' a puff of sweet-sour stomach gas hits him, and with it the feeling on his skin of a tiny spray like a sneeze. He says, 'I don't think there's much point calling a doctor,' and adds, 'It's all right, I'll stay here with you.' She stares, confusion bleeding into a new, compound fear as he pulls a chair close to her. She says, 'Please call an ambulance,' as loudly as she can, but the plea reaches him empty of fellow-feeling; he hears it like reported speech in a news story. Of course that is what she would say, this is the body in collapse, its desperate reflex in the basic state of fear. It is the physical symptoms that are most interesting. He realizes he has never seen this before, death in full assault, and it is as if what has long been present is just now surfacing, as if putrefaction started inside long ago, and now comes through where the vessel ruptures with strain. She is flat across the sofa now, still making her frantic gasping noise, still sounding surprised. So this is what happens to history and memory, her long proud catalogue of recollections sinking and silenced now, experience so gradually accreted gone in a gulp and rendered void. Tony takes her hand, which shakes inside his like a train leaving its tracks. 'I fuck men,' he tells her, 'or they fuck me, all that stuff. I've always been like this, since I was a boy.' Her expression does not change. 'It's ages since I've had my end away though. I'm going spare with it, wanking myself stupid. I could find some bloke in a toilet or whatever, I used to do that a lot, but I don't feel like it so much no more. I've gone a bit soft for my mate Dave, the one you met. It's stupid though, if anything was going to happen it would have by now.'

He drops her hand, stands. She is spent, her gaze dropped to the cushion by her head. Outside it is getting dark and the streetlamps have come on. He turns on the ceiling light and the one on the table. He picks up the flag and lets it fall open, the far edge tumbling to his feet. It is much wider than his arms can span. The material is thick and old, the design assembled in solid shapes edged with heavy stitching. Its colours and obscure stains are both faded. He asks her: 'Is this really what you say it is?' She says, 'Yes.' He says, 'I'd like to have it. Are you feeling better?' Her breathing has become shallower and less desperate. She says, 'I think the pain has passed.'

He fetches her a glass of water and raises her to a sitting position so she can drink. She takes tiny sips in between long pauses holding it in her lap. He folds the flag and rolls it in a bundle. It will fit in his duffel bag.

He says, 'You never went to Germany until after the war?'

'No.' It is a wet sound, and she wipes her mouth with the section of toilet roll he has given her.

'So you never really met anyone.'

'No. Except . . .'

'Go on.'

'When I was in London after the war, when things were at their worst, I stayed for a few days in a nurses' hostel.' Her voice is faint but calm. 'One night I dreamed that I travelled to Nuremberg. I found myself in Göring's cell. I told him that I wished I could save all of the martyrs, but I had been granted leave to help only one. I had chosen him because of his kindness to animals. I felt something in my hand – I did not know what – and gave it to him, saying, "Take this, and do not allow these people to kill you as a criminal. *Heil Hitler*."

'The next morning I woke up late, which was very unusual for me. It was raining outside, I remember, the sixteenth of October, and as I walked out I saw a newspaper kiosk. The headline was: GÖRING FOUND DEAD IN HIS CELL AT 2.30 A.M. NO ONE KNOWS WHO GAVE HIM THE POISON. POTASSIUM CYANIDE.'

'That's a strange story.'

'It's entirely true.'

'It's today's date. The sixteenth of October.'

He helps her to the bedroom. 'Should I leave the light on?'

'No, please, turn it off.'

'You should have Arthur call a doctor, get yourself checked out. It was a nasty episode you had. How much do you reckon that flag is worth?'

'A great deal, I would imagine. But only to someone who would sell it.'

'You be able to get to sleep? You should think about something nice.'

'I will think about tomorrow. I haven't seen my friend in many years.'

'How long have you known her?'

'Since 1946.'

'You two go back a long way.'

'Yes. I'm looking forward to seeing her very much.'

The Nivens do not arrive back until midnight, and there is much debriefing to be done. Niven is shaken and grateful in equal measure, and furious with Dave, for whom Tony invents a family emergency. He walks out into silence and a moonless sky. A few feet on he hears a whistle and there is Dave, sitting beneath a tree. He waves a shopping bag, which clinks: 'Had a few already.'

They walk towards the woods. Tony says, 'So how's the brave new party?'

Dave shrugs. 'More of the same isn't it. They like a good sing-song anyway. Gave out the lyrics and everything.' He digs a cyclostyled hand-out from his pocket and gives it to Tony, who stops under a lamp to read:

The time is near when those streets we'll clear / Of those foes of our race evermore. To the tune of "Keep Right on to the End of the Road." What one's that?'

'You know. Pa pa pum pa di pa diddi pum.'

'Don't know it. *Now we are coming / See them all running*. Doesn't rhyme.'

Dave smiles. 'A lot of the old BM boys were there. People I hadn't seen for a while. Might be worth keeping a toe in.'

'Tyndall's an old git though.'

'At least he's not a fat poof.'

'True enough.'

'Some of the boys are going down the 100 Club next Thursday. It's meant to be Skrewdriver's comeback gig. I might head down – you interested?'

'Yeah I'll come to that.'

They continue in silence until they are out of the houses, then settle on a verge beneath the woods and crack open new beers.

'Anyway,' says Dave, 'how was Eva Braun?'

'Well apart from her nearly dying on me we had a lovely time.'

'You're joking.'

'I'm not as it happens.'

'Shit. Well go on then.'

Tony pauses. 'I can't remember. Honest. It's like a gap.'

'You're having me on.'

'Not really. I remember her gasping a bit and I remember her looking better, but the stuff in the middle's gone.'

'That's weird.'

'It's been a weird day.'

Dave nods, takes a long pull on his beer, belches. 'What's that in your bag?' he asks, and then: 'What else did you do with her?'

'Chatted mostly.'

'What about?'

'This and that. Old-lady things. You know, cats. Holidays. Auschwitz.'

'What did she have to say about Auschwitz?'

'Auschwitz? It was the dog's bollocks.'

Dave looks down at his can. He says: 'My grandad died at Auschwitz.'

'Oh here we go.'

'No we're all dead cut up about it. Apparently he got drunk and fell out of the machine-gun tower.'

It's an old joke, but he still cracks up before he finishes the punchline.

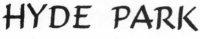

HYDE PARK OUTRAGE!

Visitors to London's Hyde Park were outraged recently by the antics of a group of boneheads holding an outdoor art class. Terror struck as a well known skin from Crayford, Kent bared all in the cause of art. The Honourable Cynthia Withers-Smythe who was exercising her stallion (you mean her old man was with her? - Ed) was accosted by the assembled mob. "This is disgusting!" she cried, "Why don't you binders Naff Orf and leave the park to law abiding boring old farts to gaze aimlessly at the boring old surroundings?" This was too much for the cropped ones who proceeded to rip off Cynthia's riding habit revealing only a sex-pistols T shirt being worn underneath. After Cynthia had been rescued by Colonel Anstruther the lads decided to wash their underwear by having a swim in the Surpentine but this drew the attention of Old Bill. "Ullo, Ullo, Ullo, what's this 'ere then. Don't you know that under bye-law four thousand, six hundred and thirty two, sub-section five, paragraph six (b), washing of soiled underwear is strictly forbidden?" On hearing this the crew decided to leg it to the nearest tube station. Continued The Aggy.

Skins International fanzine, 1983

Before the Night Falls

I woke, again, with a dead arm. I pulled it from the pillow by Adam's head and unpeeled myself from his sleeping body, hot against my front: he shifted, with a little cough. My arm lolled like a dead fish. I flapped it about to shake the circulation back, then trailed its working counterpart overboard, dragging the floor for my glass of water. In this weather Adam insisted on keeping the windows closed and the heating on, and I was always thirsty.

Around the curtains bled orange light from an outside streetlamp, fissured by the branches between. Adam's I clock-radio flashed 3:14. When I woke alone such hours had always brought with them mortal intuitions, from which being with Adam had so far protected me; for this I kissed the back of his head. Turned, as usual, away from me, his arms drawn to his chest, he resembled, with that hairless skull, an elongated baby.

I finished the water and needed more. In the kitchen, the fridge bathed my naked body in its morgue light. I replaced the Brita jug and shut it fast, and went to the warmer living room, where our laptops slept together on the dining table, mine with its soft white pulse, and Adam's, its green blink. (I'd been momentarily excited by the discovery that, filming the 1984 ad that launched the Mac, Ridley Scott had bussed real skinheads to Shepperton Studios, and I'd scoured footage of the shoot for a glimpse of Nicky: but '1984' was made in 1983, and he was in prison that whole year.)

Adam's computer winked jealously. Sometimes we'd sit across from each other, screens raised like shields with opposing ensigns, checking our messages. In such moments were his truancies arranged. When I touched Adam's laptop I saw his cat eyeing me from the sofa. I reached for mine instead.

Word was still open to my notes on the Hamborough Tavern riot, after which the *Mail* had exposed Nicky as the cover star of *Strength thru Oi!*. In the hiatus between initiating violence (smashed storefronts, street fights) and the full eruption, an oddly silent image: Asians gathered round the pub watch the skins inside write NF slogans in condensation on the glass. Then bricks, petrol bombs, 600 police, a smoking husk.

I closed Word and checked my email: only spam. I had been getting a lot more recently, some of it quite unpleasant. As part of my research I had joined a few nazi websites, and should have been more careful with my email address.

Scrolling through my purged inbox, I recognized the impulse I now felt: it was a familiar ritual at times like this, the luxury of personal archaeology. I still had Adam's first email to me ('told you research was a piss-easy job!'), and all our correspondence since: arrangements to see forgotten films, invectives about work, the occasional blush of amateur porn. And dating further back, in batches carefully transferred from older machines, earlier mail clients, most emails I had ever sent:

When you're young [I complained to Philip] and from a certain background, you're encouraged to 'express' yourself. Then you hit adolescence and the virulence of life crashes into your veins.

Everything now begins to encourage you against yourself. Your fellow adults lock themselves down into a death-rictus washed by the thick current of cathode fantasy. They will brook no attempt to disrupt this.

Do you remember what I said to you last summer? Because I was right and have forgotten. Something almost happened to me, and I've slipped back.

Confirmation emails for flights long past. Exchanges, clumsily intimate, with boys met online. One American, younger than me and closeted, had talked of suicide: our correspondence tailed off.

At 3:20 A.M. there were 4,078 men logged on globally, 291 in London. I had no new messages, so browsed my tabulated fellow citizens. At this hour their profile taglines became more urgent, more despairing. *Anyone up 4 it now? Horny and waiting in SE8! Looking for meet this eve.*

COME ON GUYS WHERE ARE YOU

I edited my own to read *Everything now begins to encourage you against yourself.* Underneath, my portrait, snapped by Sarah at a family gathering, smiled unaffectedly back at me. It was two years old: false advertising.

Adam, I saw, had new photos. *Horny 25yo sub skin in Kennington. Into BDSM, CBT, CP and more. No BB. Have great BF only looking for fun.* He stood shirtless in boots and combats by a low hedge, grinning and squinting at the sun behind the camera. In the background were what looked like the sails of an old mill. The ground at his feet was thick with grass. Where had it been taken, and by whom?

You could search the profiles by keyword. I tried *windmill.* There were no results. I tried *BDSM* and got several hundred: even more for *CP.*

I tried *death-rictus.* Nothing.

I tried *LOG.* Ditto.

I tried *not even amusing myself now*.

I tried *nazi*, and the site returned fourteen profiles.

A grey man in SS leathers. More than one skinhead saluting the camera (one with the note *Vote BNP Hull, Derringham 18 Jan!*). A Jewish teacher into concentration-camp role play. Somebody grimacing in poor lighting asked, *What is the nazi leather movement?* A rhetorical question: *It is a movement for men of all races and sexual preferance!*

One man billed himself as *Hard sskin top iso ssubs who can clean boots properly, also bruders alpha dogs and m88s. Whites only. Stay safe to stay pure.* Later I would search for *bruders* and *m88s*, and get several results for each.

The last profile of the fourteen used the handle 'arealnazi.' There was no photograph. The text said: *Nazi skinhead thug, fat, middle aged, tatts, will abuse worthless scum. I will hurt you & rape you if I want & take your money if I want & leave you bleeding. If thats not what your looking for fuck off. If your going to ask for a photo fuck off. I am not play acting I am a fucking nazi.*

'Come back to bed.' Adam stood in the doorway.

I closed the laptop. 'I couldn't sleep.'

'Look at yourself.'

'What?'

'Nothing. I'm not saying anything.'

Under the duvet he said, 'You're freezing. Why couldn't you sleep?'

'How much are boots?' I asked.

'What sort of boots?'

'Proper boots. Like yours.'

'Good night.' He kissed my hand.

I said: 'It says on your profile that I'm a great BF.'

'I've been meaning to update that.'

In the morning we went shopping. Philip was due for dinner with his new boyfriend Tom, to whose irritating vegetarianism

I felt the need to respond with some sort of casually achieved triumph, as if by providing better food than he was surely used to I could allude to pleasures beyond his prim horizons. But my couscous didn't turn out as I'd imagined. 'Sorry it's rather tasteless,' I said. Tom, blond and three years my junior, smiled cutely: 'It's very nice.' He had expected nothing better.

'Oh,' said Philip, 'I'm always up for couscous.'

I said, 'Well, if you will date vegetarians.'

He ruffled Tom's hair. 'I fry myself a steak once in a while.'

'When I'm not around he does. I can't stand the smell.' The grains were claggy and dry, and the vegetables that sat on them harsh with raw spice.

'So,' said Philip, 'have you actually written anything yet?'

'I've made a lot of notes.'

'James is writing a screenplay,' he told Tom.

'Probably.'

'A screenplay probably. Or a novel possibly. Or a performance piece or maybe a haiku. He hasn't decided. But he's made *a lot of notes*.'

'What about?' Tom said.

'Don't get him started,' Adam advised him.

'Actually,' I said, 'it's been getting quite interesting.'

Among the 'special material' in the library I had located certain underground texts of the British Satanist group the Order of Nine Angles. Their author, who signed himself 'Anton Long,' was widely identified as David Myatt, the neo-nazi ideologist whose writings had inspired the London nailbomber David Copeland. Myatt had disavowed more than a brief, youthful involvement in the occult, and repeatedly denied being the same person as Long, but Long's satanic autobiography read like a dark-glassed version of Myatt's own, and in it he claimed authorship of poems and translations of Greek classics published in Myatt's name. Some of the library's texts had been numbered or amended by hand, in the same script with which Long signed himself. This, and their content, had made the experience of reading them quite unsettling.

Long (I told the others) elaborated an extensive system of Satanism, the Seven-Fold Sinister Way. It was a process of individual personal development, which demanded rigorous self-testing, pushing limits on both physical and moral planes: on the one hand, for example, walking fifty miles over hilly terrain, and on the other conducting human sacrifice. This last, he insisted, was central to satanic practice; he claimed to have performed it more than once.

'*Nice*,' said Tom.

'I thought you were writing about Nicky Crane,' Philip said.

'I am.'

'It doesn't sound like it.'

'Putting it together is the fun part. It's degrees-of-separation stuff. Like, what has David Myatt got to do with Nicky? Nothing directly – well, they were both in the British Movement—'

'I can't keep track of all these groups,' Adam said.

'I don't think anyone can. Probably including the members. The factions split every three weeks, and they're all named using some combination of the same ten words. I wouldn't bother, frankly: just go with the flow . . . Anyway, back to my Nicky–Myatt degrees-of-separation thing. There's a guy called Tony Williams who was Myatt's protégé in the National-Socialist Movement – the '90s NSM, which splintered out of Combat 18, not the '60s NSM run by Colin Jordan and John Tyndall after they were kicked out of the BNP – which is not today's BNP, which was started by Tyndall after he left the National Front. The '60s NSM is what became the British Movement. See, *I* can keep track of them. So, it was Williams who let Copeland into the NSM. But a few years earlier, Williams had helped organize Rock Against Communism and

Skrewdriver gigs – the Nicky link. It was also Williams whom Colin Jordan sent as his representative to Savitri Devi's funeral. Jordan' (I footnoted for Tom) 'is basically the godfather of British fascism, and she was this mad Greek Hindu woman who created a sort of Hitler religion – Hitler never died or was coming back or whatever – but Savitri Devi did – die I mean – on a visit here in '82, on literally-and-I-am-not-making-this-up the very same night that Skrewdriver held their comeback gig at the 100 Club. Death and rebirth, see? In fact that was probably the concert where Ian Stuart finally came out as a nazi; he gave a *sieg heil* salute and sang "Tomorrow Belongs to Me," which of course is actually a pastiche nazi song from *Cabaret*, written by two Jews . . . You see, the stuff's all *there*, I'm just tracing connections.'

'You're writing conspiracy theory,' Tom said.

'Well, speculation. Or alternative history. I mean, technically speaking it's fiction, so you have a lot of leeway. You just ask, what *might* have happened? Like suppose Savitri Devi was spreading some much darker, secret tradition that went back to the Third Reich – she was totally plugged in to the Odessa network through Otto Skorzeny, so it's entirely plausible. And maybe through her connections over here that stuff gets passed on to Anton Long, who works it into the Seven-Fold Way. Then maybe Long gets obsessed with Nicky Crane. After all, Myatt idolizes skinheads – calls them heralds of the new aeon – and Long says the aim of Satanism is to produce a new species, a master race to inspire fear and admiration in the supine majority. Doesn't that sound like Nicky to you?'

Philip said, 'If you're using Myatt, sweetheart, I'd consider changing his name. Besides, isn't this all rather juicy? I thought your interests were a bit less . . . you know, Channel Five.'

'A bit of meat won't hurt. Besides, my whole point is that all of this stuff actually existed together. I haven't made up the Order of Nine Angles any more than I have the BNP.'

'Do you have a producer or something?' said Tom.

'It's all early stages so far.'

'And are you working as well – I mean, a job?'

Philip shook his head and mouthed, Parents.

'*Ah*,' said Tom. 'One of those.'

'An honourable tradition.' Philip topped up his wine. In the gesture I saw the four of us, suddenly, as an illustration: the modern gay dinner party, as conducted on a certain budget. Two couples: an anthropological commentary would elaborate on the nature of open relationships, the ostensible ease with which the participants accommodated a complex network of prior and ongoing interactions. Or had Tom turned Philip monogamous? It had happened before, with these young boys. That brought to me with a jolt that I had never thought about the obvious likelihood of sexual history between Philip and Adam – had never thought to ask either of them. The voiceover in my mind now murmured that Philip was the only one to have slept with everyone else at the table; Tom the only one tied by just one thread.

'I joined Stormfront too,' I said cheerfully, and Philip groaned.

'It does sound unhealthy,' Tom said. 'Like it's getting inside your head.'

'I'm not going to become a nazi just by reading about them.'

'Are you sure? I mean, sorry, but you sound obsessed. Not to be rude or anything, but these people are losers. Wankers and nut-jobs. Just because one of them blows people up or thinks he's a Satanist doesn't make them interesting.'

Tom was getting on my nerves. I thought of Long's advocacy of the selection of opfers – his term for human victims – through a series of tests. 'Opfers,' he wrote, 'are examples of human culling in action.' I shrugged and played with my wineglass. 'Maybe you're right,' I said. 'I don't *feel* like a nazi, but . . . I have been having weird dreams.'

'What kind of dreams?'

'Like . . . I'm walking through a town centre late at night. All the locked shopfronts with their merchandise lit up to deter thieves. And I know that I'm just going to start killing people.'

'Killing people?'

'Taking them out. Ten or twenty at a time, whoever comes along.'

Adam frowned: 'That is a bit fucked.'

'How do you kill them?' asked Tom.

Why had I told him that? I frowned, considering. 'I poison their couscous. Would you like some more?'

'Unfortunately I'm stuffed. In fact will you excuse me?'

When Tom was in the bathroom I told Philip, 'He seems nice.'

'Fuck off.'

'He does. For a twelve-year-old.'

'He *is* nice. He's very sweet and sexy and I like him quite a lot actually, so watch it.'

'What do you do in bed? Teach him to read?'

'Enough now, thanks. Besides, he rather had a point.'

'Funnily enough I did dream about Charlie Sargent the other night.'

'Is this another joke?'

'Scout's honour. He accused me of stealing his Smirnoff.'

'What did you say?'

'That I didn't drink vodka. And if I did it wouldn't be a cheap brand like his.'

The young man on screen wore a QUEER AS FUCK T-shirt. 'Jesus,' said Philip, 'those were the days.' We saw a skinhead follow him menacingly down an alley. Once inside it they kissed.

'See?' I said. 'You need to see things from more than one angle before you can truly understand them.'

'Very deep.'

'What are we watching?' asked Tom.

'The Channel Four programme where Nicky came out,' I told him. He was at one end of the sofa, fondling Philip's leg; I perched by Adam on the other arm.

'*Oh*,' said Philip. 'I thought you were showing us one of his porn flicks.'

'I would if I had any. I have been looking – I mean, I've asked in a few shops. I don't know how you track down old amateur porn.'

'Well, you've lost my interest now. Although: what the *fuck* is Patrick Harrington doing there?'

Harrington, in a jacket and tie, was telling the camera, 'I think that the skinhead image is a potent image of working-class aggression.'

Tom asked, 'Who?' and Philip told him: 'He ran the National Front in the '80s, with Nick Griffin and some other lunatics.'

'There was a big fuss,' I said, 'when he was studying at North London Poly. Harrington's fellow students picketed to keep him out. The Front took photos of the student leaders, and the judge – who by the way was one Justice Mars-Jones, father-of – ordered the lecturers to name them. They refused and it went on for ages. Anyway, the Front had collapsed by the time they filmed this.'

'The average skinhead on the street, I would say,' said Harrington, 'would react emotionally against any homosexual behaviour.'

'Father of who?' Tom muttered to Philip.

From Harrington the tape cut to Ian Stuart, who seemed to be sitting outside a pub. 'I don't think a gay person should be a skinhead at all,' he said. 'I just don't think it's got anything to do with skinheads, gays.'

'This,' I said, 'from the man who got a makeover from Steve Strange.'

'*No.*'

'Honest to God.'

'He had a nice voice, didn't he?' said Philip. 'All Northern and gentle.'

I said, 'He's coming up now.'

Nicky sat in what must have been his Soho bedsit, illuminated dimly behind him. A television, a cupboard in dark wood veneer, square silhouetted items on a shelf. He wore a green camouflage T-shirt and pants, hands folded in his lap, his posture that of some guru of hard-won knowledge. 'Adolf Hitler was my god, he was sort of like my *Führer* and my leader, and everything I done was like for Adolf Hitler.' We panned over what must have been his scrapbook. Cuttings from local newspapers – HITLER BIRTHDAY TRICK; SKINHEADS IN RACE RAMPAGE. Something, amazingly, from *Socialist Worker*. I wondered, again, where the book was now.

The camera lingered in close-up on Nicky's hands, his tattooed arms. I had watched this section frame-by-frame when I got the video, noting the visible tattoos. There were nearly thirty, swastikas and slogans like I HATE NIGGERS, and various insignia of the British Movement. One I couldn't interpret: the initials LOG, the O quartered into a sunwheel. When I pointed it out now, Philip said, 'League of St George, maybe?'

'I thought that too, but wouldn't it have an S?'

In close-up you could see moisture on Nicky's upper lip, but he spoke with astonishing calm: olive-green eyes steady at the camera, at you. Adam was stroking my arm. When Nicky said, 'It's actually then that I started to feel like a hypocrite,' furrows of concern appeared between his brows, his eyelids lowered, and he glanced down and to his left: the direction associated with remembered feelings and internal dialogue. Ian Stuart, by contrast, seemed jumpy as hell. In the time it took him to say, 'To me, what a skinhead . . . part of being a skinhead is to be a nationalist, to be patriotic,' his gaze swerved left and then forward three times in a row, and on the word 'nationalist' his eyes lurched so far to the right (the direction of lies and invention – assuming Ian was right-handed) that his head turned to follow them. Had he known, when this was filmed, what it was for? ('Mr Stuart, we're from *Out*, the Channel Four slot for lesbians and gay men, and we'd like to interview you.') Had he known of Nicky's involvement, of his announcement? This statement of Ian's was later used on a neo-nazi DVD, which did not cite its source.

Sonny, Adam's cat, wandered in from outside. He walked in front of me, brushing my feet with his tail, and I held out my hand to him. He moved past, nuzzling Philip's legs for a moment before jumping up and settling across his lap and Tom's. 'He likes *you*,' said Adam. 'He's normally shy with strangers.'

'Cats do,' replied Tom, stroking him. 'Like me. Hello,' he told Sonny. 'Hello, you.'

Nicky said, 'A lot of people who I used to hang around with like, they did sort of, like, hate, as I said, queers, and would go out queer-bashing. It was something, like, that I never did myself.'

'Oh, *listen* to him.' Philip was rolling a spliff. 'Bless. Sumfink I never did.'

A gay BNP member spoke next, his face in shadow. 'When I get a partner they want to be pissed over, scat over, beat up, whipped, whatever, strapped up and abused and that.' I squeezed Adam's hand on that.

Nicky: 'Once I just walked into the toilet to go for a piss and this black man followed me in, he actually went down on his hands and knees and like started licking my boots and I was actually very embarrassed' (here his face broke into, very precisely, an embarrassed smile) 'and just walked straight out of the toilet.'

Three black men now stood with folded arms. 'If a skinhead said to me . . .' one was saying, 'I would put it back on to him . . .' He enumerated oppressive structures on his fingers. Philip said, 'You have to stop this now. It's too painfully '90s.' He lit up and took a drag. 'Christ, we were fucking humourless.'

The youngest black man said, 'I can't shed my skin so I think these skinheads should take their fucking uniforms off.'

'You and me both, sweetheart,' Philip yawned, passing Tom the spliff.

'See?' I told Adam, stopping the tape. 'When you go out in your gear you're the oppressor. When you go to your *club*.'

'Not these days. Not in London. Anyway, at least I smile at people.'

'I smile,' I said, lying on the floor, and Philip said:

'Ha!'

'What club?' asked Tom.

'Adam' (I inhaled and coughed) 'goes to a skinhead night. In Vauxhall.'

'That sounds fun,' said Philip. 'What's it like?'

'I've not been.'

'Oh, you have to, surely.'

'I'm not sure I'm invited.'

'Of course you are,' said Adam. 'But you'll be disappointed again.'

'Again?' Tom asked. (God, I thought hazily, you *are* on the ball.)

'So what goes on at this club?' Philip said.

'Not in front of the child,' I told him.

'James . . .'

'Is it like a sex club?' said Tom.

'I wouldn't say that.' Adam smiled at him in a way I didn't much like. 'More a club with sex.'

'So *that's* what the nazi obsession's about,' Tom murmured to Sonny. 'James is jealous of his boyfriend, fucking all those skinheads.'

'Nah, I'm way too busy fucking yours.' This sounded louder and less casual than I had intended.

'That's not funny, James,' Philip said, and told Tom, 'Ignore him, babe.'

Adam stroked my head. 'James is tired. He hasn't slept much recently.'

'Imagine,' said Tom, 'how he'd cope if he had a job.'

There was a general silence at that. Eventually I asked, 'Shall I put some music on?'

'Not,' said Philip, 'if it's fucking Skrewdriver.'

'I was thinking Tom Robinson. I found him on iTunes.'

'Darling, I remember him from the first time round. He was shit.'

'He was *lovely*. I want to marry him.'

'He *was* lovely. And very important. But the music was shit.'

I reached for the joint and smoked, regarding him. 'It's weird thinking you were around for this stuff. You remember the Winter of Discontent.'

'I was *twelve*. Not exactly manning the barricades.'

'It's just, you get into this mode, reading about it, where it's all like history. You know? And then you think Oh, hold on, I was fourteen when Nicky died. Tom Robinson's on the radio. Pat Harrington has his little website. All the nazis are still around. Nick Griffin's still going, John Tyndall.'

'It wasn't that long ago.'

'Yeah, I know. Did you see they got arrested? Griffin and Tyndall?'

'Fat lot of good it'll do.'

'What time is it?' Tom asked.

'Oh yes,' I said: 'where do you live again? Catford?'

'Greenwich.'

'Only my geography isn't very good outside London.'

'It's Zone Two. Like here.'

'James knows where it is,' said Philip, standing up. He massaged Tom's shoulders. 'Anyway, *this* one's coming to mine.'

'That's good,' I said. 'I'm not sure how late trains run to Kent.'

As he put his coat on Philip said, 'You know what you've done? Speaking of history: it's exactly what you've lost sight of. Nicky wasn't an *Übermensch* conjured up in a black mass on some moor. Skinheads were produced by socioeconomic circumstance, like every bloody thing else. The Blitz. The redevelopment of the East End, which dismantled old social networks. Post-war immigration. Teddy boys, mods and rockers, rude boys, hippies, punks. Unemployment. The collapse of the social contract.'

'I know that. It's why I was reading about the strikes. But it's not enough. It explains why people like Nicky existed but not what it was like to be Nicky.'

'Then focus on that. Not the bloody occult. Nicky's out with his mates and they start queer-bashing. What goes through his head? He's in a club and sees a black and a white man snogging. What does he think? No, fuck "think": what does he feel? Does he feel sick, does it turn him on? Both? What's it like to be Nicky *in his body* – fucking and fighting? But enough with the magick, because if one thing's obvious from that programme, Nicky was a very pedestrian kind of nazi.'

'What do you mean,' I said, '"was"?'

Philip stared at me.

'The Register Office can't find his death certificate.'

'Oh for God's *sake*.'

'Funny, though, isn't it? Look, all I'm saying is you can't

175

separate ideas from reality that neatly. Ideas *create* reality. It's all connected.'

'Everything's fucking connected. We know that by now, surely? Chaos theory: you have a wank and there's an earthquake off Sumatra. Doesn't tell us anything, apart from maybe you should wank less. I think I'm drunk. Come on, darling,' he said to Tom. 'Let's go.'

Adam said: 'We can wash up in the morning. Let's just get it in the sink.'

'You don't think I'm turning into a nazi, do you?'

'No. But it's all you talk about these days. It does sometimes look like displacement activity. What is it you don't want to think about?'

I dreamed, not of Charlie Sargent or an urge to kill, but of Nick Griffin. I was staying with his family; I'd written an article about them that would soon be published. Now we sat round the dining table while Griffin read it. I'd been friendly with him, to get his confidence, and I knew he would feel betrayed. I wanted to say, 'I'm sorry,' but the article was honest. I stirred, pulled away from Adam muttering, 'You're too hot'; drifted off again with my back to him, staring at the fractured orange round the window frame. The smell of musk. A pearl-white manikin between a woman's thighs. Trees flashing past beside a road. *By our will, destroyed*, someone murmured – a ringing bell. I woke with an erection and a fierce thirst, peed in the dark in case the bathroom fan woke Adam. All I need now, I thought, is a black man on his knees.

My laptop glimmered with fresh proposals: to consolidate my debt, show me college boys missing their girlfriends, ask me, *Did Six Million Really Die?* One message, sent late from a Hotmail address, read simply *Stay away*. Was it from one of the message boards? I typed a reply – *Stay away from what?* – but thought better and deleted it. Instead I logged on to the website and, with Long in mind, tried new search terms, and got a few results. *Friends of the Dark Lord especially welcome*, read one. *10 mins from M25 junction 8.*

I had bookmarked arealnazi's profile. *Skinhead thug*, I read again. *Hurt you & rape you & leave you bleeding. I am not play acting.*

Nicky in his body.

I clicked on Send Message. I wrote: *Hi.*

RAC News

SKREWDRIVER LEAD THE WHITE BACKLASH!

NEARLY FIVE HUNDRED people turned up to see Skrewdriver and two other bands play a concert for Rock Against Communism last month.

The concert was held at Stratford in East London and the number of people who turned up exceeded all expectations.

The first band to play were a group called **Peter And The Wolves**. They played a fast and furious set which went down well with the crowd.

The Ovalteenies were next on and they really got the crowd going. They have a hard-core following of White racists who even hired a coach to get them to the concert. Mick, the lead singer, finished the band's set by stripping off his Ovalteenies t-shirt to show off the 'White Power' t-shirt he was wearing under it.

By the time **Skrewdriver** came on the crowd were really warmed up. They opened their set with the last single, *Back With A Bang*, and continued with a string of old favourites including *Anti-Social* and *Boots And Braces* from the *United Skins* LP.

But it was the newer, more political numbers which seemed to go down best with the crowd. *Shove The Dove, Tomorrow Belongs To Me, Voice Of Britain, Smash The IRA* and the next single, *White Power,* all guaranteed that any Black-lovers in the audience had a heart attack!

All in all it was a very successful and enjoyable evening and hopefully it will be only the first of many RAC gigs to take place in the future.

BE THERE!

The next Rock Against Communism concert will be held very soon. Anybody who wants to see Skrewdriver and other patriotic bands live should write to *Bulldog* and we will let you know where the next gig is to take place. Write to *Bulldog*, 50 Pawsons Road, Croydon, Surrey CRO 2QF.

SOUNDS LIKE WAR!

THE Black-loving scum in the music business are trying to destroy Skrewdriver. They have been trying to smash the band ever since they found out that Skrewdriver support the National Front.

Perhaps the group's biggest enemy is Gary Bushell, the Features Editor of *Sounds*. Bushell declared war on Ian Stuart and the other members of the band as soon as they refused to toe the line. Ever since then he has done everything he can to ruin the band's chance of succeeding.

He put a news black-out on anything to do with Skrewdriver appearing in *Sounds*.

He banned Skrewdriver from advertising their future gigs in *Sounds*. He blackmailed shops, such as Small Wonder records, by threatening to black their adverts in his paper if they didn't stop selling the group's records. Finally, he tried to get Skrewdriver banned from playing live dates by making threatening phone calls to the owners of all venues where the band have played.

In short, Bushell has declared all-out war on Skrewdriver. But if Bushell wants war he can have it. The White Backlash in the music industry is just beginning!

THE WHITE BACKLASH!

THERE ARE only two things that White racist bands can do when they are faced with attempts by the music business to smash them. They can either give up or fight back.

It's about time Skrewdriver and all other patriotic bands started to fight back!

OUR OWN RECORD LABEL

A NEW independent record label is being set up especially to bring out records by patriotic White bands. It will be called White Noise Records and the first single on the label will be White Power by Skrewdriver.

OUR OWN LIVE DATES

THE Rock Against Communism concert held last month will only be the first of many to be held in future. If nobody in the music business will handle concerts by racist bands then Rock Against Communism will just have to organise the concerts itself!

OUR OWN MUSIC PRESS

ISSUE FOUR of *Rocking The Reds* is now out. It includes a full-length interview with Ian Stuart of Skrewdriver, as well as news, reviews and an article on Rush. It is available from RAC, 50 Pawsons Road, Croydon, Surrey CRO 2QF. Price 20p plus 12½p postage.

OUR OWN FREEDOM

BY producing their own records and organising their own gigs, patriotic bands will at last be free to say what they like. They will no longer be at the mercy of the reds and rich bosses in the music industry.

Skrewdriver
OUT NOW! 12" SINGLE
GET YOUR COPY | MAIL ORDER HOTLINE
FROM ANY GOOD | & ENQUIRIES
RECORD SHOP | 01-684 0271

BACK WITH A BANG

DYNAMITE!

Bulldog 33, circa April 1983

IN FINNEGAN'S WAKE . . .
**SKREWDRIVER: White Power
(White Noise) When the NF
unveiled their election manifesto
on TV the camera cut from the
press conference to talking head
Fred Emery who was giving a
typically complacent English
smirk. It's not so easy to laugh
when you're confronted with the
stark reality of the placid,
'reasonable' front. Preaching
damnable lies and sheer hatred,
'White Power' is the ugliest and
most evil deployment of youth
music I've ever come across.
Frightening to think how many are
going to buy this record,
frightening too to think how many
are going to ignore it and the
implications it carries.**

New Musical Express, 30 July 1983

Hill Farm

It is Saturday, 29 September 1984, and the coach, heavy with sour air, makes a left turn out of the valley road that a few skins who have been here before recognize as the last. They cheer as it begins to climb, and empty beer cans roll haphazardly down the aisle.

Tony stretches. His calves feel thick inside his boots, as if his blood has pooled in them. 'Fucking made it,' says Glenn happily. Tony turns to face him. 'Yeah,' he says, and looks away again at the ploughed earth that runs beside the road in broad tracks, like an ancient motorway.

Before the crest of the hill they pull in, and drive round the farm buildings to park on the grass behind. Another coach is here already, and there are cars and minibuses and a burger van, which even at 11 A.M. has a queue. The skins stand, grabbing bags, and someone farts loudly and laughs. Ahead, Dave stuffs away the *Searchlight* he was reading. A man in glasses meets them off the steps. 'Have your tickets ready as you come down, please lads,' he calls through the door. 'If anyone doesn't have a ticket I can sell them one now for a fiver. If anyone doesn't have a fiver they can sod off back to London.'

*

Glenn says: 'How many people do you think are here?'

'Fuck knows.' There must be at least 500, mainly skins but others too, older and in average clothes, who stand in clusters of their own sipping from polystyrene cups: Front activists. A few women, also, and skin girls, and girlfriends who aren't skin yet.

Glenn tails Tony round the complex. There are more buildings than he expected, quaint old ones and modern additions. Sellotaped on the back door of the main house is a notice, PRIVATE, and underneath: TOILETS AVAILABLE IN CAR PARK. In a corner of the abutting courtyard large wooden doors open on a barn, where a stage has been set up. Men in jeans are hanging flags: Union Jacks, long banners with the NF logo. Glenn winks at him.

Outside, a tug-of-war is taking place. 'That's Ian Stuart,' says Glenn, and runs to join the onlookers. And it is him, at the head of one team: boot heels dug into mud, angled like an inverse Soviet statue, comfortably tossing out asides. Even if you didn't know who he was you'd sense the presence he carries so easily, holding the crowd's attention. At the rear of Ian's team, Steve strains at the rope with almost the same psychotic energy he had as a teenager, any shortfall made up for by his increased mass. Stripped down for the effort, he displays his black Skrewdriver Security T-shirt taut around his belly. Nicky Crane's, on the other hand, is presumably still zipped under his bomber jacket. 'Get a move on you cunts,' Nicky yells, grinning from the sideline, and the other team's leader, who Tony doesn't recognize, calls over his shoulder: 'Come on, we've nearly got them.' With a shaky lurch they gain an inch or two. 'I'm not fucking having that,' says Ian. 'All right lads, one last push. One, two—' Glenn cups his hands to his mouth and shouts, 'Go on Ian!' But it doesn't decide the match, and Tony, who has spotted Dave at the bookstall, leaves Glenn watching.

The stall is three tables in a row. Posters hang from their edges and the wall behind. There are piles of *NF News*, *Nationalism Today*, *Holocaust News*, something called *Rising*. At least fifty copies of one booklet, *Yesterday & Tomorrow: Roots of the National-Revolution*, are displayed in neat stacks. Tony picks up a magazine called *The Scorpion*, whose cover shows a good-looking couple in camouflage. But inside are long essays in close type: 'Who's Afraid of Ayn Rand?,' 'The One-Dimensional Philosophers.'

'There's a song I wrote in there,' says a young man behind the counter.

'Oh yeah?' Tony flicks through it again, but instead of lyrics he finds 'Interview with Doctor Ishakamusabarashango' above a picture of a black man in a bow-tie and specs. He puts it down. 'That one any better?' he asks Dave, who looks up from his book, *The Turner Diaries*, and laughs.

'Yeah it looks good,' he says. 'It's a novel about race war.'

'Go on,' says the young man, 'it's only a quid.'

Tony says: 'There any action in it?'

'The hero flies a plane into the Pentagon.'

'Spoiled it now haven't you.'

The salesman laughs. 'Actually, it's well worth reading. The author is an exceptional mind. It's very honest about what the revolution will be like – not for the squeamish. But you don't look squeamish types. You ex-BM?'

He is mid-twenties, somewhere between Dave's age and Tony's, in an open-necked shirt and student jacket. With some facial hair he could be a communist. Dave says, 'I don't like to say "ex."'

'Fair enough. But you're not paying dues any more. You thinking of joining the Front?'

Tony says, 'We're just here for the music.'

'You should think about it. We need more people like you.'

'What, skinheads?'

'We had an article a while back: "Skinheads, the New Warriors."' He looks the two of them over, as if deciding whether the phrase applies. 'The Front's not what it used to be,' he adds, 'a bunch of reactionary old Tories. It's changing. We've got rid of Webster and a young leadership, a radical leadership, has taken over. We're building a real revolutionary organization. We're going to need soldiers.' He puts out his hand. 'I'm Nick, by the way.'

'Dave.'

'Tony. Thought I recognized you. This is your place isn't it?'

'My dad's.'

'It's fucking huge.'

'It's average for a farm around here. I'm serious about joining. We need a different kind of member now. We're not interested in pissing about. Take a copy of the paper. You can pay me later. Have you got any questions I can answer?'

'Yeah,' says Tony. 'Where the fuck are we?'

Nick laughs again. 'Come on,' he says, 'I'll show you,' and steps out from behind the stall. 'Bring the book,' he tells Dave, who is putting it down. 'We can sort that out later.'

He leads them up the hill, away from the farm buildings, where sound tests have now started. Tony is starting to feel hungry. He lags a few feet behind; Nick is striding forward and Dave keeping up, asking some question. Dave has filled out a bit in the last year or so, still slim but no longer skinny. It's a few days since he last shaved his head; the stubble reaches down his neck in a pale orange V. The gap between twenty-eight and twenty-two seems somehow greater than between twenty-three and seventeen.

They stop at the top of the hill, Nick stamping his feet as if to mark the spot. 'Right,' he says, like a teacher on a school outing. 'You're in Suffolk, which is part of East Anglia, right, the big bulge on the right-hand side of the map? Named after the Angles, Anglo-Saxons who settled here from Germany around the fifth century. If you head that way' – he points across the road – 'for about ten miles you hit the North Sea. Nearest small town is Huntingfield, over to the north-east, nearest big town is Ipswich, which you probably drove through, to the south. This is Hill Farm, and down there is, you'll never guess, Valley Farm. Down the hill that way is Ubbeston Wood, which is ancient forest, symbol of what the Front stands for. Other direction, a bit down the coast, is Sizewell nuclear power station. Symbol of what the Front is against.'

Dave looks across the field. 'What do you grow here?'

'Me? Nothing. My dad's an accountant. But anyway, this land's between crops. See how it's ploughed up? They just harvested the sugar beet and in a while they'll probably plant wheat. This is clay land, good arable country.'

The expectant soil rolls away from them to the west, the east.

Nick says: 'Breathe in. Go on. Look around you. This is what it's about. This is what we're fighting for.'

He tells them: 'If you think things are bad now, they're going to get a lot worse. Immigration's not going to slow down, capitalism's not going to slow down. Ten years from now we'll have massive unemployment, a much more repressive state, terror in the inner cities – and the oil we're pumping from the North Sea over there is going to start to run out. The white people of this country will be very poor, and nearly outnumbered. Now that's the moment, when things are in crisis, when large numbers of whites might rise up and fight back. But they'll only do that if there are people to lead them.

'So whose job will it be? It could never have been the old National Front. They didn't have an ideology, they just knocked together whatever mishmash of policies made their supporters happy. The BNP's no better, just smaller. Tyndall doesn't have a revolutionary bone in his body. But we do – the new NF leadership. We're a new generation. We're revolutionaries. For the first time in its history the Front really knows where it's going.'

Tony says, 'What's the difference?'

'Ideology. Hard work. Listen, I joined the Front ten years ago and in that time we had I don't know how many marches and rallies. But as for actually thinking about and discussing what we stood for, I can remember three one-day sessions. Three, in ten years. Now we take ideology seriously. We've got day-long seminars every month when we actually sit down and read thinkers like Julius Evola and Franco Freda. We seriously debate alternative systems: distributism, feudalism, Strasserism, Nasserism. We're taking all these ideas and we're bringing them together into something new, into a fully developed ideology. Look,' he says to Dave, 'what do you stand for?'

Dave pauses before saying: 'Britain.'

'And what does Britain need?'

'To get rid of the niggers and Jews. And the reds and the Pakis.'

'Because?'

'Because the blacks are taking things white people need – British people. They're taking jobs when there's millions of whites unemployed. Taking council houses white people can't get. Making Britain foreign.'

'Exactly. That's exactly right. Well, for the old Front, that turned into "I fucking hate blacks." But *it's not the blacks' fault*. It's capitalism's fault, it's the international moneymen and big corporations that bring them here to undercut British workers, because they'll work for half the wage a white man will.

'And I'll tell you a secret: the blacks don't want to be here either! You look at surveys and the majority of blacks, when given a choice, say well hang on a minute, actually I *would* rather go home. And why wouldn't they? They'd have to be mad not to. It's not their country, it's not their culture, it's a lot more bloody sunny in Africa, and people here don't like them.

'Now in America a group of blacks have got together and said enough's enough, we don't want to be mixed against our will into white culture any more, we want to be separate. And what we say to them, the Front, is: good on you. You're black nationalists, we're white nationalists, we both want the same thing, which is to preserve our own people, our race, against the international capitalists out to destroy both of us. So let's see how we can help each other. How we can learn from each other, and share our ideas and our experiences.

'The old Front would never have done that. The old Front would have said, "Oh, this bunch of niggers, we'll have nothing to do with them." And that's the difference. Because we're national revolutionaries, because we have a programme of ideological development, we don't do what's easy, we do what's right – even if it's difficult, even if it's the exact opposite of what Tyndall's Tory Front would have done. So that means forging links with the Nation of Islam, it means supporting the miners who want to stop the closure of British pits, even if we don't agree with their tactics or their leaders, it means going back to the land, to the earth, here, this stuff, and learning to use it again, to live from it, and defending it against capitalism and industrialization and pollution, and getting involved with people like the Greens and anarchists and animal-rights activists, helping them out, exposing them to our ideas and ideology. Because all these different things are part of getting back what we've lost as a race – a tradition and a way of life; and all their enemies, Thatcher and the bankers and the nuclear industry and the people behind vivisection and kosher slaughter, they're our enemies too.'

Nick stops and smiles, as if embarrassed by his passion but still proud of it. In the silence they hear music starting down the hill. It is lunchtime proper now. Tony says, 'You want to unite with the blacks?'

'Not unite with them. Stand alongside them for our right to stay separate. It's easy to say send them home, but it's stupid to ignore the fact that's what they're asking for. That's reactionary. Now most of the guys down there, the skinheads' – he points towards the farm buildings – 'are basically reactionaries. They'll beat up the odd Paki and sniff a bit of glue, but discipline and ideological development is too much for them. We need something better. We're building a revolutionary organization and that means starting with a revolutionary cadre body. A highly dedicated political middle management. People who will come to the sessions, and read and learn and train, and stick at it, and not give up, not accept second best.

'I wish you could read – my colleague Derek's written, we're about to publish, a really inspirational booklet. It's about the political soldier – it's a phrase from Evola, but Derek really explains it, puts into words what we're about. He goes back through history and looks at examples like the Spartans and the Crusaders. There was this guy in Romania, in the twenties, Corneliu Codreanu. His country was being destroyed by immigration, filling up with Jews, and he started a revolutionary movement, the Iron Guard. They had an oath: to defend their country, defend their race and their soil. They said, we'll make a permanent sacrifice. No pissing around: we'll be poor, put everything into the movement. And we'll never compromise. The oath ended: "Long live Death!" That's how Derek ends the booklet, "Long live Death." Well, that's what we're about. Devoting ourselves, devoting our lives, to the revolution.

'Look what happened in Lebanon. The US went in to help the Zionists. America is one of two world superpowers, a massive military machine armed to its teeth, and the revolutionaries were penniless. But they still kicked them out.

Because the Yanks were fighting for their wage packets and pensions, and the revolutionaries were fighting for an ideal. They said OK, we don't have planes, so we'll drive truck bombs straight into your camps. And yes, we'll die, but we don't care, because we're fighting for something more important. That's what the Iron Guard meant when they said, "Long live Death." Not desire to die, but contempt for death. That's what makes a political soldier. That's why they won. And that's why we'll win.'

'Bloody hell,' Tony says.

He has been watching a figure climb the hill towards them. He knew who it was long before he could see him properly. Now, as he approaches, Glenn's smile wavers before firming, like a radio tuning in.

'All right Glenn?' says Dave.

'I wondered where you was,' Glenn says, broadening the 'you' from Tony to include Dave with a sudden zigzag glance. Nick smiles up, a look that makes clear he has already decided not to include Glenn in his recruitment pitch.

'It's started,' Glenn tells them. 'You're missing it.'

When Tony arrives the courtyard is filling up. He doesn't recognize the band on stage, but a banner behind them says OFFENSIVE WEAPON. The singer sounds Irish. He cannot yet be twenty, and is tall, with a round face and a toothy, childlike grin that appears from nowhere as the song ends. He says, 'This next one's for our boy Joe,' and on the intro his smile drops quickly and he bounces on his toes to the beat, like a boxer limbering up. When he starts to sing he breaks into a ferocious, spittly rage. He yells into his microphone and bounds about the stage, kicking at the air and his band-mates, who kick him right back. The bass player, a short lad in bleached jeans and braces, mauls his guitar, brown and white with black strings. When the singer gets near him they spit at each other. With his accent, drunkenness and limited ability, and the way the mike sways past his mouth as he bounces and kicks, the lyrics are hard to make out, but when the chorus comes some of the crowd join in on the key word, and swap *sieg heil* salutes with the band. '*Bulldog!*' they all shout, and the singer adds 'something something-ay.' *Bulldog!* – it's here to stay. *Bulldog!* – something stand, something fight. *Bulldog!* – something Britain white.

Glenn makes brief forays to the jumping cluster at the front and pulls back again. There aren't enough people yet for Tony to want to join; it's just some younger lads so far, the rest of the audience more or less still around them, at most nodding a bit and saluting for the chorus. Ian Stuart is here, drinking with his musicians, giving the younger band public support. Nicky Crane stands with them, pulling at his can and laughing at something, and Steve, too. It would be nothing, really, for Tony to go up and join them. They might even welcome it. He could walk straight over across the space, say, 'All right,' nod. Steve catches Tony looking and says something visibly loud over the band, and the others laugh. Nicky flicks Tony a glance, and Tony turns away. 'Going to get more beer,' he mouths to Glenn and Dave. The song finishes behind him in a crash of yells.

Dave joins him in the queue. 'Set's over. Nothing more for a while.'

'What did you think of them?'

'They were all right.'

'Yeah. Seen Glenn?'

'He's with some of the lads I think.'

'Thank Christ for that. He's doing my head in.'

They buy beers and sit on the grass at the churned earth's edge, watching the crowd. Under the flat autumn sky, in this interstitial moment, the other skins look unexpectedly lost, like animals waking in a foreign zoo; they pad the field aimlessly, with involuntary darting looks at nothing in particular, and an air of having forgotten something, of which only a troubling nag still lingers. There are pockets of laughter and a couple of tetchy brawls, but even these look like manufactured distractions against the vast oppressive silence of the countryside, which swallows the sounds and leaves only their pale echo. Tony and Dave drink. After a while Dave says, 'It's all right out here, isn't it?' and Tony says, 'I couldn't live here though,' and then they drink some more.

'Look at Steve,' nods Tony. 'Fucking giving it.' He is walking with the Skrewdriver boys, looking ostentatiously around as if any second he will need to wrestle a mad fan to the ground, take a bullet for Ian.

Dave smiles. 'He's enjoying himself isn't he?'

'Oh he loves it.'

'How long's he been doing it now?'

'I don't know. A few months. Since Nicky come out of prison.' Ian and Nicky are pretending to fight: there are inflated postures, yells, and then some mutual feint, too minor to see from here, into laughter and a short, aggressive hug.

'How well do you know him?'

'What Nicky? To say hello. I joined up before he did, so. You must have met him when you joined, he was Leader Guard then.'

'Yeah. He was all right. Quite friendly really.'

'Not what you expected?'

'Well, after all I'd heard. Is he as mad as they say?'

'He's a good fighter. He stopped some nigger knifing me once. Back when we had that do at the Odeon, you remember. One minute the cunt was all white eyes in my face and it's me thinking I'm for it and the next Nicky sweeps him aside like he's a fucking, I don't know, packet of crisps.'

'Don't think I noticed him that night myself,' Dave says.

'That last Sham gig at the Rainbow, I think that was first time I saw Nicky really go for it. I've got this picture in my head now of him like charging through the crowd towards the stage, picking up anyone in his way and just chucking them over his shoulder, like the Incredible Hulk. It can't really have been like that but it's how I remember it. Just like, *aaaar*.' Tony mimes the throwing action: left, right. 'Cra-a-ne-e-y!'

Dave smiles. 'I heard about that. I mean the night. I wish I'd been there.'

'It was a good night.' He nods. 'I went outside after, when it was over. Everyone had fucked off and I didn't know where they were, I was trying to find them. I went out the back and I seen Jimmy Pursey.'

'Really?'

'Sat on some steps with a beer. Wasn't no one else around, just him sitting there. He looked at me but he didn't say anything. Swear to God he was crying. I thought, We fucking shut you down mate.'

'You didn't say nothing?'

'No. I felt a bit sorry for him. He was all right, Jimmy. I hung around backstage with him a few times in the old days, back in '78 or so. With the old Mile End boys, Steve and that lot. We used to drink all his beers and argue with him about politics. Steve and them lot would be all, Adolf Hitler, Adolf Hitler, and however much he went on Jimmy would never just say shut it, he'd always argue, like he could really convince us or something.'

'Do you think he recognized you? Outside the Rainbow?'

'I don't know. Probably. Sham were good though once.' Tony drains his can and opens a third, mumbling, 'Jimmy Pursey is innocent' in vague tune.

Dave grins: 'I've still got that T-shirt if you want it back.'

'Nah fuck it, I wouldn't wear it now.'

'I hung on to it for you.'

'Used it for a wank rag probably.'

'Fuck off.' Dave throws his empty can at him, not hard. From the direction of the courtyard comes the noise of another band starting.

'That's not them yet is it?' says Tony.

'No, there's three more supports first.'

'Any good?'

'We'll hear it if they are.'

'Yeah.'

Dave says, 'I thought you might start doing that.'

'What?'

'You know. Skrewdriver Security.'

'No. And no one's asked me have they.'

Tony looks at the ridged ground, from which insects slowly distinguish themselves. Dave leans back with his hands flat beside him, facing the sky. He says: 'What did you make of that stuff earlier?'

'What stuff?'

'About the Front. How it's going to be different now. All that.'

'I don't know. It sounded a bit daft to me. I mean, I'm here because I'm a fucking racist, I don't want to start holding hands with Arabs do I. What's the point of that? And all that reading and ideology sounded like a lot of shit.'

'Yeah I suppose.'

Tony shrugs. 'Student isn't he.'

'Don't you get frustrated sometimes though?'

'What do you mean?'

'Well I've been doing this for five years now, it must be six or seven for you, and we're not getting anywhere are we? I mean we'll have a march and we'll have a fight and that but we're not changing anything.'

'Yeah I'll give you that much.'

'Maybe we do need to think more. About how we're going

about it. I liked what he was saying about getting serious, you know, devoting your life to it.'

'I'm not driving fucking truck bombs for nobody.'

'But he's got a point. Don't he? If we really want to change how things are. We need to do something. I don't want my kids growing up in a country like this one's turning into.'

'Is that what's brought all this on? You get some bird pregnant?'

'No leave it out. I'm serious. I'm going to have some one day aren't I. And if I want them to have a proper home I'm going to have to fight for it. Because no one else is going to do it for me.'

'Want their dad alive,' says Tony, 'won't they.'

Dave says, 'Maybe it's different for you.'

'What do you mean?'

'I don't know Tony. I mean, I can't see you with kids.'

'Why not?'

'I just can't imagine it really. No offence or nothing. I mean you'd be a good dad if you wanted to.'

'Yeah well.'

'No you would.' Dave drains his beer. 'But I do. You know what I mean? I do want kids. So.'

He stands, unreally tall against the dimming sky.

'I'll see you later yeah? I'm going to have a piss.'

You see: blankness. Only grey with a memory of blue, and darker grey scrolling in from the left. The thinnest fringe of a breeze just starting up the hill and brushing your face. The impossibly muted sound of music, doll's-house bangs and shouts. And nothing and noise and nothing.

And you're twenty-fucking-eight.

'Oi! What are you doing down there?'

'Oh bang on fucking cue.'

'Fuck off.' Glenn mugs a grimace, then grins and sits. 'Brung you a beer.'

'Cheers.'

'What have you been doing anyway?'

'Nothing. Drinking.'

'You missed the Die Hards. And Public Enemy.'

'Who's on now?'

'Brutal Attack.'

'They're not bad.'

'I know. I'm going back in a minute. You coming?'

'In a bit.'

'How pissed are you?'

'A bit.'

Glenn drinks. 'One of the drummers was all right.'

'Don't start.'

'He was.'

'Yeah.'

'He had his shirt off and he was fucking wet with sweat.'

'Leave it out. I'm serious.'

'No one can hear us.'

'These are my mates all right?'

'They're my mates too. Imagine what would happen.'

'Shut your cakehole.'

'They're looking at us now. Shane and Martin. All right lads? They think we're talking about Skrewdriver. Imagine if they knew. How I drive my fucking skrew. If I leaned over and snogged you.'

'You're not funny.' But at his crotch, amazingly, a rodent tug.

'I tell you what's not funny is how fucking randy I am right now. Just lean forward twenty-four inches and kiss you. They'd fucking crucify us. I want you so badly now. I want to strip you naked and come all over you.'

'Piss off right now,' says Tony, 'or I'll kick your head in. And I will not fucking care. I'm not joking neither.'

Glenn whispers, in his Barbara Windsor voice, 'I want to get me smackers round your knackers.' Then he laughs and stands. 'Don't be too long eh? You'll miss the headliners.'

Now, heading back to the courtyard, where music has again started, the uneven ground keeps tilting towards him, and the sky seems to dip close when he's not looking, with sudden lunges. The grass is pockmarked with trash, discarded cans and wrappers, in a pattern that scrolls jerkily down as he walks. The unevenness of the ground travels up his legs, their suspension system dulled by drink, and he feels it bump his solar plexus, a reminder that he needs to piss. He veers away from the looming courtyard and round the side of the building, remembering as he parts his fly the pasted imprecations to use the Portaloos and spattering the whitewash with satisfaction.

As he stands, focused on the middle distance, he hears voices and laughter approach and there are new presences on either side, talking across him as they ready themselves at his improvised, now shared, urinal. There is movement he will not look at and 'Fucking wankered' pronounced in tones of surprised, nearly joyful introspection. Tony stares determinedly ahead, blocking the stereo siren call, so aware of the corners of his eyes they almost itch. His flanking companions sound young; the one on his right belches, spurring a shared shout of laughter, and Tony, charting at the most functioning level of his thought the route between prurience and blank hostility, allows himself an indulgent smile at this, zipping up as he does and turning to go with such efficiency of purpose that he almost doesn't see the trio of skins sprawled in his path a few feet ahead. He stops just in time, over the aerial view of one of them holding white plastic to his mouth like a horse's nosebag and staring back at him with a kind of glassy, dazed benevolence.

The boy is perhaps fifteen, with a snub nose, freckles and

close-cropped hair. Thrown from his purpose by having to stop so suddenly, Tony keeps looking at him, and the boy gazes back with peaceable curiosity, as if trying to answer in his mind some tiny but elusive question. Then, slowly, he extends his arm, lifting the bag from his face and silently offering it, a diver sharing his supply of oxygen. Tony says, 'You're all right,' but the boy doesn't react, doesn't retract the bag. Tony takes in for the first time the boy's companions, of a similar age and in the same state, all now looking at him with this well-meaning, strangely underinvested interest.

Tony feels like a squirrel being tested with a proffered nut. He notices the recent silence, which was internal to him, only as it is ruptured: his companions from the whitewashed wall talk loudly as they pass, a noise that slashes the seal of the moment and lets the noise of the gig flood back in. The bag hangs from the boy's outstretched hand, weighted by the sludge at its bottom and rippling like a standard for something. Tony sits. He steadies himself, facing the boys. 'Go on then,' he says, reaching for the bag. He tells them: 'I was your age once.'

He holds the bag to him, feeling the creased, cold texture of its kiss, moisture from the boy's mouth, and breathes in hard. It's like diving, except the rush comes with the inhalation and not after, and there's the instantly familiar shock of the foreign chemical element so immediately invading and inhabiting you, staking its territory, swelling against the inside of your skull. Tony lets the bag drop and the world sways after it with a new lightness: the six eyes of his companions are bright marbles on a mobile. He hears his own slowed breath, as in a brass helmet, underwater: the boy was a diver after all. He takes another pull from the bag: the second dose is less violent, a confirmation almost, reassuring. When he stands he feels breached liquid tumble down his sides. He tosses the bag back. 'Yeah,' he says. 'Those were the days. Cheers lads,' and walks into the shaky projection of the farm.

In the courtyard a song has ended, to fading cheers. In the gap before the next one both the band on stage and the crowd facing them stand awkwardly still, as if he, Tony, has interrupted something. It is not yet getting dark, but it will be in a couple of hours at most; there is an atmosphere of climax and things finishing. The space to the right is bounded by a long low building with a sagging roof, on the near slope of which a vast Union Jack is spread. Tony's gaze follows it round, above the sheared heads of the crowd, to the taller structure from which NF banners hang, and which, before him, opens on to the stage. At its rear the familiar backdrop has been hung, a huge black cloth with SKREWDRIVER in white like blown-up, badly photocopied text. Ian Stuart stands stage front, in a short-sleeved black shirt not quite flattering to his almost pudgy figure, but redeemed by the sheer confidence with which he faces the crowd. He is flanked by his guitarists, both taller than him. The drummer is barricaded upstage behind his kit, and they are surrounded on the periphery by other skins whose roles are less clear.

Waiting for his moment, Ian passes the mike from hand to hand. He speaks to the drummer, and when he turns forward again there is a burst of feedback. 'It's nice to see . . .' he says, 'it's nice to see so many people here to celebrate GLC anti-racist year,' and grins briefly, and there are shouts of entertainment at the joke and disgust at its subject. He waits for them to quieten down, and goes on: 'Now I'm sure most of you have heard about a certain young student, Patrick Harrington, and the trouble he's been having from the reds, who are trying to get him kicked out of class because he's a nationalist. Patrick's had to go to court to defend his right to study, and even though he *won* the commie bastards are still threatening him. Well, a few of us have been down to back him up. We're restraining ourselves now but when he's finished his course we'll go down there and' (louder) *'annihilate that filth.'* Again he lets the shouts abate, then lifts the microphone. 'This is another song from our new album. It's about the threat to this country from immigration, and how we've got to do something about it before it's too late. It's called "Before the Night Falls."'

He turns and nods, and the drummer taps out a couple of bars of beat before he and the guitarists come in together on the introduction. The knot of boys up front, who had been stilled by the silence, immediately start to pogo again, jumping up and down and pushing themselves up from each others' shoulders, amplifying their momentum like trampolines. Tony should watch how he stares, but his caution is washed over by the glue and music, by Ian's growly, slightly American-sounding singing voice.

> *'They come here to this country from the jungles and from*
> *   trees*
> *The traitors in the parliament give them a better deal*
> *Spend the nation's money, to cater to their needs*
> *They all accept our charity, then bite the hand that feeds.'*

On the chorus – *'Before the night falls, heed the White call!'* – Ian takes the mike in his left hand and gives *sieg heil* salutes with his right that are returned by the crowd and by Tony, who now pushes forward a little into it, as if the arm is pulling him, as if the mirrored salutes attract like magnets. The core of jumping boys is swelling, pulling the crowd around into its turbulent vortex. Glenn and one of his mates, Martin, have broken free of the agglomerating mass, and bounce crazily through it in a unit, face to face with hands on each other's shoulders, cutting swathes through the audience as they go. From the front of the stage, off to the side, Nicky Crane watches.

'Our forefathers fought in two world wars, they thought to
  keep us free
But I'm not sure that in those wars, who was our enemy
The Zionists own the media, and they're known for telling
  lies
And I could see, that it could be, we fought on the wrong
  side.'

As Tony pushes deeper in he sees Dave and Nick by the wall, conferring through the noise near a pair of skins who stand *sieg-heil*ing in unison to the beat, in and out from the elbow, so that they look, he thinks, like synchronized swimmers, or formation disco queens. Nick grips Dave's shoulder and yells happily into his ear, and Tony decides suddenly that he is fed up with Nick's academic niceties, and has the vision, which he feels he can reach out and take, of that neat hair wet and hanging over his face.

'Oi!' Tony surges out of the crowd and puts his hand against the wall over Nick's shoulder, pinning him in place. Dave looks at him in surprise, Nick with a flicker of alarm that quickly hides itself. 'Hello, Tony,' Nick says.

'Don't you ever stop talking?' Tony yells over the music. 'It's fucking Skrewdriver up there. All these people have paid to come to your farm and hear them and you're nattering away like you're better than us or something. Don't you ever fucking shut up and dance?'

Nick looks at him with animal calculation. Tony can see him trying to gauge the seriousness of this unexpected attack – how in control of himself Tony is, the degree of physical threat – and then, in rapid succession, like pages quickly turned, the merits of the suggestion itself, what harm there could be, and (a politician) what benefits might accrue. Unwilling to let him have the dignity of a visible decision, Tony says, 'Go on get your fucking feet wet,' and grabbing

Nick's neck pushes him forward into the crowd, which is now almost entirely taken over by the spreading movement. Tony turns to Dave and says, 'You won't be twenty-two forever you cunt.' He rubs his knuckles hard against Dave's bristled scalp, then bounces backwards away, grinning, and turns towards the wild turbulence of the dancing skins. He pushes forward hard into it, between precipitous outcrops of saluting arms, crashing against other bodies, sinking down sides, heaving forward. A boy in braces ploughs past, shoving his arms before him in alternating salutes like a front crawl, and is lost in a swell. Tony sees Nick nearby, moving determinedly up and down with a fanged grin of performed enjoyment, his eyes ranging across the crowd, notching up gazes. With his limited careful motion, Nick is being pushed to the periphery by the big waves from the centre, to which Tony now, with all his energy, propels himself, into the heart of the maelstrom, where everything is both repulsion and embrace, the arms of strangers grabbing his shoulders and pushing off against him. *Before the night falls, heed the White call!* He grasps around him for leverage and support. His arms press against the wet slide of skin and at the feeling something in him wants to blush: it must be obvious, what else this is for him; he thinks of Glenn: 'Imagine if they knew. They'd fucking crucify us.' Men's bodies jostle, lift, force him under, and it seems that he might be ripped to pieces by the consuming flood. Heaving up, gasping for air, he sees Nicky Crane holding position at the front of the stage: poised, erect, his hands held down by his sides and slightly out, as if he might take off. Like the figurehead of a ship, tossed up against the thunderous sky above the roiling surface of the crowd. Tony tenses, strains forward at this mirror of how he should be, shoring himself up against the seething mass. He will not drown; he is a rock; the waves break over him. Then something pulls him beneath the surface, into airlessness and compression, and when he rises there is Dave, bobbing before him, the crook of his right arm warm round Tony's neck and his left stretching out in salute, yelling against the music and into it, shouting and saluting over and over with the loudening beat. Tony salutes too, and yells, and the crowd does the same around them, heaving, pushing, and Tony sees himself repeated in every direction like a hall of mirrors, and understands that this will not wreck him, he is not distinct from it and floating fragile on its surface, but rather it is him, of him, and he is part of it, the shouts, the salutes, the *sieg heil*s coming from within and around him alike. With one force, one voice, he fills the courtyard.

GIVE US WAR!
A N D W E'L L G I V E Y O U
F R E E D O M

NEVER MIND WHAT THE PEOPLE SAY FROM THE CHOSEN PARTYS. If we are toever be set free
WE THE NATIONALISTS MUST take power away from the goverment elect who ever they may
be. We all know what sort of state our land is in, we all know what that mess that is
like that the reds and all the hangers on are causing. So what can be done?......

for a start we can forget all the pointless campaigns that our leaders are asking us
to carry out. These campaigns just arnt helping us, there aint a person in the land
that is taking notice cozë every time we get up they the papers knock us down every
thing we do they the papers twist it, every thing we do is SLANDER'D . LETS AV' THE
BASTARDS if you find your self up against a black thug who is only interested in
robbing or cutting you make sure you get him before he gets you in fact just do
what i do cut them anyway. ▆▆▆▆▆▆ you dont have to be some great big muscle bound
geazer coz a knife does the work for ya.

Also wreck everything that is organised by the Reds i.e. Carnivals, concerts, meetings
and that sort of thing. Do IT or you will NEVER GET ANYEHERE THE WAY THINGS ARE GOING
NOW.

 M O R E A B O U T
W A R

THE MAIN RED BAND AT THE MOMENT ARE THE REDSKINS
THEY ARE FOREVER PLAYING GIGS ALL OVER THE PLACE
THEY ARE ALWAYS SLAGING US OFF
THEY HAVE BEEN KNOWN TO SLAG OFF SCREWDRIVER
TO THE SKINHEADS AMONGST US LETS ALL GET TOGETHER
AND WRECK THEIR GIGS WE CAN GET INTO THEM QUITE EASY
SO LETS ORGANISE YOURSELFS AND WRECK EVERYTHING THAT
THEY DO LETS USE THE ONLY BIT OF POWER WE HAVE OUR
STRENTH AND OUR LOYALTY. IF YOU THINK YOU HAVE THE
BOTTLE TO CARRY OUT THE ABOVE GET YOUR MATES TOGETHER
AND LET ME KNOW (Terry London) AND I'LL PASS IT ON TO
OTHERS AND WE'LL ALL GET TOGETHER and smash the DIRTY
LOWLIFE SCUM. Some people say that the Oi scene was
killed by violence well this is true. So lets give the
REDSKINS a bad name, people dont like violence so lets
give it to them. The Oi and Skinhead movement were
attacked by the Reds so let the Oi and Skinheads Fkill
the Red Movement TODAY.....................
LET ME KNOW IF YOU ARE INTERETED IN THIS
WRITE TO TELL ME IF YOU HEAR OF ANY REDSKINS CONCERTS.

White Rebelion [sic] fanzine, *circa* 1984

Rabies scare: Crane on the loose

Nicky Crane is on the loose again. The admitted leader of a violent attack on the Hank Wangford band during a Greater London Council sponsored day for London's young unemployed last summer has just been released after a six month prison sentence, following a fracas on a London underground train in which he was arrested in possession of an offensive weapon.

Last time he came out of prison he lost no time in returning to battle. After serving a sentence for a serious assault on police officers during a British Movement riot against black people in south London, he was soon to be seen leading various violent actions in the company of the boot boys of the National Front's Instant Response Unit.

Despite clear photographic and eye-witness evidence of Crane's role in the South Bank GLC day disturbances, no police action was forthcoming. The offensive weapon charge arose out of a different activity.

Last Christmas *Searchlight* received a card from Crane, then a prisoner on the Isle of Wight. Although he got only six months the authorities chose to send him to one of the most secure prisons in the country — a clear indication of Crane's violent nature. In his card he explained in graphic detail that he was not a member of the National Front but followed in the British Movement tradition, i.e. violence against just about everything. He also laid claim to his part in the attack of last summer.

Searchlight believes that the GLC and the people who were attacked should demand that the police charge Crane for these assaults in which people were badly injured.

Since arriving home from the Isle of Wight Crane has returned to his old stamping ground of south and east London. On Thursday nights he can be found at the Heaven disco at Charing Cross.

Searchlight, April 1985

Old Albion

At the library, whole years of *National Front News* turned out to have disappeared entirely. When I enquired about them the Indian woman at the desk told me, 'Well, don't expect me to help you!' She added, 'I'm only joking,' but was clearly discomfited, because after making a few suggestions she said, 'If you do find them make sure you tell them an Indian helped you, so we're not all bad.'

'Jesus,' I said, 'I hope you don't think I'm reading this stuff out of *sympathy* for the—'

'No,' she said hurriedly, 'no, I just needed to say something.'

We were both embarrassed now, visibly, shakily so, and I ended the conversation as quickly as I could. Describing it later to Adam and Sarah, as we walked the Regent's Canal, I kept going over her odd formulation, 'tell them,' who *they* might be simultaneously obvious and baffling: did she believe that fascists had sent me to find their paper? 'I needed to say something,' she had explained, as if by just referring to the Front I had somehow helped it breathe.

Sarah's completion of her PhD had made good the prospect, which she had long been nurturing, of a research post at the London School of Hygiene and Tropical Medicine. Her team was to investigate what she glibly described as 'the sex life of malaria.' It was led by an old colleague of her supervisor, with funding underwritten by the Gates Foundation. I felt oddly excited that my sister's salary would be met by the world's richest man, but Sarah was more preoccupied by her switch to a 'mainstream' parasite: she had a proprietorial attachment to the undistinguished trypanosome whose promastigote stage was the subject of her thesis, and was sorry to be moving on. When I suggested malaria was big money for a reason, and that no matter how small the part she played, the possible glory of an eventual vaccine would be large enough to share, she claimed that 'her' organism still killed several thousand people a year, and that measured by, say, dead humans per researcher, she was almost certainly losing out. Still, the job, and her consequent return to London, deserved celebration, as did the news that same week of John Tyndall's death, so I had suggested the canal, which had long been on my list, for a Sunday walk. 'We'll end up in Limehouse,' I had added, 'so we can go to the White Swan for amateur strip night.' That had long been on my list as well.

We started at the earliest point possible, where the canal emerges from its passage under Islington, and a gate in the road above the tunnel opens on to a path that seems to promise a secret garden: you have to part thin, dangling stalks of trees and swarming midges on the steep descent, and there's the sudden ancestral comfort of woodsmoke from the houseboats moored below.

'The thing is,' I was saying, 'when I started I thought the point was that Nicky lived this amazing double life – neo-nazi by day, homosexual by night. Deceived his comrades for years and devastated them when he finally came out. Right? But it doesn't hold up – *Searchlight* outed him from the beginning. There's an article from '85 about how he's been involved in various attacks and so on, which ends something like: "On

Thursdays you can find him at Heaven in Charing Cross."
That's within a *year* of the first time he had gay sex. Later they
do an exposé on a security firm he works for, and it turns out
that Nicky and some other nazis went on the Pride march
under a "gay skins" banner. Later again they say he's building
up this gay skins movement, which meets on Fridays at the
London Apprentice.

'They out him *over and over again*. And not just vague
rumour: they say these are the clubs he hangs out in and these
are the nights he's there. Well, all the fucking nazis read
Searchlight. They were obsessed with it. It's basically impossible that the stuff in those articles wasn't widespread
knowledge among the right, the way they always knew about
Martin Webster. So I've begun to think that the story isn't
about Nicky *hiding* his sexuality, it's about his nazi mates
ignoring it. They had to know, all of them. They knew all
along.'

In the summer evening the towpath was busy with families,
groups of teens, shirtless joggers with iPods strapped to their
arms like medical devices or tefillin. A young couple passed us
in three-quarter-length trousers, with a young boy in tow and
a baby in an expensive stroller, and I thought I saw Sarah
frown at them. 'So it was all one big gay club,' she said.

'Well, exactly. I mean obviously it wasn't. But you do feel a
bit *Pink Swastika* after a while – you know, all of them fairies.
There's a group of out gay nazis in the States – of *course* there
is – who insist that Ian Stuart himself was gay. Stewart Home
implies the same thing.'

'Do you think he was?' said Adam.

'Unfortunately, no. Though I am starting to wonder about
Savitri Devi.'

'You,' said Sarah, '*love* her.'

'Well, she gives good subject matter. Her marriage was
never consummated, by mutual consent apparently. And in

her account of being imprisoned in Germany after the war, when she was done for spreading Nazi propaganda, the mad old bitch, she goes unbelievably *Cell Block H*–lyrical about a fellow inmate who'd worked at Belsen. You know: her pale blond silky hair, her beautiful blue eyes . . .

'*Meanwhile*, she had a close lifelong friendship with one Miss Muriel Gantry, also unmarried. Which despite Miss Gantry's evident dislike for her friend's rampant Nazism lasted until the moment she died, in Gantry's house, in 1982. Now, Muriel Gantry is an interesting figure. She was a "theatrical costumier" who published a novel in the '60s. I read it in the library – well, scan-read it. It's called *The Distance Never Changes* – rather feverish story of ancient Crete, *very* Mary Renault, who apparently rather liked it.'

'Who's Mary Renault?' Adam asked.

'Google her later, I'm on a roll. So the heroine of this novel is a young girl who dresses up in boys' clothes and ends up in an explicitly non-sexual relationship with a boy who sleeps with other boys—'

'Do you think,' interrupted Sarah, 'that you might be overdoing the research just a bit? So Savitty-thingy wore comfortable shoes?'

'Actually, right into old age she claimed she'd never had intercourse. Maybe that's true. All I'm saying . . . she was an old lady who was fond of cats. I mean, I know all ideologies embody contradiction, but neo-nazis do take it to extremes. You know: the Holocaust never happened but it was *completely brilliant*. Queers are *Untermenschen* and can I suck your racially pure knob?'

After delivering this pre-prepped punchline, which fell flatter than I'd hoped, I felt suddenly empty and fell into a vague, embarrassed silence. I had been planning to outline to Sarah the wilder aspects of my developing plot: the clandestine order, Lanze O-something Geheimgesellschaft, custodians of the true

Spear of Longinus, as used in Himmler's most secret rituals at Wewelsberg and transported in the final days of the war by U-Boat to the secret Antarctic base of which Dönitz had hinted in his speech at Nuremberg; retrieved in 1979 on the orders of Hans-Ulrich Rudel, the Nazis' most decorated fighter and Hitler's own intended successor as *Führer*, who later, sensing his own death just months away, entrusted it to Savitri Devi when she visited him in Kufstein in 1982; and upon her own unexpected death in Sible Hedingham soon afterwards, recovered from among her effects by an emissary of Colin Jordan. Jordan had already begun to develop his masterplan, as later published (perhaps in muted form) under the auspices of the League of St George, for his élite task force of guerrilla activists modelled on the *Werwolf* of Otto Skorzeny; and with his guidance the spear, and the traditions and esoteric wisdom of the LOG, found a new home among the strange nexus of skinheads, political-soldier revolutionaries and nazi occultists that emerged during the Thatcher years. Was the astonishing possibility of Nicky's continued survival somehow linked to the fabled powers of the spear?

But now the energy of performance had ceased to drug me. I thought how hopelessly arcane all this was, not to mention silly; and how only someone already seduced by the minutiae of fascism could think, like a stamp collector or a comics geek, that normal people might find it interesting. I felt like a child at a family gathering, grabbing at adult attention with a card trick and realizing, with a flood of shame, that what I got was only charitably given. We approached a bridge, where steps led up to the road above, and for a moment I thought I might run up them and flee. 'When Nicky was my age,' I said in the echoey space beneath, 'he had nine years to live.'

'Adam's gone quiet,' Sarah said. She nodded to where he walked ahead of us, with that familiar, toe-rocking gait. His braces, hanging down, swung gently around his arse, and his head rocked from side to side, as if there were a rhythm in it. It wasn't like him to be so unsociable.

'What's up with him, do you think?' I asked.

'Just a guess, but really: "Google her later, I'm on a roll"?'

'Oh.' I shrugged. 'Maybe you're right.'

'How are things with you two anyway?'

'Good.'

She squinted at me.

'No, they are.' And it was true, I thought; what fallout there had been from our failed experiments had not lasted long. That we could not do together all we hoped had perhaps disappointed Adam, but affected not at all, it seemed, his broader commitment to me. He simply went out, every now and then, on one of his hook-ups, or to the skin night he still visited monthly, and if I had not yet made peace with that I was getting used to it. Besides, these days I often took the opportunity afforded by his excursions to expand my online communion with arealnazi.

We had exchanged several messages since my initial *Hi*, and true to the uncompromising stance of his profile he had told me almost nothing of himself while demanding ever more of me. In particular, this involved my sending him photographs of myself: full-body, face visible, in postures of mounting, pre-scribed humiliation. The sheer inequitable riskiness of this (I had not so much as a cropped-torso shot in which to ground my idea of him) excited me more than anything had for a while. I told myself it was research, and indeed did ask him the odd question, though with limited success.

What does LOG stand for? I tried once.

where did u see that

On a tattoo.

After a pause: *i never heard of that*

Oh.

show me ur arse again

*

Victoria Park spread out on our left beyond a low fence. To the right, where the canal dropped abruptly in a lock, two old black men sat fishing, swapping laconicisms like a nascent sitcom.

I watched Adam step aside to let pass an old Asian man in a kufi, holding by the hand a young boy who was presumably his grandson. Doubtless I only imagined something anxious in the man's look at Adam: he was far too neat a skinhead to carry much historical threat. But maybe the man was unusually alert: two weeks earlier a middle-aged Muslim had been beaten to death in Nottingham; there had been arson attacks on mosques and Asian homes, and thousands of death threats. Still, the press insisted on commending our restraint, and avoidance of some more drastic 'backlash.' Another day spent not smashing a Muslim's head in with a brick, you were rather encouraged to feel, another small achievement.

For the BNP this couldn't have been better timed, coming as it did on the eve of Nick Griffin's long-awaited race-hate trial with his protégé Mark Collett: one charge involved Griffin calling Islam 'a wicked, vicious faith.' Within days of the bombs, leaflets had appeared with pictures of the exploded bus: 'Maybe now's the time to listen to the BNP.' They urged their supporters not to victimize 'moderate Muslims,' but those supporters could have been forgiven confusion when the party's website simultaneously read: *War has come to our city streets. Blood is flowing. The time for action has come. Words are not enough.* Three days before our walk, Griffin and Collett had pleaded not guilty. It was hard to imagine how what had started a weak case could now possibly succeed.

So what tattoos do you have? I had asked.
  ill show you when we meet
I had furnished my faceless correspondent with an extensive gallery of commissions by now, and recently, with my purchase of a webcam (whose sudden, parasitical crouch on my laptop

screen Adam had let go unremarked), we had graduated to more immediate interaction. It was still an unequal exchange; arealnazi claimed to own neither camera nor microphone, and so I would speak to the lens and perform before it in counter-point to his still-typed conversation and commands, at which, with my glasses (as he had taken to requiring) removed, I had to squint from a close distance.

A couple of weeks before our walk, I had been extricating myself from the awkward perch upon the dining table into which he had directed me when an intimate tickle made me jump. Recovering from my pratfall, I scooped up Sonny and kicked him from the room. When I looked at the screen it read: *nice cat*

I apologized with a mimed laugh, then watched the screen awkwardly until I saw movement again. Leaning forward and wrinkling my features I made out:

do u have pen

'Yeah,' I said, 'I should imagine so. Any particular sort?'

marker pen

'Hold on a sec.' I walked off-screen to the kitchen, where I scrabbled in the drawers until I found a thick black number bought, though rarely used, for freezer containers. 'Is this the kind of thing?' I asked the webcam, and after a moment the non-sequitur came:

show me ur cock

I made the appropriate adjustments.

want u to draw swastika on it

'You're joking,' I said, but it leaped disloyally.

fuck off and do it

'It's a permanent marker.'

u have 15 secs

It was something I could only achieve by ignoring, indeed by harnessing, the knowledge of how hard it would be to remove. Later, even after considerable abrasion, I kept my underwear on with Adam for a day or so, relying on his apathy in the wake of his own activities. For a shift of gear, this transaction had impressed me considerably; as for where it was heading, I could only know if we met, something that arealnazi now regularly proffered, and I put off as flirtatiously, and apparently endlessly temporarily, as I could.

In the park, the evening sun cosseted the trees. A pair of boys in trackies approached the other way: they looked like brothers, perhaps thirteen and sixteen, pale skin elegiac in the advertising light. As they passed, the older one said from beneath his baseball cap: 'It's the best time to do it, 'cause you're half asleep and not thinking about it.' I turned at this, but as they walked away any potentially elucidating reply was quite inaudible. Sarah made a noise of delight and nudged me.

'What?'

'This. London. Ach, you take it for granted.'

'You'll be back here soon.'

'I know. It's why I'm smiling.'

'I still can't believe you have a job. And you're Doctor Sarah now. I can't do anything.'

'You can! You could go on *Mastermind*. Specialist subject, Paki-bashing cocksuckers. Anyway, boyfriend beats job, so stop complaining.'

'Yeah – how are things on that front?'

'The usual desert. With the occasional slightly grubby oasis.'

'That doesn't sound so bad.'

'It is when you're thirty-one.'

'Why?'

Sarah looked at me. We crossed the start of the Hertford Union Canal on to turf dry and patchy in the summer heat. With the paucity of trees, and the buildings across the canal low and industrial, it seemed that the city was being squashed flat under a sloping ceiling, and we would soon have to stoop.

'You're joking,' I said, realizing.

'Not really.'

'I didn't know you *had* a biological clock.'

She was silent for a moment, then pointed ahead of us. 'You should talk to him,' she said.

Adam was sitting on strip of lawn beside the water. As we approached he pulled a blade of grass from the ground next to him and rubbed it between his fingers. I sat down beside him. 'Hey,' he said.

'So this' – I checked the map I'd printed – 'must be Mile End Park. Looks rather nice.' It ran ahead of us as far as I could see.

'Lots of green,' said Adam.

'It's still new, I think. Put together out of little bits of land patched together quite slowly since the war. Used to be all buildings and bombsites. They only managed to finish it as one of the big millennium projects. All very eco.'

'Half a century,' he said, 'to make a park?'

'Things move slowly out here,' said Sarah, who was standing over us. 'I'm just going to go and . . . feed the birds.' She wandered away on to the grass. I looked at my map again, and pointing over to Queen Mary College told Adam how it had, like the park, been assembled piecemeal from adjacent plots acquired over years. The largest had been a Sephardic burial ground, purchased under a special act of Parliament. Most of its residents were disinterred in the mid-'70s and reburied, anticipating the 'white flight' of their living neighbours, in Brentwood, Essex; but 2,000 graves still occupied a lacuna in the middle of the campus, invisible from where we sat, but a stark prospect, presumably, for readers in the new library alongside. 'The library was modelled on the old Reading Room of the British Museum. The London Psychogeographical Association says it's the start of a powerful ley line used in the sacrifice of Ian Stuart.'

'Scary,' he said gently.

Dull green growths as big as we swayed beneath the surface of the canal, their shapes like ink dropped in water. Adam poked at them with a long twig. We sat like that, silently, for a while; I feigned hypnosis at the slow, subaqueous dance, and looked now and again to where, in the park, Sarah watched shirtless teenagers improvise around a football.

What would we do, I had asked arealnazi, if we met?
what ever i want to, he replied.
How could I be sure I was safe?
you wont
And later, when I had thought to ask:
yeah i knew nicky

'I'd like to come with you sometime,' I told Adam, 'to your skinhead night. If that's OK.'

He looked up from the water and smiled.

After some time the current brought, brushing against the canal wall so it got stuck immediately before us, a floating polystyrene tray not quite a metre square: a moulded insert from the packaging of a TV or stereo. Into its raised edge cut stems of roses had been pressed, so the dying flowers, their reds and yellows still intense, formed a sagging perimeter. In clusters on the surface of this little raft lay bananas just beginning to go brown, a pair of oranges, dried slices of mango, perhaps, flat leaves, and bright round sweets; the whole was further strewn with flowers, and there were, now that I looked closely, even striped birthday-cake candles between the rose stems.

'What is that,' I said, 'some Hindu thing?'

'Guess so.' Adam stood and nudged the vessel on with his foot. Then he held out his hand, and pulled me up.

A huge brick column, storeys high, streaked along its length with white like smeared chalk and marked at the base with graffiti tags, rose inexplicably from the ground where the park finally tailed off, like the chimney of some massive, now absent, factory. Directly behind it, and from this perspective far smaller, appeared the skyscrapers of Canary Wharf; with all of this I was looking up and not, at first, at the man who now approached along the towpath: lurching, unbalanced, his head dangling from his neck, too drooped to see where he was going. I had been half aware, in my peripheral vision, of people clearing his trajectory, but properly registered him just as, tripping on uneven stone or in some private spasm, he pitched suddenly forward, hunching a little as he fell, and flopped into an unmoving heap ahead of us. He let out a moan, less of pain than of vatic foreboding, which continued, unvarying in pitch or volume, with just short breaks for breath. Sarah rushed forward and tried to uncurl the man from his huddle. 'Are you OK?' she asked him, and after too long a pause the man shouted, 'Yeah yeah,' and raised his head, revealing the shock of a face that glistened almost black with blood. He began to lift himself, pushing his heavy body off the ground so it swayed above the four points, too closely clustered, of his hands and feet. He managed a few seconds of this unlikely suspension, then collapsed again and was immediately still.

Sarah made a face at us. The moaning did not resume. Bystanders, pre-empted like me and Adam of involvement, watched from the perimeter. She shook the man and spoke loudly in his ear, and he stirred and resumed his struggle. 'You're bleeding,' she told him, 'quite a lot.'

'I'm all right,' the man yelled to the pavement against his face, somehow wobbling up again to teeter on his feet. He moved down the towpath like a latter-day leper, bent nearly over, improbably avoiding what seemed his inevitable keel into the water. 'I'm all right,' he kept shouting, warding people off. A patch of still-fresh blood the size of his face pooled like melted sorbet on the stone.

*

Philip had spoken salaciously of amateur strip night at the White Swan in Limehouse, where improbably young scally lads, thin and pliant as the stalks of plants, competed, or so he claimed, entirely for the money. The blacked-out corner pub certainly seemed to hold such promise as we approached: it could almost have been made of gingerbread. But as we neared it a man yelled something I couldn't process, and assumed to be abuse: it was only later that I worked out what he had said, some minutes after we had paid three quid each, at the counter inside, to a big man in a polo shirt. I ordered drinks and we leaned against the bar watching the dance floor. The song was one I knew, 'The Closest Thing to Crazy': not the Katie Melua original, but a cover version shoehorned improbably into waltz time. The dancing couples' movements were formal and precise.

'I don't see any teenage strippers,' murmured Adam, and I put my face in my hands. 'Sorry, folks, I ballsed up. That's what the guy outside was saying: "Tea dance." Clearly we didn't look the type.'

But as the waltz ended and the spinning couples slowed like a fairground ride, it became clear there was no type. Some parted with kisses or hugs and others moved off together, but the DJ's announcement of a Boston two-step brought nearly everyone back. In pairs, and one trio, they span in a huge circle, advancing and retreating with extraordinary, anachronistic grace. There followed a foxtrot, and then a line dance, with everyone clapping their hands, which finally drew a pot-bellied Indian man out of his wallflower hesitation.

Later, when we'd bought more drinks and declined various invitations to dance, there was another waltz: the song 'Once upon a Dream' from Disney's *Sleeping Beauty*, which I had first seen with my family when I was two or three at the big cinema in St Martin's Lane; I could still remember how it transported me. I tried to remind Sarah but she shook her head blankly.

Yet personal though my reaction was, it was clear this was a big number for everybody, for to the few red and green spots that had so far illuminated the floor were added the thousand swirling particles into which the mirror ball exploded the lights now aimed at it, and which fell, in countermovement to their circulation, across (among others):

— an elderly, big-eyed tranny in a plain skirt, with his own hair falling to his shoulders, whose thin-lipped mouth looked toothless until I saw him speak, who left the quite ancient woman he had been seated with, whom I assumed to be his mother, to take to the floor, as the song started, with a short man in his fifties, with gelled, dyed hair, a sly smile, and a hunchback;

— a tall man, with a big smile and spiky, receding hair, nimbly following his shorter, fatter partner, whose goatee and blue short-sleeved shirt convinced me for no good reason he was a train driver, the pair accelerating with breathtaking nimbleness into sudden sweeping arcs across the floor;

— a pair of lesbians, one comfortingly social-workerish in a red dress, another with a pigtail and glasses and a body like two balls separated vertically by a pole, holding each other slow and close;

— a man with a pencil moustache and Brylcreemed hair in full ballroom attire – black glittered shirt, tight trousers and special shoes – precisely leading a muscle Mary in a baseball cap and ripped-sleeved, red-checked shirt;

— a middle-aged Chinese man in a slinky, slutty transparent top with a heavy and perspiring partner of the same age in everyday work suit and glasses;

— and an amazing look-twice transvestite with perfectly bouffant hair, in gorgeous make-up and a pristine, elaborately detailed *Gone with the Wind* ballgown of staggering diameter, paired affectionately with an old gentleman dressed with beguilingly enigmatic intent: glasses, long white ponytail, vest and thin baby-blue bloomers that billowed around old-man legs gripped to just below the knee by white socks; who, like most of the others, was a remarkably good dancer, his work-shoed feet, as the music swelled, plotting a rapid exuberant pattern on the floor in dialogue with hers;

and I found myself, witnessing this secret rite, reaching, without looking for it or planning to, for Adam's hand, and gripping it tight for moorage as a great swell of unanticipated, and perhaps later to be embarrassing but now unarguable and obvious and fully justified – no avoiding the word – *joy* came rushing to carry me.

SANCTUARY

TERRORISTS WALK THE STREETS OF LONDON

Roberto Fiore
SENTENCED in his absence by a Rome court to nine years for subversive conspiracy. Original charges included attempted murder. Works as mini-cab driver in Streatham. He is 26

Stefano Tiraboschi
SENTENCED in his absence to eight years and two months for conspiracy. Original charges included four armed robberies. Pizza parlour manager in Kilburn. He is 24.

Marcello de Angelis
SENTENCED in his absence to six years. Originally alleged to have been involved with Fiore, in attempted murder. Works for a printing firm in Finsbury. He is 25.

Massimo Morsello
SENTENCED in his absence to ten years. He was originally being charged by the Italians with a raid on a gunshop, an attack on a school. Part-time mini-cab driver. He is 26.

Marinella Morsello
SENTENCED to two years and eight months for conspiracy. Accused of gunshop robbery, and throwing Molotov cocktails. Lives with husband in Crystal Palace. She is 25.

THESE FIVE people are Italian terrorists — and they are walking free on the streets of London.

Mrs Thatcher pledged last week that there would be 'no haven and no escape' for terrorists, yet all five have been convicted in Italy.

They were found guilty of *'associazione sovversiva e banda armata'* — loosely translated as subversive conspiracy and membership of an armed gang.

All five say these charges are 'political'. And all five have managed to fight off extradition proceedings to the anger of the Special Branch. For it is feared that some of these members of an ultra right-wing Italian terrorist group have involved themselves in the British Fascist movement.

This week Home Secretary Leon Brittan faces demands for action. But to the fury of Italian Prime Minister Bettino Craxi, who last month personally asked Mrs Thatcher to deport them, he will refuse to step in.

This is despite Italian insistence that they are front-line terrorists who ought to be serving long prison sentences.

The Special Branch also believes that the group is behind a recent 'palace revolution' in the National Front leadership, which has left that organisation even more militant and racist.

Martin Webster, the NF's overweight national activities director, has a paranoic hatred of Italians. But a group of NF leaders were attracted by Fiore's Third Position and together, they conspired to expel Webster and his supporters.

Webster said: 'The Italian cell has now taken over the National Front and Fiore is the major influence.'

The NF member Fiore has been living with at Warwick Square is Martin Walker.

Camps

He has also met a leading Front member Nicholas Griffin, 26, a Cambridge graduate and son of a wealthy Suffolk farmer. The group set up a magazine, Rising, full of vicious racist propaganda.

Shortly after Rising was established in August, 1983, Griffin and Fiore began to organise weekend 'training camps' at large country houses.

Mail on Sunday, 21 July 1985

The Craven Club

It is Thursday, 25 April 1985, a quarter-past seven in the evening, and it has just started to rain. Tony walks faster past identical black-railed Georgian houses. He stops at the door of one and is reaching for its bell when a voice behind him says, 'Excuse me?'

At the foot of the steps is something thin and broken in a wheelchair. Behind it stands a man in his thirties with a poof moustache. He must be the one who spoke, because he now looks at Tony through the drizzle, taking in his tattoos and the patches on his jacket, and says quickly, 'It's nothing, sorry.' Tony turns away, but before he can reach the bell again the one in the wheelchair calls his name.

His face looks hastily assembled, the skin rough, unevenly coloured, stretched too thin. He wears huge, medical spectacles, a patterned sweater, a baseball cap: all too big for him. 'Tony?' he says again.

Tony's arms prickle with damp. He says: 'I don't . . .'

'I wouldn't recognize me neither.' He smiles, good teeth splitting the surface. There is a patch on his lower cheek, towards his mouth, that looks like someone has taken sandpaper to it.

'Ryan,' he says. 'Used to be mates with Dennis. You remember. What's it been, ten years? More. You haven't changed.'

Tony does remember: a ginger teenager, a particular shy smile in the front seat of a green convertible. He is not sure if he can see the smile's echo now, or is just imagining it through the torrent of difference.

'Ryan. Yeah.' He hugs his stomach against the rain. He feels suddenly, prodigiously embarrassed, as if it is he who is a freak. 'You all right mate.'

'I've not been well Tony.' Ryan smiles again, the awkward rupture repeating. 'Never guess though would you?'

'Yeah sorry to hear that.' Moisture gathers in a drip under Tony's nose. He scans the road to see if anyone is coming. A businessman regards them in passing but does not stop.

'But I've got such lovely mates, looking after me.' Ryan smiles up at his companion. 'Can't complain too much, can I? This is my friend Andy,' he tells Tony. 'This is Tony. From the old days.'

'All right,' nods Tony.

Andy puts a hand on Ryan's shoulder. 'It's wet,' he says. 'We should get you inside.' He stands before Ryan and extends his arms. Ryan leans forward and Andy grasps him under the shoulders, hauling him into a clumsy, close embrace. Ryan makes little noises and his legs quiver. Andy puts his right arm around him and holds the left out low like a bar on which Ryan leans. The arrangement looks precarious, misconceived.

'OK?' says Andy.

Ryan nods, panting. He asks Tony, 'Could you get the door for us?'

Tony blinks. He looks around him, thrown, before thinking to ring the bell; then frowns at the camera mounted above, which examines him in silence. He imagines its view, the rickety clutch of men over his shoulder. There is a beat, ten seconds, twenty, then a buzz.

Holding the door, watching the effort of their advance, Tony feels the massive loom of the staircase at his left. The wheelchair stands abandoned on the pavement, rain pooling on its seat. It looks like bad poster art.

The men seem to swell into the doorway. Tony presses back against the wall but still they brush him, breathing heavily. Andy's elbow nudges his stomach. Andy looks everywhere but at Tony.

From the foot of the stairs Ryan says, 'Would you do us a favour Tony?' His voice is wobbly with exertion. 'Would you bring the chair up?'

Andy says quietly, 'I'll do it.'

'Tony won't mind, will you Tony? He's going upstairs anyway.'

Tony says, 'It's all right.'

'It folds up,' Andy tells him. 'If you look in the middle of the front bar there's a catch.' As Tony goes out he calls, 'It's very kind of you. Thanks.'

The door swings shut behind him. He squats in the street before the wheelchair, examining its front. Blebs of water cling to the metal, from which his fingers gather smeared dirt. He pokes and fiddles but nothing seems to give. The rain patters his scalp. Eventually he gives up and pulls the chair behind him as it is. He rings the bell again and stares at the camera as if daring it to ask why he's still outside.

He shoves the door with his shoulder and drags the chair backwards over the sill. Andy and Ryan are only halfway up the first half-flight of stairs. Andy watches him. He seems to wonder whether to repeat the information about the catch and decide to leave it.

When they have rounded the corner Tony hauls up the chair. It is just narrow enough to fit. It bashes banisters, scrapes the wall.

He waits on the landing until they reach the top. When he

follows them up, the chair keeps catching. His armpits are wet.

Andy lowers Ryan, panting and sweating, back on to his seat. 'It's not worth all that effort this place,' Tony tells Ryan.

'I'm not that bad Tony. Looked harder than it was probably.' His breath heaves, then settles. 'You look well though. Strong and that.'

'Getting a beer gut.' He pats himself.

'It's good, a bit of fat. Means you're healthy.'

'Yeah well.'

Ryan says, 'You go on first Tony. I need to clean up a bit anyway. Wouldn't help your pulling power, going in with me.'

They look at each other. Tony says, 'Yeah. All right then. Cheers. I'm . . .' He searches for a formula. 'I'm sorry you've been sick and all that.' At the door he turns. 'Ryan mate. Do you know if Dennis . . . Do you see him ever?'

'I haven't seen Dennis for years Tony.'

'Yeah thanks.'

'He was doing well last time I saw him. And I haven't heard anything, on the grapevine. I imagine I would have, if . . . I bet you he's right as rain wherever he is. You know Dennis. He's probably met his Prince Charming and lives in a palace in France knowing him.'

'Yeah,' says Tony. 'Probably. You take care of yourself eh? Cheers Andy.'

Andy catches his eye and looks quickly away. 'Thank you,' he says, with a careful lack of inflection, 'for your help with the chair.'

Inside the club it is still fairly quiet. One or two people have been drinking since lunchtime. Tony greets some skins he knows and gets a round in quickly so he can be talking to them when Ryan enters. He tries not to watch when it happens but can't help shooting the odd glance. One of his mates looks too and mutters, 'Jesus Christ.' Neither Ryan nor Andy tries to acknowledge Tony. The barman seems to know Ryan, who chats to him happily.

At a table by a window is a boy who can't be more than twenty. He looks like a student on a night out: jeans, white shirt, floppy blond hair. He is talking to his friend, an older cardiganed queen, but keeps looking in Tony's direction. The fourth time, Tony meets his gaze and the boy looks quickly away. He says something to his friend, clutching his hand across the table, and laughs.

'He was eyeing me up earlier,' says one of the other skins. 'Lost interest when you come in. Fucker.'

'Jailbait anyway,' says Tony, 'isn't he,' but he keeps an eye on the boy.

By nine the bar is filling with the pre-Heaven crowd and Tony has had a few drinks. When the boy next goes to the bar Tony follows him. The old queen watches anxiously.

Tony stands next to the boy, who is slurring his order – more drunk than he looked, Tony thinks – and stares at him, waiting. 'Hello!' the boy says when the penny drops, and then 'Oops – thank you,' to the barman. While he waits for change he leans into Tony's jacket, eyeing the patches myopically. 'Skroo-drai-vaa,' he says. 'You're not really into that stuff?'

Oh well, thinks Tony. Worth a try anyway.

'Yeah,' he says. 'I am. So why not piss off before I kick your head in.' He turns to face the bar. The boy takes his drinks away in silence, but a few minutes later Tony sees him looking again.

Some time after ten, Ryan and Andy start to leave. They clear a path slowly through the now crowded room. As they approach the door it opens, and Nicky Crane walks in.

He still has it, that presence or whatever that makes people stare. If Tony hadn't been watching Ryan he'd still have looked up, at the drop in volume. Nicky enters the room, Tony catches himself thinking, like an Olympic diver into water: hard and smooth, raising waves from the quick displacement. Sometimes you forget, and then you see him like this— Nicky, seemingly oblivious to the crowd's involuntary tribute, is talking over his shoulder and nearly walks into Ryan's wheelchair. They stop within inches of each other. Nicky stares down at Ryan for a beat, and then at Andy, before stepping slowly, parodically, aside. The guy Nicky was talking to, who Tony now sees is of course Glenn, mimics this in the doorway, and as Andy pushes Ryan out, as fast as he can without looking cowed, Nicky says loudly: 'These fucking spastics should have all been in the camps.'

One of Tony's mates chuckles. 'Way to make an entrance isn't it.'

Nicky and Glenn drink their pints by the pool table, silently encouraging the conclusion of the game in progress. Glenn spots Tony looking, and nods to him across the room, so Tony has to say hello.

'How are you doing,' he asks Glenn, 'OK?'; and adds to Nicky, 'All right mate?' in a tone that signals no conversation is expected, or perhaps desired. Nicky smiles and Glenn says, 'Yeah good Tony thanks.'

'Been up to much?'

'Same old stuff. You know. How about you?'

'Not bad.'

'Yeah well. Good.' Nobody says anything for a long moment. Then Tony says, 'Anyway, I should . . .' and gestures. 'You going to Heaven later?'

'In a bit. You?'

'No I'm just in for a drink. Well. Have a good evening. Cheers.' He walks straight to the boy's table. The boy and his queen friend both look up at him. Tony tells the boy, 'I'm going for a piss and then I'm going home. If you want to come be ready when I'm back.'

Entering the toilets Tony has the extraordinary conviction that Nicky will come in after him. He can almost hear the loud bang of the door, and even the idea of trying to piss while Nicky stands alongside watching, casually loosing several pints of beer, blocks him up for a long, anxious moment. In his mind's eye Nicky notices and winks at him.

When he returns to the bar the boy and queen are whispering. The boy makes a face at the queen, who stands up. He is shorter than Tony, but looks him in the eye. 'I'll remember you,' he says. His voice wobbles. 'I'll be able to describe you exactly. So don't . . .' He trails off and tries to imply his demand with a teary look.

Tony says, 'Yeah calm down you old fairy. He'll be all right.'

He nods to the guys he was drinking with, then looks at the boy, who stands up shakily. He follows Tony down the stairs in silence and stays half a step behind him on the walk to Charing Cross. In the station Tony says, 'Do you need a ticket?'

'Yes.'

He nods at the counter. 'Woolwich Dockyard. Quick as you can.'

As they walk down the platform, he says quietly, 'I ain't going to shit on you or nothing if that's what you're looking for.'

'No. God, no, I'm not into anything like that.'

'Good because nor am I.'

'That's a relief.' The boy smiles, the first time since they spoke at the bar. 'Although I wasn't really worried about it, you know, as a possibility. I mean until you mentioned it.'

'Well,' says Tony, reaching for the door, 'it's funny what some people expect, do you know what I mean?'

'Oh, I know. Some people can be right wallies.'

When Tony opens the train door six young blacks look

baldly back at him. 'Maybe not this one,' he tells the boy. The carriages are divided crosswise into separate compartments. Each has doors on its sides to reach the platforms, but there is no connection internally. The next compartment's only occupant, a middle-aged woman in office clothes, looks nervously at Tony but stays seated.

'You a student?' Tony asks the boy as the train pulls out.

'Second year. I'm at UCL.'

'Illegal then.'

'Technically.' The boy smiles again and blushes. The woman stares determinedly through her window.

'Does that queer always pimp for you like that?'

'No, he just . . . he likes to look after me.'

'Got bollocks hasn't she.'

'Oh, he's great, Ed. He's my best friend.'

They lapse into silence. The train fills up further at Waterloo East, then rolls out among the roofs of Southwark. The boy stares self-consciously out. The woman keeps glancing at Tony – his boots, jacket, scalp, but never his eyes – and quickly away again.

When they arrive at London Bridge, there are jeers and yells from down the platform. The carriage door is opened by an Asian man looking nervously in the direction of the noise: he turns, sees Tony, and walks on. Hearing the gang approach, the boy is visibly anxious. Their chant of 'Hitler was a skinhead' – in which Tony recognizes at least one voice – becomes a chaos of abuse when its authors discover the blacks next door. But the yells abate, and it must be the skins who backed off, because Steve is now climbing through the doorway. 'Oi oi,' Steve says as he spots Tony, 'look what's behind the square window,' and Tony manages to smile. Four more skins follow. They drink beer from cans and loudly establish their domain. The woman, and the boy next to Tony, both stare at their feet.

Steve stands over Tony with his group around. 'All right Tony,' he says, 'been a while,' and they all shake hands. Tony does not look to his right, where the boy is sitting: it is as if he has engaged a catch that prevents the rotation of his gaze beyond a point just past straight ahead. Of the ten seats in the compartment only three were occupied when Steve came in; it must be obvious that Tony was not beside the boy accidentally.

'You been out then?' asks Steve.

'Yeah I had a few drinks.'

'Where did you go?'

Tony thinks. 'The uh—' What the fuck is there near Charing Cross? Near Waterloo? 'The you know the Princess Louise.'

'What up on Holborn?'

'That's it.'

'It's all right that boozer. Who was there?'

'Oh some of the lads. How about you? What have you been up to?'

'We bought a few cans. Been for a wander.' He looks at his watch, a Rolex or a copy of one. 'Left early didn't you?'

'Knackered mate. Getting old.'

'Yeah well,' says Steve, in the tone of someone setting up a joke, 'you want to watch it when you're tired. You let your guard down.'

'How do you mean?'

'Sat next to a fucking AIDS carrier aren't you mate.'

The boy is staring terrified at the floor. Steve says, 'You're in my seat you queer bastard,' and prods him with his boot. Without looking up, the boy stands. He opens the door while they are still pulling in to Deptford. One of the skins shoves him as he descends and the boy stumbles on to the platform.

Steve stretches his legs in the vacated seat. 'You want to watch yourself Tony. You don't notice these things.'

Abruptly, the woman stands. 'Excuse me,' she mumbles,

and Steve winks at her and pulls his legs in very slowly. She gets off as the train begins to move.

'You're too innocent,' Steve tells Tony. 'That's your trouble.'

Tony wonders if all this has been Steve playing a game with him. The gentleness with which Steve nudged the boy's leg troubles him. He says, 'Good thing you're keeping an eye on me.'

'I'm a dad now aren't I so I'm always on the look-out. I don't want some pervert coming up my little boy's arse.' And he *winks*.

'Don't see as much of you these days do we Tony,' he says.

'Well I haven't gone anywhere mate.'

'Don't suppose you have.'

There's not much to say to that. Two of the skins mutter, laugh. Tony is here as long as they want him.

'I thought,' says Steve eventually, 'you might have joined the Front. Like Dave and them lot.'

'Too much like hard work isn't it. Anyway I thought you had. What about Skrewdriver Security and that?

'Plenty of hours in the day mate.'

They pass Greenwich. Four stops left.

Steve says more quietly, 'You heard anything about these Italians?'

'What do you mean?'

'You know with the Front. I heard they were running training sessions. Paramilitary stuff. Sounded interesting.'

'No one tells me that shit. You'd hear about it first.'

'Dave hasn't said nothing then.'

'Haven't seen him for a while as it happens.'

'Yeah.'

Steve is being fucking strange. Tony wants to get out but Maze Hill comes and goes and he is still stuck in the skins' improvised airlock.

Steve says, 'So you're officially unaffiliated.'

'Free agent you might say.'

'Yeah well.' Steve considers the ceiling. 'Listen. There's a few of us never left the BM in the first place, do you know what I mean? Just because that Scouser pillock of a milkman wanted out.

'We kept it quiet for a bit, had to sort a few things. But we're growing now. Slowly. Telling some of the old members as and when. Blokes with experience. Do a bit of business on the side, if you follow me.

'There's some good stuff on the burner. Country sports you know? Gun clubs. Got some lads in the TA and all. Defence begins at home so they say.'

'You've been busy.'

'Just help out where I can mate. Anyway what I'm trying to say, I could mention your name if you're interested.'

Westcombe Park has come and gone. If Tony doesn't leave at the next stop they will be getting off together. 'Sounds interesting,' he says. 'Definitely. But tell me more next time, I'm getting off in a minute.'

'Isn't Dockyard better for you?' says Steve. He leans in confidentially. 'Thing is mate that pack of niggers in the next compartment – you must have heard our little set-to at London Bridge. Well they haven't got off yet. They won't have a go as long as we're together and if they do we'll have them, but if they spot you jumping off alone they might fancy their chances. Not that you couldn't take six jungle bunnies single-handed or nothing.'

Tony grimaces: 'Fair point.' Steve is right: it would be asking for trouble.

But as they roll into Charlton Steve pats his knee. 'No,' he says, standing up, 'you get off where you want to mate. We'll keep them entertained. What you want to do,' he tells Tony as the train stops, 'is come round Kings Cross some time. The Ferndale Hotel in Argyle Square. You must have heard of it.

I'm usually there on a Sunday. There's people you should get to know.' They are on the platform now. Steve marches straight to the blacks' compartment. 'Get yourself some kip,' he tells Tony, then throws open the door and declaims, 'Bloke walks into a pub with a crocodile, goes up to the bar and says, "Do you serve niggers in here?"'

To the blacks' almost dutiful sounds of outrage, Steve climbs inside with his mates following.

'Governor goes, "Course we do, we're not racist." So the bloke says, "I'll have a pint of lager and a nigger for the crocodile."'

Closing the door behind him, the last skin gives Tony a flat look through the window that could signify either brotherhood or contempt. As the train pulls away Tony hears the blacks shouting, Steve's burlesque surprise, the overture to a proper fight.

When it has gone Tony stands with his hands on his knees. 'Fuck,' he says. 'Jesus. Fuck.' Blood pulses in the full of his face, a hot mask squeezing him. 'Shit': only barely not yelled. His eyes are prickling; he might really cry. He kicks the nearest thing hard, a waste bin. It gives a dull brief ring. Grow up, you cunt, he thinks, and walks on, but his legs are shaking stupidly and soon he sits straight down on the platform. He wipes his eyes. Just give it a minute and he'll stand up.

It is Steve's wink that keeps coming back to him. It was nothing probably, but still, how fucking *strange*. And that talk about his boy getting buggered, of all sick shit. Jesus. The kid's only three or something.

Just one more minute. It's good he got off at Charlton, being stuck with them any longer would have done his head in. At least if someone comes out and calls you queer you know where you stand.

Somebody is watching him, approaching down the platform. Tony looks up. The boy from the Craven Club.

'What do you fucking want?' says Tony.

'You invited me home with you.'

'Yeah well.'

The boy looks up at the sky. He says, 'Your mates – were those your mates? They nearly kicked my head in. They were close, weren't they? They could have killed me. Really killed me. Would you have done anything?'

'I wouldn't have let them.'

'What would you have done?'

Tony looks at him. 'Thought you got off at Deptford.'

'I got on another carriage. It's lucky I saw you, I was waiting for Woolwich Dockyard.'

'You'd have run into all them lot probably.'

'Oh God.' His voice shakes at the thought.

'No, they'll be busy with the niggers now.'

'Jesus,' the boy says.

'What?'

'Nothing. You really talk like that. Do you think I'm a queer bastard AIDS carrier too?'

'I hope not.' Tony gives a sort of laugh. 'If you're still coming I mean. Are you?'

'Half of me,' the boy says, 'wants to beat the fucking shit out of you.'

'You wouldn't get very far but you can try if you like.'

The boy sits down next to Tony. 'Well,' he says, looking straight ahead, 'I suppose I was originally hoping for the other way round.'

'What really? Beat you up?'

'Not . . . seriously. You know, just a bit.'

'Slap you around a bit.'

'Not seriously or anything. Not like them.'

'Well this is it.' Tony holds the door for the boy, whose name is Chris. 'Luxury accommodation isn't it. Do you want a drink?'

'Are you having anything?'

'Don't laugh but I'm having a cup of tea. But I've got beer if you want.'

'Tea's perfect actually, thanks.'

'Milk and sugar?'

'Just milk please.'

He has to wipe out two mugs. The teabags float half out of the hot water. He forces them down a couple of times to stew better but they keep bobbing back up. Witches, he thinks. Burn them all.

In the bedroom Chris is looking at his walls: posters for *Hail the New Dawn* and the Waffen-SS, Union Jack, small portrait of Hitler. 'Thanks,' he says, handed the tea, and sits next to Tony on the bed. They sip slowly, waiting for it to cool.

Tony says, 'One of the blokes I was talking to at the bar said you was eyeing him up and all.'

'The one with the boots on his T-shirt?'

'Paying attention wasn't you?'

'Just a bit.'

'Bit of a skinhead thing going on.'

'I was only looking at him until you came in.'

Tony says, 'Put down your tea a minute.'

Chris's mouth tastes of milk and cigarettes. His head trembles in Tony's hand, which pulls it against him, lacing fingers through wads of hair. Tony's tongue is a thug against his.

Tony says, 'You're a good kisser aren't you.'

Chris smiles as if to say that's not all. He pushes himself back from Tony and lowers himself off the edge of the bed to the floor, where he kneels. Supporting himself on his balled fists, he leans forward and kisses Tony's left boot, about halfway up, looks back at Tony watching him. He repeats the kiss a couple of times, then licks the same place gently, just a small patch on the side, a taste. He grips Tony's booted leg in

234

both hands, his left on the back of Tony's calf, his right anchoring the toecap to the floor, and in a series of overlapping strokes pushes the wetness out from its starting point, slightly further each time. He is working himself up to move down towards the feet, along the gradient of accumulating dirt.

Tony reaches down to touch his head. He says, 'Come back up here.'

'What are your tattoos for?'

'I'll show you. Look. This is the first one I got, this is Borstal tears. When I was inside as a kid. A lot of lads who've been to Borstal have them. Some people just have dots, but in the same place, it's the same thing. They're fading though because it's only biro ink.

'This symbol's for the British Movement. I got that done in '77, a couple of months after I joined. How old were you then?'

'Eleven or twelve.'

'Yeah well I'm not saying nothing. Couple of swastikas here and here. They're from around the time that cunt Thatcher got in.

'That one's just a picture I liked, it don't mean anything.

'Skrewdriver, here, I know you know who they are. I got that when their album come out last summer.'

'Is that it?'

'For now yeah.'

'None hidden away? That's a pity. What are you going to get next?'

'I don't know. Nothing for a while.'

'You should get that one with the dotted line across the neck' – his fingertip traces it – 'and CUT HERE written on it.'

'You'd like that would you?'

'God yeah. I think those are fucking sexy.'

'Yeah well it's not you has to wear it all the time. You got any?'

'Tattoos? Course not.'
'Show me then.'

Chris's body keeps surprising him in its simplicity, the way it offers a kind of rediscovery of something forgotten. Like a flower, thinks Tony, trying to pinpoint it, like a spring flower after winter, and then, confusing himself a little, like a glass of milk, or one of them yoghurts that aren't flavoured. Like a bath. But Chris, blind to the timelessness of his body's simply being, wants other stuff, has the restlessness of a scavenging animal. He keeps turning to expose himself, he unfolds urgently, like a blank page that wants marking. Tony keeps holding and kissing him but the moment he lets up his grip Chris is diving again, this way, that, in his earnest semaphore, and there is the constant tug back to Tony's boots, which Chris won't let him take off, which draw Chris like a scent obsessing a dog: you yank it back with the leash and it seems to concede but in another moment there it is, off again. How do you keep a boy like this? In the end he lets him go, and Chris gives a little indulgent giggle as if to say, There, I knew you wanted it, almost a snigger, really, something foul about it, and he is down on the boots like a limpet and giving them intense attention, incredible, a huge fucking turn-on of a sight, but frustrating, because your boots can't feel anything can they; you'd rather have him back up here doing it to you. If you could only hold him, if you could grasp what he has to offer that he doesn't seem to notice, let alone value, it could really be something; and Tony suddenly has this bizarre vision of himself in a student bar, at the centre of a crowd of, Jesus, students, girls with hammer-and-sickle badges and attentive Chinks and even blacks, blacks with glasses and books, and they're all watching Tony with smiles as he says, 'But then I met him,' squeezing Chris's knee, 'didn't I? And now here I am' . . . the life, it must be, contained in that little balled-up body down there, if you could only reach out and take it, the body that is giving you regular polling glances between its fervent local application, begging glances, and when you reach down and touch its cheek the reaction is so immediate, the little anticipatory wince, the gasp, that it's clear what it's begging for; well, you have to start with where you are, you know why he went for you. So Tony slaps him, not hard, across the face, and immediately the boy's full attention snaps on, like something plugged in, the eyes fixed on you, the connection made; and so he slaps him harder, and Chris's whole body, vindicated, begins to vibrate with excitement.

Tony grips him by his hair with his left hand and with his right hand he fucking belts him one.

Some time later Chris says, 'Wait. Have you – have you got any more stuff?'

'What do you mean?'

'Any more nazi stuff.'

'What for?'

'Just to have out. To look at.' He smiles. 'It's a big turn-on.'

'Oh.' Tony relaxes his grip. 'I've got some magazines . . .' Then something occurs to him: 'Hang about. Stay there.'

He pulls a chair over to his cupboard, stands on it (aware of the sight he must be from that angle, the wobble of his arse) and reaches for the bin bag. 'Stand up,' he tells Chris, climbing down again. He rips the black plastic, too tightly knotted to untie easily, and slides out its contents. He unbundles the flag – he'd forgotten how heavy it was – and gripping the long edge shakes it out and lays it flat on the bed like a sheet.

The flag creates silence for a moment.

'Jesus,' says Chris. 'That's amazing.' He puts a finger to it. 'It looks really old. Is it real?'

'Course it's real.'

'How did you get this?'

'An old lady give it me.'

Chris strokes the flag. He traces the black piece, with its border of heavy stitches. 'It's amazing,' he says again.

'Go on,' says Tony. 'Lie down.'

And again, later still: 'Wait.'

'Too much?'

'No, I . . . I don't know if you should do that.'

'Don't you want me to?'

'God yes.'

'Well then.'

'No, but I just – I'm not sure it's a good idea.'

'Why not?'

'You know . . . Health.'

'Oh.' Tony sits.

'I didn't want to make you stop.'

'Yeah.'

'I just think we should . . . sorry.'

'It's OK.'

Chris says, quietly: 'Shit.' He reaches for Tony, who takes his hand and lifts it off again: 'Give it a bit.' In the silence they newly hear the faint thud of some neighbour's stereo.

Tony stands. He fetches his cigarettes from the kitchen. 'Want one?'

'Thanks.'

They sit, smoking: Tony on the edge of the bed, Chris on the flag-draped mattress with his back to the wall and his knees drawn up. After a while, with his big toe, he tentatively strokes the small of Tony's back. 'You OK?'

Tony exhales smoke. 'I saw this bloke today I used to know. Outside the club. He was sick, he looked fucking horrible. He didn't say but it must have been . . . He came inside, the one in the wheelchair? I carried it upstairs for him. It was probably stupid but I thought I should.'

'I'm sure it's fine. You just carried his chair?'

'Yeah.'

'Well, then. And you washed your hands after?'

'I mean after a while I did.'

'Anyway I don't think you get it from that. You get it from – you know. This.'

'Brilliant, thanks.'

'But not if you're careful. I mean, they say unless you're *really* promiscuous then you should be all right, if you avoid anal sex. You know, fucking. Which is why I . . . and just make sure the guys you have sex with are in good health and aren't promiscuous either. Oh, and avoid people who've been sexually active in America. You haven't have you?'

'Never been.'

'Well then. That's it basically. Listen to me, I sound like *Gay Times*.'

'That's not so—'

'No, see?'

'But how do you know if someone's – they say "in good health"—'

'Well, it's not, they're not worried about a cold, are they? The guy you saw today, in the chair, you wouldn't have slept with him, right?'

Tony manages half a laugh, and Chris smiles: 'So.'

'And besides that you can—'

'Yes. I mean, technically they've found HTLV-3 in saliva, so even snogging you can't be sure, but I think at a certain point what are you supposed to do? If you follow the main guidelines. That's what I'm doing . . . It could turn out to be a big fuss over nothing, anyway. All this talk about how the numbers are going to skyrocket, there's no way they can know that.'

'Saliva's spit, isn't it? Fuck knows what I touched.'

'But I'm saying. If you got it like that half the country would be dead.'

'Yeah.'

'Wow. Really killed the mood, haven't I?'

Tony smiles. 'Sorry.'

'Tell you what. Just lie down and close your eyes. Go on.'

.' . . I'm quite tired mate.'

'Oh, *poo*. Well, that's age for you.'

'Fuck off.'

Chris says quietly, 'Are you sure?'

'Yeah I should get some sleep.'

'Do you want me to go?'

'You don't have to.'

'OK.'

'But stand up a minute. I should move this.'

They get off the bed and Tony lifts the flag by one of its shorter ends. 'Can you help me fold it?'

Touching his corners to Tony's, Chris asks, 'What are these stains on it?'

'Dead men's blood.'

He starts. 'You're joking, right? Don't try to scare me, I'm serious.'

'I didn't kill no one you soppy cunt. German blood. National Socialists.'

'From the war?'

'From before the war.'

'I don't understand. What is this? How come you have it?'

'You wouldn't believe me if I told you.'

'Try me.'

'No. I'll tell you one thing though. Hitler's held this flag.'

'Now you are kidding.'

'Swear to God.'

'Fuck. *Fuck!* . . . How much is it worth?'

'Enough.'

'Aren't you worried someone might steal it?'

'For a while I was. But I don't think no one knows about it. Except you. That old lady who give it me died soon after.'

240

Chris uses the bathroom. When he comes back he says, 'I should go.'

'You don't have to.'

'I know, but . . . I've got classes in the morning.'

'Trains have stopped.'

'I'll find a night bus or something.'

'Up to you anyway.'

When he has gone Tony wraps his legs around the bundled sheets and murmurs to them in the dark as if they were Chris, staying.

SKINHEAD PRODUCTIONS
BY SKINS...4 SKINS
PRESENTS......

skinhead   boot-a-gram!

If you want to shock your boss or friends this Christmas, then call us
to deliver your Christmas present or card. We'll send round two or three
rather large Real Skinheads, covered in tattoo's and not the sort of lads
your boss would like to meet in a light alley-yet alone a dark alley!

So give us a call and we'll do the rest. Phone: 04024- 58552 (24 hours)

Flyer, *circa* December 1985

WHY I'M A

BY THE BROTHER

Sometimes I feel I already live in the future, where every joint and tenon of society has cracked off and the whole edifice disarticulates and crumbles away, leaving us squabbling on a bare plain, naked as the ancestors they keep digging from the Olduvai Gorge. I walk down the street and the paper-thin frieze of building societies and unisex hairdressers is a film they're showing me. Behind the screen we're all animals.

I grew up in remotest and desolate suburbia, a cold, clever little boy who was older than his parents by the time he was 10. Untidy, shy and eccentric, I was at first bullied then ignored. I had no friends from 11 to 16. In my bedroom I was a space captain. I wandered lonely as a cloud on my bicycle and discovered by looking through the right holes what respectable suburban men did with each other in toilets. I joined in with enthusiasm. At school I was Charles Laughton. In the cottages I was James Dean. The human, sociable me was the fat boy who got picked last for the football team. The animal me was a sweet little angel of sex who galvanised lonely, guilty men for a few minutes and then vanished with a grin. I've felt better as an animal ever since.

The skinhead is beyond fashion and cannot be assimilated. If he is stupid he is a black hole, an anti-human, sucking in all the abundant hatred that lies to hand and re-radiating it. He exists only in the mirror of other skins' faces. If he is clever he is the eternal outsider, using his image to constantly vary and contradict himself, able to walk anywhere, his passport the astonishment of the sharp mind in the brainless stereotype. His clothes have not the sameness of a uniform, but of a hide; they are anti-clothes, reduced to the function of an animal's coat; his boots are his hooves. This animal's only secondary sexual characteristics are his braces, worn up to exaggerate the width of the shoulders, down to emphasise the curve of the bum. He is pure sex because no intellectual drives can be read into him, not the mod's urge to conform and better himself, not the punk's longing for integrity. He is an anarchist not because he rejects rules but because they cannot be applied to him. They slip off.

Square Peg 12, 1986

ⓝⓕ ENTERPRISES LTD. IN ASSOCIATION WITH

MOLOTOV PRODUCTIONS.

PRESENTS

RACIAL ATTACK AGRAM

NIGGERS JUST MOVED IN THE AREA?

INDIAN TAKE AWAY SERVING CAT AGAIN?

DONT GET EVICTED. LEAVE THEM TO US!

send them a SMASHING message

Flyer, Manchester area, 1986

ABOVE THE RUINS......

I RECIEVED THIS TAPE OF PATRICK HARRINGTON AND WAS QUITE SUPRISED TO HEAR
WHAT I HEARD. SIDE ONE OPENED WITH "WAITING" IT IS A SLOW NUMBER WITH A
REALLY GOOD BEAT TO IT AND BRILLIANT LYRICS. THE NEXT TRACK IS "STORMCLOUDS
OVER EUROPE"WHICH IS ABOUT THE BERLIN WALL AND HOW EUROPE HAS BEEN RAPED
BY THE DISEASE OF COMMUNISM. "ROSES"THE NEXT TRACK IS ABOUT A SOLDIER DYING,
THE NEXT TRACK "LAST RITE IS AN INSTRUMENTAL WHICH IS VERY TUNEFUL. THE
LAST TRACK ON SIDE ONE IS "UNDER WESTERN SKYS" WHICH WAS VERY GOOD. SIDE
TWO KICKED OFF WITH "SONG OF THE WOLF"WHICH IS THE TITLE TRACK OF THIS
CASSETTE L. P"100 FLAGS"THE NEXT TRACK WASENT REALLY MY CUP OF TEA, BUT A
LOT OF PEOPLE WILL LIKE IT THE SECOND FROM LAST TRACK "PROGRESS"IS ONE
OF THE BEST WITH LYRICS LIKE"ITS BEST TO BE HUMBLE AND DO AS YOUR TOLD,
TO SPEAK AS YOUR TAUGTH AND DIE WHEN YOUR OLD, FOR SUCH IS THE MEANING
OF MARX AND HIS,WINE FOR THE REDS AND CHAINS FOR THE HERD". THE LAST TRACK
"MAKE US STRONG"IS VERY POWERFUL AND VERY GOOD. THE ABOVE THE RUINS "SONGS
OF THE WOLF TAPE IS VERY GOOD AND WELL WERTH BYING.

SONGS OF THE WOLF BY; ABOVE THE RUINS, IS
AVAILABLE FROM; BCM GRIMNIR, LONDON, WC1N 3XX. PRICE
£3,30 INCLUDING P&P. CHEQUES OR P.O.s SHOULD BE MADE
**/ABLE TO; GRIMNIR.

English Rose fanzine 3, *circa* 1986

Boots and Braces

A man in his sixties left the shop as I approached. He wore full skinhead gear: red-laced boots, bleached jeans, black jacket open to a vest that made the shape of his torso, with its wrinkled dugs, uncomfortably explicit. He stopped in the street and raised his left hand before his face, then gripped it hard with his right. He was in pain, arthritis perhaps; he grimaced as he squeezed, endlessly adjusting his grip, until he was almost in tears with distress: as if the pain were a blister he had no strength to burst. The walls of the shop were hung with netting, and gas masks stood on display. The twenty-hole Rangers I tried first seemed too big, but unwilling to repeat my blushing farce of lacing, painfully exacerbated by the assistant's sympathy, I bought them anyway. They cost considerably more than I had expected.

Later that evening, looking at myself in the mirror, I was mortified by their naked fetishism. Their brand-new gleam, fresh from the box, insinuated hours of devoted burnishing, and they climbed high up my calves with a shameless plasticity. With a pair of jeans rolled above them and a black Fred Perry, both borrowed from Adam, my lack of authenticity seemed horribly visible, as if quote marks swarmed about me like moths.

'It's not very you,' said Adam. But it is you, I thought, watching him get ready with a dreamy anticipation untainted, for once, by the knowledge that I could not follow. Usually, when he dressed for a night like this, or some private meet, I would be struggling not to manifest my exclusion, and the absence of that familiar anxiety was almost numbing. I ended up drifting through the flat after him in a haze of pleasure, or rather the promise of it, still frustratingly intangible, which I tried to reify by inventing new rituals of intimacy: offering, for example, to shave Adam's head. He said no, but seemed happy for me to watch: his fingertips, checking for completeness, made confident, musical patterns on his scalp. Afterwards he stood quite still beneath the shower, letting the flecked suds roll before its enveloping sheen. Not for the first time I was taken aback by this slim, quietly muscled body and my claim on it: if not exclusive then at least unique. On his left shoulder, unmarked except by the pale bump from his BCG injection, he had been talking about getting his first tattoo, from which might follow the whole foreign syllabary of possible piercings. I pictured us entering the club in our similar gear. I had only a vague conception of the place, but I thought we might be young for the crowd. I imagined kissing Adam there and perhaps, in that environment, more: saw us spotlit, and aspired to.

When Adam was dry he put on a red jockstrap and long socks; then combat trousers, cropped and bluntly stained. He fastened his boots with none of my neophyte fumblings. A trail of hair emerged from his groin like an access route, but the chest above it was shaved as usual. He harnessed his T-shirt in place with red braces and fastened a wide leather cuff round his right wrist. He pulled on his bomber jacket and checked his reflection. 'Are we off then?' he said.

Adam planned to drink, so we took a minicab, for which I was grateful; on the bus my outfit could have precipitated in me a surfeit of neuroses. Inside we deposited our coats and paid the entrance fee to a goateed man with whom Adam exchanged a few familiar words. There was a mirror by the coat check: Adam examined himself again, and produced a length of metal chain from his pocket, which he wore as a necklace, linking its ends in front of him with a padlock that he left unfastened. He saw me beside him in the glass and said, 'No specs.'

'I won't see anything.'

'You'll see enough.' He lifted them off, folded them and put them in a side pocket of his combats: 'That's better.' I could see his smile, but everything beyond had collapsed into a defocused haze, no man's land fizzing with noise where sharp edges had been. I could no longer read the notice on the wall that outlined the dress code, the restrictions, the limits of responsibility.

I followed Adam in. It seemed tiny at first: a good chunk of the railway arch it occupied was taken up by the cloakroom and entrance area, from which we emerged against a bar wedged beneath the curving wall. Its ranged, illuminated bottles, simplified by my blurred vision into uniformity, like a kaleidoscope effect, reminded me for reasons I couldn't grasp of the silent movie *M*, which I had seen at college and hardly thought of since. Before the bar was the narrowest of spaces, which extended into a corridor that grew quickly dark as Adam led me down, so architecture became hard to distinguish. I saw brick at times, in the red trickle of occasional dim lights; dividers of mesh and corrugated metal gave a maze-like atmosphere through which silent figures moved. Even with my glasses I would barely have seen them until they were next to me (with every man you passed there was a pause, a glance, like a factory conveyor halting for quality control); as it was, my short sight reduced people to their most cartoon attributes: heavy earring; beard; inked skull; leather cap. I thought: Isn't it all skins, then? The muffled beat of music pulsed like blood in the building's walls, as if we were inside the head of someone listening. I was just thinking how all this was like a bad movie cliché of itself, and trying to decide if that disappointed me, when Adam rounded a corner and the space opened up around us. We had emerged into a second arch; I saw another bar, more comfortably proportioned, lit up like a town approached at night. This was the source of the music, which was revealed – as the dampening effect fell away, and with it any potency – as generic hard beat.

'They're here,' Adam said ahead of me, waving, and pushed through to the bar. I kept my hand on the small of his back so as not to lose him, and eventually made out Philip and Tom leaning against the counter. We kissed hello, and Philip said, 'Why, Miss Jones, you're beautiful.'

'Ha ha.'

'Are you wearing contacts?'

'You know I don't wear contacts.'

'Can you see that?' pointed Tom, and I squinted at the screens behind the bar: 'I can see bodies,' I said, 'but not what they're doing.'

'Lucky you.'

I looked them up and down. Both wore ankle-length Doc Martens, jeans and short-sleeved shirts. It was the bare minimum: skin-casual. Philip at least had braces (just visible beneath a combat jacket) and, of course, cropped hair: as for Tom, I asked: 'They let you in with all that on your head?'

'Look around. It's not unusual.'

I could see enough to tell that he was right, as had been my impression in the corridor. Of our nearest neighbours I counted three skins, two guys in leather, and a tall black man in a rubber apron, like something from a camp musical remake of *The Texas Chain Saw Massacre*.

'I thought it was a skin night,' I complained to Adam.

'It is. It just affects the proportions.'

'But they're not even bothering with the music.'

'What were you expecting? Reggae?'

'Yeah. You know' – I did a little movement – '"I want all you skinheads to get up on your feet." Or at least a bit of Cockney Rejects.'

'You really have no idea, do you?'

Next to me a man with a shaved head, heavily tattooed muscles and mud-spattered hobnail boots asked the barman for a single Sapphire and tonic. 'Life,' I said, 'is endlessly disappointing.'

'Don't knock it too much,' Philip said. 'We're all here on your account.'

'My apologies.'

'Oh, *I'm* all right. I'm reliving my youth.' He had been a skinhead of sorts, in his queer-activist days: it was the subject of an Ellen Marsh photo. He had been rather beautiful then.

The music thumped away; various blurred abstractions bought various blurred drinks. Everything was black surface, pinkish flesh. We looked vaguely about us; no one could think of much to say. After a while I announced brightly: 'Theweleit says that the very prohibition of gay sex in the Third Reich made it a key area of transgression into which the fascist power élite had to be initiated.'

'Who says what?' said Tom.

'Klaus Theweleit. Because the anus, you see, is the ultimate sluice.'

'They did put gay men in concentration camps, James,' said Adam quietly.

'So is that what we're here for,' Tom said, 'your research? You going to "interview" some leather queens in the back room?' He smiled sweetly, as if I was imagining any nastiness. For my best friend's boyfriend, I hadn't seen much of Tom since that dinner nearly a year ago. Either I deliberately saw

Philip alone, or Tom was said to be busy in advance, or Philip simply turned up without him, alleging some work panic or stomach bug. How Philip felt about this I didn't know: my own irritation at being snubbed was more than compensated for by Tom's absence. I decided to ignore his dig.

'Perhaps I should. I could march in and shout, "Take me to the LOG!"'

'You're still running with the conspiracy plot?' Philip said. 'Is there anyone you haven't implicated yet?'

'I'm struggling to squeeze in the political soldiers.'

'Oh, that's *easy*. Griffin, Fiore, Evola, Kali Yuga, Savitri Devi. Bish bash bosh.'

'The problem is, Evola's rather boring.'

'I'm relieved to hear you say that.'

'Actually, I'm getting slightly creeped out by the real connections.'

'Between the Front and the occult?'

'Between fucking everyone. I was reading the *Scorpion*, this would-be-intellectual journal put out by Michael Walker, who used to run a tour company with Nick Griffin and Roberto Fiore. So in summer '93, just before Nicky died, Walker published an article by Stephen Cox, who ran something called the Jarls of Bælder, which as far as I can tell was a sort of occult, quasi-nazi homoerotic naturist group. Bælder had, or has, a secret inner order called the Fraternitas Loki, devoted to "covert aeonic action": aeonics is a key Nine Angles term, and in Norse mythology Loki was the father of Fenrir, the wolf, right? The Above the Ruins album was *Songs of the Wolf*, and *Fenrir* was the in-house journal of the ONA . . . Anyway, Cox's piece is this barking analysis of European history that says we need to reappraise the Third Reich and seek our destiny among the stars. And it's illustrated with diagrams that say, at the bottom: copyright Order of Nine Angles. So this is *explicit* Nine Angles material appearing in *the* major British journal of the new right. They're all over each other. Actually I was going to have the L in LOG stand for Longinus, because my plot's based around the Heilige Lanze. But maybe Loki makes more sense . . .'

'And on *that* note,' said Adam, 'I'm having a look round.'

'I'll come with you.' It got darker the deeper we went into the arch. Under the higher part of the roof, metal dividers grew to a raised gallery. I followed Adam up the stairs, where I brushed against a descending skin, thirty or so, and caught his eye; at the top I looked back, but couldn't see, in the unlit blur, if he was reciprocating.

The structure trembled under our boots. It could have been the prow of a ship: men promenaded (one even led an exposed, cowed creature on a leash), peered over the railing at the turmoil below or stood in close pairs, muttering over obscure interactions. Adam found a place at the rail. I stood next to him and put my hand against the small of his back. He kept looking down.

'Kiss me,' I said.

Adam pulled a face.

'Go on.' I kicked his ankle gently, with mock/real peevishness. 'Kiss me.'

He did. We stood for a moment, and he smiled at me. Then he said, 'I'm going for a wander, OK?'

'I'll come.'

'I'll see you back at the bar.'

'Ads . . .'

He fingered my – his – Fred Perry. 'This *so* isn't you. Look at that.' He pointed down to where a shadow seemed to move around a source of light. I squinted hopelessly. 'What is it?' I asked, but he had gone.

I blinked around me at the milling figures. One or two got close enough to catch my eye: I dropped my gaze; they walked on. I could make out the illuminated cluster of the bar, its light reflected in shaved heads, and thought I should go back to Philip and Tom, but when I made my way there, moving uncertainly down the metal steps (which seemed newly steep), I couldn't find them. I bought another beer and investigated the warren of space beneath the gallery. Like a tourist at a spice market, nervous of being trapped into purchasing, I was careful to look across people rather than at them, and avoid staying in one place too long. I pushed through gaps, ducked round corners. The music's unrelenting beat insisted it was a soundtrack to all this, and kept tricking me into believing there was a shape to my movements; when I noticed this I played a version of a game I'd once invented on a train, watching the landscape pass with my headphones on: to make myself perceive sound and action separately, in their utter lack of relation. I failed at this, as I always did.

I stepped into an alcove to let someone pass but he followed me in. It was the skin from the stairs.

'Got a light?' His accent was south London, or maybe East End.

'I don't smoke, sorry.'

'Yeah all right, geezer.' He smiled as if I'd made a joke, and didn't move. We looked at each other for a long moment. He said, 'Having a good evening?'

'Not bad.' I swigged my Beck's. His eyes were close enough to see now, pale and blue. 'How about you?'

'Yeah likewise. Just checking it out, you know, seeing who's my type.'

'So who is your type?'

When he rested a hand on my midriff I didn't flinch. I could make out his freckles and orange stubble. There was a certain deliberate resolve to the set of his chin, as if pre-emptively forestalling some quibble.

He said, 'You are.'

'In what way?'

'Well now. Young and cute, for a start.' He touched my face. 'Fit but not a muscle Mary.' My arm. 'Cropped. Pale.'

'Pale? Thanks.'

'Yeah, I like pale skin.'

I couldn't stop myself: 'Not too big on black guys, then.'

The skin smiled and looked at the ceiling. 'We-l-l,' he said, stretching it out. 'Yes and no, fella.'

'What do you mean?'

'Well I definitely don't find them a sexual turn-on.'

I smiled: 'As opposed to?'

'What do you mean?'

'As opposed to what kind of turn-on?'

He frowned, as if it was me that was thick. 'I mean I don't fancy them.'

'OK.'

'No,' he said, 'I like white lads, me.'

'Right.' I thought: Please stop talking now and touch me again. But I had started a chain of thought, and I must have seemed too open to ideas, or perhaps, after that last exchange, in need of education, because he went on.

'Just don't like the black attitude, you know what I mean?'

With what I hoped was edge I asked: 'What's the black attitude?'

'You know. Kissing teeth and all that. And the overall appearance.'

'I didn't know there was one.'

'Oh definitely. Mind you, I do have black mates.'

'Well there you go.'

'But they've rejected a lot of that stuff.'

'Have they.'

'Says a lot I think.'

'It does.'

'So anyway.' He smiled. 'What's your type?'

I said, 'Yeah. Actually I think I need to find my friend, sorry.'

He raised his eyebrows and shrugged. 'No worries, fella.'

I ducked out of the alcove without looking back and squeezed between the men lining this section of the corridor, aware that my constant use of 'Excuse me' was inappropriate but unable to restrain it. A few metres on someone grabbed my shoulder.

'Who was that?' Philip said.

'Who was who?'

'Your little friend just now. You looked cosy.'

'Oh. Turns out, a racist prole. Why are people such stereotypes?'

'Because that's how you want them. Did you get off on it?'

'Don't be silly.'

'Hmm,' he said. He reached down for me and winked. 'Liar.'

'Where's Tom?' I asked.

'Good question. Where's Adam?'

'Gone for a *wander*.'

He pinched my cheek. I said in a pissy whisper: '"They *did* put gay men in concen*tration* camps, James."'

'Naughty,' muttered Philip, and pulled me against him, hard. I opened my mouth. I closed my eyes. The beat was not our soundtrack. His chest hair tickled me through his shirt's open neck. I fingered the long furrow of his spine, and tried to trap his tongue with mine when it came in quick sly swoops. My hands moved round him and down his front, grasping his braces like a ladder's sides. Feeling his tug at my waist I grabbed his fly and got it open: worked my fingers inside, towards warmth and tackiness. I hooked two of them round my target and worked it gracelessly out; shook hands briefly to renew acquaintance, then looked down, breathed in, dived. But seconds later he was pushing me off again, and I strained my knees to stand. He said, 'Tom's over there.'

'Where?'

'Don't look.' He gave the inside of my mouth a final, furtive lick and said, 'Find us at the bar in a bit.'

I walked off in the other direction, only realizing as my jeans sank around me that he'd unfastened them. Zipping up, I thought the action was garnering me credit, as if I had done what I'd set out to. In any case I needed to pee; I found my way somehow to the toilets, but as I waited, unzipped again, for the usual pause to pass, I felt a nudging against my shin that made me think of Adam's cat. Beneath me a squatting figure, naked but for a jockstrap, was nuzzling my boots. As I looked down he smiled back with incongruous affection. He was South Asian, probably, thirty or so, with a scraggly mop of hair brushing the urinal and gap teeth revealed by a mouth so far open that his pleasant face contorted around it. With glasses on I could have seen his tonsils.

'Go on,' someone said, 'it's what he wants,' and in apparent agreement the crouching man widened his maw further, twitching its corners in a grin and lolling from it a shadowy tongue.

'It won't cost you anything,' said the voice.

'Sorry,' I mumbled ashamedly to the waiting man, 'I can't.' At once his expression turned flat and bored. He shrugged, and shuffled off.

The entrance to the smaller arch was framed with slouching figures like warnings or advertisements, who watched in lazy synchrony as I pushed my way between them. I progressed to its further recesses, registering with uninvolved curiosity the various shrouded gestures, the transactions and refigurings, taking place on the margins as I passed. A Socratic beard munched pedagogically on a glabrous nipple; a testis demonstrated its resilience; tattoos stretched and strained. What had I imagined: that I would discover beneath Vauxhall railway the persistence of a subculture unaltered by time, like a movie hero uncovering the rituals of the exiled Reich? At the threshold of the final room, the level of illumination was, perhaps in reward, very slightly higher, so that its shape was more apparent: a brick chamber, relatively large (or so it felt after the constriction of the approach), suspended in a haze of the ubiquitous, uninspired red light. My eyesight had not, of course, improved, but I had rather got used to it, so that the vague apprehension I had of my surroundings now seemed about right, as if it would have been presumptuous to expect more detail. No, the blur was . . . *appropriate*: with this saturated palette it looked not so much like watercolour as long photographic exposure, and lent a particular expressiveness, but also a certain discretion, to the pair of shadows in the corner, studies for a more developed allegory of subjection and compliance; and the quicker host around, action sketches of grasps and nods. Much closer and more clearly visible was the man who stood with his back to me, his posture as legible as the others' but more banal (shoulders – in a leather jerkin – slouched, head to the side, one booted foot tapping); and I realized why I had paused in this doorway: I had joined, unconsciously, the back of a queue. Peering past him I saw five or six men also waiting, the ubiquitous mix of skinheads and leather queens, their costumes progressively less discernible to me as they approached the object of their patience, a repeating and instantly familiar pink spasm in the corner. I put a hand on my neighbour's shoulder as I passed, with the nonsensical impulse to reassure him I wasn't jumping the line; and proceeded, slowly, along the wall of men, touching each in my partial blindness, and regarding their faces in profile: there was a heavily veined neck; one of those massively distending ear piercings (a huge black ring with the lobe stretched thin around it, like a rubber guard); a weak chin and prominent Adam's apple; someone, with concave cheeks, wiping his nose. And then I was at the front, where an overfilled, checked short-sleeved shirt kept up a grunting totter against a thin, braced body that I knew. As I moved round to look at him (both of our heads touched the wall now – my ear, his brow) I saw that the padlock that linked his necklace had been fastened shut; it bounced and jiggled in the space below his chin. Adam had taken his shirt off, and his combats hung down over the tops of his boots. 'I need my glasses,' I told him, 'I want to go,' and he muttered, 'For fuck's sake,' but I was already crouching to retrieve them. His braces trailed on the floor, and in the triangular space under the quaking little lean-to that he made I had to root for his pocket among the folds of cloth. Looking up I noticed that he still wore his jockstrap. I put on my glasses and stood. As I walked out I was careful not to hurry. Most of the still-queuing men avoided my eye when I looked at them, with a focus that now seemed hallucinatory.

I couldn't find Philip. Outside I called Sarah and told her I was coming over. 'What's happened?' she asked, but I just said, 'I'll see you soon.'

The tube had long stopped running: I took the first night bus across the river, sitting behind two boys who began, the moment we left the station, to kiss. They looked like a photograph, their clothes cheaper and more stylish than I would dare, and I imagined that I could catch, where I sat, the evanescent limit of their melded breath. It tasted of their evening just gone – lager, fags, pie and chips: harsh and warm like a fart.

NF dispute spills over into bar-room brawl

By David Rose

The National Front is in the throes of a deep internal split, with rival factions seeking expulsions and High Court injunctions and indulging in bar-room brawls.

At a meeting on Saturday, the NF's executive council voted to suspend the membership of the party chairman, Mr Martin Wingfield, his predecessor, Mr Ian Anderson, and another former chairman, Mr Andrew Brons.

Mr Patrick Harrington, the NF spokesman, said yesterday that he intended to "prosecute" the three and another senior member at a party tribunal and attempt to expel them. He claimed that they had been disloyal in revealing the contents of meetings of the party leadership.

Last week, the faction led by the now-suspended group attempted to take out an injunction freezing party funds. Mr Harrington confirmed that there had earlier been a fight between supporters of the two groups in an east London pub. "There were a few bruises. The police weren't called," he said.

The roots of the split appear to lie in the close association between Mr Harrington and his allies and a group of Italian fascists in London wanted for questioning by the Italian police in connection with terrorist bombings. The connection was a matter of embarrassment and concern to the more traditional faction.

There were further disagreements over discussions held with the Ulster Defence Association in the wake of the Anglo-Irish agreement.

Mr Wingfield said he was hurt and surprised: "Three weeks ago the NF bulletin said I was a martyr for going to prison in defiance of the Race Relations Act. Now they claim I'm in the pay of the Jewish Board of Deputies."

Guardian, 23 May 1986

The truly disruptive purpose and nature of the " N.F.Support Group" can be seen very clearly by examining how the reactionaries have set up their own seperate organisation and the sort of things they do to advance their aims.

They have their own paper THE FLAG. This is in direct competition with NATIONAL FRONT NEWS and was deliberately launched at a time when NFN needed every ounce of the movement's effort put into the drive to make it fortnightly.

* * *

We now have an idea of how far the enemies of Revolutionary Nationalism will go to try to stop us. Fortunately the recent upheaval has purged the movement of the last reactionary elements who always act as their fifth column.

This means that the next moves against us will have to be made openly, with repressive laws and brutal policing. This will inevitably cause us setbacks and suffering, but at least the battlelines will be clearly drawn and the attacks will only serve to strengthen our resolve. We will make whatever sacrifice is necessary for the salvation of our Race and Nation. We will do so without hatred and without fear. And we will win.

To the enemies who have failed to destroy the National Front by guile we give this message: now you can only use brute force, so go ahead and use it. Even if you kill us, you cannot kill our Revolution. Your corrupt System is doomed to collapse, but we will build a new world above the ruins....

* * *

Nick Griffin,
Chairman, National Directorate,
National Front.

This statement was unanimously approved by the National Directorate and written between 1st - 5th August, 1986.

Attempted Murder: the state/reactionary plot against the National Front, 1986

BEHIND THE RUINS

AN interesting new association emerges from a few enquiries into 'Above the Ruins', an NF supported band which is trying to break into the market for racist rock music opened up by the unsavoury likes of Ian Stuart's 'Skrewdriver'. 'Above the Ruins' is not entirely unknown to the NF's current thug-in-chief, Nicky Crane, gauleiter of their Avenell Rd, north London rat hole.

A broadsheet advertising their album is published from a British Monomarks box number in London. And it turns out to be that of ever-so-respectable new rightist Michael Walker, editor of *Scorpion*. He has been, readers will recall, host to convicted terrorist Roberto Fiore, who shared his Pimlico flat.

Searchlight, October 1986

Ian Stuart Donaldson is on the verge of launching a new nazi party along with fellow boot boys Nicola Crane and Des Clarke. So far the party has no name but its publication will be called *Blood and Honour*.

Stuart's main claim to fame is his association with the sick nazi music scene via groups like Skrewdriver and Skullhead.

Crane, the right's finest example of a clinical psychopath, is also engaged in building a "gay skins" movement, which meets on Friday nights at the London Apprentice pub in Shoreditch.

Stuart's existing group, closely linked to the Holland/Griffin faction of the NF, is the White Noise Club. This organisation boasts support from as far away as Chicago, Stockholm and Hamburg. Violence follows them wherever they perform. Their London operational base is the Prince Albert pub in Kings Cross.

Stuart's latest project could well be the next stage of the NF's master plan — the creation of a street fighting crew that can be distanced at least on paper from its NF puppet masters.

Searchlight, October 1987

Bressenden Place

Steve says: 'It's all fucking going to pieces.'

'Come on Steve mate,' says Dave quietly, into his pint.

'Nutty Fairies. Fuck's sake.'

Tony waves at the barman. 'Do you want another?'

'Yeah go on. Look at this mess though. It's a joke.'

'Dave?'

Dave lifts his glass, still half full. 'No I'm all right cheers.'

'Can't even fucking drink properly any more,' says Steve. 'That's your first fucking problem.'

'Two more pints please mate.'

'I mean what the *fuck* is going on out there?'

It is a fair question. Among the troops in the Stag an easy truce operates, but in the street outside a dumb-show of factionalism is being staged by their respective leaders, who stand clutching their flags in little clumps, with occasional waved gestures or messengers scuttling between them: these, and the half-arsed, smirking arbitration of the police.

'It was bad enough last year. Two National Fronts: taking the fucking piss. But last time we marched with you lot and now we're with the others. How fucking stupid do you want us to look?'

It is Sunday, 8 November 1987.

Through the window, they watch Nick Griffin confer with Pat Harrington. Griffin keeps checking his watch. He has grown, Tony notices, a moustache. The effect is strange, but far less than that of Dave's neat schoolboy hair. And his *tie*.

('When did you grow that then?' Tony asked when they saw each other.

'Couple of months now.'

'You trying to go respectable?'

'If you really want to change society your haircut's probably not the single most important thing,' Dave said equitably. 'Is it?'

'Nice suit and all.'

'It's Remembrance Sunday. We're meant to be paying respect.')

Outside it is beginning to drizzle. Two policemen are talking to the leaders of Dave's party: Griffin; the Front's new chairman, Derek Holland, with ugly glasses and a pale, girlish scarf, holding a wreath; and Harrington in his long black trench coat, who dangles a megaphone at his waist, listens to the police, nods. Steve says: 'I see his arm mended.'

'What Herr Flick?' Tony says.

'Yeah. There's a glorious national revolutionary for you. He's going to fucking bottle it if some copper even pulls a face at him.'

Dave smiles. 'I doubt it.'

'Look at him. "Yes officer can I clean out your lovely arse-hole with my tongue please officer." Thieving little prick.'

'It doesn't hurt to look reasonable,' says Dave.

At a table in a corner of the pub a man is sitting alone with a pint of bitter. He must be forty or fifty, clean-shaven and with neat black hair, eyes big like a fish's behind gold-framed spectacles, a dour flat mouth and delicate, pointy ears. He wears a long, dark raincoat that needs a clean; an expensive-looking umbrella with a carved wooden handle is propped up next to him. Every time Tony has glanced in his direction, the man has been looking straight at him. Now it happens again and Tony looks aggressively back, but the man seems quite unfazed and regards him levelly, even raises his glass and sips. Tony would swear he's seen him around before. You'd think Special Branch or something, except they don't dress like that and with all the cops here what would be the point?

'Here.' Dave, who has been digging in his pocket, produces a creased leaflet from which he reads: '"Any attempt by the police to interfere with our traditional rights will be rejected. The non-political parade, the short religious service at the Cenotaph, and the political rally at the end of the activity will all go ahead *regardless* of any possible state bans, police harassment or violent attacks by communist thugs."'

'Believe it when I see it,' says Steve. 'Fucking student politics.'

'Come with us then,' Dave tells him. 'Why not?'

Tony says: 'They wouldn't have us mate. Sully your image and that. Anyway we're independent now aren't we.'

'I don't know who "we" is any more to be honest Tony. What are you these days, BM again is it? BNP?'

'"We" is Blood & Honour.'

'Oh B and H. I thought that was a record club. Or Benson & Hedges. All these Bs I get confused. BHS. B. B. King. Bebop-a-loo-bop.'

'I'll tell you what B stands for,' says Steve. 'British.'

Dave smiles: 'Thought it stood for Blood.'

'*British* Movement. *British* National Party. British. Ring a bell does it?'

'What National Party like National Front?'

'*B* not *P*.' The last letter is spat. 'Right? BM, not PL fucking O. How much did your dues go up last year? Ten times?'

'Something like that. Got to keep out the timewasters haven't we.'

'And did that go to Palestine too or was it just the Skrewdriver money?'

'You got a problem with supporting Palestine?'

'Oh I'm sorry. I thought you was a nationalist.'

'Who's fighting the Zionists Steve?'

'The Zio-whats? You know mate I still remember you fighting the Yids.'

'Crapped my nappies once too. You grow up don't you.'

'And the niggers. Remember them? Can you even say it now? Say "nigger."'

'Come on Steve.'

'Say it. Or have you been brainwashed? Go on. Nig-nig-nig—'

'Nigger. Woo, scary. Nigger wog coon Paki kike. That helping is it?'

'There you go. I knew you had it in you.'

'I can say *sieg heil* too if it makes you happy.'

'How about towel-head?'

'*Sieg heil. Deutschland über alles*. Ten pints of cider and a bag of glue.'

'Towel-head. See? Filthy Arab. Pal-est-inny-un.'

'Pakis are smelly and Hitler lives in Dagenham. *Sieg heil, sieg heil*, let's all go down the pub.'

A general silence follows Dave's improvised song. Tony sees the man with the umbrella leaning over a table at which sit some of the older and more violent *Flag* skins. He mutters something to them and they laugh, then walks out, nodding at Tony as he leaves.

Tony asks: 'Is anyone else hungry?' He watches through the window as the man walks to an old Morris Minor Traveller with a wooden frame, parked where it probably shouldn't be. He drives off without looking at Tony again.

'What time is it?' says Dave.

'Gone half-two.'

'Shouldn't your lot be setting off?'

'There's a Burger King opposite the tube entrance,' Dave tells Tony. 'Or a Casey Jones in the station.'

Steve belches. 'Lesson three. Have a go at this one. Can you say "queer"?'

'Steve mate give it a fucking rest.'

'Go on, say "shirt-lifter." Say "arse-bandit."'

'Hang about,' says Tony, 'something's up.'

'Oh it's us,' says Dave. 'I thought we were going second.' But outside, the police, quite independently of Griffin and his colleagues, are assembling that group's supporters into a waiting queue in the north end of the street. Other officers, some distance behind, marshal together the rival *Flag* group. 'Right,' says Tony, and drains his pint; they wander out. It is getting damp and Tony lights another cigarette. Then he nods to Dave – 'Better get on with it' – and walks with Steve to join the skins among the *Flag* faction. 'Miserable isn't it,' Tony mutters to placate Steve: he nods and wrinkles his nose in response, which is better than nothing. They wait in silence for some moments, and then Steve says, 'They're on to it already, did you see?'

'On to what mate?'

'*Searchlies*. On to Blood & Honour. Big story in the last one, you can't have missed it. Fucking zine's barely out yet.'

'Quick sometimes aren't they.'

'Yeah well you have to wonder who their sources are.' He regards Tony uninterpretably. 'Course they took the chance to call Craney queer again.'

'Did they?' Tony looks back blankly.

'Won't leave it alone mate. Must have been trying that one on for years. Ridiculous isn't it.'

269

'Pathetic is what it is.'

'Can you imagine it, though, Nicky Crane taking it up the arse? Nicky fucking Crane bent over for some old nonce? Oh yeah Daddy yeah fucking give it to me.'

'Want to destabilize us don't they.'

'Oh yeah Daddy that's it oh don't fucking stop Daddy. Eh?'

Steve is getting louder and attracting attention. Tony tries a restrained smile, as if to say he gets the joke but it could have been done better, when suddenly the guys around them start trudging forward, and they follow suit, until the front of their queue has met the rear of Dave's faction ahead. The two clusters of leaders, who stand apart from all this watching, are beginning to frown.

Steve asks someone next to him what's going on, and he shrugs: 'We've all got to go together.' The policeman with Harrington must be saying the same thing, because Harrington now looks unhappy and says something back, then lifts his megaphone, steps forward into an emptier space, and announces: 'We're being told we have to combine the marches but we in the National Front refuse to march alongside people who are wearing swastikas.' At this there is laughter even from his own supporters, much louder from the *Flag* half of the group, who yell insults and start short-lived chants.

Steve shouts: '*Heil Hitler!* You fucking ponce.'

'Bit of a mess all this,' says Dave, as he reappears beside them.

The *Flag* leaders are remonstrating with nearby police and gesturing at Griffin and Harrington, to whom a policeman in an officer's cap talks with his hands in his pockets while Derek Holland stands apart in silence. Tony gives Steve a cigarette; Dave declines. A slow hand-clap builds from the rear of the crowd. Tony wonders if he has time to run to Burger King. It is nearly three-fifteen.

The officer abandons Harrington and talks to his sergeant, who beckons his constables over: they listen, then fan out along the line of waiting marchers, touching arms and speaking quietly. A couple leave the crowd; others argue. When the news reaches Steve he says: 'You're fucking joking.'

'What?'

'They're saying it's rained off.'

Tony says, 'What the whole thing?'

'Shit . . .' says Dave.

Tony says, 'Fuck's *sake*.'

'What fucking rain?'

Steve says, 'Let's see them try to shift us then.'

More policemen are arriving, trying to move the crowd on. Harrington steps forward with his megaphone. 'Here we go,' says Steve.

Harrington is saying: .' . . members of the official National Front that we reassemble in Sloane Square for a drink at seven-thirty this evening. For now if we could all move away down Vauxhall Bridge Road as per police instructions. That's seven-thirty in Sloane Square in Chelsea, thank you.'

He drops the megaphone, stands in place for a minute and raises it again: 'To be clear, this does not contravene police instructions, it's not a political meeting but just a social gathering. Hope to see you all there.' He turns away.

Dave frowns. 'Is that it?'

The people in front begin to disperse. Most wander off in the direction they have been given.

Dave says: 'I don't believe this.'

'Told you he didn't have any bollocks,' says Steve.

'People have come down from all over for this. Midlands, Yorkshire.'

Behind them, most *Flag* supporters have not moved. Several skins try to get a chant going. The *Flag* leaders form a furious circle with the capped officer. One, with a beard and zipped beige coat, grabs a megaphone and strides towards what remains of the crowd, yelling invective against Harrington and his gang of perverts, who have betrayed the movement; his colleague stands awkwardly, clutching the wreath he was meant to lay. Someone else strides along the queue shouting: 'All ex-servicemen to the front of the march please, we're getting ready to move. Ex-servicemen first,' until four policemen frog-march him off.

At this the remaining crowd gives up. A pair of young skins wanders into the distance, still holding between them a banner that even in this mist is thin enough to read, in mirror writing, from behind: ƧЯAW Ƨ'ЯƎHTOЯꓭ ƎЯOM OИ.

Steve says, 'Let's go back in the pub.' But the entrance is guarded by policemen who tell them to move along that way now please lads.

'Right then,' says Tony. 'Burger King.'

Later, Steve and Tony are walking through St James's Park. A small group of old men in uniform stands near the bank of the lake, watching the birds. Steve, who seems cheered to have seen his predictions vindicated, calls out: 'All right grandad?' A pair of veterans look at them: shake their heads, turn away.

Steve says, 'Mate of mine was up in York last year on the BNP march. Says it wasn't bad. Quite a good ruck before except some of the lads got done. Anyway the ones who aren't nicked, they've all met up in some car park for the march, right, and this old geezer starts giving it all this, what do you call it with Hitler at the rallies, blood-flag stuff.'

'*Blutfahne*,' says Tony, and Steve looks at him.

'Blood touching blood,' Tony nods, 'isn't it. Power and that.'

'Well it's all right at Nuremberg. But not in a fucking car park in fucking York. Anyway this geezer, he gets out what he says is the flag of the original BNP, you know from the '60s, and he makes everyone else who's got a flag come forward. And he starts touching them all with his one going, "The flag is the strength giver, the flag is the strength giver."'

'Christ.'

'On the other hand at least they had a fucking march.'

'Not our biggest success today was it.'

'It's not over yet mate.'

In the Store, on Beak Street, Steve's mob is drinking with men in tops by Armani and Marc O'Polo, jeans from Chipie and Chevignon.

'Come on,' Steve says. 'I'll introduce you to some Chelsea fans.'

So after a few more pints it's down Regent Street again and on to Haymarket, walking fast on a new determined wind fuelled by beer and this group, one big gang of booted skins and Headhunters in, well, Timberland moccasins, mainly, or trainers: not much help with kicking but they don't seem worried which you can understand given their reputation. How many guys in total? Sixty, more? Rounding the corner into Trafalgar Square, singing and chanting: everyone gets out of their way except a few tourists without the language to be frightened who let the mob engulf them, pop out bobbing and startled in its wake. In the pub they heard that unlike theirs, the reds' parade was allowed to go ahead: 2,000 Asians and white race traitors polluting the Cenotaph, 'Anti-Fascist Action.' Well now. Round two.

In the far corner of the square, past the column and fountains, a crimson banner marks the picket where it always is, on the pavement by South Africa House, a gaggle of students and dykes shouldering rabid placards. But the interesting bit isn't the picketers, it's whether the would-be hard nuts from the red march have kept their promise to protect them. As the mob enters the square everyone's keeping an eye out. They cross the road and head along the top, not dropping past the balustrade into the sunken central section but staying where you're not so easily walled in. Tony breathes, bounces a little on his toes, prepping for a fight. One of the Headhunters calls out: Tony looks where he's pointing and there, on the steps of the church ahead, is gathered the waiting opposition.

'Come on then you red faggots,' yells Steve, gesturing at them over the heads of the approaching mob, and Tony echoes, 'Come on you cunts.' One of the casuals he was talking to in the pub, Terry or Gary or something, pushes to the front and produces from somewhere a bottle, which he lobs in the reds' direction. It smashes in the road just shy of them and the space clears efficiently of bystanders. Some reds are yelling back, 'Fascist scum!' or whatever; a few stand on the railings making come-hither signs. They're low-budget versions of the Headhunters, mainly, with the usual few commie skins, like looking in a soiled mirror. It's hard to tell how many there are and Tony wonders if he should have found a weapon. But once you're stuck in it comes pretty easy, and he's one of the minority with steel toecaps.

Gary or Terry, up front, squats like a constipated frog. He parodies the reds' come-here signal, clicking invisible castanets, and bellows, 'Fucking come and get it then.' For a moment there's no response; then with – to give them credit – impressive calm, the commies on the church palings jump down and saunter forward, and their mates behind climb over and follow. Some in this next line are pretty big, and some are smirking. When they're over there are more behind.

The guys keep moving, yelling abuse. The gap's a couple of hundred feet now and Tony's starting to have doubts. He shouts a bit to get himself going and clenches his fists. He steals a few glances at the lads round him; one or two look uncertain but the rest don't seem much bothered. He gets the usual watery feeling before a fight and is scanning the commies, still ambling with parodic nonchalance towards them, for the ones to avoid. A couple at the front look like real bruisers; there's one in a ropy old jumper and jeans with a dent in his forehead, not young, some grey hairs, with an almost cannibal grin, close enough now to catch Tony looking and blow him a casual, vicious kiss. The number that have leaped the railings is a shock; the dark shelter of the church was deceptive. Someone lets out an unwitting 'Fuck': Tony's not the only one recalculating odds. Sixty feet.

Then a Headhunter just ahead, one of their faces, running things, makes a decision. 'Not happening,' he yells, 'run!' and turns as he does, pushing through the left flank of his firm and looping back across the road before cars jolted into quick reaction. The others try to follow, but it's difficult to execute a one-eighty in this formation: they're not a flock of pigeons and there's a lot of stumbling and knocking each other. Tony fudges a swivel and nearly trips into the guy behind. A howl of ridicule from the reds builds into a battle cry as they accelerate in pursuit.

'Split up,' somebody shouts, and some lads drop into the square while others head round the National Gallery. Tony runs straight for a bit, then decides to cross the road too, scrapes past a braking taxi as he does, gets a flashbulb close-up of its yelling driver. He tears up the alley towards Leicester Square: a glance back grants the appalling vision of pursuing reds reaching out, zombies in a video nasty. He runs on. Something hits the back of his head: not hard, but there's a sharp cold feeling like a cut behind his right ear. Shouts and laughter. He didn't see anyone from his crew when he turned and there's none ahead either, only bystanders and tourists who stare like dumb animals.

Slogging uphill through this improvised obstacle course, Tony feels heavy with beer, retarded by it, and also like a balloon of the stuff has exploded in his guts and wants to flood out. He barrels into the square, knocking over a small kid with a green plastic toy who for some reason has backed into him; registers the yelled outrage of its off-screen parents. He runs through crowds, out the top of the square and left-right into Wardour Street: bang on whatever hour it is, because when he passes the Swiss Centre its puppets start their jangling pageant above. All the people and the dusk are to his advantage; he hasn't heard a red shout for at least two minutes, but there's no point looking back, he should clear more distance first. There's a chance, too, they might regroup and patrol the area, picking off dispersed nationalists one by one, which is why splitting up was stupid without a place to reconvene – but the reds don't know that, don't know they won't mob up in greater numbers and go back to the picket, so they might decide to keep guarding it, which would be good.

He's in Soho now. He could stop in the church gardens for a breather but it's too much of a risk because he might get cornered. Still, he slows to a fast walk, looks behind at last. Nobody. His breath is heaving. What he wants is a piss and a stiff drink. A pub would be good but none nearby will want him; he's covered in sweat, too, and might be bleeding, though when he touches a hand to his ear it seems OK.

There's that pub on Old Compton Street that went queer. The reds wouldn't look there, but what if his own lads see? He'd be safe once he was inside. That kind of relaxation would be good right now, welcome, and touch, the possibility of human touch, also. But dressed like this they won't let him in and if they do the other punters will be too much bother.

He ducks under Raymond's into Berwick Street, past the closed garment shops and doors open on to lit stairs up to tarts' flats. In his mind's eye Steve wanders out of one, fiddling with his belt, and then a whole queue of his colleagues from the football firm. Laughter – 'Told you I was a man of taste.' It's quieter here; he's covered some distance now. In Great Marshall Street, almost empty but for a smashed crate of cabbages abandoned for some reason in the slimy gutter, he allows himself a full minute to breathe.

Black railings surround the steps to the men's toilets at the corner with Carnaby Street. As he descends the air becomes improbably warm, building towards the entrance to a close, humid stink. The light inside is poor, the room cramped and awkward, as if its walls have buckled before subsiding earth. When he enters a short man, Chinese or something and middle-aged, is at the urinals to his left. He looks at Tony and immediately away, staring down at the drainhole he is putting to no use. Tony passes him, close enough to brush in this claustrophobic architecture, and stands a clear distance away, at the other row of pissers in the corner. He relieves himself in protracted luxury, and when he looks up the rattled Chinaman has gone.

Afterwards Tony stands in place, with a sense of the time so far lost to him as having palpable density, calcifying in some vein or organ, quiet, relentless. He feels beneath his top for the hairy droop of his stomach and strokes it pensively. He has pulled that trick of bringing himself here without thinking about it, thinking in fact of anything else, like someone talking loudly as they walk you to an ambush. Well, he's here now, and it's been a while. But first things first: he zips up and goes to wash his hands. There's no soap and nothing to dry them on so he flicks them about and wipes the residue on the thighs of his jeans, making them briefly clammy.

He leans in to the grubby mirror and squints at his ear. He runs his fingers over the patch of scalp the bottle hit and when he examines them they have brought nothing back. He rinses his face and dries it on his top.

He loiters at the sink, dragging out a protracted hand-wash, but nobody arrives; eventually he heads back past the entrance and takes up position at the front, where the Chinaman was. He unzips his fly and stands. The urinal is streaked with mineral deposit. Cars pass overhead in an irregular pulse.

Footsteps shuffle down the stairs: a homeless man, bearded

and dressed like a TV scarecrow, in shapeless tattered layers. Passing Tony, at whom he does not even glance, he exudes a sharp smell. He heads straight for one of the stalls. His loud self-ministrations are punctuated by an irregular hacking cough.

In the middle of this someone appears in the doorframe, sees Tony, leaves. From what he saw they looked young. Tony's outfit isn't helping: well, he can't change it now. He stares at the ceramic, finds patterns in the stains.

After an age the tramp flushes, after another emerges from the stall. At the sink he turns the tap by pressing his sleeve to it with the heel of his palm.

Tony sways on his feet. It is all he can do not to lean forward, prop his forehead on the wall above the urinal, close his eyes. But not yet: not a third concession in one day.

The tramp abrades his soapless hands in the running water until it seems the palms might bleed. As he finally closes the tap he looks baldly at Tony, as if forming some kind of judgement, and stomps up out of sight.

After another interval a boy in jeans and blue rain-jacket enters, stops on the threshold when he sees Tony. When after several seconds the boy has neither entered nor retreated, Tony looks at him. He is twenty or so, fat with a pimply forehead, his chin an indented bump like the button on a mattress, pinning the flesh beneath the gassy puncture of his mouth. Under Tony's level gaze the boy does not immediately bolt. At other times Tony wouldn't be considering it but now he thinks, Well at least he's young, and swivels his torso towards the boy and back, holding his gaze so the boy's eyes lower first. After an uncertain pause the boy walks past Tony without looking at him and goes to the urinal at one remove. He fiddles clumsily with his fly, straightens his spine militarily, closes his eyes against the awkward silence before he can pee. Tony turns his head to look and the boy seems to wince, sensing it.

The boy finishes. He does not move, nor yet look at Tony, who has begun to touch himself. His tug on the boy's peripheral vision is almost sensible. Tony is about to step into the gap between them when there are footsteps. He faces his urinal. The boy tenses, coughs.

The new arrival is in his late thirties, a gym-goer, broad shoulders in a leather jacket trim at the waist. He catches Tony's eye and then, past him, the boy's. Satisfied, he walks behind them and stands at the other row of urinals, in the corner. He is only a couple of feet from the boy but Tony has to twist his neck to see that the gym-goer has begun to play with himself for the boy's benefit. Tony moves over next to the boy, but it is too late; the boy in the same movement steps away, towards the gym-goer. The gym-goer turns towards the boy. The boy kneels.

For a minute, Tony simply watches while the boy jiggles on his haunches like a space hopper and the gym-goer looks steadfastly across him at the corner of the ceiling: unable to hold this gaze forever, he catches Tony's eye for a moment and Tony takes a step in their direction, but the man looks pointedly away with an audible tut.

Tony zips his fly. He really could kick both their heads in. Instead he goes to the sink and makes a perfunctory show of hand-washing, for the benefit of nobody here, really, then walks into the end cubicle furthest from them and locks himself in. Exhausted, he stands before the bowl for a moment, then hangs his jacket on the hook that has somehow survived, and sits.

The door in front of him stops far off the ground, leaving a gap almost to the height of his knees through which the stall's occupancy can be monitored; conversely, the partition that divides this cubicle from the next reaches nearly to the floor, to prevent significant transaction beneath. Someone has started to gouge a hole but it will not yet accommodate more than a squint.

Tony lets himself close his eyes and listen, vaguely, to the sporadic noise of the pipes, the ventilation, the muffled traffic above, and what he can hear of the blow job taking place ten feet away: very little, mercifully, except the squeak of sole on floor. Inside his eyelids, in purple and red, runs the pulse and blush of visual noise.

When he jolts awake he has no idea how long he was sleeping. The first thing he sees is his jacket hanging on the door, which in the blur before his conscious focuses he thinks is someone poised to strike, Steve or a Headhunter or a red. He breathes again and takes in the silence, straining to hear if the coupling is still in progress. There is nothing audible.

On the partition to his left someone has written *I am 15 and a Rick Astley fan and I only shag the best. If interested leave details.* To this someone else has appended *I buy his posters they are great.*

Tony should go home, but doesn't have the energy. He wonders what would happen if he just sat here. Would anyone notice? Does the place close?

After some time come the footsteps of a new arrival. They stop at the entrance, then like a showroom demonstration of stereo technology move to his left, to the sink area, pause, and cross to his right, passing through the space before the first urinals to reach those at the end: so the fat boy and gym queen have finished and gone, and this man is scoping the place out. He stops outside Tony's stall; he must be leaning down, to see his boots through the gap.

Now he moves into the stall next to Tony's and shuts the door. There is the sound of unbuckling.

He could have taken the next stall along.

There follows a silence long enough for Tony to be clear that the man next to him did not enter the cubicle to take a shit.

Tony shifts his right leg a few inches so his boot rests against the partition. He quickly feels, on the edge of his foot, a recip-rocal touch.

The hole in the partition is obscured by something that darkly glints. Then it clears and there is rustling, variations in different textures.

Before the toe of Tony's right boot, something folded and white appears on the floor, delivered under the partition by fingers briefly visible. He leans forward to pick it up. The sheet is lined, with a ripped perforation at the top.

What are you looking for? it says.

Tony reaches for the back pocket of his jeans, where he always keeps a pencil. It is not there. He leans forward, takes his jacket off the hook. Nothing. It must have dropped out, perhaps when he ran from the square.

He folds the paper and pushes it back. There is the sound of its retrieval, unfolding. It reappears shortly, with a second question mark appended.

He returns it again and as he does says under his breath: 'Pen.'

There is a grunt on a rising note, a noise of enquiry.

Tony coughs and repeats, more loudly, 'Pen.'

He waits. The paper reappears. Its inscription has not changed.

New footsteps arrive and move squeakily to the urinals. Tony keeps still.

Something pokes through the hole between the stalls, inches from his face. It is a biro. He takes it. On the back of the paper he writes *Any thing you?* He pushes it under the partition.

The man outside goes to wash his hands.

There is a cough from next door. Tony sticks the pen in the hole and it is quickly retrieved. After a pause the sound of paper being torn is bizarrely loud: there is a startled beat between the footsteps of the third man, now exiting; but only a beat, and then he is gone.

The new sheet of paper says *I'm Colin. I'm 28. What do you want to do and where do you want to do it?*

The biro jiggles naggingly in its aperture. Tony takes it, then puts his eye to the hole. He has a view of white cotton, a hand on a bare crotch.

He writes *Ive got a place but its in Woolwich! I dont mind too much am open minded ~~can do any~~ be honest what I realy want is a snog. Dont fuck any more scared of AIDS sucking OK. Tony*

He pushes the message back under for Colin to read, resting the biro on the lip of the hole and waiting for its acceptance. He is trembling slightly at his answer, hoping he hasn't put off Colin with the snog bit, but fuck it, down here, now, he's not the only one who will be making compromises.

Colin has not yet taken the pen. Perhaps he is making his mind up about something. It would be good if he had somewhere to go closer than Woolwich.

Now there are new sounds: parting Velcro, Colin murmuring, the crackle of a radio. Tony scrambles up, grabs his jacket and runs up the stairs, but before he reaches the top two policemen have blocked his exit.

NOTICE.IMPORTANT NOTICE.IMPORTANT NOTICE:
Because of Ian Stuart's slandering of the N.F.
and White Noise,all units of the N.F. and W.N.
have been told to clear all stock bearing
the name of the nazi band "Skrewdriver".So,
all the T-shirts of the band are being "sold
off" for just £3.50!Send your cheques/P.O.s
to:"Lambeth T-Shirts"P.O.Box 220,London,
SW9 OBJ,England.

Welsh Leak fanzine 1, *circa* 1988

L.O.G.

League, Loyalist, Liberty/Liberatio?
Guido vOn List. GeOrge Lincoln Rockwell.
Likes Older Guys. Licks Out, Gratefully. Let's Off Geldof!
L–(Z)OG?

L	O	G
Longinus	Order (The)	GLadiO
Lionheart	ODESSA	Guard (Iron?)
Lebensraum	Occult	Gothic (Ripples)
Lanz(e)	Odin	Guénon
Lightning (& Sun)	Odal (rune/Ring)	Golden (Dawn)
Loki	Oak (Cato)	Glyndwr (Sons)
LaVey	just Of? (or Ov)	Greensboro (Cov>C18)
Lucifer	S. O'Hogan	Ganymede (J. Martin)
W. Landig	Oi!	Greenshirts (T. Chadwyck)
C. Lassen	Ostara	Gnosis
A. Long	Ordo Novi Templi	Grail
λύκος	" Templi Baphe-metis	Gibor

Linz, Leonding, Landsberg am Lech. (Obersalzberg, Germany/Germania.)
Lancashire, London, Libya. Greenwich.
Göbbels, Göring, Gaddafi. Lecomber, Owens, Griffin.

Larry O'Gable!

Order of Nine Angles (not angels but ...)
Otto & Gregor
Opfer??

Hail the New Dawn

The bus was heading on to Camden. I got off past Warren Street and wished I'd done so earlier: the West End, through which we had passed, and where the snogging boys had happily descended, was still busy with people; but here the pavements were quiet, and those who did walk them I felt an urge to avoid: a jerking man dropped his trousers by the Wellcome Library entrance and liquid crashed to the pavement from some part of him. I sped past: there would be minicabs by Kings Cross. Heading east I felt the rush behind me of each solitary car as it swept fast from the underpass, only to halt with a certain bathos in the middle distance, at one or other traffic light.

I was passing the shabby patch of grass outside Euston when my mobile rang. I thought it would be Adam, home at last and discovering my absence, but the number was withheld. 'Hello?' I asked, and hearing no answer repeated myself. Still no reply, yet the connection was real: I could hear noise down the line, the base susurrus of another place. 'Ads?' I said, and made out what seemed an intake of breath, like a stifled laugh or sob. Perhaps it excited the lungs, or brought the phone's mike closer to a mouth, for controlled breathing was now unmistakable.

'Adam,' I repeated angrily, but knew by now it was someone else. 'I'm hanging up,' I said, and did, adding, 'Shit!' quite loudly as the call was cut, which seemed to trigger a brief, harsh laugh nearby; turning, I saw its source, a man in a pale trench coat passing under a streetlamp ten metres behind me.

On my left now were the tall main gates of the British Library, wrought thin and the top and thickening towards ground level into solidity. How much time had I spent in there, the last – what – eighteen months? By now I had hundreds of thousands of words of notes: a chronology (detailed in places but with large gaps) of the years of Nicky's life and Ian's; my own Skrewdriver gigography; endlessly reworked diagrams of the implausible links between people and groups: Above the Ruins, Current 93, the Church of Satan, the Werewolf Order. By the bus stop, dead flowers were taped to a dented lamppost. A picture of a black boy in his teens – a school portrait, probably, with one of those sponge-painted skies that always look oddly overcast – grinned from its stapled vantage on the wrapper.

The trench-coated man was still behind me; when I turned again he caught my eye. There was no sense, I knew, in my alarm: this was the main route after all, and walking behind someone I might absently watch them too. Still, I crossed the road (easy with so few cars) and turned down a side street, and the next time I looked the man was gone.

The houses here were all bed-and-breakfasts, with plastic illuminated signs: Florence, Fairway, Central Hotel. VACANCIES, it said on the door of one in a jaunty bubble script, whilst its ground-floor window was taped with printed notices there was no light to read. I rounded a corner, intending to loop back to the station, and found myself in a square above which huge trees hung like spiders, black and massive against the gaseous haze of sky. Diagonally across from me the St George's Cross glowed over a lone illuminated window, and from it came a low thud of drums that I knew only my imagination, inspired by the flag, made sound like Skrewdriver. Nearing the building, I read the sign on its side and felt a thrill of genuine unease. FERNDALE – SO this was Argyle Square: I had known it was near Kings Cross, but in all my time here never thought to look for it. It was in this building that Ian had lived for much of the '80s; this door that loosed gangs of skins on violent rampages in the area. I had the fantasy of simply ringing the bell, but instead stood close to the door and peered through its glass. Through the small gap in the curtains behind I could make out the base of some stairs, and one of those statutory notices about fire escapes. The small panes were filthy with dust: I traced my finger over one, brought back a grimy smear. The bass upstairs continued unabated. NICKY CRANE, I wrote in small capitals on the dusty glass. I considered this for a moment, then added IS ALIVE.

My mobile rang again, its shrill immediacy slicing through the drums above. As I scrambled for it I heard the music quieten and, stepping back half tripping from the porch, saw shadows move against the window's light. I turned away quickly, whispering to the phone an urgent 'Hello?,' and headed down the street without looking back. Ahead I could see dingy lights around the station, the miniature late-night border town that fed on it. 'Who's there?' I said, but once more had no reply. The caller's number was blocked again. I turned the phone off, a process retarded by my trembling hand.

By the time I had found a minicab office and waited for a car, my abstract panic had abated, and in the space that it left the events of earlier that night reasserted themselves. As the driver sped us through the back streets of Islington, my mind kept veering to the vision of Adam at the front of the queue, then flinching away with directionless embarrassment. 'Now then,' I muttered involuntarily, as if to distract myself with some imaginary agenda: 'so, so, so.' I lowered the window for air and saw the driver watching me curiously in his glass.

*

'Wow,' said Sarah, when she opened her door. 'That's . . . quite a look.' I had forgotten what I was wearing, and peered in surprise at where my boots met the jeans rolled over them.

'We went out,' I told her vaguely.

Sarah was dressed for bed: a pair of man's boxers and a tank top that showed the sides of her breasts. Beside her on the sofa, I frowned at them, wondering if it was the shape they made without a bra that so drew my attention, or simply such an exposure of flesh. She gave me a look and stood to make us tea. Returning, she said, 'So did you have a fight?'

'Sort of. Not really.'

'Well, come on then: details.'

.' . . I don't really want to talk about it. Do you mind?'

'I thought that's why you were here.' She worried at her teabag with a spoon. A minute later she asked if Adam or I had been 'having an affair,' a concept that seemed so incongruous, from another world system entirely, that despite everything I laughed. This angered her, and soon she wrinkled her face in frustration and said, 'I don't know why you find it so hard to talk.'

'I don't want to think about it. It's just . . . nice to be here.'

It wasn't that I didn't want to tell Sarah, more that I didn't know how. The whole context of what had happened was so far removed from how she must think of me and Adam ('Are you having an affair?') that I couldn't now imagine making such a transition. For all the glee once generated in her by my gonorrhoea, I suspected that Sarah's exuberance around my sex life was as touristic and circumscribed as a hen night's at a gay disco. Instead I said, 'I got a bit weirded out on the way over. I found this building where Ian Stuart lived. Totally by accident. I just found myself standing outside.'

'Where?'

'A square near Kings Cross.'

'I've been waiting up since you called. Why were you

wandering round Kings Cross?' She shook her head impatiently. 'How is all that – the nazi stuff? Are you close to finishing?'

'I don't know. It's all getting quite . . . complicated. I mean, the research is fascinating but I don't know if I can keep it under control.' I looked down at my jiggling boots. My legs ached with tiredness and I couldn't keep them still. 'Sometimes,' I told her, 'I wonder if I'm just wasting my time.'

'In what way?'

'It can seem a bit recondite.'

'Really.' She sounded irritated. It had been a mistake to come over like this. I should go home. At the very least, Adam and I needed to talk. 'Mum and Dad remortgaged the house,' Sarah said abruptly. 'Did you know that?'

'No.' I sat up. 'Why would they do that?'

'Oh, I don't know. Maybe for the same reason they went to Spain last summer instead of the three weeks in Bali they'd planned.'

'I didn't know they were going to Bali.'

'They didn't. Be a shitter if the market tanks, though. The remortgage.'

'Yeah.' I couldn't sit still. I risked closing my eyes and thought I reopened them immediately, but found images lingering as if my mind had had time to wander: kissing boys on the top deck of the bus; liquid guts splashing on the Euston Road; flowers for a black kid, taped to a lamppost. How do you drive into a lamppost, anyway? Car crashes, flowers, funerals. Derbyshire in the early morning: fog, a Volkswagen Polo spinning off the road. A group of men facing a camera. I blinked and shook myself. 'They're *old*, James,' Sarah was saying. She sighed noisily: had I missed something? 'They should be buying a cottage for the weekends, not going back into debt.'

'Well exactly. So why should they . . .' I trailed off again. I saw the conversation veering away ahead of me, a track from which my carriage had come unfixed.

'Because you're their son and they still believe the horseshit that some day you'll produce this masterwork you claim to be working on, and which is much more important than anything so humble as getting a fucking job.'

This brought me back. I sat upright and looked at her. 'Are you . . . angry about something?'

'Oh, I can't fucking imagine. Jesus *Christ*, you're a solipsistic prick.' She reached for her cigarettes and lit one clumsily, and when she continued her voice sounded ready to crack. 'I'm thirty-two next year, we *talked* about this, I'm all alone and I want kids. I'm going to need financial support from somewhere. You've spent the last – how many years? – pretending to be a bloody artist, and apparently now you're suddenly agonizing that *maybe* it's all a big waste of time. Well I'm sorry but apart from you and our deluded fucking parents, I think everyone came to that conclusion ages ago.'

She gave a moan of frustration and subsided into muffled sniffs. I stared at the floor, trying to unpack my reaction. Was she really accusing me of spending her unborn child's school fees? There was no point in shouting, and besides, I was too tired. In the end I said dully, 'I don't think it's a waste of resources.'

'Who's going to fund this film of yours, James, when you've finally written it?'

'There's various—' I began, and shrugged. 'There's no point talking about it when you're like this.' This she acknowledged with a bitter, tearful smile.

I sipped my tea. It had gone cold.

'I've stopped using condoms,' Sarah said eventually. It was so quiet I took a moment to register.

'What?'

'Not that it happens that often. I tell them I'm on the pill.'

She sniffed. 'I had thought that maybe Adam . . . well, it's not like you two could have kids. But maybe he's not going to be around now either and God knows we don't want you feeling responsible.'

I closed my eyes and let them stay that way. I could hear a truck passing somewhere near by. Sarah was still talking, apparently about some man she had briefly seen. 'But I *don't*, you know?' I heard her say. 'That's not what I'm looking for. But if I'd *told* him that . . .' What friendship did we have, outside the roles we played for each other? She knew nothing of my life. Blu-tacked over her desk was a photo of the Bodil Manz ceramic that had been our joint gift to Mum and Dad a few Christmases back. It had gone down well: a particularly filial gesture, successfully to assume your parents' taste.

At some point she told me she was going to bed. 'We'll be OK,' she said. 'We should talk to each other more.' Though my inclination was the opposite I nodded and let her hug me. When she had closed the door I lay on the couch with my boots, which I had no energy to unlace, hanging off the end. But it was getting light, and I was too tired to sleep. I went through to her bathroom, where I looked at myself in the mirror for a long moment. Then I left as quietly as I could.

It was past six by now, and the streets floated in tenuous, grey light. I walked north up the Holloway Road. So early on a Sunday the traffic was sparse; two men loudly raised the shutter on a convenience store, but most shops and businesses looked like they had been closed for months. I felt hungry but there was nowhere to eat. I passed the graduate centre that Daniel Liebeskind, the architect of the Jewish Museum in Berlin, had built for what was no longer North London Polytechnic, where students had once picketed to demand the exclusion of Patrick Harrington. Its silver angles dull with exhaust grime, it looked like a cheap, stunted rip-off of Liebeskind's own work, or one of those cardboard models of famous buildings you buy in museum shops: clumsily assembled, badly glued.

Men facing a camera. A wooden marker. The side of a road: the A38.

Where had I seen it? Some website, a nazi one. Some time ago: two, three months? On a terminal, in the library. *Comrades from*, I don't know, *Sweden* or *Germany* or wherever *pay their respects at* – not *Ian's resting place*. At *the site of Ian's – falling? murder? martyrdom?*

At the site of his *sacrifice?*

An early jogger overtook me, did a double-take at my outfit as he passed. I smiled at him and walked faster. I had my ending; I knew what LOG had achieved. The road curved west, the buildings before me lit now by the sun almost risen at my back.

You're HIV-positive in 1993. What you need is a magician.

The side of the road, a grass verge. A group of men salute the camera around a wooden marker in the ground: like a cross but with arms pointing diagonally up.

Perhaps Nicky Crane disappears without explanation for several days. Perhaps he is found to be missing from his hospital bed. His friends and the doctors panic, then wonder if he has gone off quietly to die. But when he comes back he says he is feeling better, that he has finally had the one man he always wanted. His friends notice the mud on his clothes and boots but do not say anything.

The houses lining the road had gone; it led now between wild grass and trees. I had the intense feeling that I was walking back through history and might never see a town again, before I realized this was Hampstead Heath. The sun made occasional low winks through the trees to my left, and shone off the bodies of passing cars, which I took as confirmation that I was still in the same time after all. There was a strange, mounting silence, less an absence of noise than a thing itself, swelling thickly into space. I could feel its substance as I stepped into it: it shivered, as if living. I felt the need to get away from the road; I thought that way I might longer preserve my grasp on this palpable silence-thing, and somehow examine it. I stepped off the path into grass and mud, lurched a little as I remembered to attend to where I walked. What I saw ahead could have been the entrance to a forest: it was not a London park of level surfaces and formal plans; it was barely London at all. As I stepped between the trees I had the vague idea of news reports, the bodies of lone ramblers, victims of malefic rituals or damaged minds, and wondered if now was the best time to be doing this; but if there was a threat I could not feel it. Yellow light rippled across me in patterns; the bark of trees was damp and scarred; my boots churned the mud, where water glinted in tiny pools. The land rose sharply and took effort to climb. The sun came through gaps, heating patches of air like puffs of breath warm on my face. I passed over whole dioramas of labouring insects, with their vast appalling discipline, and there was a scent building, rich, sweet and heavy, as if it were summer and this a field of flowers. Ahead of me, on the crest of the rise, the sun glowed through bare branches so vividly they thinned into absence before it; as I walked they moved across its surface, and it pulsed. I didn't have the vocabulary to tell myself what I saw; I had never paid attention to the garden at home, didn't even know what trees these were. I grasped at names: oak, elm, hazel, ash; fern and ivy; peonies, dandelions, daffodils. What did you call these bright yellow autumn flowers? The silence was unbroken and yet also filled with the manifold hum of bees – was this even the time of year for bees? I felt them anyway, an impromptu retinue, rustling the air at my neck. The sun that waited at the top of the slope was full in my face and gave off an unexpected heat. Dark green needles of grass wove vivid carpets on the higher ground. So this was how it felt, revelation: shimmering light on the beckoning crest of a hill, the colours of things saturating, a fine accruing surface detail, as if looking close at a familiar painting and seeing for the first time the texture of the oils. That inner intensity you knew as a boy and had since forgotten spilling and flooding into the physical world, into warmth and colour, the vibrant thrum of awoken nature. I stumbled up, found the summit, swayed in place as the sunlight pounded me. The land fell away ahead, and all across it I could see meadows unfurling in emerald and gold, thick mantles of trees, their dense canopies merged, falling and rising over distant hills. A vast flock of birds swirled in the sky; a squirrel nudged my feet without fear; a pair of dogs, their fur thick and black, and the size, it seemed, of donkeys, lumbered from nowhere up the path towards me, smelled something on the wind, gave a laughing bark, were gone, plunging through waist-high stalks like the waves of the sea. I walked forward in their wake; the ground dipped and rose; I bobbed in the tall grass. I knew what vision I had been granted: Imperium, the new dawn, the Satanic aeon; the return of the golden age long lost to algebra, industry, abstract thought, foolish insistence on the pre-eminence and commonality of man. The dogs were wolves, the wolves what men could be, and they chased the power to conquer galaxies. Nicky Crane was alive, and before me, now, the city burned: I had reached another crest and there it was, far below and tiny, its dull anaemic greys glistening with the reflected red of the flames consuming it, the air, even here, thick with the caramel taste of burning flesh. And through its smoke, the risen sun. The old age never died; it was in retreat; it slept, while all the time its ancient guardians, LOKI OKKULT GESELLSCHAFT, LUPINÆ OPERÆ GERULI, LEGATI ORDINIS GALAXICI, tended it with secret rites, sacrifice magnified by powerful relics passed on in unwritten rituals of initiation. The martyrs of the Munich *putsch*, Röhm at Stadelheim, Himmler at Wewelsburg, Savitri Devi at the Externsteine, Anton Long by the Stiperstones, and Ian and Nicky – where? – blood touching blood, energies presenced and channelled, death turned to immortality, until dawn rises on the new race: skinhead, *Werwolf*, *Homo galactica*.

Climbing down into Kentish Town, which was no longer ablaze, across a once more wet and muddy heath, I struggled to keep the details of the vision in my mind. On the tennis courts ahead of me the first players of the day were limbering up, men who had risen early to fit the game into their crammed weekends. Before I reached them I saw the dogs again, half the size I had thought, happily following a woman in a Barbour from whose left hand, hanging at her side, trailed the loose edges of crumpled plastic bags.

On the tube I fell asleep, and had to double back to my stop. It was only as I walked to the flat that I remembered to turn my mobile back on, and got the voicemail that Adam had left me hours before, and the several that followed. I listened to the first, then ran the rest of the way home.

Adam had somehow managed to fall asleep. He lay on top of our bed, still dressed, in his usual foetal curl. In the crook he made lay Sonny, whose cut paw he had cleaned and bandaged, and who watched me silently as I inspected it.

The heat had been turned up high, but the living room was still freezing. Glass sparkled in shards across its floor. The brick that had shattered our window lay like a trophy on the table, weighing down the paper it had been wrapped in. It was an ordinary A4 sheet, the kind any office stocks in reams. The side facing up was decorated with swastikas drawn in red ink. On the other each corner was marked by a circled pentagram, and large capitals at its centre spelled out L. O. G.

Outside a wind was picking up. The newspaper Adam had taped across the frame rustled, and now and again thudded like a drumskin. I wasn't as scared as I thought I should be.

The shock of discovery had come in a great cold rush, but of vindication as much as surprise, and my head now buzzed with inferences. Another, more detached part of me remarked on this already detached reaction, and wondered if I was in shock. But I knew, now, where things were heading.

As soon as I touched him, Adam opened his eyes. 'Hey,' he said, reaching out to me. He looked shockingly vulnerable, as he often did when I woke him; I used to wonder if I had been hurting him in his dreams. It was familiar, this anxious, expectant expression, as if waiting for me to say – what? There's been a phone call. I just saw, on the news; I heard a noise. There's been an accident. There's been an attack. It's your mother; it's your home town; it's outside; there's someone here. I'm sorry; you're going to die now; go back to sleep, it's nothing; I'm so sorry.

Blood & Honour

The Independent Voice of Rock Against Communism

40p

NEW ALBUMS –
SKREWDRIVER
BRUTAL ATTACK
NO REMORSE

COMING SOON
The Klansmen
Sudden Impact

SWEDISH
INTERVIEW
Agent
Bulldogg

RAC Charts
White Whispers
and More . . .

AGAINST RED FRONT AND MASS REACTION

Blood & Honour 8, 1989

Blood & Honour 8, 1989

'ZINE SCENE

RADI-KAHL £1.00 from PLK, Nr.064435C., 8500 Nurnberg 45, West Germany.

PRIDE OF THE NORTH £1.00 inc P&P, C/O Chad 54, Storey Square, Barrow in Furness, Cumbria CA14 2DL.

BOOT BOYS 3 International Postal Coupons to: Boot Boys Postboks 72, 3053 Steinberg, Norway.

THE TRUTH AT LAST B.C.M. Box 5103, London WC1N 3XX. Available for 6 issues - Britain £3, Europe £4, World £5.00.

PITBULL BOY 941 W Leonard, Grand Rapids, Michigan 49504, USA. $2 inc p&p for sample copy.

OFFENSIVE WEAPON BM Box 46, London WC1N 3XX. Clockwork Orange videos, Richard Allen Skinhead books for sale. Articles on tattooist Lal Hardy, Link Records, Brutal Attack, Vicious Rumours etc. Send 50p and SAE.

BOOTS & BRACES Available for 75p inc p&p from Tasha Walker, 41, Palmerston Road, Bowes Park, Woodgreen, London N22 4QH.

HAIL VICTORY PO Box 7467 Dearborn, Michigan 48121, USA. Send $2 inc p&p for sample copy.

ALL OUT ATTACK Bellini Massimo, Via Zardo N.20, 36100 Vicenza, Italy. Send 3000lire for sample copy.

DE LEVENSWIL C/O, Kruisstraat 1A, 1740 Ternat, Belgium. Available for 50 Belgian francs or £1 for 2 copies.

NO SURRENDER C/O Via Piacenza 5A/85, 16138 (Molassana) Genova, Italy. Available for 3000 Lira or 20,000 LIRA for six issues.

NORTH WIND Apartado 162, 2700 Amadora, Portugal. Send £1.00 for sample. Issue 2 features Plastic Surgery.

NATIONS PRIDE NSF, C/O Fabri Francesco, Via Giacomelli N4. 35126, Padova, Italy. Send 3000 lire for sample.

BOOTBOYS P.O.Box 72, 3053 Steinberg, Norway. Send International postal coupon for sample.

BRITISH PATRIOT MAGAZINE P.O.Box 57, Norwich, Norfolk NR2 2RV. Available for 50p plus SAE.

VIT REBELL ZINE Sample copy 15 Swedish Crowns, from P.O.Box 6035, 151 06, Sodertalje 6, Sweden.

QUERSCHLAGER 2 German Deutschmarks, inc P & P. Send to: FAP. (Essen), PLK - Nr. 01 57 26c, Hauptostamt, D-4300 Essen 1, W. Germany.

KAHL SCHLAG 2 DM inc P & P. To Unter Deb Burg 16, 2120 Luneburg, W. Germany.

CANADA AWAKE 2 Dollars (3 dollars for 2 copies). Send to P.O.Box 5475, Station C, Montreal, Quebec, Canada H2X 3M3.

ROCKING THE REDS ZINE 80p inc P & P to 185, Baberton Mains Drive, Edinburgh, EH14 3EL.

SKINHEAD Send £1.00 for two copies to P.O.Box 94 100, 08080, Barcelona, Spain.

IMPACT ZINE Available for 70p inc P & P from 51, Sudbury Heights Avenue, Greenford, Middlesex NB6 0ND.

VIKING REVIEW 70p inc P & P from P.O.Box 3, Rochdale, Lancs OL11 5LG.

STORM TROOP GPO BOX 1595P, Melbourne 3001, Victoria, Australia. Send 2 Aus.$ for sample. Issue 4 features No Remorse, White Lightening etc.

VENTO DO NORTE (Northern Wind) Apartado 162, 2700 Amadora, Portugal. Available for 200 Es cudos in c P & P.

EISENSCHADEL C/o SG Graf von Moltke, Str.5, 2012 Luneburg, Germany. Available for 5DM, inc P & P.

FANZINE WRITERS If you want your zine advertised on this page then send us a copy, plus the price (including postage). Send to **Blood & Honour, BM Skrewdriver, London WC1N 3XX.** We will only continue to feature fanzines that appear regularly.

Speakers' Corner

The surface of the water is scummy with rinsed shaving foam and stubble from his face and scalp. When he gets out this gunk clings like film to his ankles, sealing the hair against the skin in tapered verticals, so, with the bath drained, he holds each foot under the running tap, flicking water about to wash dirt from around the plughole.

He pulls on clean underwear, sealing inside a climate still slightly moist; next, bleached jeans, old ones and getting tight, into which he tucks an even older *Bulldog* T-shirt – with the original logo of the crouched and slobbering beast, almost collectible now – hooking his braces over. He unwraps his new white laces and ties a knot at one end of each, to anchor them in the bottom outside eyelets of his boots. He threads each to halfway up in a single zigzag line, pulls the boots on and laces tightly to their penultimate holes. He wraps each untethered end several times around the top of its boot, threads it through the final hole, doubles back, threads it through again, and tucks it in.

He tips old biros from a jam jar to reach the sharpener inside and carefully trims with it an HB pencil, which he puts in his back pocket. He pulls on his jacket. He looks in the mirror. He checks his watch.

It is a few minutes past four in the afternoon on Saturday, 27 May 1989. In less than a month he will be thirty-three.

In the street it is warm – not the killing heat of earlier this week, but a good day for it none the less. A few doors down, at the entrance to her front porch, a small girl sits in a ruined pink armchair: ancient, disgustingly stained. Her knees can't reach the lip of its seat, so her calves extend horizontally, poking out over the pavement. She watches him approach, and as he passes he winks at her.

At the end of the street a dark blue car pulls up. 'Hello Tony,' the driver says. 'Going to the gig?'

He leans inside. 'Piss off will you.'

'Now don't be a bitter old queen. Hop in. You're getting a lift.'

'So where's the concert happening, Tony?'

'If I knew I wouldn't be going to the redirection point would I?'

Novak smiles. 'I'm only kidding with you. It's at Camden Town Hall. Not any more, of course. They cancelled the booking. But you've got to give them credit for a sense of humour, haven't you, those Skrewdriver boys? Trying to host a nazi shindig with a loony-left council. Expensive joke, mind, if they don't get their deposit back.'

'They'll have back-up venues.'

'Course they will. All part of the game. It's like they say: not over till the fat bonehead sings.'

'Yeah.' Tony stares through the passenger window, avoids looking at Novak. They are on Blackheath, moving along Shooters Hill like a pulled zip severing the vast flat fabric of the grass. Someone's kite-flying is reduced by distance to its barest schematic: two points, one static, one vacillating, an implied line between. Nice area this, thinks Tony meaninglessly, a reflex action of the mind that triggers actual introspection as he wonders when he last heard from Niven. Is it really a year? But if Niven knew anything there'd have been consequences by now.

All at once the green is pulled out from under them and they are falling towards Deptford. Near New Cross Station, Novak says, 'That reminds me. What were you doing on the eighteenth of January, oh . . . eight years ago?'

'Having a better time than this.'

'Go on, confess to a bit of arson. Make my day.' Novak's aspiration to comedy is the most aggravating thing about him, probably. He pulls in by the next Paki shop and says, 'Do us a favour, Tony. Pop and get me a Fruit and Nut and a can of Lilt. Didn't have my lunch today.'

'Are you taking the piss?'

'And whatever you want for yourself.' He holds out a ten-pound note. 'You can keep the change.' He watches Tony's hand take the money and asks, 'That a new tattoo? Charming.'

'True isn't it.'

Tony buys himself a can of lager and gets Novak his chocolate bar and a Tango, which he shakes next to his thigh as he approaches the car. He lies: 'They were out of Lilt.' Novak eats the chocolate first: the drink has settled by the time he opens it.

They turn up the Old Kent Road in silence. Novak has still not said why he picked Tony up, and Tony is not going to ask. Near Elephant and Castle, under a billboard that reads E.LIF: CAN ANYONE MAKE SENSE OF IT?, the traffic slows to a baked and fuming stasis.

'What time are you due at Speakers' Corner?'

Tony looks at the clock. It will soon be five. 'Now,' he says.

'Until when?'

'They'll be done by six.'

'Got your ticket already?'

'Yeah.'

'We might have to sort you a refund.'

'Just let me out here,' says Tony. 'I'll get the tube.'

'Can't do that. I'm taking you to meet someone.'

Tony mutters, 'Wanker.' Novak complains to his walkie-talkie about the traffic and gets a scratched response. 'Ah,' he says, digging around his feet for something which he puts through the open window: it lands on the roof with a magnetic clunk. He presses a switch and a siren starts; a few cars in front of them move vaguely aside, and they force their way slowly through.

Alongside the Imperial War Museum, Novak kills the noise and comes to a halt. The junction ahead is clogged with Asians, arriving from the distance in a steady stream and filling up the small park around the building. They are all men, some in suits and others those white sheet-like dresses they wear, with beards and little round hats. Most smile and chat; a few look determinedly dour. They hold banners in awkward, formal English: SACRILEGE CANNOT BE GOOD BUSINESS. PENGUIN DO NOT BECOME GUTTER PRESS.

'There's only fifty thousand of these jokers between here and Hyde Park,' Novak says. 'Shouldn't slow us down too much.'

The tail end of a group of old men shuffles past to reveal quite different marchers behind. They are in their twenties: they have moustaches and permed hair, pale jeans, the odd nastily patterned sweater. They are chanting in call and response. 'Rusty – *bastard!*' it sounds like. 'Rusty – *bastard!*' Some punch the air on the chorused answer. One catches Tony's eye through the windscreen. He says something to the man next to him and points.

Novak is smirking. 'Just let you out here then, shall I?' he says.

Using the siren when it suits him, he presses on through the traffic and over Waterloo Bridge. By the time they cross it is gone five-thirty. The redirection will be over soon.

Novak says, 'Do you know where they've all come from? Hyde Park. And where are you lot gathering for Hitler's hundredth birthday party? Hyde fucking Park. You couldn't make this shit up.'

They give up on a packed Strand and cut through to the river, but the embankment road is blocked at Westminster by a police cordon. Novak could presumably get through, but there is nowhere to go; the bridge, and the road into Parliament Square, are solid with people: marchers, policemen in riot gear gathered round their vans. Novak stops the car.

'How much was the ticket again?'

'Fuck off.'

'Stretch your legs if you want. We'll be here awhile.'

'What for?'

'I'm not driving round half of London to bring you to Special Branch. If Muhammad can't get to the mountain because his fucking followers are in the way, then the mountain's going to have to walk.'

Tony gets out. Looking down at the river, he is ambushed by the memory of standing somewhere like this with Dennis, waiting for that queer photographer. Were they having an argument? Novak is talking on his radio again; Tony knocks on the window, gestures for a cigarette. He lights it and watches the bridge. The crowd is stationary, not moving forward into Lambeth; indeed, most face back in the direction they came. New arrivals from the north halt uncertainly upon reaching them. A few policemen are visible on the far side of the bridge, where some marchers are sitting in the road. It looks like an attempt to negotiate: there is clear disagreement, almost mimed. Eventually the police withdraw and return to where their troops are assembled, alongside the closest section of the march.

There is a noise behind Tony and he turns to see more vans parking in the empty street: scores of policemen get out wearing helmets and shields, and are led off quickly. Meanwhile on the bridge some younger demonstrators have surrounded a police van, yelling: after a couple of minutes of this a group of about thirty riot cops, who have been standing off to the far side of the march, abruptly charge them. There is panic as people try to get out of the way, some scrambling over the crash barriers between them and the road where Tony stands. A young Asian in a leather jacket, having cleared the barriers, runs in Tony's direction, pursued by a yelling policeman. They are ten feet away when the policeman catches up. He reaches for the Asian, who turns at his touch, and the policeman punches him hard in the face. The Asian stumbles back over half-turned legs and the policeman jumps him and pushes him against the road. There is a struggle in which the Asian is soon cuffed, then dragged over tarmac to the nearest van. Other marchers harangue the police as they force the handcuffed Asian inside. When the doors close they back up their shouts with hurled sticks and soft-drink cans. The police take cover behind the vehicle. Groups of riot cops make sorties into the crowd, targeting youths whom they seize one by one, pinned and wriggling on the black wall of their shields, and shove into vans. Tony grinds his cigarette into the pavement.

Novak stands next to him. 'Are we winning yet?' he asks.

'No.'

'We will. They're doing better than your mates, though, these Pakis.' He waits for Tony to ask what he means, so Tony doesn't. Eventually Novak gives up. 'Yeah,' he says. 'I was just talking to some of the boys over Speakers' Corner. Turns out a few hundred lads from Anti-Fascist Action had the bright idea of occupying the redirection point before Blood & Honour turned up. They've been picking off boneheads as they arrive, beating the crap out of them. Blood all over the shop. Bit less of the honour . . . Course, our boys would love to keep the peace

306

and protect your poor defenceless mates, but we're a bit over-stretched today so AFA have free rein, basically. They're a scary crew when they're properly tooled up. Terrible business.' He tuts, smirking again. 'Not to worry though, we'll drop you up there soon enough, you can come to the rescue . . . Oh dear. Quarter-past six.'

Tony says, 'You found out where the gig is?'

'Oh yeah, apparently that Nicky Crane turned up with a minibus of élite fighters or whatever and a minute later they were all running off like this.' He flails his wrists. 'Here, have you and him ever done the dirty?'

'Piss off.'

'Don't be a sour old bitch, you'll get wrinkles. No, I'm only kidding with you. Except the running-away bit, I had that from the lads up Hyde Park. Eyewitnesses. Honest Injun.'

Ahead, a hundred or more policemen have massed into formation and begin to move against the crowd, trying to herd them across the bridge. Their riot shields merge into an unbroken plough, over which long truncheons threaten vigorously. The closest marchers are forced to move, but those further on hold their ground, and some who were sitting at the far end now press the crowd in the other direction. From the crushed centre come cries of mounting panic, and everyone is shouting, in English and in other languages.

Tony says, 'Why won't they move forward?'

By the nearby crash barrier, where police hold back the later section of the march, a white man emerges, heading for Novak and Tony. He is forty-something, with a grey suit and receding hair, and a plastic folder under his arm. 'How's it going?' he asks, shaking Novak's hand. 'And you must be Tony. I'm Bruno. It's my surname, I'm not being friendly. Let's go for a drive.'

Novak has reversed the car into a turn, his left arm across the passenger seat, looking through the rear window, when he says, 'I don't believe it. Look at this.' He gets out, and the others follow.

On the bridge, the police charge has abated. The marchers stand with their backs to Tony, leaning forward at the waist, as if mooning him *en masse*. After briefly holding this position they stand again, then promptly kneel and, still facing away, prostrate themselves on the floor. With the lowering sun cutting across them from the right, they could be neat rows of huts on a beach at evening. They sit up straight, prostrate themselves, stand back up. They raise their hands. All of this is more or less coordinated, and seems, from where Tony watches, to be entirely silent. The police stand off to the side. The response of the majority is invisible behind their helmets; of the others, a few look awkward, and several laugh.

Bruno says, 'So what's your take on all this then, Tony?'
  'What?'
  'That. Karachi Central.'
  They are driving away from the march, up into the West End. Tony says, 'Well they shouldn't be here should they?'
  'Who shouldn't?'
  'None of them. Them ones or the wog wrote the book.'
  'Fair point.'
  'They should be having it out in Delhi or wherever.' Everyone will be heading to the gig now. 'Mind you it might be a good thing.'
  'What?'
  'All this. When the British people see how many are over here. All in one place like that. People might wake up.'
  Bruno smiles. 'You've got it all worked out, haven't you?'
  'It's not complicated.'
  Bruno unzips his folder and leafs through the papers inside. Without looking up he says, 'So what's your position on the fatwa?'

'The fat what?'

'Come on, Tony. From what I hear you're not that thick. Death sentence, courtesy of the beardy git on the placards.' Maybe he's got a point – I've heard the guy's a moany cunt.'

'I'm not interested in Arabs.'

'Khomeini's not an Arab. I thought you knew that stuff. Or' – he takes a magazine from his folder – 'did your subscription lapse?'

It is a copy of *Nationalism Today*. The cover is the usual green and white, its strap line *A Call to Arms, a Call to Sacrifice*. Novak says, 'This is last month's issue. We get it in the post.'

Tony says, 'I don't read that shit.'

'Really? You're missing out.' He holds out the magazine: an article called 'Iran: An Assessment,' a young boy pictured with a massive gun.

Tony scans the page. It looks typically unreadable, all italic quotes and exhortations in boldface. Subheadings are scattered throughout: '*A Godsend . . . Yankee hypocrites . . . Revolutionary future*.'

Bruno says, 'You really don't read this?' He turns the page and reads: '"Reflections from a National Front prisoner." This one's fun. "Either you are with us or against us. There is no third option. To reclaim that which is rightfully ours, we shall fight to the end. Long live Death!"'

'Am I being thick,' Tony asks, 'or have you not got a point?'

Novak is driving them, apparently randomly, round Covent Garden. He seems in no hurry to get to Hyde Park. Bruno says, 'Want to know a secret? We don't think Lockerbie was the Iranians at all. The Americans are pushing that line but it's politics. We're pretty sure it was Libya.'

'Is there a difference?'

'Actually that's no secret, it was in the papers. You do read the papers?'

'I read my horoscope. Today it said you will have your

entire fucking day wasted by coppers who talk bollocks for hours, and miss Skrewdriver.'

Bruno produces another document: 'This one we had to intercept.' NATIONAL FRONT says its letterhead in huge type, and underneath, *The Movement of the Future*. Bruno reads aloud: '"Dear Comrade Colonel.

'"Let me first extend to you National Revolutionary Greetings from the National Front in Britain and express the sincere hope that the spirit encapsulated in *The Green Book* continues to inspire the revolutionaries and people of your country.

'"Your book, a seminal work by any political criterion, has been subjected to rigorous analysis within the Movement for the greater part of the last two years, in response to the political, historical and philosophical needs of the Third Position in this country," blah blah. We'll both fall asleep if I read the whole thing . . . "They degraded and exploited the mass of our people" – can't imagine who "they" are, can you? – "in the horror of the Industrial Revolution: a horror so vile that it would bring true tears of pain and sympathy to your eyes; they destroyed the pristine purity and beauty of the Gospel of Christ, perverting it and harnessing it to the service of the minions of the Dark One . . ." Well, you get the idea. Have you seen the photos of their trip? Griffin, Harrington and Holland standing like tiny pillocks before pictures of Gaddafi the size of Tripoli?'

'I've never been in the Front.'

Bruno zips his folder and looks out at the weekend crowd. After a while he says, 'Do you know how many people died on that plane? Two hundred and sixty. Not including the folks on the ground. Long live Death, eh? Bodies and wreckage across eight hundred square miles. Bits of head and spine in people's driveways. Burst stomachs in flowerbeds. Have you seen the pictures? No, even if you read the papers you haven't, because they weren't in the papers. But I've seen the pictures.'

'I've never been a member.'

'Fucking journalists still pilfered from the bodies of course.'

'British Movement all the way. I hate Arabs.'

'Course you do. You're an old-fashioned thug. As a matter of fact I can understand where you're coming from. I'm not saying I approve of how you go round expressing your opinions, but at least you're loyal to Britain. Shit-hole wanking aside. No, it's your boyfriend I'm interested in.'

For some reason, for the last minute or two, since Bruno started going on about body parts, Novak has been driving them in circles round Seven Dials. The theatre keeps flashing past, SHERLOCK HOLMES — SHERLOCK HOLMES, and Tony has begun to feel sick. He mumbles: 'But . . . he's out of it.'

'Can't hear you mate.'

'Glenn? He's out of the whole thing. I mean from what I heard he joined those SHARP wankers. Skinheads Against Racist Prejudice or whatever. He's practically a red these days. I don't want nothing to do with him any more.'

'Who's Glenn then, Tony?'

At last Novak breaks his tight loop and takes off for Shaftesbury Avenue. He grins into the mirror: 'How many boyfriends have you had, you slag?'

'Who do you mean,' Tony insists, 'my boyfriend?'

'I mean Dave Masters,' Bruno tells him. 'Who do you mean?'

Tony stares at him. The mention of Dave's name has dramatically amplified his motion sickness. He says, 'You're talking shit.'

'Come on, Tony, do you think you're the only snitch we've got?'

'Dave? He's never . . . he isn't. We've never— This is bullshit.'

Novak pulls into an alley behind the cinema, where a tiny park hides. The policemen get out and Bruno holds Tony's door until he follows. They sit on a bench under a tree, watching a woman push her child on a swing. Novak gives Tony a cigarette. In his grip it exaggerates the tremble of his fingers.

Bruno says, 'You'd be doing him a favour if you helped us out.'

'You've got it so fucking wrong.'

'He could end up put away for life, Tony. He could end up dead.'

'But he's normal as they come.'

'It's OK you trying to protect him. Listen. The Front's on the verge of collapse. After that they won't even pretend to be legitimate. These people are going underground. Does he talk to you about his cadre training?'

The woman is still pushing the swing. It goes higher each time. Tony imagines the kid falling, flying away.

Bruno says, 'I don't have to tell you who their backers are, it's in the magazine. I know they look harmless with their little copies of *The Green Book*, but for Christ's sake, Gaddafi's just built a massive chemical-weapons factory. If he'll take down a passenger jet, what do you think his friends over here could do with a bit of ricin? In that cinema on a Friday night, say. Or the tube at rush hour. You can't tell me that's what you want.'

'You don't really think they'd do nothing like that. The Nutty Fairies? They couldn't organize a piss-up in a brewery.'

'That's what everyone always says, until the bombs go off. Don't tell me you haven't read *The Turner Diaries*. It nearly happened in America a couple of years ago. Fellow travellers of yours hoarding thirty gallons of cyanide. Now we've got long live Death, hooray for Palestine, little Pat Harrington defending the IRA. Don't be so blind, Tony. It doesn't suit you.'

'You sound like fucking *Searchlies*. They don't support terrorism. They've said that.'

'I don't support adultery. Ask my wife how reassured she is.'

Tony says, 'Oh this is fucking crap.'

'Why are you pretending,' says Novak to Bruno, 'you're asking a favour?'

Bruno says, 'I'm just trying to be polite.'

Novak tells Tony, 'He's not asking a fucking favour.'

'I've been helping you out for a fucking year. How long does this go on?'

'Who said it stops?'

'Have you got another fag?'

'You've been fuck-all use so far, you know that? The little you do tell us we already know. Blood & Honour's leakier than a rusty barrel these days. We've been doing *you* a favour and you haven't earned it yet.'

Bruno says, 'Never been in *Searchlight*, have you, Tony? We could put a lovely spread together. Copy of your conviction next to a blurry photo of you and the BM boys. You and Ian Stuart in a pub. With some sarky caption, they're good at those.'

'Stick in that note you wrote,' says Novak.

'Oh yeah,' says Bruno. 'What was it again: "Come over here and fuck me up the jacksie"?'

'"Don't fuck me, I'm scared of AIDS."'

'Oh that's adorable.'

'"Sucking OK."'

'What happened to that case up near Kings Cross?' Bruno asks Novak. 'Ian Stuart cutting that poof's throat?'

Tony says, 'He never done it.'

'Not enough evidence,' says Novak.

'Have you got another fag? Please.'

Bruno tells him: 'I want to hear who's gone where and who they spend time with.'

'I haven't even seen Dave in months.'

'Well get back in touch and make fucking nice then. Buy him chocolates and put your frilly knickers on.'

'You don't listen do you?'

Novak says, 'Are you working these days?'

'You know what I'm doing. You know when I take a fucking dump.'

'Because there are certain things we have a responsibility to inform your employer about. Or potential future employers.'

Tony says, 'I know the fucking threats by now.'

Bruno stands up and pats Tony's shoulder. 'Then we'll leave you to ponder them on your own.'

'Are you OK for money?' says Novak.

'I've never been OK for money.'

'Here's forty. If you need more you know how to get it.'

'Thing is,' says Bruno, 'if you don't come up with the goods, if anything does happen and maybe if it doesn't, everything's out of my hands and into MI5's. Including you. And believe me: that you do not want.'

Tony is alone. The woman with the child has gone. He walks to the swing and touches it. He hears the car start, then stop again, and Novak returns.

'Breaking news,' he says. 'We found the concert. Northfleet in Kent. Back all the way we come and same again. Ironic isn't it?'

'Thanks for telling me.'

'You might make it if you hurry. These things never start on time, do they? But the pub holds four hundred people and there's twice that heading over. Capacity issues as such.'

Tony looks at the sky.

'Tell you what,' Novak says, 'you could always run away with him to Denmark. They're letting poofs get married there now. As of yesterday, which I know because I do read the papers. And it's crawling with boneheads, that place. Be the bloody promised land for you.'

'Are you still here?'

'What happened to you anyway, Tony?' asks Novak. 'You used to be one of the smart ones.'

'Yeah fuck off,' says Tony.

314

Anti-Fascists Jailed

Just recently three anti-fascist militants were sent down for a total of 11 years (4,4,3), one of whom had no previous record.

They were arrested after this year's "Bloody Sunday" march for an attack on Nicky Crane, a well known racist and nazi. Despite what **Searchlight** reported, he did not lead an attack on the march, he was spotted in the area and dealt with. His previous history and convictions for racist violence are reason enough.

There will be no bleeding-heart liberal campaign protesting their "innocence" for we believe fighting fascism is no crime. There is a fund being set up called the "Anti-Fascist Defence Fund" and money will be greatly appreciated.

Those who make the decision to fight these scum must be prepared for the risks involved. We send our best wishes to those convicted.

For more info on the prisoners, the Fund and AFA, write to: AFA, BM 1734, London WC1N 3XX.

WE'RE IN HERE FOR YOU

YOU'RE OUT THERE FOR US

The colleague I had entrusted certain matters to on my departure was not present for my arrival, and I was glad, for I found it difficult then to speak to people. It felt like a burden, after so many months alone. But when I did see him, some days later, I was surprised that he understood. But he always was sensitive, and a little in love with me. During my absence, he hadforged my signature every two weeks to obtain by a small deception a small amount of money for himself according to my plan. I had used this ruse before, a few times in the years of my political work, to provide an alibi of whereabouts should something of what I had then been doing while away be discovered. But this time, it was for him. That night, for the first time, I was tempted to fulfil his hope of our relationship and sleep with him, for I felt aroused, both physically, and emotionally. It did not last - but brought an understanding.

In the morning, he left, as I did, to resume another life.

Anton Long, *Diablerie: revelations of a Satanist*, 1991

The Road to Valhalla

It was gone eleven by the time we set out, and the streets had thickened with traffic. We stop-started over Vauxhall Bridge, sped up encouragingly past Hyde Park, then crawled round Speakers' Corner to see metal packed the whole interminable length of Edgware Road. Neither of us had really slept, and near-immobility kept encouraging into catatonia my dull stare through the windscreen, until the memory of our situation startled me loose again. When that happened I would glance around in a sudden panic, to find Adam still somehow awake at the wheel.

'Are you going to tell me what's going on?' he said.

For no good reason, neither of us had changed. We had told each other we were too tired, or didn't have time, but perhaps the truth was more that our outfits felt appropriate. I had queried Adam's ability to drive in his boots, but he told me he was used to it.

All at once, it seemed, we were near Hendon, accelerating alarmingly as our road became the start of the M1. As we drove fast into it the rain fell harder against the glass. The wipers scooped and smeared it in patterns that distorted in turn the quickening world outside. Reality, thus liquefied, melded with the strange detritus of my waking dreams.

I said, 'I thought I was just making stuff up.' But it was noisy on the motorway and perhaps he didn't hear.

Later he said, 'We should have called the police.'

He had had Sonny since he was a kitten: nearly five years. Under other circumstances we would have found an emergency vet.

'Come on, Ads.' I imagined the conversation: I see, sir; and what is the purpose of this research, exactly? And how long have you been doing it? 'I don't want them going through my . . . fucking laptop, you know?'

'What have you been up to?'

'*Nothing*. Nothing that you don't . . .'

'Fuck,' he muttered, when I tailed off.

.' . . I've been talking to this guy.'

We stopped for food at the services at Newport Pagnell, spurning the coffee-bar clone for Burger King. We sat by a window eating burgers from a smeared sheet and drinking the hot, dirty water they sold as coffee.

'Thanks for doing this,' I said.

'What else would you do, hitch-hike?' Adam dumped sugar into his drink. A minute later he said quietly: 'Last night. I mean at the club . . .'

'Can we talk about it later?'

'You wanted to come.'

'Let's not do this now.'

He blinked and the skin tightened against his lower jaw. 'I don't know what it is you want.'

'Please, Ads.'

'It's only sex.'

I looked out to the car park, on which the rain seemed to

descend like fixative, so that a hundred years from now it would be quite unchanged, the same Morris Minor estate still parked at the same hurried angle.

'I can't give you what you need,' I told him.

His reply was so low I had to strain to hear: 'You always did.'

In the toilets, miniature advertising billboards displayed a pair of fat, headless breasts above each urinal.

Past Coventry it stopped raining, and the dark grey clouds that had tamped our surroundings opened into a strange yellow hiatus above our heads. Its reflection shimmered on the wet surface of the road so we seemed suspended in alien light.

'I don't know what we'll find,' I told Adam, 'but it's where everything points to.' Perhaps it was exhaustion, or stress, but names and places, patterns and dates were aligning like sheets of tracing paper in my head.

Ian had left London for good in 1989, after the public humiliation of having his redirection point for the Main Event concert taken over by Anti-Fascist Action and turned into a battering-ground for nazis. They had attacked him in person, too, several times, and on one occasion 'fucked up his fingers with a hammer.' As for Nicky, I lost track after January 1990, when he was 'dealt with' by AFA during the Bloody Sunday March. By one account, they threw him 'through a bus shelter,' by another, slammed his head in a taxi door until he blacked out. With the political soldiers meanwhile heading underground, it might have felt for a while like fascism was in retreat. But Skrewdriver carried on playing – Staffordshire, Nottinghamshire, Newcastle – and Ian made Derbyshire his new home.

'Take the next turn-off,' I said. 'The A511.'

Burton upon Trent had not been good to Ian; he had been injured here on one occasion, and on another, when trying to

319

leave it, he had died. Adam pulled in by a newsagent, a plain two-storey brick building with a canopy in filthy red-and-white stripes. I sat in the car while he went inside for drinks. Ahead, in a gap between buildings, an advertising hoarding had been erected flat-on to the road, its wood since warped by time and weather into concavity, so that from this angle I could not see what it sold.

I am not play acting.

If your going to ask for a photo fuck off.

'Is this it?' Adam said when he came back.

'It's the start.' I pointed. 'We want the A38 northbound.'

'What are we looking for?'

'There'll be a marker, made of wood. Like a pointed cross.'

Friday, 24 September 1993, the early morning. A Volkswagen Polo headed down this road, carrying Ian and his mates home from a night in Burton, a few pints at the Royal Oak. It was foggy, the small car heavy with five men, most of them drunk. Did they open a window? A dull route, it now turned out: the road curved, it rose and dipped a little, but there was rarely more to the side than steep grass verges, trees, the occasional glimpse of fields. Grass grew along the central divider; overhead, concrete bridges delimited distance.

Who was travelling with Ian? I recited the names in my mind: Stephen Lee Flint, Richard Hill, David Roy Mee, Robert Sherlock. Stephen Flint, called 'Boo,' was a young Nottingham skinhead. Richard Hill was a Klansman from Ilkeston, who had put Ian up when he first moved north. 'Cat' Mee was a long-time BM activist and member of Skrewdriver Security; his parents ran the Red Lion in Heanor, the pub above which Ian lived. Robert Sherlock did not appear in my notes.

There was no mystery about what had happened. The steering wheel caught (a blow-out), the car turned over and left the road. Boo died instantly; Ian was cut from the wreckage and taken to the Queen's Medical Centre in Nottingham, where he was pronounced dead later that morning. The other three survived. 'We were doing fifty-five mph,' Cat told the papers. 'It was as if someone up above had put their hand inside the car and said: "Come here."'

I watched the roadside on my left, trying to picture the crash-site photograph. A group of men facing the camera: the sky beyond, a backdrop of trees? Now the barrier's regularity was broken by a small cross fixed to its surface. It looked normal: Christian. I let it pass.

What was the mood like in the car? Maybe they'd spent the night discussing arrangements for the Blood & Honour social that was planned for that Saturday, somewhere in the Midlands. Or perhaps they'd been celebrating: just a week earlier in Tower Hamlets, Derek Beackon, the BNP's chief steward, had won the party's first-ever council seat. Ian had no time for the BNP, but this was a victory for the movement as a whole; he'd phoned a friend early in the morning, excited, when he'd heard the news. When I had first read the London Psychogeographical Society's theory that Beackon was a magician who ensured his survival through Ian's occult sacrifice, I had assumed it was deliberate nonsense. Now I thought of how Anton Long claimed to publish the truth in distorted form, to confuse and test. My eyes were closing again: if I did not keep watching the road I might miss it. Adam stuck to the left-hand lane, driving as slowly as he could. The view extended a few metres on each side: it was as if we were in a channel cut through a solid surface of trees, in which there was only the road, a strip of grass alongside, and sky.

Ian died in the same year as Nicky, or the year Nicky was meant to have died. Had he heard Nicky was ill? That alternative narrative, always present in my reading, never credible but never silent, seemed to tend to just this ending. A phone call, or perhaps a note in the post, care of the Red Lion: PRIVATE AND CONFIDENTIAL, children's capitals. *We've not been in touch but I had to let you know. It's impossible to know how long I, so under the circumstances you* . . . What he's feared for years: the cheap cliché denouement, the great unmasking, truth rupturing skin, the body's betrayal of the word. Interminable cascade of imagined consequence: comrades, fans, press; mates, family, wife-to-be. The knowledge weighing for how many weeks, slowing conversation, hampering the natural smile, the easy joke. And all at once a decision, simple and without passion in the stern clarity of morning. Nothing is not avoidable. He speeds up, grips the wheel, turns.

But I still didn't believe that. And anyway, Ian wasn't driving.

By many accounts, since leaving London Ian had begun to want out. His mother had died after a long illness; he was engaged to his on-off girlfriend and under pressure to complete the deal; the violence of the opposition was getting too much. He was 'depressed,' one friend later told a journalist. 'He was starting to doubt it all. But it was the others wouldn't let him go. People like Charlie and that.'

'People like Charlie': in the last year of Ian's life, Combat 18 had taken control of Blood & Honour; it was pulling in, by some estimates, hundreds of thousands of pounds a year. How could Ian leave? Besides, he was a figurehead for the movement; abandoning it would have destroyed people's faith as well as the business, whereas his death consolidated both. Combat 18, like Mark Collett after them, would later claim that Ian had been murdered by the state (in their jargon ZOG, the Zionist Occupation Government), but it was not the state that most benefited from his death. David Myatt had written of his own 'personal pledge of loyalty to Charlie Sargent,' and steadfastly condemned later rumours that Sargent had been a state asset.

Anton Long called acausal existence 'the secret of true Immortality.' He added that, though unusual, 'consciousness can be transferred to inhabit another causal body.' Long wrote: 'The ideal candidate for Satanism is the individual of action rather than the "intellectual."'

Skrewdriver was reborn on the night Savitri Devi died. What, or who, was given new life by Ian's death?

So what tattoos do you have?

ill show u when we meet

There was a blow-out. Ian grabbed the wheel. The car lifted, span.

A flash of red and white on our left. 'What was that?' I asked Adam. He signalled and slowed, pulled into a lay-by twenty metres ahead. 'Wait here,' I said, and got out of the car.

Where we had stopped, empty lager cans surrounded a sign: NO LITTER, PENALTY £100. There had been a gathering here, not long ago. I walked back towards the thing I'd seen, along the strip of wild grass that fringed the steep incline of the bank. There was no barrier; cars and lorries came past barely metres away, at speeds around seventy. I was walking as carefully as I could, but in my tiredness seemed to tick left and right in my boots, like the needle of a metronome. The bank on my right was thick with nettles and hawthorn bushes from which random trash sparkled, garish flies in their web.

The St George's flag lay in the grass where I had seen it. It was thin, cheap plastic, its white barely dulled by the layer of moist filth on its surface. Untangled from the twigs it clung to, unfolded, it was slightly smaller than an A4 sheet. I held it by my side, wondering how this looked to the passing cars, and scoured the scrub for something more, without success. A small printed note nearby briefly intrigued me until I got close

323

and saw it was a packing slip for some building product – PRE-CAST CONCRETE and then something illegible – perhaps a remnant from work on the highway.

I stood with my back to the road, looking up at where thick trees lined the ridge. I could spot no runic totem, nor any person watching.

'Maybe it's not the right place,' I told Adam. 'Or maybe the marker got moved. There's all these beer cans where they'd have stopped, and I found this lying on the ground.' I showed him the flag.

'This came off a car,' he said.

'Perhaps it's still ahead.' But we didn't see anything else before the turn-off to Heanor, which Ian, on his drive, had never reached.

Without signs the town would have been indistinguishable from the muted continuity it was part of, brick homes and businesses long drained of ambition. We left the car in a small, empty lot behind a boarded house. Across the road another, larger St George's cross, ripped and frayed at its free edge, flapped on a pole above someone's garage. We walked back to the main street, which sloped steeply down. The Red Lion stood on one corner of a T-junction, opposite a tanning parlour and a café unconvincingly called Happy Chef. It was the town's oldest pub, a two-storey building bigger than the local average, but in the same rust-coloured brick. There were large windows on the upper floor, behind which, I'd read some-where, Ian had practised martial arts. In this building, too, he had been initiated into the Klan.

'It's a bit *Wicker Man*,' whispered Adam as we entered.

'It's a bloody Wetherspoon's. When did *that* happen?'

Shortly after five, the pub was still quiet. The barmaid met our request for two pints of bitter with little expression. The drinks seemed cheap. We carried them to a table in the huge, roped-off 'family area,' which was nearly empty; I wasn't sure if we qualified, but no one challenged us. A brace of slot machines lit up in elaborate, compulsive patterns that repeated without end: they could have been animals performing a mating dance long fixed in their genes. Everyone ignored them. I had been preparing myself for BNP leaflets by the door, clusters of men, whose visible tattoos I would anxiously parse, muttering and shooting glances at the skin gear we wore; but there was nothing more than a bright display of affiliated drinks brands and a handful of people starting their Sunday night early. Nobody seemed to be investing in us even the mundane hostility of the provinces.

I told Adam, 'There's something I've missed.'

'Can we go home now?' he said.

'We could check that stretch of road again.'

'James. There was nothing there.'

'There's not *nothing*, Ads. There was a brick through our window and I've been having online sex with Nicky Crane.'

Adam frowned at me, as if he had been missing something himself.

'*What?*' I said.

'He's not . . .' He spoke carefully, as if to an invalid. 'Whoever this guy is he's not *Nicky Crane*, James.'

I shook my head, impatient. 'I don't know who he is.'

'Nicky Crane is dead. He died of AIDS.'

'Don't patronize me, Ads. You don't know everything, OK? There's some fucked-up stuff involved. I've been trying to . . . protect you.' But when he heard that he looked more worried about me than himself.

'Protect me from what?' he said.

I began to answer, then breathed out and shook my head. This wasn't the time to explain about the Death Ritual and aeonic manipulation.

Adam said, 'Someone's been fucking with you. James, what

325

are we *doing* here? Jesus, I thought . . . We go home, now, OK? And we go to the police.'

'That's right,' I said quietly, 'you go find some real men,' and Adam gave me a nervous, frowning smile and said, 'What?'

The barmaid was finishing a barrel. Its dregs hissed and spattered from the tap. 'Go on then,' I told him. 'Go home.'

'Don't be silly. Come on.' He put his hand on mine.

In a tone I hadn't known I was capable of, I said, 'Fuck off, Ads.'

His whole head jerked, and his eyes filmed suddenly with water. He stood up and grabbed his jacket, trying to get out before I saw him cry.

TELL US YOUR FEELINGS ABOUT THE SUBJECT OF NICKY CRANE, ONCE A CLOSE FRIEND, AND THEN TURNED OUT TO BE A GAY.
I feel more betrayed by him than probably anybody else, because he was the head of our security. I actually used to stick up for him when people used to say that he was a queer, because he convinced me that he wasn't. I always used to ask him why he worked at these gay clubs, telling him that he'd get a bad name. He used to say that it was the security firm that he used to work with, that they used to give him the jobs there. I accepted him at face value, as he was a nationalist. I was fooled the same as everybody else. Perhaps more than everybody else. I felt I was betrayed by him and I want nothing to do with him whatsoever. He's dug his own grave as far as I'm concerned. He has actually been in touch with me after the program was aired, he wanted to assure me that he wouldn't sell out the nationalist cause, which I wouldn't expect him to do anyway, considering that he went through so many things for nationalism. It's a big shame that he turned out to be a homosexual because he could have been a good nationalist. It just goes to show that nationalism and homosexuality do not fit in together, because nationalism is a true cause and homosexuality is a perversion. Nicky Crane left, and I think that it was the best thing he could have done, but he should have left a hell of a lot earlier. He was living a lie for all of them years. I've got no respect for the bloke anymore.

Ian Stuart, interviewed in *Last Chance* fanzine 13, *circa* 1992

The Yorkshire Grey

It is Saturday, 12 September 1992, and he is nearly at the top of the escalator when loud noise startles the surrounding chat. Shadows, massed against daylight above, steam into the lads up front, who react with jerky panicked yells. The assault is transmitted through the packed line of bodies: Tony grabs the handrail as the man in front stumbles back. A rain of missiles: something hard and heavy strikes his head; his skull rings with a dull interior sound. Glass explodes next to him on the ad for *Miss Saigon*, spraying his shoulder and the side of his face, his eyes automatically, mercifully, closed. Impacts echo up the long enclosure. The force of a renewed attack piles others back again and knocks him, tethered by his gripping hand, flat against the side. His legs scrabble to stand as one of the guys from the tube falls backwards past him in a mess of flailing. There is a cracking noise and a short slide and the man is prone against the moving stairs. He tries to sit up, disengaging whatever kept him in place, and slips again, arse and coccyx bumping hard on steps till his arms make a jamming brace beneath. His comrades rush forward, yelling in German. Tony sees the guys ahead huddling in a tortoise formation so when they come off the escalator they can force themselves far enough that they're not shoved down it again: he runs to join it and in a blind push they stumble over the top and out on to the concourse, where the cluster comes apart and Tony, reeling in the sudden space, tries to take in what's happening.

Waterloo Station is an arena of shouts and chaos. There are people running in all directions, groups joining and splitting, and scores of fights up and down the length of the concourse: one-on-ones and five-on-ones and ten-on-tens. Under the repeating brown-and-orange logo of Smiths, scruffy figures boot one skin against the lowered shutter's rattling base. Three policemen struggle to subdue a bearded man just feet from Tony: one grips him from behind with his arm round the man's neck and his knee hammering his spine, while his colleagues pull back one arm each, producing a cruciform position in their opponent that seems designed to display his T-shirt, which says THE ONLY GOOD NAZI and then a graphic of a skewered swastika and then IS A DEAD ONE. Three blacks now occupy the top of the escalator: one swings a crowbar at the void, from which angry yells emerge. Some skins try to intervene but before Tony can see what happens his vision is thrown into an unwilling spin by a hard punch to his right cheekbone. A kick to his calf tries to trip him, but he stays standing: the blind instinctive swipe of his arm connects ineffectually with something oddly soft but buys time to face his attacker, a man in his forties with long artless hair and a white top under a padded waistcoat: perhaps what Tony hit. He fixes Tony with an exhilarated grin and starts punching at his head and stomach, yelling 'Fucking nazi scum' in a Brummie accent. Tony tries to get in a kick at his balls but there's not enough room: the commie's legs are in his way and vice versa so all they can do is mutually kick shins, beating each other ineffectually and collapsing inward as they do; nearly embracing now, an intimate exhalation of warm mint, each pair of hands moving to bash and scratch the other's head. Tony grips the man's ears in a hot squeeze and with a little bounce and tug tries to head-butt him, but the other reacts too quickly, and with guts, actually moving closer so that instead of Tony's forehead smashing his nose in, they impact messily, with an agonizing crack above Tony's cheekbone. He hears the noise in his whole head and loses vision in that eye, he is stumbling, but before his attacker can take advantage a policeman jumps him from behind. Tony backs off as the officer gets eagerly astride the man, shoving his face at the floor and scrabbling to cuff him.

Tony's eye feels horribly squashed. Sight is returning in ebbs between dark purple pulses and there is the pink shimmer of blood. He puts his hand to his face and despite the pain probes the socket for looseness, but the bone feels whole. He covers the eye and looks around. He is backed into a corner of the station, almost offstage; can hear his own gasping breath. From what he sees (with one eye working and the other making glitches like television interference) the skinheads are badly outnumbered, dispersed like morsels for the mass of reds, which has somehow occupied the entire station, to forage. The only challenge to them, and a welcome distraction, is the police. They don't have the numbers to corral all the commies but are making violent token arrests, beating individual targets far past the point of just subduing them, to intimidate others into leaving. The blacks who had taken the top of the escalator, he's pleased to see, are now a choice example of this . . . but before he can enjoy the display of truncheon work someone is out of nowhere beside him and saying, 'Excuse me.'

Tony starts, before processing the lack of threat in the words, the suit and hovering microphone. '*Sky News*,' says the man, pointing to his camera-hefting colleague. 'Are you with Blood & Honour?'

Tony squints at the lens. 'I'm just here to catch a train.'

'Don't worry, we're not filming – put the camera down, Mike, would you? We're looking for the organizers of this concert, or whatever it is. Do you know where we can find them?'

Tony spits the excess liquid from his mouth. 'Can't help you mate.'

The reporter looks annoyed. 'They said they'd be available for interviews now. Waterloo Station. How are we meant to find them?' He looks around, demonstrating the problem. 'I guess they weren't expecting this.'

'They better not have been is all I can say.'

'Thanks. Shit. Mike, can we get some more of the riot from here . . . ?'

They walk away, ignoring him now. He is watching them frame a shot when he hears shouting: 'Over there!' – somehow the noise of someone singling you out is uniquely penetrating – and three reds approach, grimacing with effort. Tony turns for the exit at the top of the station, but before he gets there it fills with dogs – suddenly, as if curtains parted – a hunting pack of twenty or thirty and, gripping their leashes, more police. He lunges out of the way and they charge straight for his pursuers, the cameraman, he sees, already filming this. Then there is a hand on his arm and a policeman saying, 'Come with me, we'll get you out of here.' But instead of taking him through the exit he leads Tony, who does not argue, to the middle of the concourse, standing with him like an au pair while the dog handlers break apart and spread through the station. More policemen approach where Tony stands, some bringing other skinheads, and he sees what they're doing, gathering all the nationalists into a group they can cordon off and protect. Soon there are twenty skins, then forty, ringed by as many police again, and it feels like a school outing or something, the skinheads dazed and largely silent, several bleeding, too drained to return much abuse to the reds, who jeer from an enforced distance and occasionally lob bottles despite excited warnings from the police.

Clustered together on the wide space of the concourse, in sunlight falling through the high glass panels of the roof (where the noise of the fighting calmly echoes, and from a rafter of which descends a big orange triangle that for some reason wants to label where they stand with the letter G – a pigeon settles on this marker and launches restlessly off), the skinheads watch their escorts rescue isolated colleagues, some needing to have attackers pulled from them one by one, others emerging from hiding places (two were behind an unmanned information desk) and joining the assembly of their own sheepish accord, avoiding the eyes of officers parting to admit them.

If you look along the roof there are more of those triangles. H near where the dogs came in, and past the big central clock F, and another beyond that too far for him to read. Across the top of the Departures board runs an unbroken row of CANCELLEDS and DELAYEDS.

'All right Tony?'

'What are you doing here?'

'Coppers can't tell the difference can they?' says Glenn. 'All just skinheads to them.' He smiles. He has somehow got right next to Tony; he speaks quietly, but does not whisper.

Tony can't hack the look in his eyes and turns away. 'Wanker.'

'There's a few of us here, not just me. Well, we're on CCTV now aren't we, don't want to do nothing heavy. But the nice officers are going to walk us all outside for your safety and that. And there's no cameras out there.'

'You're a fucking race traitor Glenn.' Tony, because he doesn't know what would happen otherwise, collaborates in the conversational hush: they could be queuing at a supermarket checkout. 'You're worse than a fucking nigger.'

'If you like. I just wanted to tell you before it kicks off. There's a truce between us as far as I'm concerned. For old times' sake. But I can't speak for the other lads, so I'd run if I was you. When you get the chance. Is this bonehead wanker a friend of yours?'

He kicks both ankles of the man in front, who stiffens.

'Know him Tony do you?' mutters Glenn.

'No.'

'Good, because when we get out of here he's dead. Did you hear me you daft nazi cunt?' Glenn kicks him again. 'When we get outside I'm going to kill you.' The man is visibly shaking.

Slowly the police begin to move the group towards the far end of the concourse. Beyond the cordon, watching reds yell taunts and insults. Some get a chant going, 'Police protect – nazi scum!,' until the objects of their criticism set dogs on them. Near the driveway for postal vans two men in donkey jackets conduct – amazingly – a paper sale. 'Buy a copy, officers?' one calls as the tense formation troops past. 'Read about how workers pay for government failures. One pound solidarity price.' He waves it after them: *Workers' Power*, it says on a red background, and on black, HANDS OFF IRAQ!

Glenn mutters: 'How's your love life then?'

'Fuck off all right.'

'Touchy aren't you? Don't they know you're a poof these mates of yours?'

Tony says nothing. They are nearly at the closed-off bit where the new station is being built. In two minutes they will be outside.

'Bound to be some likely shags in this lot Tony. You know what these Europeans are like.'

From behind, Tony watches the face of the man Glenn has threatened to kill. He is listening; his pupil trembles against the corner of his eye.

'I can big you up if you like,' Glenn offers. 'You always were good in bed.'

The subdued shuffle of the skins' boots as they are herded sounds like rain against the roof.

'Better than Nicky if I had to be honest. To my taste anyway. Probably because in your own way you were even more fucked up. Did you see him on telly the other week? Bet that upset a few people.'

They file through the doorway and down the steps.

'You know what my favourite bit was? Right after you'd come. You'd always go a bit bad-tempered but I liked it. Do you still talk in your sleep?' he adds, mimicking: '"Hello? Hello?"'

They stand at the bottom of the stairs, where the sloping access road leads to the street. People are quiet: the skins, many aware by now of what is happening, waiting for the infiltrators to strike, not sure, with so many foreigners and out-of-towners, which of their neighbours to trust; the police oblivious, relieved to have got the nationalists out of the station and apparently with no plan for what to do next. You'd think they would either disperse them or at least keep moving but for now there's nothing going on.

Tony tenses, waits.

And as if at some signal (but none that he notices) it happens. The group explodes from within, like it was packed with charges, amid yells of triumph and surprise. Not expecting such a swell of force, the police perimeter strains, is breached, fragments. People are on top of each other like skins at a gig. In front of Tony, Glenn's nominated victim spots a gap and is already running, Glenn managing only an approximate blow – with a stick produced from somewhere – as he goes. Not waiting to see more, Tony pushes against the thinnest part of the surrounding crowd and breaks through.

He runs. Down the slope into the wide street below, and over towards the river. He has no plan but to gain distance. His hurt eye feels newly tight with the rush of blood from sprinting.

In the protection of the South Bank complex he slows and

335

breathes deep and long, looking about in case there are reds here too. There's no point going back to Waterloo. He could phone Steve and ask where the gig is. But when he has climbed the stairs by the concert hall, panting by the statue of the terrorist Mandela, a large crowd of skins approaches from the footbridge across the Thames. They wear jeans and black bomber jackets with patches, or camouflage, and several carry backpacks. They are grinning and chatting as they saunter towards him. One walks up to Tony. 'Hello, mate,' he says, 'are you going to the concert?' He has a foreign accent but good English. 'Is it that way to Waterloo?'

'Yeah but it's fucking chaos over there.'

'Chaos?'

'Communists.'

The man grins. 'We can handle communists. Come with us.' He holds out his hand – 'I'm Peter' – and introduces a few companions, whose names Tony doesn't take in. 'We're from Antwerp,' Peter says. 'It's in Belgium.'

'Tony,' says Tony, looking over Peter's shoulder. There are sixty or seventy men with him.

'We've come a long way for this,' Peter says.

When they arrive back at Waterloo, the base of the steps is occupied by about twenty skins: the reds have retreated inside. The skins shout into the entrance, guarded by uncertain police; one or two wave swastika flags. As the Belgians arrive, the groups salute each other across the street.

'Can't get in,' an English skin tells Tony. 'Too many reds. Coppers can't control them so they're keeping us out instead.'

'Anyone seen an organizer?'

'What do you fucking think?'

'Listen,' Tony says, 'a mate of mine should know where the gig is. He's one of the stewards. I'll try and get hold of him.'

Tony leaves the Belgians with the others and crosses the

road to the nearest phone box. He roots around in his wallet for the scrap of paper where he once wrote Steve's cellular number, and to his surprise finds it. He pushes a phonecard into the slot and dials. The display flicks on: £5.60.

A long pause, then a faint and crackly ring. Over the road, a policeman walks down the steps and speaks to the nearest skins.

No answer. Tony dials again. This time, after several rings, conversation and loud laughter. 'Hello?'

'Steve?'

'Who's this?'

'Steve it's Tony.'

.' . . who?'

'Tony.'

'Tony mate how's it going?'

£4.90. Jesus. 'Where are you Steve?'

'What? I'm in the pub mate.'

'What pub?'

'Down Victoria.'

'Victoria?'

'What?'

Down the road, a gang of forty or so casuals are approaching from County Hall. The policeman talking to the skins has gone. Nobody guards the entrance now; the skins are animated; something is about to happen. They talk or argue and look anxiously round. A group of six breaks off for the roundabout.

'Steve I'm at Waterloo. There's a hundred of us and we can't find any—'

'—mess down there isn't it?'

'What?'

'I said it sounds like a fucking mess down there. It's all over the radio.'

'Well there's no organizers are there? No one knows where the gig is.'

'—here with me.'

'What?'

'You need to get it sorted down there mate. Can't do a redirection with the reds running the place.'

£3.85.

'Can you tell me where the concert is?'

'Just get down here OK?'

'What?'

'Get yourself down to Victoria. We can't give the venue out there, it'll be overrun with fucking AFA.'

'Listen Steve this is costing me a fucking fortune—'

'I'll see you down here all right?'

'No you need to fucking tell me where the—*Shit*.'

'What?'

'They're fucking—'

A rain of bottles and God knows what else from the station entrance is the opening volley announcing a massive surge of reds from the building. They pour down the steps and pile into the skins, while others spill over the footbridge that emerges from the station's side. Still more appear on the access road. There must be, what, five hundred of them? Six?

'Steve we're getting fucking slaughtered down here.'

'So don't stay there you pillock. Get down to Victoria.'

'Hello?'

'I said get down to—'

The phone beeps and spits out the finished card. For nobody's benefit, Tony slams the handset against the glass.

The fight at the base of the steps spills into the street. No questioning that the reds have the numbers. A fleeing skin gets halfway over the road and is intercepted by a piece of fencing, swung at his chest and knocking him down. He tries to curl into a ball; the mandatory kicking begins. Along the road, the casuals are trading missiles with a gang (heavy with Asians) advancing in pincer formation towards them, when thirty riot cops appear in an urgent trot. Batons first, they force their way between the sides, ring-fencing the casuals under the foot-bridge – but haven't reckoned on the reds above, who hurl bricks and broken quarry tiles from the bridge at their now helpfully stationary targets.

The sound of brakes pulls Tony's focus closer. A Rover has swerved to avoid the fight and pulled up near his phone box. The four skins inside are debating what to do and staring at the masonry blitz on the casuals ahead: unable to warn them Tony watches a passing teenager in a hooded top reach through the driver's open window and grab the ignition key. Thus immobilized, the car is set upon by the kid and his mates, who jump on the roof and bonnet and smash the windows. The thief waves the keys cheerily at the passengers, who shield their faces from the wash of glass.

Then, as if in mimicry, the door of the phone box implodes: a great crystalline crunch and shatter. The rock that broke it hits Tony in the back, but its momentum was dampened by the glass and the impact is not more than an immediate sharp ache. The real threat is what follows: he turns to see what looks like a paper seller from the station, not that there's time to be sure, making over-arm psycho jabs with a screwdriver though the voided frame – 'I'll give you fucking Skrewdriver,' he yells; he must have tooled up with the line in mind – which Tony only partly deflects, trapped in place, pressed against the back. He tries to bash the man away with the telephone hand-set but gets stabbed a little in the neck, a gash riding over his jawbone: not a serious wound but it could have been and hurts like fuck. He tries to focus through the pain and keep fighting off these lunges, any one of which could be bad should it con-nect. The tool pistons at him through the gap, Tony dodging it or blocking the man's forearm as best he can. He could make a grab for the screwdriver but it might go through his palm. The man's elbow is bloody where, jabbing at him, it has scraped the crumbled glass fringing the door's edge: and in the moment in which that detail is distracting Tony, the man stabs him in the top of the head and like a stunned cow's in an abattoir his legs spasm and give way. In fact this isn't all bad because although he's now down in a heap and unable to fight back, or do much at all except try to shield himself, at least his assailant moves on from the screwdriver, pulling back the skeleton of the door and kicking Tony on any accessible surface, which is his legs and the side of his body and, until he raises his arms to cover it, his head, the man's boot relentless as a demolition ball, worst on the side of the ribcage, which he's worried will crack, and below that where his kidney is. Among the general variety of pain Tony is just noticing that he feels sick, when hands yank his assailant's shoulders roughly back.

Tony watches in confusion and (briefly unconcealed) relief as Glenn says something, and the man says something, and there's half an argument but not much of one. The man makes one last taunting gesture with his screwdriver at the slumped and wary Tony, kicks him one more time and is gone.

Glenn crouches over him. 'You're too old for this,' he says. 'You can't look after yourself no more.'

'I was doing all right.'

'Go home Tony.' He touches the head wound and Tony winces.

'Don't waste your whole life with this shit eh?'

.' . . It's what I believe in.'

Glenn stretches. 'We shut down Waterloo, Tony. Coppers closed the whole fucking station. And Lambeth North. And Charing Cross. And someone glassed Ian Stuart in the face last night, in a pub down in Burton on Trent – did you know that? Can you get up?'

He does, slowly. Watching, Glenn adds, as if it follows: 'Oh and you'll never guess. I had sex with a Asian guy last

Christmas. Sort of felt I had to, to be honest, do you know what I mean? But it was nice. He was really nice.'

Tony brushes broken glass off himself with the sleeve of his jacket. More of the stuff squeaks and crunches under his boots. Without looking at Glenn he says, 'Did you say you're still in touch with Nicky?'

'Yeah I still see him sometimes.'

'Do you know where he is?'

'Come on Tony. I can't give that out, not after the telly thing. He'll be fucking firebombed.'

'You know me better than that.'

'Yeah maybe.'

Two long-haired men chase a skin from the roundabout: catch up, trip and kick him; one stamps on his head. Distance and the general chaos render these actions silent.

'Why do you want to know anyway?' Glenn says.

'I just . . .' Tony is not sure himself. 'There's something he should have.'

Glenn sighs rhetorically. 'Flat on Rupert Street. Over the caff. And if anything happens to him there's a hundred of us coming for you.'

'Nothing's going to happen.'

'Yeah.' Glenn kicks the frame of the phone box. 'I'll warn him anyway. Listen. If you ever get out of all this, look me up, won't you? We'll have a drink or something.'

Peter the Belgian spots Tony lying on the patch of grass by the river, staring at the sky. There are still reds everywhere and he should really have kept moving, but either no one noticed Tony or they decided from the look of him he'd had enough. The Belgians peer down at him, relatives over a cot.

'Hello, mate,' says Peter. 'You look like shit, you know?'

Peter himself is utterly pristine.

Tony smiles up. 'Good holiday so far?'

Peter laughs. 'It's been fucking crap if you come to mention it. But neither is it over. We found out where the concert is. Now: how in Jesus Christ's name do we get to' – he consults a piece of paper from his pocket – 'Eltham?'

The toilets of the Yorkshire Grey are plastered with stickers. In the space above the urinal, through the bump and sway and self-imposed tunnel vision (there's not much space and the man to his right is bumping his side, mumbling inaudibly) Tony reads:

WHITE POWER. NATIONAL FRONT and

BRITAIN AWAKE. BRITISH MOVEMENT and

HANG I.R.A. MURDERERS. BRITISH NATIONAL PARTY and

FAITH. FAMILY. NATION. INTERNATIONAL THIRD POSITION and

JEWS OWN 75% OF THE PET FOOD INDUSTRY! WHERE ARE OUR MISSING CHILDREN? THINK. K– K– K and

KILL THEM ALL. COMBAT 18

In the pub, No Remorse are playing. To the brown curtains that hang stage rear, a single Blood & Honour flag has been tacked; too low: the musicians obscure it. The place was booked for many more people than the couple of hundred who have made it so far: the room is too big and feels empty. Still, those present will not show defeat. Paul, the singer, who edits the *Blood & Honour* fanzine and helped organize the gig, tries to whip them up between songs. He's not the world's best speaker ('Hitler and the six million Jews' – pause – 'it's all a load of shit') but the intention is there and there's a lot of good will from the concert's simply going ahead. Paul's brother, John, is at the front of the audience, waving his pint in support and slopping lager on the stage. He's Skrewdriver's drummer and due for trial in Germany: apparently he and his mates went on a bit of a rampage last year after a gig to celebrate reunification. He got the bail money from their dad, who Tony's heard is some famous artist and mortified by what his kids get up to.

342

Bored of rambling at the audience, Paul tells his band to start the next song. He shouts the words at the microphone point-blank:

'Filthy little Asian
With his corner shop . . .'

Some watching skins have already stripped to the waist. A guy around Tony's age – older? – tall and scrawny, with a hairless chest, dances in a space by himself, holding his fag and his pint. His movements are old-fashioned, with a touch of the early '80s about them – the way his arms move up and down in front of him like a marionette's – maybe even a memory of reggae. He has a big chin, and a mouth slightly open in a permanent O, as if trying to verbalize some elusive thought. The younger lads (there are younger ones, new ones, every time) are more raucous; they're not dancing yet, but keep yelling at Paul and saluting. A kid of sixteen has black hair and a Millwall shirt, both soaked with sweat. He grins joyfully and nods in endless, enthusiastic assent: if you could see only him you might guess he was at a rave instead of a B&H gig. But his friend's a skin, faithfully reproducing the old grammar in shiny new miniature: the Millwall boy puts a hand on his damp, bare shoulder to tell him something, and lets it rest there when he's finished talking.

'Sells his goods at double price
That's how he makes his bread
Filthy little Paki
Won't stop till he's dead.'

Tony heads to the bar for another beer. He's already had a few (three provided by Peter from Belgium, who clearly has money to piss up the wall), and the room is rippling gently in

343

response. The alcohol long ago took the edge off the pain: he's still aching all over, but almost pleasantly, like when you're tired from labour. A couple of lads have asked about the scab, still moist and forming on his head, but most ignore it: there are plenty of bruises and wounds on show. The train they got to New Cross was like coming back from the front, only with no women waiting. The police had cleared the platform and warned blacks to keep away. Someone on the train claimed the ethnics who worked at Waterloo had been given the day off and all . . . and someone else said they'd seen Derek Beackon, the BNP's chief steward, turning up hours after it all kicked off. Not impressive. The BNP are sharing security detail with the BM tonight, but Beackon hasn't shown his face yet. Steve, on the other hand, is walking round like he owns the joint. He keeps glad-handing people, but the greetings are too theatrical and drawn out: he is probably dealing. The casual look suits him, thinks Tony; the loose clothes are vaguer about his bulk, and if you were feeling generous you could say the hair makes him look younger. That fucking cellular is fastened at his waist like a cop accoutrement. The girl behind the bar has Tony's pint ready and has been trying to get his attention – he wonders how long she's been waiting. She winks when she takes his money, her make-up a circus clown's. He wanders away from the bar, stumbling a step and recovering, and takes a first long pull at his pint. It is bad timing: a dense, eggy fart nearby turns the beer sulphurous in his mouth, and Steve is all over him. 'Pardon me,' he laughs, clapping Tony on the back so the beer spills: 'Watch your step eh?,' and he has moved on.

Tony steadies himself and scans the room. People are still arriving, but it won't be full. In fact (he was hardly paying attention) No Remorse sound like they're finishing: a roar; a blitzkrieg on the drums; purposive, protracted claps and cheers. Paul is saying thanks and something about a bit of an interval before the main act: as he does, before him, with a growing rumble, bodies break from the stage like chunks from an iceberg and float towards the bar. Conversations resume but it's still quieter than it was – people were talking over the music anyway – and in this lull Tony has been gazing without processing it at a figure leaning by himself near the door, with a sheaf of magazines in one arm and a half-drunk pint that he sips, looking around as if deciding whether to stay. He has neat red hair and glasses; it was probably the latter that kept him so unspecific, but now he looks through them at Tony and smiles. Tony, drenched in a wash of feelings too thoroughly blended to identify, plods over, a hippo from his stagnant pond; it seems neither of them, particularly (with no hand free, between pint glass and magazines, for shaking) Dave, quite knows how to greet the other; so they just smile and nod and eventually Tony says:

'Hello.'

'All right Tony. How's it going?'

'Yeah not bad. Didn't think I'd see you here.'

Nodding: 'Didn't you?'

'Not your sort of thing no more is it?'

'Well you're right of course. But it was meant to be big so I thought I'd hand out some of these.' He bumps the pile of magazines, wedged between his hand and armpit, up and down.

'Can I have a look?'

'Go ahead.'

Dave contorts a little to release the outmost copy, which Tony pulls out. *The Kent Crusader* says the cover.

'Looks good. Is this yours?'

'Me and a few mates.'

'"In support of the International Third Position."'

Dave laughs. 'Yeah actually we're not any more. We're starting our own movement – just voted on it. But the contact address is still ours so I reckon we may as well give them out instead of chucking them.'

Tony flicks through. 'I thought you was with them for the long haul.'

'I was. It's them that changed, not us.' Dave takes a longer pull of his pint. 'It's turned into a sort of Catholic cult to be honest with you. And most of us don't like it, and they know that and they don't want us changing it, so they just got rid of the cadre system. Everything revolutionary about it's gone. We're just carrying on what the ITP was supposed to be. What the Front was supposed to be, when I joined.'

'You got a name yet?'

Dave's smile is almost shy. 'English Nationalist Movement.'

'That's not bad.'

'Well it does what it says on the tin doesn't it. There's a good few of us actually. Do you remember a chap—'

'You know what mate, don't tell me too much.'

Dave looks at him, taken aback.

'. . . I mean,' Tony goes on quickly, 'it's not that the particulars of your latest split aren't the most exciting thing I've heard in a hundred years, do you know what I mean?'

Dave smiles. 'Yeah sorry.'

'At least you're doing something.'

'You can keep the magazine if you like.'

'Anything in there by you?'

'About half of it.'

'See if I can guess which bits.'

'Have you moved or something Tony? Because I phoned a few times.'

'Did you? I've had terrible problems with that answering machine. I keep meaning to get a new one.'

'Yeah I thought it might be something like that.'

The audience starts to cheer. The Skrewdriver musicians are taking the stage and making unnecessary, crowd-teasing checks of their instruments. The microphone stand is still unoccupied: Ian Stuart might be waiting behind a door, or perhaps he's just at the foot of the stage, hidden behind the crowd.

'Here we go,' Tony says.

'Listen Tony let's have a pint sometime. It's been years.'

'Well I'll replace that machine next week so give me a ring.'

'All right I will.'

'Nice glasses by the way.' Tony winks at Dave and, with the pretence of examining them and the armour of a mocking grin, allows himself to look in Dave's eyes for longer than usual: two seconds, three. He calculates, in the very moment of wondering, that Dave must be thirty, and the realization comes like fingers on the back of his neck and silences the stamps and yells. He looks away. Ian Stuart is making them wait; the muffled thunder of boots gathers, grows. A boy sits on the edge of the stage, looking out over the crowd like a swimmer contemplating a pool. His hair is cropped but not shaved, or shaved at least a week ago, his widow's peak visible. He is eighteen, perhaps, ugly in a sexy way: flattish nose, watery eyes, heavy lips. He wears a Skrewdriver Security T-shirt. There have been a few designs in the years between, but apart from the off-centre placing of the SS rune this one looks the same as Steve and Nicky wore at that first Suffolk concert: years back.

'Did you see Nicky on telly?' Tony turns and says this with what feels like ridiculous speed, so that it seems unlikely Dave could have heard, but he pauses only briefly before replying:

'I did Tony yeah.'

.' . . Unbelievable. Wasn't it?'

Dave smiles. 'I thought it was quite funny.'

'Yeah that too.'

'We're still going to be . . . against it. In the ENM. Homosexuality and that. Nothing Catholic of course. More a sort of discipline thing really.'

'Well you have to be don't you?'

'Just to sort of have it in the law.'

The rumbling breaks into sudden thunder: Ian Stuart is at last on stage. He is dressed in black; his short-sleeved shirt bears a big Skrewdriver patch. He extends his right arm and holds it, immobile, impassive. The crowd returns the salute. The shouts of '*Sieg heil!*,' at first chaotic, converge into rhythm.

'Here we go,' Tony says again, raising his arm.

'Took his time didn't he.'

'I might go a bit closer.'

'I'll ring you next week then,' says Dave. 'Enjoy the gig yeah?'

Pushing forward, arm outstretched, Tony cannot feel the floor against his feet. The Skrewdriver Security boy regards the ranged salutes with a wary smile that he soon, upon visible reflection, substitutes with a scowl. Something about him reminds Tony of Dave at that age. Above, Ian persists in silent acceptance of the tribute. Nobody glassed him last night, Tony thinks first, in Burton on Trent or anywhere else, but then he sees that Ian's lip swells slightly at its bottom left. From this distance it could be a cold-sore scab.

Tony finishes his pint with his left hand while still holding out his right, and is already getting another at the bar when Ian lowers his salute and over the barely abating cheers nods to John, Paul's brother, who starts a fast rat-a-tat on his drums. After a moment the guitarist joins in and they go straight into – what else? – 'Back with a Bang.' When Ian opens his mouth wide to drive home the chorus, Tony sees he is missing a couple of teeth.

Ian sings 'Tomorrow Belongs to Me' and 'Europe Awake' and tells the crowd about the glassing incident and the gang of niggers that did it (they told him, 'The gig's off tomorrow, you nazi bastard,' only as Ian points out it isn't, is it, and everyone salutes and shouts again). He sings 'Streetfight' and 'The Showdown' and lays into the reds at Waterloo who tried to stop the concert. He says, 'Whatever the vermin does, we'll be there with a pint and a stiff right arm.' In support of this Tony gets another pint himself.

Ian sings 'Paranoid' by Black Sabbath and 'United' by Judas Priest. He sings two more of his own songs, 'Our Pride Is Our Loyalty' and 'Hail the New Dawn,' and in homage to a recent cross-burning ceremony up in Walsall he sings 'Johnny Joined the Klan,' which is his version of 'Johnny B. Goode'; the original is by Chuck Berry and that's quite funny when you think about it.

Tony has another pint and more guys are dancing with their shirts off. It's dark and loud and hot and Ian shouts and growls into the microphone and sometimes stops to talk politics between the songs.

Ian says: 'They keep sending us these fucking niggers, they keep sending us these Pakis, they keep sending us these dirty Jewish fuckers to take over our fucking country.'

Tony shouts, '*Sieg heil*,' and when the drums start again he jumps up and down and spills most of his lager on a brick shit-house of a German. He apologizes and buys a couple of pints for the German and his mates and replaces his own. Peter the Belgian watches with a little smile.

Ian sings 'Blood & Honour' and 'Stand Proud' and a version of 'Sweet Home Alabama' by Lynyrd Skynyrd and '46 Years' which is a song he wrote when Rudolf Hess died and appears, like 'Sweet Home Alabama,' on the album *After the Fire*, which Nicky did the cover art for, an old gnarled tree on a bleak landscape, with grave markers underneath and birds tiny against the sky.

He doesn't sing 'Justice' from *Hail the New Dawn*, a song Nicky wrote the lyrics for, about when he was sent down for that fight at the Woolwich Arsenal, only Tony always wondered if the line 'My poor mother's screams numb me with shock' was about something else as well. Nicky designed the cover for that album too.

Tony goes back to the bar and Ian goes back to the glassing incident. He says: 'Do we want these subhuman black bastards in this country? Do we fuck! It's about time the lot of them were either gassed or fucking shipped out.'

Ian says: 'Walk down the street in this country, what do you get? Some fucking big-lipped, flat-nosed black bastard walking along' (he does an impression of this, with a comic roll of his shoulders, and people laugh as well as shout and salute again) 'going, "Raas man," fucking barging the skinheads out of the way. He don't fucking do that if it was a fucking proper society.'

Ian says, 'We'll have the black filth out one day, don't worry about it. And if we don't throw them out we'll fucking gas them.'

Tony stumbles from the bar. The room is a hot dark mass of noise, the songs blending into each other now; Ian is at one point singing, '*Strikeforce!* White survival . . . *Strikeforce!* Kill all rivals,' and in what feels like the same moment but can't be because it's a different song, bellowing, '*Smash! Smash!* the I – R – A!,' with everyone yelling and stamping along. Ian gives a *sieg heil* salute on every 'Smash!' and Tony is lurching a bit as he watches and has the feeling of the movement around him slowing even as the sounds speed up; there is a mass before him that swells and threatens to engulf and then he is into it and it is soft and damp and smells of sweat, pushing him back and saying 'Whoa there' and the mass is Steve.

'Watch yourself,' Steve says.

Tony isn't sure how he wants to reply but it comes out like: 'I – ow.'

Steve squints into Tony's eyes. 'You all right mate?'

'Have you gu—' says Tony, and pitches forward a few degrees.

'Oh Jesus. OK come with me. Let's get you outside.'

Steve nudges him in little steps towards the door. Behind them, Ian is introducing another song. He says he wants to dedicate it to a new group the reds have just found out about and they're doing a good job and something about Charlie who looks like a schoolboy but there's never been anyone less like a schoolboy (Oh yeah, Tony thinks through his haze, *Charlie*) and this song is for them, Redwatch – at which Steve turns back, pulling Tony into an emetic swerve, to raise his arm in acknowledgement. As the song begins they push through the door and stagger together down the steps and fall into a seating position. When he hits the step Tony belches and he thinks he's going to be sick. He leans over and retches but the moment has passed.

Steve says, 'Think you've had enough mate.'

Tony says, 'No I just . . .' and then falls silent, looking out at the cars circling the roundabout ahead (red lights to the left, white to the right).

'Fuck,' he mumbles after a moment, blinking at his feet. The ground is slowing to a halt. He says: 'I didn't know you were Redwatch.'

'I'm not anything mate.'

'Thought you were BM.'

'Oh does that still exist does it?'

'Yeah well,' Tony says.

Behind them Skrewdriver is playing 'When the Boat Comes in.' Ian leads the whole audience in the chorus:

'Nigger, nigger, get on that boat
Nigger, nigger, row
Nigger, nigger, get out of here
Nigger, nigger, go, go, go . . .'

'Anyway,' Steve says, 'it's not called Redwatch no more. The organization I mean. *Redwatch* is the magazine.' He pulls a crumpled copy from his windcheater and hands it to Tony, who smooths it with his palm. It uses the same three-bladed swastika for its logo as Blood & Honour.

'They'll be running this lot soon,' Steve says, nodding back at the pub.

On the cover is a picture of gas canisters. Across them is written: 'ZYKLON-B: OVER SIX MILLION SATISFIED CUSTOMERS. MANUFACTURED BY COMBAT 18.'

'Very nice,' Tony says.

'We're not pissing about.'

Tony flicks through. It's just a few pages, mainly names and addresses: union reps, race mixers and the like. Haddo House, he thinks, and puts it down on the step. 'Steve have you got anything?'

'Like what?'

'Nothing heavy. I just feel a bit . . .'

'What like speed?'

Tony shakes his head.

'I've got some Diazepam.'

'That's more like it.'

'You're half asleep already.'

'Don't matter.'

'Well it's up to you. Tenner.'

Tony swallows the pills. Inside, another chorus of 'Nigger, nigger' begins.

'BM's getting sidelined,' Steve says. 'Front's finished. BNP, C18: they're the only ones doing anything. Skinheads are over: you want to grow your hair. Skinheads are wankers, they're either queers or reds. Did you see Nicky Crane on telly? The turds always float to the fucking surface.'

'I can't grow my hair. What am I meant to do, dress like you?'

'What's wrong with how I dress?'

'Can't afford it can I. All these labels.'

'A few of us went down a queer pub in Kings Cross the week after that programme went out. Squared the balance a bit. You should have been there.'

'Too old to change anyway.'

'Look at Rostock,' says Steve. 'That's the way to go. Barbecue a few gooks and they start deporting them. Gets results that Althans bloke.'

It's too early, but Tony feels like the Diazepam is already working. Sounds and objects are retreating a little. 'We'll get him soon enough,' Steve is saying, 'old Craney,' but his words are shrinking, solidifying, becoming an object themselves, a little marble Tony could flick away. He peers at it.

'Can't see me going round in football shirts,' he tells the marble.

'Well,' says Steve, blowing smoke from a cigarette Tony hasn't noticed him light, 'I suppose you never was much of a football fan was you Tony?'

'I've been Millwall,' Tony answers, 'since I was a kid.'

'If you say so mate.'

Something is uncomfortable where Tony sits, against his arse. It's not the pencil in his right pocket but something wide and thick, which he pulls out and puts at his feet. Steve picks it up. 'That yours?' he asks.

Tony squints at it: *The Kent Crusader*. He thinks, Oh right.

'Dave,' he explains. 'He's here tonight. Did you see him?'

'Still into this shit is he?' Steve tosses it to the pavement.

Inside, Skrewdriver are playing 'White Power': it must be the last song, at least before the encores.

'National revolutionary,' says Steve. 'I should go back in.'

The marble is still there, hovering about a foot off the ground. Tony could reach forward and tap it. It catches the light as it spins, distractingly.

'Why did you do it?' he asks Steve, staring at the marble.

'Do what mate?'

Tony's not really sure himself but he carries on, curious to find out:

'Tell them that about Dave and me. You knew it was bollocks.'

Involuntarily, Steve sits up.

'What did they have on you? Was it the dealing?'

He can feel Steve tensing. Steve says, 'Don't talk shit.'

'It's not his fault how I look at him. How could you do it?'

'Mate I haven't got the first fucking idea what you're on about. Go home Tony. You're wasted.'

'Yeah I will. But . . .'

Tony turns and looks into Steve's face.

'Well,' he says.

Maybe it's the way they're sitting, or maybe alcohol and Diazepam have somehow fused into a passing clarity, but it shouldn't be nearly this easy for Tony to stab his sharpened pencil into Steve's throat. He finds it already in his right hand, by his side, and just swings round and thrusts. Steve knocks him away but Tony pushes back and with hardly any apparent resistance (it feels almost exactly like popping a balloon) the pencil is stuck in the side of Steve's Adam's apple. The protruding half wobbles vaguely, a misplaced cigarette, and a small amount of blood runs from the hole. Steve hardly moves.

He stares at Tony and makes an unpleasant noise, a choking rasping glug, one hand circling nervously around the pencil but unwilling to touch it, as if the pencil is a ghost he doesn't believe is there. Tony wonders if Steve would be better or worse off pulling it out. That's not what it was for, anyway, he thinks, just to use all of a sudden, without a fight or nothing. Oh well. After a moment Steve fumbles clumsily at his pocket (his coordination has gone, he looks like a spastic doing it) and, not wanting to find out what he's going for, Tony stands and kicks him hard in the head (much more of an effort, that) and Steve rolls down the steps. Inside a song is ending; probably the last one, from the loud response. Tony is a few feet away when remembers the cellular. He leans over Steve, feels at his waist for the phone and yanks it off, snapping some attachment. Then he crosses the road away from the roundabout and heads into Sutcliffe Park.

Eltham is dark fields at random angles and houses huddled under the pensile branches of trees, and Tony walks through damp grass on an erratic surface (brittle and then a sudden sinking) or passes mainly unlit windows to the sound of muffled televisions and sometimes shouts and sobs, not running because he doesn't have the energy and he's not sure what the point is but not stopping either. The Diazepam is definitely doing something now: he's tired, massively so, as if gravity has increased its pull on all his organs, but somehow it isn't making him want to lie down or even stop; all he can do is continue at this dragging pace and let inertia play itself out.

He knows where he's going without really thinking about it and certainly without planning a route but part of him is still taken aback when after a lot of this lost time he rounds a corner and sees the vast emptiness of Blackheath – the name makes sense at night – like reaching the world's edge and peering out past. That orients his consciousness so he crosses another street and soon he is outside Niven's house. The front door is bolted and heavy, with small, dense arrangements of thick stained glass, but the kitchen door to the back garden is two long plain panes with a thin strip of wood between (and the cat-flap in the base which creaks when he prods it). With the glass broken the separator is a trifle to snap and having knocked the bigger jags from around the edge he can step carefully through. He stands in the kitchen and waits for Niven to creep down at the noise or the arrival of telephoned police but nothing happens, not in all the time it takes to drink a can of beer from the fridge, listening to its hum strain louder the longer he leaves it open for the light. There's no sign of the cat and Tony wonders if it died.

When he has finished the beer he fishes through the cutlery drawer for a knife before he notices the block on the counter. He takes a big *Psycho* number with him when he climbs the stairs. The Nivens' bedroom door is closed. He opens it and feels around inside for the light switch, finding it at roughly the same time that Niven's wife gives a little gasp, far less than a scream. When the light comes on they are both watching him.

'Don't worry about this,' Tony says, gesturing at the knife, and sits on the edge of their bed with it in his lap.

'Oh Tony love,' says Niven's wife.

'What do you want, Tony?' Niven is scared, and trying to look stern.

'Cup of tea would be nice.' Niven's wife actually begins to move at this, so he tells her, 'No, stay here.'

'Are you looking for money?' says Niven. 'Are you on drugs?'

Tony tells him, 'We're all on fucking drugs Arthur.'

It might have been a mistake to sit down; he could practically curl up between them and sleep.

'Didn't make it to the gig then,' Tony remarks.

'You know I don't like that stuff,' says Niven.

356

There is a long silence. He turns the knife about in his palm and bounces a little on the mattress. Niven mutters, 'There's . . . a hundred pounds or so in the top drawer of my desk. It's in a blue envelope.' Eventually he says, 'Tony, have I upset somebody?' He cannot prevent his voice cracking at this, and his wife reaches out to him.

'No nothing like that. Anyway I wouldn't know if you had. I just wanted to talk to you.'

Niven says, 'We could meet in the morning . . .'

'Why haven't you been in touch Arthur?'

'In touch?'

'You used to ask me to do stuff.'

'Oh, it's – nothing personal, Tony.' Niven seems genuinely confused. 'I just haven't needed very much help recently. And there were always people around.'

'I had to tell the police a few things.'

Niven says nothing. He looks surprised, though whether at the information or its admission is not clear.

'I never gave them nothing important. Things they probably knew already. I don't hear much anyway these days. I thought maybe you knew.'

'No.'

'Only they had me for soliciting you see.'

After a pause Niven says, carefully, 'Tony, why have you come here? You broke into my house.'

'Yeah sorry about that. I wanted to tell you because I stabbed Steve. At the gig down in Eltham. I don't think I killed him. Well I don't know to be honest. But he was doing it too. Grassing. I don't know why, maybe because he's been dealing – drugs I mean – and they got him. Or maybe just for cash. But he told them – you remember Dave Masters? He went Third Position – he told them Dave was with me. Which is out of order because Dave's not queer. Well I'm not having that. So. I don't know what else he said but you might want to

357

be careful because he's in with Redwatch – Combat 18 – and I know the League's been working with them so you might want to look into it. I took his phone – his cellular.' He puts it on the bed.

'If the police come round you don't need to lie. I mean I know I'll get done for this. By the law or Steve's mates or both. But I want people to know I never sold out the movement. Not really. I may be queer but I'm not a traitor. And I want them to know what Steve done. That's it I suppose. Sorry Janet I didn't mean to scare you.'

He stops in the doorway: 'I might borrow a bit of that cash for a cab if you don't mind. I'll pay you back and everything.' The blue envelope is labelled *Receipts*. Before he goes downstairs he asks, 'Did you really not know I was queer?' and Niven says:

'I don't think I ever thought about it, Tony.'

'Bye then Arthur,' says Tony. 'Sorry again Janet. *Heil Hitler.*'

Somewhere on Charlton Road he finds an open minicab office. It has peeling white-and-yellow wallpaper, a chair in crushed red velvet to wait in, and a pair of miniature dispensers that sell peanuts and bubblegum in five-pence handfuls.

The staff are all Pakis. The man behind the window says: 'We're not serving you mate.' A sticker in the corner of the glass shows the flag of St George. *England* is written diagonally across it in curling script.

'What this?' says Tony pointlessly, gesturing at his patches. 'I'm off duty.'

'I'm not doing a cab for you. Sorry.'

'I'll pay extra.' Tony holds up the wad of notes he took from Niven.

'Just find somewhere else, man, OK?'

'Look how much do you want just to take me to the West End?'

The man looks at his colleagues in the office behind and shrugs. One of the younger Pakis stands up.

'Double fare,' he says to Tony, 'in advance. And we're not having a conversation, you understand what I'm saying?'

'Let him stew why don't you,' says an older man.

'Fuck it,' replies the kid. He takes his coat from a rack on the wall and is pulling it on as he walks through to the reception. Underneath he wears a sweatshirt that says *San Francisco*.

'If you give me any shit,' he says, shrugging the coat into place, 'I'll fuck you up. You get me?'

He is probably around half Tony's age.

Tony says, 'All I want is a lift.'

He takes the cash from Tony up front and charges £10 extra to stop off at his flat. 'How do I know you'll wait for me?' Tony asks.

'Are you questioning my ethics now?' says the kid. 'Because that's a big laugh.'

Nobody is waiting for Tony outside his place, or in it.

The kid drives well over the speed limit through the Blackwall Tunnel. He plays a tape of Asian music for the whole trip, a man singing fast, repetitive songs. 'Hab-a-jub-a-jub, jub-jub-jub,' it sounds like. 'Hab-a-jub-a-jib.' He keeps turning it up. When they stop at traffic lights on Commercial Road, Asian youths on the corner stare at Tony: one leans through the window and talks with the driver in a foreign language. Tony keeps a hand on the duffel bag beside him.

The kid cuts the engine outside Charing Cross. 'That's your lot,' he says.

In Trafalgar Square Tony pauses, not sure why he feels confused, until he realizes he was vaguely preparing himself to encounter the night-shift picket outside South Africa House; of course they don't bother with that any more. He heads up Charing Cross Road and turns into Old Compton Street. The bars and pubs are long closed (what time is it anyway: two? four?); a tramp sleeps in the theatre entrance. Further down two boys crouch strangely by a doorway: when they get up he sees they were talking to a beggar huddled there. One of them waves to Tony – 'Excuse me mate, do you know where's still open?' – but his friend pulls him away, with a comment too low to hear. 'We're from Newcastle—' the first boy says, before he is silenced.

On Rupert Street, the door beside the café carries the number 47. There are several buzzers without names. He presses them in order. The first one does not reply and the second is a woman who swears at him when he asks for Nicky. When he does hear the voice he knows it immediately.

'Who's this?'

'Nicky? I'm sorry to wake you. It's Tony Crawford.'

There is a long silence.

Eventually Tony says, 'Hello?'

'Do you know what time it is?'

'Yeah I'm sorry. I need to talk. It's important.'

.' . . Tony who?'

'Tony Crawford. From Woolwich.'

'What is it?'

'Please Nicky. I come by myself. I want to give you something.'

A long pause, and the sound of movement, perhaps Nicky finding a weapon. 'Second floor,' says the voice, and the buzzer goes.

Tony pushes open the door. He lifts the bag from the pavement and hefts it over his shoulder. The bundled flag inside feels even heavier, and he moves very slowly up the stairs.

London Psychogeographical Association

Nazi Occultists Seize Omphalos

The election of Derek Beackon as a Councillor on the Isle of dogs caused shocked outrage across the Establishment. Beackon is a dedicated Nazi occultist. He graduated to the British Nationalist Party after serving his apprenticeship in the British Movement. Beackon is an adept of Enochian magic. Devised in the sixteenth century by John Dee, it was this magical system which laid the basis for the conjuring up of the British Empire. Like every other form of nationalism, British nationalism is a psychic elemental which drains energy from living people in order to maintain itself as sickly caricature of life.

From his home at Mallon House, Carr Street, Limehouse, Beackon was able to tap into the powerful leyline running through his front room. This leyline is readily visible from the Observatory at Greenwich. It goes through the macabre Queen Anne House, and guided by the symmetry of the Naval College it crosses the Isle of Dogs clipping the corner of Canary Wharf complex before exactly passing through the tower of St. Anne's Limehouse. Then it passes through Beackon's lair before going onto Queen Mary and Westerfield College.

This leyline has been in the hands of the Establishment for years. They used the Greenwich section for astrological purposes. Time and space are measured from here. The British Establishment have now gained universal recognition for their hermetic

system. Meanwhile, the other section at QMWC has been the centre of sub-atomic research. Thus Greenwich accounts for the macrocosm, while the alchemical processes north of the river account for the microcosm.

Many people believe that Greenwich is in fact the Omphalos — or spiritual centre — of the British Empire. However those with a deeper understanding of Feng Shui, the ancient Chinese art of land divination, will recognise that the actual Omphalos must be on the Isle of Dogs, protected by water on all sides. Those who visit the Mudchute — a piece of park mysteriously built as an exact replica of an ancient hill fort — will find a special staircase leading to a cobbled circle. This is the Omphalos, the spiritual centre, where the magus John Dee conjured up the British Empire in the presence of Christopher Marlowe, four hundred years ago this year. However, using the leyline for such evil purposes necessitated the sacrifice of a human life. A psychic attack on Christopher Marlowe and his friends in Deptford pub lead to a brawl in which the famous playwright died.

In more recent years the Canary Wharf tower was built very carefully. It is in fact a column supporting a pyramid at the top. This pyramid serves to represent a much larger pyramid which would be formed if the lines at each corner were stretched down to ground level. This greater 'virtual' pyramid lies with its South West corner upon the leyline. The use of such street names as Cabot and Chancellor, and Churchill clearly show the intention to make Canary Wharf a powerful totem to resist the revival of German imperialism. Wren's name is used in deference to the architect who organised the building of the Naval College, and supervised the erection of St. Anne's tower as a U-Wave conductor. The building of Canary Wharf involved several human sacrifices, passed off as 'accidents'.

However the British establishment did not think that the pro-German British Nationalist Party would challenge them on this power line. But the BNP knew what price they would have to pay. Having conducted his obscene rituals to gain electoral success, Beackon fled his home fearing the negative Karma which would result. The BNP cynically pretended that he was in hiding from some unspecified anti-racists. Richard Edmonds, another cowardly BNP occultist was so worried he arranged for some BNP moles in the police to keep him out of harm's way locked up in a cell. However the karmic law is remorseless. Having used the power of the leyline, a human life had to be sacrificed.

As the principal culprits had protected themselves from psychic attack, another top Nazi occultist would be the victim. It was Ian Stuart, lead singer of the cult band Skrewdriver. The official story is that the car he was travelling crashed, and that the two passengers in the back escaped before the car became a ball of fire. However the truth is that the driver succumbed to demonic possession before spontaneously bursting into flames.

The BNP may feel safe now that their demonic master has sated its hunger. But the BNP are mere amateurs at occultism when compared to the top experts who run the British Establishment. The more they proceed with their occult nightmare of ritualistic sadism, they more they become victims of masonic mind control.

The British Establishment is now using them to conduct an experiment on the people of the Isle of Dogs. Using the Island as crucible of social engineering, they want to test what role race riots can be used to prop up the decadent masonic system. If the experiment goes wrong, the island can be sealed off and the inhabitants isolated. If it succeeds, the state will have a new weapon in its arsenal of terror.

Already the East London Advertiser is running a competition where readers are invited to ring different phone lines as to whether they think it was right that the BNP were elected. This is simply another wing of the establishment experimenting with the Nazi impetus. We cannot expect the press to expose the evil of which they are in fact a part, albeit a different department. The same goes for the rest of the establishment, whether the police, the church, or the political apparatus. We can only move forward by having nothing to do with any of these evil organisations.

END MASONIC MIND CONTROL

London Psychogeographical Association, undated leaflet, 1993

James, darling –

Sorry I haven't been in touch in a while. You're right that I've been avoiding you a bit, though wrong of course that it's because I haven't read your script, or can't face telling you it's crap – of course I have, and of course it isn't. I do have some issues with it, and I'll tell you what they are in a bit.

But I went 'radio silent,' as you put it, for a different reason. After a truly *epic* series of heart-to-hearts, and much anger and agonizing on both sides, Tom and I are back together, I hope for the long haul. I know you won't be best pleased by that, or the fact that he's asked me not to see you – for a while – and I've agreed. I doubt I can make you understand, but please let me try.

When I first learned he'd put that brick through your window, I completely freaked – as you know. It seemed awful – inexplicable, inexcusable. Don't get me wrong, it *was* awful and it *was* inexcusable. But perhaps not entirely the other thing.

This might sound daft, but after going over it with him a lot (really a lot) I think the window was just never as huge a deal for Tom as it was for you (and Adam). God, that sounds wrong – what I mean is, for Tom it was a gesture of anger and misery and frustration – emotions he should of course have been directing at me, not you – but still a *gesture*. As awful but as *transient* as slapping someone in anger – unless you're one of those people who thinks Slapping Is Beyond the Pale. (Before you ask, yes, Tom has hit me a couple of times – literally two, in fact – and no, I *don't* think that requires me to dump him. He can get frustrated when we argue because I'm more articulate than him, and lashing out physically is a last-resort way of expressing how frustrated he is. I *almost* find it endearing. You of all people should understand that.)

Of course, for you and Adam the brick was not only scary and upsetting, but conveyed a serious threat – which I don't think Tom really *understood*, because *I don't think he ever really believed you could take that note seriously*. I don't mean for a second you *shouldn't* have taken it seriously – in your place I absolutely would have done (probably) – but for Tom, who you have to remember was never as steeped in this stuff as you or even I, it always seemed remote and silly *and obviously unreal*.

He says he tried to warn you off with an email after you two hit it off so badly, at that fairly disastrous dinner party at your place where for God only knows what reason, sweets, you told him you and I were still fucking. After that – for my sake and yours as much as his – he rather avoided you. But I wanted you both to get on, and talked him into coming to that god-awful skin night. I'm just as responsible as you for what happened there, but it was a terrible thing for both of us to do.

You mustn't underestimate how much he felt threatened by you. Not only were you my old and close friend – he knew we'd had a sort-of-thing in the past – but it wasn't easy for him to participate as an equal when we discussed things like politics. And you were, to be fair, darling, pretty aggressive with him from the start, with your digs about vegetarianism and the provinces.

So here's James, the scary brainy one with the History, belittling Tom and first claiming to be sleeping with his boyfriend and then apparently proving it in public. It's not surprising he wanted to hurt you – he should have wanted to hurt *me*, and doubtless did, but it was me he was worried about losing and you he thought might take me away. And he knew both you and Adam were at the club, so nobody would see him, and – he says just as importantly, which I believe – neither of you might accidentally get hurt.

Writing LOG on it was just him mocking you for how you'd been going on. I don't think he imagined for a moment you'd take it seriously (though perhaps he was also testing you a bit: he thought it would be ridiculous to be taken in by the note – and so at one and the same time you couldn't *really* be, and if you *were*, that was your fault for being stupid).

He was *devastated* when he found out he'd hurt Sonny. You know how much he loves animals.

Does all this make any sense? I'm not asking you to understand, much less forgive him. I just want to explain as best I can why I think I *do* understand – understand him much better now, his flaws and vulnerabilities and his strengths and the things that make him special – which is in a nutshell why we've ended up back together. He's not someone I can just let go, not at my age. Accepting his request that I don't see you – *temporarily* – in no way means I'm accepting or supporting his aggression towards you, much less acting it out. I'm just doing what I need to reassure *him*, doing something *for* him to make up for what I didn't do before, and need to now, because I love him.

All that was longer than I'd planned and perhaps a bit sterner. Sorry. So in reward for getting this far – assuming you did – let's move on to your script.

First, and notwithstanding what follows: in many ways it's very good. You clearly have talent, and imho, a good ear for dialogue.

Second: I don't think *this* script, as it stands, is likely to get commissioned.

But as you know this is not my field. I'm a journalist. I can only comment as myself, not some expert on TV drama. I know you think TV is TV. It isn't.

I was obviously surprised when you sent it. I thought you were planning a feature, which was more comfortably outside my purview! (Although to be brutally honest I sometimes dreaded that you would come to me with a pitch for *Panorama* and I'd have to explain that gay nazis in the '80s were not really current affairs.) I was hardly expecting to get, out of the blue, the full draft of a six-part, *very* post-watershed drama series. And on the one hand delighted, but on the other a bit bemused. Because, darling, if you *had* told me this was what you were planning, I would have warned you in advance that it seemed to me highly unlikely that, regardless of its quality, anybody would want to fund it. James, honey – nobody makes six-part dramas any more. And this is a *wildly* niche subject. I know *Nazis* sell, as your email sweetly trumpeted. But Nazis sell because winning WWII was the last thing of worth this miserable, relegated country did. (And the Jews control the media, ba-boom.) *Neo*-nazis are different. Hitler was evil. Griffin is an unpleasant embarrassment.

Then there's the almost *autistic* geographical specificity of the script. Have you got any idea how expensive it would be to film in all those places, let alone dress them in period? To a producer it will scream Budget Nightmare. (I have the uneasy sense that if I were to plot all the over-described journeys your characters take on a map, I'd end up with, I don't know, a picture of a swastika, or a map showing the location of the Holy Lance, or something. I assume that's not the case, but if it is you seriously need help.)

Yet this is countered by a strange vagueness about some of the larger realities of your nazis' lives. I have no idea, for example, what jobs they do. Also, the politics are oddly hard to fathom. I know where you stand on neo-nazism, but other people won't. It doesn't help that some of the nazi characters seem oddly sympathetic – not least when many of the others are, frankly, cocks.

I realize all this might sound a bit negative, and also that I've failed to address some of your specific questions. But the fact that you just sat down and wrote it is a major achievement in itself, and something to be proud of. So seriously, darling: well done.

I'm going to go 'radio silent' again now, for reasons already explained. I do feel bad about this, and do miss you, and it won't be forever – just a few months. When things with Tom are more secure and he OKs it, I'll get in touch. I might need to agree some rules with him for a while (probably things like not staying out too late, particularly if it's just you and me) – but I'm really looking forward to seeing you again. Assuming you want to. I hope you will.

I *do* think that given all that's happened a break from each other is not a bad thing. I'm not sure our old relationship was entirely healthy or grown-up. I know that – unlike me – you weren't breaking any rules, but on the other hand nor was Adam, and look what happened there. Of course I feel particularly bad that I'm not around for you now given what's happened with Adam.

I know you haven't replied to Tom's letter of apology and I don't think he expects you to. *I* certainly don't expect you to. But I want you to know he really meant it. I don't imagine you and he will ever be more than civil to each other, but I hope that in time you can both manage that, because he needs to accept that I care about you – and you need to accept that he's my lover.

Philip xx

PS the enclosed document is by way of inadequate apology, and the tape is a sort of forget-me-not – I hope it lives up to your expectations. You'll want to know how I found them both, I suppose – well, sweetheart, I *am* a journalist.

QBDX 439919

CERTIFIED COPY   OF AN ENTRY

DEATH	Entry No. 227

Registration district
    Westminster

Administrative area

Sub-district
    Westminster
                       City of Westminster

1. Date and place of death
    Seventh December 1993
    St Mary's Hospital, Praed Street, Westminster

2. Name and surname
    Nicola Vincenzio CRANE

3. Sex   Male

4. Maiden surname of woman who has married   ——————

6. Date and place of birth
    21st May 1958   Bexley Heath Kent

8. Occupation and usual address
    Club Securityman
    47 Rupert Street W1

7 (a) Name and surname of informant

(b) Qualification
    Present at the death

(c) Usual address

8. Cause of death
    Ia. Bronchopneumonia

    Certified by S Smith MB

9. I certify that the particulars given by me above are true to the best of my knowledge and belief ....
Signature of informant

10. Date of registration
    Seventh December 1993

11. Signature of registrar
    C Christofi Registrar

*See notes overleaf

CERTIFIED to be a true copy of an entry in the certified copy of a register of Births or Deaths in the District above mentioned. Given at the GENERAL REGISTER OFFICE, under the Seal of the said Office on   2005

CAUTION: THERE ARE OFFENCES RELATING TO FALSIFYING OR ALTERING A CERTIFICATE AND USING OR POSSESSING A FALSE CERTIFICATE ©CROWN COPYRIGHT

WARNING: A CERTIFICATE IS NOT EVIDENCE OF IDENTITY.

GCJ

Back with a Bang

I read Philip's letter several times. I did not recognize the informant's name on the enclosed certificate; for his 'qualification,' it simply said 'Present at death.'

At the back of the drinks cabinet I found an unopened bottle of single malt on which it seemed appropriate to make a start. I sat in an armchair with my drink and watched the video Philip had sent from beginning to end. When it was over I phoned Sarah. 'What happens,' I asked, 'when you die of bronchopneumonia?'

'You do *know* I'm not a medical doctor?'

'Yeah, but you know that sort of thing.'

She sighed. 'I think you can't breathe, basically. You get liquid on the lungs and run out of oxygen. You lose consciousness, wait longer and longer between gasps for air, and eventually stop, and then you're dead. Why?'

'I just wanted to know.'

'Are you all right?' she asked.

The last traces of visible surface had long eroded from the plants in the garden; through the front windows Blenheim Crescent glowed silently. I topped up my whisky and watched the ten o'clock news. More newspapers had published the

Jyllands-Posten Muhammad cartoons, and protests were spreading. The jury in Nick Griffin's trial had been discharged, after finding him and Mark Collett not guilty on various counts of inciting racial hatred, and reaching no verdict on others: I watched them greet cheering supporters outside the court, but turned off the TV when Griffin began to speak. Instead I played Tom Robinson through the stereo, to whom, with nobody watching, I danced with a kind of clamped intensity, throwing myself hard into postures in which I tensely froze before moving again. I kept this up for several tracks, and had begun to sweat by the time the pace of the album slowed for 'Martin,' to which I shuffled and chorused along, waving one of Dad's crystal tumblers carefully so as not to spill my drink, and adding my own little cheer to the recorded crowd's when Tom sang, 'I'ad to punch a few policemen before I was nicked.' I switched it off after that song, refilled my glass and logged in to the website.

Adam was online; I clicked on his profile before remembering it would show him I'd done so. Well, it was too late now. He had changed his selection of photographs, recycling some that I recognized, but I saw none that were new. Nor had the text altered much: he was now listed as single, but still 'mainly looking for fun.' I was scrolling through the other men online when he sent me a brief message to check I had the post he'd forwarded: I answered, *yes thx*. He didn't reply to that.

Across the city, a thousand men faced analogous displays. We appraised each other in batches of twenty, listed by proximity of interest; then degree of financial commitment to the site; then chosen nickname, ordered alphabetically. The most dedicated users had names beginning a1, or aaa1, or even ..1a – the full stop, someone having previously discovered, bearing the lowest ASCII value of any permitted character. Insensitive coding shrank everyone's photo, whether portrait or landscape, disproportionately to the same square ratio for the indexed thumbnails: a catalogue of the bulbous and the racked. With each picture was shown name, location, status line. The latter came in various genres: most were variants of *horny top looking for action in E5 now*, but there were also *ask for more info*s and *mature teacher very discrete*s and *let me take your mind beyond the infinite*s. I was trying to compose a polite snub to the mature teacher, whose boilerplate approach I had received at least twice before, when a pop-up alerted me that arealnazi had logged in. There were still no photographs on his profile, nor had he edited the text since I first discovered it:

Nazi skinhead thug, fat, middle aged, tatts, will abuse worthless scum. I will hurt you & rape you if I want & take your money if I want & leave you bleeding. If thats not what your looking for fuck off. If your going to ask for a photo fuck off. I am not play acting I am a fucking nazi.

I looked through the photos I had sent him that summer, before I got confused about who he was. It had been strange, my sojourn into commissioned pornography; seeing the pictures now I felt a bit giddy, but also a bit sentimental. Without glasses, I tended to squint at the camera in whatever contrived position (raised on books on the dining table; balanced on the bathroom sink) I had put my laptop: assuming arealnazi's prescribed postures, displaying his marks.

It was strange, too, to be seeing Adam's flat like this.

I sent a message to arealnazi: *Evening*. After a minute or two there came confirmation that he'd read it. I stared at the screen, reloading the page every few seconds to accelerate my receipt of his reply, but apart from the schoolteacher's worn acknowledgement (*I understand, thank you for your consideration*) nothing more arrived. I sent another: *You ignoring me?*

After a while he answered: *sorry not interested in time wasters* Timewasters?!

games playing

I poured myself more Scotch. Really, I'd had enough of people's judgements for one night. I said: *What makes you think I'm playing games?*

I waited until he'd read it, then went to the bathroom to pee and look at myself in the mirror. When I came back he still hadn't replied. I hit Reload a few times and watched the message window reassemble itself in flickering stages with each press.

'Fuck it,' I said out loud, and wrote: *All right then. I'm free right now if you are. Can accom.* I pressed Send before I had time to think.

give me ur adress he said.

Let's agree some ground rules first, OK?

give me ur adress or fuck off

So I did, and he said, *ill be there in an hour*, and then he logged out.

I stayed where I was for a few minutes, clicking randomly on bookmarks and links without reading the pages they led to. I wasn't quite sure what I had just done, or whether I had really done it. It was just before eleven; at ten to twelve, or thereabouts, he would arrive.

The website, like most of its genre, offered guidelines for meeting strangers. Choose a public place, a busy time; bring a friend. Nobody bothered with all that. But: *hurt you & rape you & leave you bleeding* . . . I had no mobile number for him, no way to back out except turn him away at the door. At the very least, it would be sensible to let someone know. In other circumstances I would have told Philip, or maybe even Adam (who would certainly have told me). I thought of calling Sarah back, but such conversations remained unimaginable.

At 11:10 I went upstairs. I tidied the mess in my room, fishing old underwear from the bed and straightening the sheets. I put the cash Dad had left me in the top drawer of his desk, and locked it. I showered; dried and moisturized; gargled mouthwash in lieu of brushing; put clean clothes on. I went downstairs again. Somehow all this had only taken fifteen minutes. In a no-nonsense burst of resolution, I called Philip. It rang three times and went to voicemail: he had diverted my call. I didn't leave a message. I saw my parents returning from holiday in just a few days, suitcases on the front step, the key in the lock, the view from the doorway. My stomach felt fragile. I turned the music back on, realized Tom Robinson wouldn't do, tried to find something appropriate: Depeche Mode. I listened to about a minute of 'World in My Eyes' and switched it off. I re-read arealnazi's profile several times.

An hour came and went; seventy minutes; eighty. I sat on the sofa with more whisky, and put on Philip's tape again with the sound down. It was the last of several generations of amateur copies: the image was badly degraded and glitching; the colours bled. Every few seconds a wave of noise would ride up the screen, and sometimes break over it.

A nondescript domestic interior. The Union Jack hung on the wall to the top right of the picture. Before it, centre screen, stood Nicky and a younger, slighter boy. They faced the camera with their arms round each other. They both wore skin gear: jeans, red braces, T-shirts. The camera panned slowly down their jeans (the boy's were bleached, Nicky's plain blue) and found the tops of their boots. The image popped. Now we saw their upper bodies again. Still holding each other, they gave nazi salutes to the camera with their free arms. The image shimmered as if the air before them burned. The doorbell rang. I jumped in my seat; my skin shrank tight around my face and neck. I stopped the tape and turned the TV to standby. My hand gripped the remote. I looked over to the front door, but with the lights on inside and darkness without,

I could see no shape at the window. The bell rang again. I stood as quietly as I could.

He knocked, paused, knocked louder. Then there was a metallic slapping sound that I didn't recognize, until I saw that he was pushing in the flap of the letterbox and letting it spring closed. Through the gap I saw the ends of fingers invade, retreat again. When I walked towards the door my shoes struck the wooden floor. He must have heard, because he stopped knocking.

The man waiting on the doorstep looked older than I had imagined: in his mid-fifties perhaps. His head was shaved, its skin slightly mottled; there was perspiration above his jowly mouth. His boots were ankle high: he wore combat trousers tucked into their tops, and his zipped black jacket cradled a substantial paunch. Over his shoulder he held a large duffel bag. He looked me up and down without comment, and as I stepped aside to let him enter, he similarly appraised the room.

'Nice place,' he said, stepping into it. He walked forward to the base of the stairs and set his bag down with a slight groan. He turned to look at me.

'Would you like a drink?' I said.

'Yeah go on.'

'Is Scotch OK?'

While I poured it he sat on the sofa. It was a big piece of furniture; he sank into it a bit. The fingers that took the glass from me were tattooed between their knuckles: A C A B. The light showed faded marks by his left eye, which I had not noticed when I opened the door.

He asked, 'Is this yours this place?'

'My parents."

'Thought you lived with your boyfriend.'

'We split up.'

'Oh . . .' he said uninterpretably, and after another sip added: 'House must be worth a few bob.'

'Property prices round here have gone nuts. We've lived here for decades though. Since it was cheap.'

'Oh yeah?' He stood up, still carrying his Scotch. As he got near me he extended his free hand towards my face and I winced. He gave a small grunt. I held myself as still as possible as he took hold of my glasses by one arm and lifted them off at an angle; my vision skewed wildly, then blurred.

'Where are they?' he said. I could see him watching me, but barely made out his expression.

'Where are what?' For some reason I thought he meant my glasses, and that it was a trick question.

'Your parents.'

'Oh, they're on holiday.' The answer was automatic, an unthinking reaction to my delayed understanding of his question, and I immediately regretted it. They're out, I should have told him: they'll be back later.

He put my glasses on an arm of the sofa and came close again, sipping his Scotch. He kept coming until we nearly touched; the detail of his face clarified once more, and I thought of those precise, monochrome moonscapes in the weekend supplements, all basins and rifts. I caught his eyes and quickly looked away. He frowned at me.

'You Jewish?'

'No.'

'Because you look fucking Jewish.'

'I'm not.'

He shrugged: 'Don't matter anyway,' and sipped his drink. His eyes closed in synchrony with his swallow. He put his other hand in his pocket, seemed to reconsider, and took it out again empty.

'Take your shirt off,' he said, and stepped back to watch. After a moment I did so. Even in the room's warmth I shivered a little. We stood like that until, to get some space, I told him, 'I should shut the curtains.' I pulled to the ones at the front, trying not to look at his bag as I passed. I walked back past him to the rear, began closing the curtains there. The black garden fell away.

When I returned he was again on the sofa. I stood in front of him, unable to think of anything to say. He sat, watching me. My upper body shook violently, as if I were very cold. I tried to control it and failed.

He stood. He held out his hand, and ran a finger down the side of my face, my neck, and then the left hand side of my chest, which continued to buck and spasm of its own accord.

'Fucking little queer,' he said.

He took hold of my earlobe and, twisting it, forced me down, until I yielded to a kneel. He pulled my face against his crotch. His clothes smelled like they hadn't been washed for a while and I tried to breathe more lightly. For an odd moment I imagined killing him (some brave, startled struggle with a knife, his stomach split like rotting fruit) and wondered where I could hide the body.

He pushed back my head so I was looking up at him, said, 'Fucking little stay-at-home mummy's boy,' and slapped me across the cheek; I wasn't sure how hard it had been, but it jolted me all the same, and stung my skin.

He brought his knee up under my chin, nudged it so I was looking up again, watched me adjust to the new information. My whole body was shaking now, twitching asynchronously in different parts, as if reacting to tiny, randomly distributed explosions inside.

He pulled a small vial from the pocket of his coat, unscrewed the top and held it under my nose. It gave off a harsh, chemical smell.

'Sniff,' he said.

I said, 'I'm not sure . . .'

'Fucking sniff it.' He put his free hand over my mouth. I held my breath for a few seconds and inhaled cautiously. The smell filled my head. I reeled a little and concentrated on staying upright.

'Again.' With the hand that held the bottle he pressed my free nostril closed. Then he kicked me, not hard, in the ribs, and I breathed in sharply. My skull felt like hands were pressing it, or lifting it perhaps; my thoughts went slow and fuggy. I heard him say, 'That's better.' He took away the bottle and I thought he sniffed from it himself. I looked up at him, wondering what he was going to do.

He trod on my hand and said something that sounded like 'Fucking nigger,' only I wondered if it had been 'nigger-lover,' which made more sense. He ran his finger down my cheek again and I saw the stained lines of his tattooed skin. I thought of marked flesh, unwilling, like a branded calf, and then the symbols I had drawn for him, the swastika I had carried secretly for days, watching it slowly fade.

I said, 'Can I have another sniff?'

'Yeah go for it mate.'

I exhaled, rammed the vial up my nostril and breathed in as violently as I could. It burned the lining of my nose a bit but that feeling was soon lost in the rush of the rest; I felt hot and giddy, like I was tipping constantly backwards; my head swelled and was pressed; my skin prickled, pulsed. He said, 'Can I have some more of that Scotch?' and I said, 'Help yourself.' The glug of its pouring ran behind my sight of things in hazy, cropped fragments: the tall still curtains, his combats' scuffed knees.

'That's it,' he said, 'lick my boots you fucking cocksucker.'

In the toe of one I saw my face, a hazy fish-eye distortion.

'What's in your bag, anyway?' I said, and added, 'I've got Skrewdriver somewhere,' but had second thoughts about drawing attention to my iPod and decided to drop it.

At some point then he was pacing around me, around the room, which I saw from my lowered, listing perspective in exaggerated angles and cartoon foreshortening. 'How much cash have you got?'

'What?'

'I said say *heil Hitler*,' he said, or maybe it was me.

'It doesn't matter,' I said, and took off the rest of my clothes. I said, 'You can hit me again.' When he did my jawbone buzzed in reaction and my ears also separately rang.

'Fucking little queer,' he said again.

His finger ran down my neck.

.' . . . aren't you?'

'Yeah.' I looked up. He breathed, looking back at me. I thought I could see him thinking. He seemed a bit stuck. I asked, 'Have you got a blindfold?'

'No sorry.'

'I thought there might be one in your bag.'

'No.'

'Oh,' I said. The image came to me of Mum and Dad, a few weeks back, when I went in to say good-night: her reading, and him with something to shut out the light. 'I might have one,' I said.

'Only that's not exactly my cup of tea do you know what I mean?'

'Oh,' I said. My knees were hurting and I sat back on the floor. 'OK.'

'No but I mean if that's what you're after . . . Tell you what how much cash have you got?'

'Cash?'

'Only I'm a bit short. Listen why don't you go and fetch your blindfold and get me like fifty quid at the same time. You can lend me that can't you?'

'Um.' I said. 'Yeah, OK.'

I felt detached from the stairs, like I was floating up them. Halfway up I turned and asked, 'Did you really know Nicky Crane?'

'We was in the BM together mate. Down in Woolwich. I knew him for years. And Ian Stuart too. Skrewdriver. I knew all them lot.'

In Dad's study, I stopped and listened a few times to make sure he hadn't followed me, and when I'd locked the rest of the cash back in the desk I put the key behind a book on the shelf. I rooted in my parents' drawers but there was no sign of the blindfold I was picturing, and I realized they'd probably packed it. Just as I was giving up and regretting the now point-less concession over money I found another, some freebie from a long-past Virgin flight. Printed across its front was the phrase BEDDY BYES. The elastic was old and brittle and it kept slipping down my face. He adjusted it hopelessly: it felt like a hat from a Christmas cracker. 'Bollocks,' he muttered the third time it fell. He looked tired and upset, like an old person realizing they have forgotten something.

I said, 'Give me that bottle again.' Its edge tickled my sting-ing membrane and I could hear myself grunting as I inhaled; then my brain was air on one side and brick on the other and the imbalance made me slump. I doubled over and caught the floor as it came for me. I hovered above it, drooped over my locked arm, which still shook with the impact.

'Go on then,' I mumbled at the planks, 'be a fucking nazi.'

'What's that mate?' I looked up. He was taking the money from the side table and folding it into his wallet: 'Can't go for-getting that.'

'Well then,' he said, and with an air of desperate improvi-sation kicked me in the crotch. I shouted, 'Ouch! – shit.' The pain rose up my abdomen in a hot flush. I felt a bit sick.

'I feel a bit sick,' I said, and with a surge of surprise puked briefly on his leg.

'Shit!' He jumped back. I stayed where I was, panting at the floor.

'Sorry.'

'Only I'm not into that you know what I mean?'

I burped. 'Nor am I.'

'Yeah. Is there more where that came from?'

'I don't think so.'

'Don't move.' I heard him opening cupboards in the kitchen, and then he was back and putting a mixing bowl in front of me. 'Stay where you are for a minute or two,' he said. 'Going to find a tea towel or something.'

In the metal bowl my face appeared with the opposite of the earlier fish-eye effect: features tiny in the centre, edges stretched crazily towards me. After a while I felt stable enough to sit down where I was, but I kept the bowl close.

He came back with his boots off and the lower part of his trouser leg drenched. 'Did it come out?' I asked. He sat on the sofa, raised the leg and sniffed: 'Not all of it.'

'Sorry.'

'You not used to poppers?'

'Not really.'

'Want to take it easy the first time.'

His stretched his wet leg from the sofa and stroked my knee with his toe.

I said, 'I might lie down for a bit. Do you mind?'

'Did you grow up in this room then?'

He was standing in the doorway.

'Yeah.'

'Nice isn't it.'

'Well, it's been redecorated since then. It's a guest room now.'

'Still. Somewhere to come home to.'

'Yeah.'

'Anyway,' he said, and patted his thighs. 'Guess I should fuck off.'

'Sorry,' I smiled.

'Might hold on to that fifty for now if it's all right.'

'Sure. Of course.'

'At least I finally got to meet you anyway. Thought it was never going to happen.'

I smiled again, politely.

'I've left my number,' he added. 'On the table downstairs.'

'Thanks,' I said. He gave me a little nod and headed off down the stairs.

After a minute he reappeared. 'I see you got a washing machine down there. Only would it be all right if I did those trousers quickly? Save me taking them to the launderette.'

I asked if he wanted a shower while he waited, and he said he'd prefer a bath. I watched him undress; there was something unexpectedly shy about it. His belly sagged over old, thinning boxer briefs that had torn away in places from the waistband; with my glasses back on I could read the text that ran around it, CALVIN CLASSICS. 'Might as well stick this lot in and all,' he said. When he was gone I put on a T-shirt and some boxers, and when I heard him safely in the bath I padded downstairs to the kitchen. He'd found the washing tabs: the box stood on the counter. The machine quivered as it ran, and through the door I could see it had been loaded almost to maximum. His duffel bag sat open on the floor beside it; left inside were more dirty clothes, a pair of trainers, two fist-sized bundles wrapped in shopping bags, a brown bottle containing a few pills.

He took a long bath, perhaps listening for the machine to stop, and I was half asleep when he came out. He had my bathtowel wrapped around him. It started at his belly button and fell clear of his legs in front of him.

I said, 'Can I see your tattoos?'

He sat on the edge of the bed, held out his arm.

'I know what most of them are,' I said. 'That one on your

383

fingers. And that symbol's the Celtic cross, probably British Movement. Swastikas, Skrewdriver, White Power . . . all self-explanatory. How about this one?'

'That one? It's just a picture I liked. Don't mean anything.'

'Were those Borstal tears?'

'Yeah. That was a long time ago. They're nearly gone now.'

'How long have you had the spider's web?'

'Ten, twelve years. Something like that.'

'I won't ask what it's for.'

He looked at me. 'We can still do something if you want,' he said. 'Reckon I owe you. Wouldn't mind either to be honest.'

I smiled. 'Thanks. But I'm pretty tired.'

'Up to you anyway.'

After a while he said, 'I should move that stuff to the dryer.'

I found him crouched at the machine, frowning at its controls.

'Do I just press this?' he asked.

The machine began to turn: quietly, almost tactfully, with none of the moans and jerks of Adam's cheap washer/dryer.

I gave him one of Dad's dressing gowns to wear. It was too small for him and looked like a pinny. As he put it on I said, 'Can I ask you a question?'

'Yeah go on.'

'What do you do? I mean, like your job, or whatever?'

He laughed, I think for the first time.

'Fuck off,' he told me.

I poured him another Scotch and he sat on the sofa sipping it.

'Do you really not know,' I said, 'what LOG stands for?'

'You asked me that before didn't you. I never heard of it.'

I put Philip's tape back on.

'That's Nicky,' he said.

Nicky wore a T-shirt with ACTION MAN 80 written in stencil

384

above his photo from the *Strength thru Oi!* cover. He was trying to replicate for the camera the pose in the photograph: teetering on one leg, the other out as if to kick, scowling, his clenched fists raised.

'Where did you get this?'

'A friend gave it to me.'

'I heard about this stuff but I never seen it.'

I fast-forwarded ('Jesus,' he said a couple of times) to a section where Nicky showed off his tatts to the camera, and paused on the pan down his left arm. The image was frosted with noise and kept jumping, but the yellow shimmer of his inked skin was still visible.

'There,' I pointed.

He frowned and leaned forward. 'That's not an O.'

'Well, I know it's a Celtic cross, but it's still says LOG.'

'It's just LG,' he said. 'Leader Guard. With a British Movement sign. Leader Guard is what Nicky was in the BM.'

The obviousness of this was too much for me. I sank on to the sofa. Eventually I laughed and he asked what was funny. I told him, nothing.

He said, 'Put it back on Play then.'

'What was he like?' I asked. We were at opposite ends of the sofa. Nicky, on screen, was snogging some boy.

'He was all right.'

'Did you two ever . . .'

'No we never done that.' He looked at me. 'That's what you wanted with me wasn't it? Sort of daisy-chain back to Nicky. Blood touches blood and that.'

'No.'

He nodded. 'He had a mate of mine once. Well more than once. So there is a chain there if you add that in. Only my mate had me first and Nicky after so the order's a bit out. But it nearly works doesn't it.'

He settled further into the seat. Now the boy was licking Nicky's boots. 'Go on,' Nicky told him. 'Lick all the dry blood off. Lick all the blood and shit off. Go on, keep fucking licking it.' He was a bad actor, and trying not to laugh. 'Go on. Lick all the fucking shit off of it. And all that nigger blood.' The boy looked up and smiled. Soon my visitor fell asleep and I turned down the volume on the tape. I reached along the back of the sofa and rested my hand against his upper arm; he shifted at the touch and his own hand came to find me. The flesh under his skin yielded to my fingertips; the dryer maintained its faint, rhythmic thrum. Looking over to it I saw a scrap of paper on the kitchen table: his phone number. I would throw it away in the morning. I must remember to wash my own clothes tomorrow, I thought, wondering how many tabs were left, and Bounce. I should do a big shop before my parents came home, make sure the house was properly stocked: perhaps an Ocado order. Nicky was saying something to the boy. I thought of him in his hospital bed, his lungs filled with fluid, heart and brain starved of oxygen, gasping, unconscious, dead, and Ian in his coma, in intensive care, kept going briefly, pointlessly; even Savitri Devi, puking, trembling and shitting on her friend's mattress, over towels and a plastic sack, the next day snoring, and then silent. I was fourteen when I thought clearly of death for the first time. It was lunchbreak at school and I was eating a packet of salt-and-vinegar Hula Hoops. Whenever something upset me as a boy I could step back from it, mentally: I knew the bully would move on; the unhappiness pass; there would be time for reconciliation and amends, the love and comfort of my parents. But from this, I remembered thinking, alone for some reason at the buttery table: from life, consciousness, there was no stepping back, no greater context; this was my limit; it was where I stopped. After a few minutes he murmured in his sleep: 'Hello?' His fingers twitched and tightened against my thigh and subsided again. 'He wasn't alone,' I said quietly, 'at the end. There's a name, on the certificate. Present at death.' But I don't think he heard me. I stroked his fingers with my own. I had been missing it, I thought: touch, human touch. And I missed Adam's in particular. My visitor sighed from within some passing dream of safety, and Nicky, on the tape, gave a final glitch and was gone into the long white noise.

Acknowledgements

This book owes its existence to China Miéville's relentless encouragement, my family's extraordinary support and the collections and staff of the British Library. My own existence, during its writing and since, has benefited greatly from the involvement of Bruno Moser.

Andrew Kidd not only believed in the manuscript, but resolved its most intractable problem. I am fortunate, and thankful, to have him as my agent. Sara Holloway at Granta sensitively and patiently shepherded the book to completion. I am grateful to them and to Amber Burlinson, Matthew Caldwell, Mic Cheetham, Amber Dowell, Mulaika Hijjas, Sven Immisch, Simon Kavanagh, China Miéville, Vaughan Pilikian, Moby Pomerance, Natasha Soobramanien, Jesse Soodalter, Liv Stones, Sarah Thomas, Luke Williams and Chris Woods for their comments on various drafts; and to Vicki Harris for copy-editing the last one.

For advice, information and access to materials on a range of topics, and for space to write, I am indebted to many of the same people, as well as to John Acord and David Guiliano, Caroline Boileau, Adam Balic, James Bridle, Allan Brown, Phil Brown and the late Derek Draper, Christabel Cooper, Katherine

Coyne, John Cranmer of Maya Vision International, Isabel Dakyns, Richard and Melanie Essex, Julian Grainger, Jim Haynes, Tim Hayward, Stewart Home, Sarah Ichioka, Taimour Lay, Simon Majumdar, Tom Masters, Vanessa Parrott, Adrian Rifkin, Brian Robinson, Markku Salmi, the train planners and driver managers at Southeastern and Tim Winter.

This is not the place for a bibliography, but I owe a particular debt to work by Edward William Delph, Nicholas Goodrick-Clarke, Dave Hann and Steve Tilzey, Murray Healy, Dick Hebdige, Larry O'Hara, Nick Ryan and the *Searchlight* organization.

The alarming gaps in the British Library's 1980s gay-press holdings were mercifully filled by the Hall–Carpenter Archives at the London School of Economics.

There has never been any confusion about Nicky Crane's death certificate, but I am grateful to Madeleine Brammah of the General Register Office for describing the information given to customers if a search does fail.

Grateful thanks to all those who generously gave permission to reproduce copyright material, much of which appears here in abridged form.

Bexleyheath & Welling Observer © Archant Regional.

Lyrics to 'Where the Hell Is Babylon?' © The Cockney Rejects.

Daily Mail and *Mail on Sunday* © Associated Newspapers Ltd.

Daily Mirror © Mirrorpix (Mirror Syndication International).

Articles from the *Guardian* and *Observer* are copyright Guardian News & Media Ltd as follows: 'Mr Tyndall "Expelled"' and 'Mr Tyndall Insists: "It is Colin Jordan Who is Expelled"' © 1964; 'Right Off' (extract) by Maggie Gillon © 1974; 'Extreme right-wing racialists are preparing . . .' (extract) by George Brock and Kirsty White ©1980; 'NF Dispute Spills Over into Bar-Room Brawl' by David Rose ©1986.

Extract from 'Reformed Fascist Ready to Admit Homo-sexuality' by Martin Wroe, the *Independent* © Independent News and Media Ltd.

Melody Maker and the *NME* © NME/Melody Maker/IPC+ Syndication.

Searchlight © Searchlight Magazine Ltd.

Photographs and layouts from *Skins International* © Martin Dean.

Sniffin' Glue © Mark Perry.

Sounds © Bauer Consumer Media Ltd.

'Nazi Nick Is a Panzi' by Brandon Malinsky, the *Sun* © NI Syndication Ltd 1992.

Zipper © Millivres Prowler Group.

Thanks to 'the brother' for the extract from 'Why I'm a Skin' from *Square Peg;* to the London Psychogeographical Association for 'Nazi Occultists Steal the Omphalos'; and to the Direct Action Collective for 'Anti-Fascists Jailed' from *Direct Action.*